PRAISE FOR *Whe*

"Bob Bergin has woven historical fact ⟨...⟩ ⟨...⟩ng novel. It will grab your interest and hold ⟨...⟩.' – **Bob Layher**, Flight Leader, 2nd Squadron "P⟨...⟩ ⟨...⟩ars," AVG Flying Tigers

"Old Asia hands love Bob Bergin's novels because the author's adventures help stir up memories of their own. The sights, sounds, smells, and feel of the Far East come alive on his pages. In *When Tigers Fly*, Bergin works another element into his exciting storytelling: expertise in aviation and its role in winning the Pacific War. Buffs of history and fiction will have an equally hard time putting down the book." – **Brett M. Decker**, former Editorial Writer and Books Editor, *The Asian Wall Street Journal*, Hong Kong

"Bob Bergin has made good use of his long experience in Southeast Asia and his knowledge of the Flying Tigers. He has written an exciting warbird adventure – full of details that put you right into the middle of the action." – **Group Captain Veerayuth Didyasarin**, RTAF (Retd.), President, Foundation for the Preservation and Development of Thai Aircraft

"A story that shows great imagination. It's set in exotic places that are remarkably well-described. The characters are fascinating, the plot moves quickly and leads to a surprising climax. The AVG background is a great touch. In my opinion the details are very accurate. A very interesting book." – **Ken Jernstedt**, Flight Leader, 3rd Squadron "Hell's Angels," AVG Flying Tigers

"The plausibility of finding original AVG P-40s was handled well. To me, as a historian of the AVG, the plot at first seemed far-fetched. But Bergin even had me going at times: 'Hmmm, maybe it is possible! Aww, come on!' I really enjoyed it." – **Frank Boring**, Co-producer of "Fei Hu," The Story of the Flying Tigers documentary

ALSO BY BOB BERGIN
Stone Gods, Wooden Elephants

"A fast-paced page-turner by an old Asia hand with an insider's knowledge of the intricacies of the antiquities trade. A good read for the armchair adventurer." – **Sylvia Fraser-Lu**, author of numerous books on Asian arts and antiquities, including *Silverware of South-East Asia* and *Splendor in Wood: The Buddhist Monasteries of Burma.*

"An adventure story with a delightful twist. Bergin leads you through the jungles of Thailand and the world of antiquities with a steady hand and a sharp eye. A good read." – **Richard Rashke**, author of *Escape from Sobibor* and *The Killing of Karen Silkwood*

"A great story that captures the total sensual package of being in Southeast Asia – negotiating the complexitites of social relations, colliding with street-level life, peering down the small side streets shrouded with ancient patinas, and stumbling into the riot of every-day adventures, some soft and quiet, others loud and threatening, but all of them worth the price of a return ticket." – **Lew Stern**, Department of Defense Southeast Asia Affairs Specialist and author of many books and articles on Asia

"A surprise at every turn. A pleasant surprise to find that Bob Bergin has written a fascinating mystery in an area where he has a wealth of knowledge. He has been traveling in Asia for many years searching out art and antiques. Weaving his expertise in this area into an incredible story of rare art, smuggling, and deception – while keeping the vision of the lush jungles and klongs of Thailand – proves a rapid pace of intrigue, rushing waters, elephant trails, and mystery." – **Dick Rossi**, President, Flying Tigers Association

"*Stone Gods, Wooden Elephants* has most everything a reader could want – quirky characters, an exotic locale, and an interesting story. I was familiar with Bob Bergin's nonfiction writing, as he is a valued contributor to some of Primedia's historical magazines, so I expected a novel by him to be well worth reading. But I was impressed by this engaging and well-imagined tale." – **Nan Siegel**, Primedia History Group

WHEN TIGERS FLY

A Novel

Bob Bergin

IMPACT PUBLICATIONS

MANASSAS PARK, VA

When Tigers Fly

Liability: *When Tigers Fly* is a work of fiction. None of the characters or incidents mentioned in the book are real or based on real persons or events. Any resemblance is purely coincidental. The author and publisher shall not be liable for any presumptions on the contrary.

Cover Photo: Flying Tiger pilot Bob Layher, Flight Leader, 2nd Squadron "Panda Bears" AVG, standing in front of his P-40 Tomahawk in 1942.

ISBN: 1-57023-221-0

Library of Congress: 2004104214

Publisher: For information on Impact Publications, including current and forthcoming publications, authors, press kits, online bookstore, and submission requirements, visit the left navigation bar on the front page of our main company website: www.impactpublications.com.

Publicity/Rights: For information on publicity, author interviews, and subsidiary rights, contact the Media Relations Department: Tel. 703-361-7300, Fax 703-335-9486, or email: info@impactpublications.com.

Sales/Distribution: All U.S. bookstore sales are handled through Impact's trade distributor: National Book Network, 15200 NBN Way, Blue Ridge Summit, PA 17214, Tel. 1-800-462-6420. All special sales and distribution inquiries should be directed to the publisher: Sales Department, IMPACT PUBLICATIONS, 9104 Manassas Drive, Suite N, Manassas Park, VA 20111-5211 USA, Tel. 703-361-7300, Fax 703-335-9486, or email: info@impactpublications.com.

For the American Volunteer Group (AVG)

Flying Tigers

whose adventures in Asia

inspired mine

When Tigers Fly,

The heavens quake

At their thunder!

Michael Wang
(Translated from the Chinese)

The events and characters in this tale are fictitious. The American Volunteer Group (AVG) Flying Tigers whose aircraft inspired the tale are very real indeed. Fewer than 100 pilots and 200 support personnel comprised the group. They existed as a combat unit for only seven months. During that time they were credited with destroying 297 Japanese aircraft in the air and another 150 probably destroyed, which makes the AVG Flying Tigers one of the most effective units in the history of aerial warfare. Their exploits, as discussed by the characters in this novel, are described as they actually happened.

WHEN TIGERS FLY

Prologue

I nteresting," Harry said, for lack of anything else to say. The six photos spread out on the table before him were well focused, if not particularly well composed. Each was a clear, detailed scene of an open field with heavy foliage and small, roughly constructed buildings in the background. Each scene contained one or more airplanes. One photo showed two aircraft partially hidden under camouflage netting. The photos were of a kind familiar to anyone with an interest in aviation history. Harry wondered why the man across from him had bought him an expensive lunch to show him these photos. As the man sitting across from him did not comment, Harry continued.

"I say they're interesting because I've never seen them before. But there must be a lot of other photos like these that I haven't seen either."

"There are no others like this," Riley said finally. "I guarantee it. But you're the expert, Harry. Tell me what you see." Riley reached for his drink and added, "Or what you think you see."

"What I think I see?" This sounded like a challenge. Harry smiled the weary smile of an expert dealing with one of the more commonplace aspects of his field. He would spell it out. He leaned in toward the photos and started.

"Okay. What I think I see: In the center of each photo is a parked airplane. In a couple of the shots there are two. The airplanes are P-40s, an American fighter airplane that was built in great numbers during World War II. Although each photo seems to show a different airplane, each one has a shark mouth painted on its snout, and a winged tiger jumping through a 'V' painted on its side. Those markings are very distinct and very famous. I would say that each photo shows a P-40 'Tomahawk' that belonged to the 'AVG', the American Volunteer Group – or, as they were better known, the 'Flying Tigers'."

Riley was smiling. "Sounds good ... as far as it goes. When do you think those photos were taken?"

"By the looks of the background in each shot, I'd say they were taken in Burma, probably at the AVG's airfield at Toungoo." Harry looked down at the photos again. "By the length of the shadows I'd say it's late afternoon of a sunny day in November 1941."

"Why November 1941?"

Harry looked at Riley and shrugged. "Elementary, Doctor Riley. The Flying Tigers had their aircraft assembled and ready for business in early November 1941. Then on 7 December 1941 came Pearl Harbor day and the war started. The Flying Tigers went into combat not long after that. The aircraft in the photos look reasonably clean. There's no sign of damage or hastily done repairs. Even the paint looks good. So, I would say that these photos were taken before the Tigers went into combat, probably November 1941."

Riley's eyes held Harry's for a long moment. "I'm disappointed, Harry. Buzz Dorkin said you were a real expert. Particularly on the Flying Tigers." By the time he finished saying this, Riley managed to look completely exasperated. "Look a little harder, Harry. You're missing something."

Harry put on a crooked, slightly embarrassed smile. "Missed something, did I? Must be those shadows. Too long for November are they? How about 7 December 1941? Right on Pearl Harbor Day...." And then, looking down at the photos again he suddenly saw it. "Christ.... " He stared at it, and finally, with a tone of slight disgust in his voice, said, "Cheap trick."

Riley came right back at him. "No trick, Harry. But I'm still not sure you're getting the picture. Tell me what you see."

"All right," Harry said. "What I see – in the midst of a classic 1941 airfield scene – I see peeking out from a goddamn hangar the fender of a modern day car." He put his face closer to the photo. "Christ, it looks like the new Mercedes SL, the 2003 model."

He brought his face up from the photos and looked Riley square in the eye. "I'm not sure what you're getting at, Riley. Why create a classic World War II scene and then plant a 2003 Mercedes in the background? To see if my eyes are still sharp?"

"Don't flatter yourself, Harry. But actually I did have that scene set up. It's supposed to tell you that what you're looking at is a half dozen AVG P-40s parked in the present. Not 1941. The Mercedes is there to show that the time is now."

Harry thought about this. "What you've got is a 1941 scene with some restored P-40s – or maybe fiberglas replicas that have been painted to look like AVG Tomahawks. And somebody forgot to move his fancy car. I must say Riley, you did a good job. It looks very World War II."

"I guess you're not hearing me, Harry. Those are AVG P-40, 'B' Model Tomahawks."

Harry folded his napkin and pushed back his chair. "Thanks for lunch, Riley. I enjoyed it." Standing up, he added, "As far as the original Flying Tiger P-40s go, they were chopped up into pots and pans 60 years ago. Not one of the original AVG P-40s survived."

Riley motioned for Harry to sit down. "Wait, wait. Don't take it so personally. Seriously, Harry, if – and I said IF – if one of the original Flying Tiger P-40s survived until today, what would it be worth?"

Harry did not need to think about it. "It would be an icon. Easily be worth a couple of million. With some collectors you could ask what you wanted. A couple of million and maybe a lot more. Old warbirds are big business." Then the implication of what Riley was getting at struck him and he sat back down. "Are you tying to tell me that an original AVG P-40 survived?"

Riley gestured to the waiter to bring fresh drinks. Then he turned back to Harry. "No, I'm not going to tell you that. I'm

going to tell you that about eight of them did. At least those six,"
Riley said, pointing a finger at the photos on the table. "And we
think maybe two more." Riley raised his hand to hold back the
words that were about to pour from Harry.

"Wait, Harry. Before you say anything, let me tell you a story.
You've heard the tales about old World War II aircraft that are
still standing where they were abandoned on airstrips in now
inaccessible areas of Burma, Indonesia, and New Guinea?"

"Yeah, for years, but...."

"You visit Asia a lot. Have you heard stories more recently
about World War II aircraft flying in the skies of Burma and
southern China?"

"Yeah, I've heard those too. And I'm even less inclined to believe them."

"Right. Well, I don't know about any aircraft parked at their
old World War II airfields, but I know for a fact that some of
those old birds have been flying."

"Come on, Riley...."

"I said I would tell you a story. Once upon a time, about a
year ago it was, the people I'm associated with started hearing
stories of old World War II airplanes flying in the skies of Burma
and southern China. They decided to run down these rumors
and put me in charge. An old China hand I know put me in
touch with a former Burmese Air Force officer, an old guy, but a
smart guy who could travel easily around the countryside. I made
him an offer he couldn't refuse, and I got him a camera. I told
him I wanted proof, if proof was there to be had, and that I
needed photos of the aircraft, if they existed. I also needed something contemporary in the photos, something to prove the photos were taken now, not in 1941. I was thinking in terms of a
newspaper with a readable date lying on the wing. But some
guy parked his Mercedes in the scene. Anyway, out of all this
effort came a lot of waiting – and finally these photos. In a round-
about sort of way."

"Photos can be faked."

"Sure they can. But these were not. I've had them looked at by
experts – photo experts and airplane experts. The consensus is

the photos are real and the airplanes are real. In blowups, they tell me you can see the stuff that makes these airplanes genuine original P-40 'B' models. Tomahawks. All the markings on them – serial numbers and what have you – authenticate them as Flying Tiger aircraft, part of the original 100 P-40s that were sent to Claire Chennault in Burma during the summer of 1941. The site where these aircraft were photographed was not the AVG's old airfield at Toungoo, as you suggested. It probably is in Burma, someplace really remote, or maybe someplace in southern China. And people in those areas don't build fiberglas replicas."

Harry sat quietly, trying to look cool while feeling completely overwhelmed. Finally he said, "Who has these airplanes? Some cargo cult?" It had made Harry think of the Stone Age tribes in New Guinea, beneficiaries of U.S. cargo drops during World War II, who still revered aircraft, the bringer of this bounty.

"Maybe. Actually, what you're saying is not as silly as it sounds. You saw that fancy Mercedes. It's the new SL, a year 2003 model. It was probably first available in Asia in late 2002. The particular car with the P-40s was photographed with them in the summer of 2001. What does that tell you, Harry? What it tells me is money. Big money that can get you what you want when you want it. And an interest in classic machinery. Who would know about stuff like that? Who could afford it up in that rustic, remote, and mysterious area of Southeast Asia? Eh, Harry, you're the 'old Asia Hand'. You tell me who these people would be."

"If what you're talking about has any basis in reality, there would be only one match: the drug lords, the opium warlords."

Riley shrugged. "Now you know as much as we do, Harry. Essentially, what we have is six, or maybe eight very desirable airplanes, in a remote and dangerous area of Asia, and owned by the baddest guys in the neighborhood. And that's where you come in, Harry. What I and my associates would like you to do is to find those airplanes – and arrange their acquisition."

"Arrange their acquisition? You mean buy them, steal them, or what?"

"Whatever."

Harry managed a weak chuckle and shook his head. He sat quietly looking down at the photos and thought for a while. Finally he said, "You're not sure if the airplanes are in Burma or in China? Can you get a better fix from your photographer?"

"We'd like to, but we can't find the gentleman. He took the pictures. Got the film on its way to us – and then he disappeared. Maybe he got run over by an elephant or something."

Harry thought about this. Then he asked the question that had been bothering him: "Tell me, Riley, why me?"

"My associates speak highly of you as an Asia expert who also knows a bit about airplanes. We've all heard how you have experience moving ancient artifacts across borders. Unobtrusively."

"Exactly. I'm a dealer in art objects, not airplanes."

"It's all the same. You just called these airplanes 'icons'. Well, an icon is an artifact. So look on these airplanes as artifacts. They're certainly worth as much as some of the art you deal with." While he let Harry think about this, Riley took a big swallow of his drink. Then he continued.

"The group I represent really wants those airplanes. They are willing to pay well for them. On the basis of some strong recommendations, you are the prime candidate to find those airplanes and get them out of Burma, China – wherever they are. And get them out intact. Intact is very important, Harry."

Harry was trying hard to think this through. "I don't think I want to get involved," he said finally. He did not sound very convincing, even to himself.

Riley smiled a small smile and shrugged. "The money's good, Harry. The members of my group are all well fixed; they're not into this to make a profit. They love airplanes and history and what these Flying Tiger airplanes represent. They figure each of these P-40s is worth a million plus. You'd be the CEO of the whole operation. Your cut would be a healthy percentage of the market value of whatever you bring out, plus expenses. Think of it as a free vacation in Asia."

"A healthy percentage of market value. I like that kind of talk. You have my attention, Riley."

"Good. I'll go over the financials later. You won't have any problem with them. But first, let me tell you what we expect you to do...."

Chapter 1

Harry scrabbled over the top of the cliff on his hands and knees. He crawled well away from the edge before even glancing back at the water rushing by far below. "How do I get myself into these things?" he asked and pulled himself to his feet. Once upright, he turned back to face the river, cupped his hands at his mouth like a megaphone, and shouted out over the gorge, as loud as he could:

"We're the Fuckarewe!"

Now that felt good. He was just a kid when he first heard the old joke about the lost tribe. He had laughed and laughed when he finally understood it. In these last few days he had certainly earned his membership in the tribe of the Fuckarewe.

He took a single careful step closer to the edge and looked down. Not far below, his two companions were slowly edging their way up the narrow steps cut into the face of the cliff, clutching the rusty cable that served as a handrail as they came. He had not intended to leave them so far behind, but his interest in getting to the top had grown more intense the higher he climbed. Now that his ordeal was over, he was pleased. The backs of his legs felt tight, but he was not winded. He must be in better shape than he thought.

There was a sudden explosion of sound right above him.

Whirrrrr!

He snapped his head back to look up. The banners! They were directly overhead, just feet above him. Dazzling red and rustling

1

in the wind. Seen from a great distance down river they had been a flashing blaze of color above the grayness of the gorge. Stretched out by the wind now to their full length, he could see what he had not seen from below. Each was decorated with a row of yellow Chinese characters. He would have to ask Mouse what the writing meant.

He turned back to survey the top of this cliff he had just climbed. His eyes slowly swept the area off to his left – and suddenly locked with a pair of intense black eyes. They were set deeply in a fleshy Chinese face. It was a big man, dressed in dazzling white. He stood not a half dozen paces away. Harry and the man regarded each other for a long silent moment.

"Hi," Harry said. He raised his hand in greeting. What else was there to do? In response the big man raised his hand, held it above his head, and shook it. What he shook, actually, was a meat cleaver grasped in his big fist. He was shouting something now. To Harry it was just noise.

"Do you want a beer, Harry?" A different voice asked that question. It came from just behind him, female, familiar, and calm. "He wants to know if you want a beer? A cold one?"

Harry threw a quick glance over his shoulder to where his female companion had just arrived at the top of the cliff and was now casually brushing her hands on her jeans. It was decision time. Harry turned back to face the man with the cleaver. He looked him straight in the eye and said, "Beer," without a tremor in his voice, "beer for everybody." Keeping a careful eye on the man, Harry lowered his voice so only the young lady behind him could hear. "Who the hell is this guy, Mouse?"

"The cook. He said this is his restaurant."

"Restaurant?"

The big man lowered his cleaver and stood silently watching them. Mouse stepped right up to him, smiled, and said something melodious in an Asian language, although Harry was not sure which one. The big man smiled. He listened carefully to Mouse, then he nodded and lumbered off toward a small building with mostly open sides that stood at the far of the clearing. Less distracted now, Harry saw that the flat area right under the banners was occupied by a dozen or so long wooden tables and a collection of assorted stools. It was a restaurant. The small building where the big man was headed was probably the kitchen.

Harry grabbed a stool, dragged it to the nearest table, and sat down. Mouse sat down across from him. She took off her red baseball cap and shook out her long black hair. She looked cute in the cap, beautiful without it. Her face was Asian, young, and very pretty. The eyes that watched Harry were alert and intelligent.

Harry turned to look back at the deep river gorge, then he leaned back in his chair and sighed. "So, Mouse," he said, "this is what we have come to: a Chinese restaurant. All those days fighting our way up the river, and here, at the end … a Chinese restaurant. I guess that's what the banners say."

Before Mouse could respond, a movement to the side caught their attention. A head poked over the edge of the cliff. Anxious eyes swept the area and fixed on Harry.

"What's happening? Why is everyone shouting?" The questions were asked in a very soft tone and the language was Thai. It was the final member of the crew, and up to now the most important one, Wit, the captain of their boat. Harry responded in Thai, "No problem, Wit. Come on up. We're having a beer."

Wit pulled himself over the edge and walked to their table. He sat down, but watched uneasily as the big Chinese cook approached with a tray from which he unloaded three large bottles and three glasses filled with jagged pieces of ice.

After the cook walked away, Harry put a finger on one of the bottles and said, "Warm." He picked up the glass and, with a practiced flick of his wrist, pitched the ice out over the river. Mouse shrugged. She and Wit poured their beer over the ice in their glasses. They tipped their glasses to each other and then to Harry and drank deeply. Harry carefully examined the rim of his glass. Then he pushed the glass aside and took a big drink right from the bottle.

"Beer is best when it is cold," Mouse said. She took another big swallow and added, "The little things that live in the ice will make you stronger."

"You mean they will make me sick."

"A little. But you will be stronger for it."

The three of them sat quietly, drank their beer, and contemplated the river below. They were all a bit exhausted, a little numb. The last two days had been rough as the river narrowed and the current their small boat pushed against grew stronger. The banks of the river turned into stone cliffs that grew higher with every mile they made. The going was slow and they probably had not covered as much distance as it seemed, but the constant "chug, chug, chug" of the engine and the absence of a beach where they could put in had wearied them. The red banners had beckoned them from a long way off. When they finally saw the small rocky beach at the foot of the cliff below the banners, and the steps cut into the stone, the decision to go ashore was quick and unanimous.

After a long time Harry said, "Where do you think we are, Mouse? China? Burma?"

"I don't know. Maybe China. But it could be Burma. There is nothing on our maps I could recognize. What the cook speaks is some Chinese, some Burmese, some tribal language. He says China is up the river."

"Always up the river. The maps aren't worth a damn here. They stopped meaning anything five days ago. Nobody has been up this way in a long time – at least nobody who makes maps."

Harry looked over at Wit, who had said nothing, but appeared very relaxed. When he caught Harry looking at him, he raised his glass and tipped it to Harry with a big smile.

"Wit, you look happy to be off the river," Harry said. "Too happy."

Wit smiled some more and said a single word, "Aroy," the Thai word for "delicious." The bottle of beer in front of him was empty.

"Mouse," Harry said, "why don't you order Wit another beer. And find out what's on the menu."

Mouse called for the cook, and in moments the two were deep in a discussion of food in a language – or languages – that were beyond Harry's ability to identify, let alone comprehend. After a while Mouse announced that steamed dumplings was the dish to order. "They are made with the meat of a big fish that lives in the river. And we will have chicken with chilies, and some vegetables and rice. And more beer."

Wit's comprehension of English was not great, but it was good enough to catch the universal sound of the word "beer," and he smiled when he heard it. At least Wit was enjoying the beer. To Harry it tasted funny. Too warm, maybe. It was surprising though, how relaxed it had made him when he really had not drunk much of it at all. It must be the long slow days spent on the river, he thought. Beer had never had much effect on him before.

Harry shrugged philosophically and looked back at the river. It was pleasant up here. The breeze was gentle and steady now, and from this height the river looked clean. There was none of the boat traffic that he would have expected to see on any river in Asia. In the last two days of fighting their way upstream, they had seen few boats going in either direction. On the lengthy stretch of river he could see from here, there was a single boat, pushing its way upriver. Probably the same small craft they had passed yesterday.

Harry stood up to get a view of the small rocky beach right below them, where their own little vessel was beached. It had a tiny cabin, a faded blue hull, and a tough little engine that beat its single note relentlessly, hour after hour. One day when the going was particularly tough, Wit said that in his life as a boatman, he had never seen an engine so strong, so sure of itself. Harry knew Wit was right. It was a special engine, he told Wit. Under his breath he said a quiet "Thank you, Sato–san."

The food arrived and the fish dumplings were indeed excellent. And the food revived them. Over the meal, Mouse and Harry argued about the most interesting and amusing things they had seen on the trip so far. There were few such things, in fact. It had been a boring, monotonous journey. One incident had been notable: Two small ferry boats collided on the only day that Mouse appeared on deck in a bikini instead of jeans. It was amusing enough, but cost them a couple of hours while Harry and

Wit fished some of the passengers out of the river and took them ashore. Mouse maintained that she was not responsible.

"A woman's body is the same everywhere," she insisted then, and repeated to Harry now. "To see a woman's body does not make boats crash."

"I agree, Mouse. It wasn't seeing a woman's body that distracted the boatmen. Seen one, seen them all. Nope. It was the bikini. That flash of fashion never before seen in this region of the world. It distracted them. It probably inspired them. On our way back we'll probably see all the ladies wearing bikinis."

Sitting across from them, Wit ate and drank heartily and seemed to be amused by what he understood of their conversation, but he had little to say. He smiled and bowed his thanks when Mouse put a dumpling or a choice bit of chicken in his dish, but otherwise seemed lost in his own thoughts.

Over dessert that was a great mound of papaya, watermelon, and pineapple, Harry turned again toward the river. The small boat he had noticed earlier was still in almost the same place, beating its way against the current. Farther downstream, a speck on the surface caught his eye, another small boat probably, making its slow way up the river. Those were the only things moving. Looking upriver, there was nothing at all to be seen.

As he slipped a chunk of golden yellow papaya into his mouth, Harry happened to glance downstream again. The small boat was still in the same place, and the speck farther off in the distance was there, but bigger than before. Even as he watched, it grew bigger. He reached for his beer and sipped while keeping his eye on it. The speck was not only growing, it seemed to be levitating, rising above the surface of the river. Harry's eyes stayed fixed on this phenomena for only a few seconds more before he turned to Mouse.

"Airplane," Mouse said, answering his question before he could ask it.

Of course it was an airplane. Mouse had good eyes. Harry looked back, and the speck had grown big enough for him to distinguish the tail and an engine on each wing. The aircraft was coming their way, moving fast, just skimming the surface of the river. And with it came the sound of engines.

Mouse and Harry both stood up to watch it go by. The aircraft was so low that it passed well below them. It was a big airplane, painted the drab green of a distant jungle. A single Chinese character was painted in bright red on its nose. The roar of its big engines shook them as it went by, then faded into a dull rumble that followed the airplane out of sight.

"Wow!" Harry yelled. "Damn! Did you see that! Incredible! I cannot believe it!" Mouse watched with some amusement and a question on her face as Harry danced a small jig and punched at the air. She had never seen him so excited. He looked ready to leap over the gorge. "Did you see that, Mouse? A C–46! I cannot believe it!"

"It is not the airplane we are looking for," Mouse stated, with a small uncertainty in her voice.

"It's not." Harry had a grin from ear to ear. "It's not the one we want, but it's an omen. It's a good sign."

For the first time in the weeks that he had been on this quest, Harry felt he was headed in the right direction. "It's a C–46, Mouse, a big old cargo airplane. It's not what we're looking for, but it's from the same era, the same war. The C–46 was used a lot in this area during World War II, and right after it. As far as I know, there's only one in all the world that's flying. And that one is nowhere near here. What we just saw is a museum piece of an airplane that nobody knows about. Just flying along, just going about its business. It's something I just never expected to see. It gives me hope that what we came out here looking for is really here."

"Vroooom!"

This noise was loud, and it came from Wit. As Harry turned toward him, Wit laughed, and then yelled, "Airplane!" With his arms stretched out to his sides, Wit ran a quick circle around a table. "Vroooom!" he cried again. This was so unlike Wit that Harry and Mouse just stood and stared.

"What the hell got into him?" Harry asked as Wit upset a chair making an unsuccessful landing attempt.

"I think he's drunk," Mouse said.

"Drunk? He's only drinking beer! And he didn't have much of that."

"Walk Like Elephant!" Wit shouted this in English. He belched, smiled an apology, and ambled off into the bushes.

There were two empty beer bottles on the table where Wit had been sitting and Harry picked one up. "The beer did taste kind of funny," he said as he examined it. "I don't know what kind of beer it is, Chinese probably." The label had a full face view of a trumpeting elephant. Around the elephant was a ring of Chinese characters, and around that, a ring of Burmese writing.

"Hey, Mouse, come look at this. Can you read any of this label?"

Mouse studied the label for a few moments. "This character is used for beer." She put her finger on it. "And this one is sometimes used for elephant."

"And it's a goddamn African elephant, Mouse. Look at the size of those ears. Can you read any of the Burmese?"

"I cannot recognize Burmese words when I try to read it." She turned the bottle, as if looking at it from a different angle would make the label comprehensible. "Maybe," she said, "they use the Burmese sounds to make Chinese words." She tried to mouth the sounds that the Burmese alphabet made. It was less than melodious, and finally she shrugged. "I cannot make Chinese words from the Burmese letters."

Harry looked at her thoughtfully for a moment. "Read those words again, Mouse. Out loud."

Mouse's face frowned as she concentrated on pronouncing the Burmese alphabetics. "Pack. Add. Durm," she pronounced. And at last: "Beer!" Mouse smiled. "The last letters make the sound for the English word 'beer'."

"It's all English, Mouse. What you just read, it's all English. Do you know what you just read?"

"No," she said, looking a little puzzled.

"What you just read were the sounds for two English words: 'Pachyderm beer'. The name of the stuff in the bottle that Wit's been drinking is 'Pachyderm beer', the beer of the elephant. Pachyderm, for god's sake."

Harry stared at the bottle in his hand. He shook his head. "This is a day for omens. Who is the one man you know who calls an elephant a pachyderm?"

"Aloysious!" Mouse clapped her hands. "Your friend, Aloysious! His company in Chiang Mai was named 'Pachyderm Tours'. Before. When the two of you got in big trouble with the Thai police."

"He's the one. 'Walk Like an Elephant'. That was his motto."

"That's what Wit said! Does Wit know something?"

"Maybe, but I think he just recognized the long–eared elephant on this label. I think it's the same one Aloysious had on his T-shirt. Wit was just quicker than us to pick up on it."

"Do you think this is Aloysious's beer?"

Harry paused for a moment before speaking. He shook his head. "I'd say it's an omen, Mouse, a sign that we're on to some-thing. But it would be too much of a coincidence to expect Aloysious to be involved with this. Life just doesn't work that way."

"But you were expecting to see him in Burma. You told me that when the Thai police were after you, you escaped in Mr. Sato's helicopter, and the helicopter dropped Aloysious near the border so he could sneak into Burma."

"I would love to run into Aloysious in Burma. He'd be a big help. But I'm not really expecting to find him. Nobody's heard from him in a long time. I checked."

"But, Harry, you said he was going into Burma to make beer."

Harry pondered this and the evidence before him. "You know, Mouse, you may have something. We've probably come as far up the river as we can. It would be rough going, pushing farther up the river from here. But it's sort of what Aloysious would do – go as far as he could – and if that happened to be the edge of the world, which is where I think we are, he would feel safe and maybe just hunker down. It's not like he had a lot of places to go."

Harry put one of the Pachyderm beer bottles to his mouth.
What a vile taste. He put it under his nose. Oh, lord, it smelled
worse than it tasted.

Harry shook his head again. "This is nothing Aloysious would
drink. But then Aloysious never had much respect for other
people's taste. The whole idea is so outrageous that it just could
be Aloysious making this crud." He looked around, briefly surveying his surroundings where he stood at the edge of the gorge.
This was indeed the edge of the world. It was as he had just said
to Mouse: It was not like Aloysious had anyplace to go.

"I think you may be right, Mouse. We need to find out what's
going on. We need a plan."

             *   *   *

It was not much of a plan, but at least they had one. Mouse
would try to find out where the Pachyderm beer was coming
from, while Harry would try to find where Wit had gone off to.
It was well past noon now, and the restaurant had been doing a
good business. Almost all the customers were men, hardy types
who looked like they spent their lives working under the sun
and were completely comfortable there. They came via a road
that approached the restaurant on the side opposite the river
where small hills could be seen off in the distance. Some walked,
a few rode motorcycles, but most came by twos and threes in
battered pickup trucks. No one came from the river.

Most of the diners ate quickly and departed. A few small
groups remained, talking quietly, except for one table where five
young men were drinking, laughing, and generally being very
loud. Every table had a bottle or two of Pachyderm beer on it,
but the rowdy table had a collection of Pachyderm beer bottles
encircling the center of the table like a brown glass picket fence.

Harry found Wit quickly. He had not gone far. He sat at a
table away from the other patrons. One arm propped on the
table held his head up. When Harry got closer he saw his eyes
were squeezed shut and he might have been dozing.

"Wit, what's happening?" Harry asked in Thai, trying to sound as sympathetic as he could.

Wit's eyes opened slowly to regard Harry. "I don't know, Mr. Harry. Maybe river fever. My head hurts. My stomach feels like a small animal is inside and fighting to come out."

"Does your mouth taste like that small animal did something dirty in it?"

"It tastes like a not–so–small animal shit in it."

"Ah, the defining symptom, Wit. I'm afraid it's not river fever you have. It's a hangover."

"Hangover?" Wit rubbed his temples with both hands. "Why? Why would I have a hangover?"

"The beer. It's not very good. It tastes like what the animal did in your mouth."

Wit looked Harry right in the eye. "No, no, Mr. Harry," he disagreed, "the beer is good." He looked ready to continue his defense of the beer when Mouse walked up.

"Wit," she said, "you look like you need to go back to the boat and get some sleep."

"Wit's got river fever," Harry said. "He'd never make it down those steps. You just rest here, Wit. What did you learn, Mouse?"

"I learn from the cook that every day a truck comes with rice and vegetables and chickens. That truck also brings the beer. It will come today, maybe in one hour."

"Good show, Mouse! Now, what do we do when the truck comes? Mug the driver?"

"I think I can talk to him. He will tell me where he gets the beer. I will get ready now."

"Get ready? Okay. I hope the driver speaks a language you do."

"I will find out," Mouse winked and thrust a shapely hip in Harry's direction. Then she flicked him a snappy salute and strode off in the direction of the restaurant's small building. "I bet you will," Harry said, watching her go.

Glancing back toward Wit, Harry noticed a child, off by itself a small distance behind Wit's chair, playing some sort of game. It wore a long sarong and, although he could not be certain,

Harry thought it was probably a girl. He watched her toss a ball
in the air, then run a small circle, trying to be under it when it
came down. Harry had no great interest in children and would
not have given her further thought, except that every toss of the
ball brought her closer and closer to Wit. When she was almost
close enough to touch him, she reached her hand out – but was
just not close enough to touch Wit's back pocket, where a lump
showed he kept his wallet. One more toss of the ball and the kid
would reach it.

Harry had seen enough of the poor regions of the world not to
be greatly surprised. Any enterprising kid would take advantage of the windfall that Wit in his current state represented.
Harry sighed. He felt responsible for Wit. It was probably best to
intervene. He approached the child quietly from behind and got
within an arm's length without being noticed.

"Okay, kid," he said, and grabbed the child's shoulder. She
lurched forward, but Harry held on. This is one strong kid, he
thought as she twisted and squirmed. When she seemed to realize that she could not break free, she suddenly turned on him.

Harry immediately dropped his hand from the child's shoulder. "God! What an ugly child!" He said it aloud. The face of this
child was old. The skin had the deep furrows of an 80-year old.
And the nose! The nose was big and gnarled and red. The child
ran off, looking back, grinning – and cackling. Harry shuddered.

Aware now of Harry's presence, Wit mumbled, "If I eat something – and drink a beer – I will feel fine."

"I'll get you a coke, Wit. And rice or something." Harry was
not particularly concerned with Wit's needs at this point. Still
recovering from his encounter with the ugly child, he now saw
a transformed Mouse exiting a door near the kitchen. Gone was
the baseball cap; waves of glimmering black hair fell over her
shoulders. The baggy cotton shirt she wore seemed to have gotten tighter and clung to her slim torso and her finely shaped
breasts. Where two top buttons were undone was a glow of
golden skin. Her jeans fit better too and followed closely the graceful curves of her thighs and sleek tail. From the sometimes rowdy

shipmate of the last two weeks, Mouse had turned into an attractive and exceptionally healthy–looking young woman.

As she walked up to him, Harry said, "You look great, Mouse. I guess you're serious about getting us information."

"Thank you," Mouse said modestly "The truck is here. I will have to go."

Harry felt a twinge of uneasiness. "Good luck," he said and watched her walk off.

He moved to a table from where he could see a beat–up white pickup truck being unloaded by the big cook and one of his helpers. There were baskets of vegetables, bundles of squawking chickens, and a dozen assorted crates. At least a half dozen of the crates bore the stenciled red head of a trumpeting elephant.

At first he did not see Mouse at all. When the truck was unloaded, the cook, the helper, and the truck driver walked back to the kitchen. Minutes later, the truck driver reappeared, walking back toward the truck. He was about to climb into the cab when Mouse materialized alongside him. Harry was too far off to hear, but she must have said something. The driver glanced back, then turned completely around to face her. Mouse moved closer, and soon the two were talking. All smiles now, the driver led Mouse around to the other side of the truck, opened the door, and helped her in. He walked back to his side, climbed in, and within moments the truck drove off. Harry's last glimpse of Mouse was of a young girl brushing a strand of hair away from a face that wore a tight little smile. She looked vulnerable, out of her depth. Oh, my god, he thought, and felt a little sorry for the driver.

Chapter 2

A short way down the road from the restaurant was an old tree. Harry sat in its shade and waited for Mouse's return. Every once in a while the sound of a poorly muffled engine in the distance would signal an approaching vehicle and he would sit up and wait expectantly for the white pickup. And usually it was a white pickup truck that came along. He eventually decided that here at the edge of the world, all pickup trucks were painted white and all were beaten with the same giant mallet. He slowly came to realize that he probably would not recognize the truck that had carried Mouse off – if it did ever return. With that thought he got concerned, just as another pickup sped by. Just past him it braked to a stop and then reversed. Mouse was at the wheel. No one else was in the truck.

"Nice wheels," Harry said, as casually as he could. "Did you buy or lease?"

"I borrowed it," Mouse replied. "The driver won't need it for a while."

"Is he okay?"

"Maybe. He has to sleep for a while." When it was apparent that this did not satisfy Harry, she added, "He is in a shed for animals. By a house where no one lives. He wanted me to go into the house with him. I told him I had a better idea."

Harry shrugged. "How about the beer?"

"I know where it comes from. In a village, maybe ten kilometers from here. There is a shop that sells food in boxes and cans and soda. They have the beer. It is a poor place. An old tribal man is the owner."

"Did you talk with anyone there?"

"Yes, but it is difficult. Everyone speaks pieces of different languages."

"Doesn't sound promising."

"Maybe, but it made me think, Harry. Here they sell only elephant beer. Before I put him in the animal shed, I asked the truck driver to stop at a snack bar on the road and buy me a soda. At the snack bar they sell only elephant beer."

"That's not so unusual in a place so far from the rest of the world."

"Yes, but they had many other things from China and from Thailand, things less important than beer. I asked if there was other beer. The man at the snack bar said everyone wants the elephant beer. It is so strong. So good."

"It must get to taste good here at the edge of the world. I thought it was crap. Maybe we should poke around the village."

"Yes, I think we should. Maybe you will see something I did not."

Mouse drove and they headed down the worn dirt road that was the only road going anywhere. There was little to see. Except for the hills in the distance, the country was flat and worn out looking. Scraggly trees grew here and there. They were the survivors, not attractive enough to catch the eye of the children charged with gathering firewood. There were low-growing shrubs with thorns that warded off the creatures that might otherwise be hungry enough to eat them. What grass there was, was dried-out looking and had the gray-brown color of the ground it grew on. The edge of the world was a very unattractive place. Recalling his encounter with the ugly child, it struck Harry that to survive here, maybe a thing had to blend into the general unattractiveness of the place.

The road met a smaller one that was even more rutted. Where the two roads crossed was the village, a small gathering of drab wooden huts faded to the gray-brown of everything else. Just beyond the crossroads was a petrol station where gasoline was pumped by hand from large, rusty metal drums. There were few vehicles to be seen, and no cars, only white pickups parked in the shade of the occasional tree. Almost no people were in sight. An adolescent petrol attendant dozed near the gasoline drums. Sharing the shade of his tree was a pair of old men playing chess with bottle caps. Across from the petrol station was the shop that sold Pachyderm beer. Harry and Mouse crossed the street. They did not bother to look both ways.

As he stepped into the shop and out of the sun's glare and the heat that drenched the street, Harry experienced a brief moment of relief. But even before his eyes could adjust to the darkness of the shop, he felt an even greater heat. The air was heavy and full of the sound of flies. It was a barrier he had to push through.

The proprietor was strategically placed to guard the only door. He sat at a scarred old wooden school desk. The T-shirt he wore looked grimy, and the faded face of a famous French cartoon character was barely recognizable. In his clenched fist he held a plastic fly swatter that he used as a fan to push air at his face, and as a weapon to wave menacingly at flies that intruded into his air space.

Harry looked around the store in wonderment. If you lived at the edge of the world, this must be desirable. Shelves lining the walls displayed smaller items, haphazardly stacked tin cans and cardboard boxes that looked faded and worn. Long tables in rows along the floor held bigger items: stacks of red and yellow plastic pans and dishes, pairs of antique-looking high-top sneakers, piles of faded green field jackets from an army whose sole decorative element was a red star. Other tables held food specialties, dried out things mostly, heaps of fish and squid flat and brown like old cardboard, red and green mounds of chilies of different sorts and sizes, and little multicolored hills of spice.

Harry walked slowly through the shop, looking as he went. At the rear, he stopped to examine a table heaped with brightly colored bags of banana chips, taro chips, shrimp chips, and even potato chips, all fried and bagged in China and Thailand. He brushed the dust from the label of a bottle of classic French mineral water, tested a made-in-China nail clipper, and peered through a pair of magnifying spectacles to watch two flies wrestle. He took a final look around and turned to Mouse, who had been keeping close behind.

"There's no beer. Where does he keep it?"

"The truck driver said he picked it up at the back door."

"Okay, tell the old man we want to buy a case of Pachyderm. God knows what we'll do with it."

Mouse walked over to the proprietor and said something, but the old man seemed not to hear. His eyes were fixed on a flight of flies engaged in convoluted aerobatics just over his left shoulder. Mouse tried again, perhaps in a different language, Harry thought. This time the old man turned to listen. When she finished, the old man said incomprehensible words in a croaking voice. Mouse bowed to him and walked back to Harry.

"He said to pick it up at the back door. His boy will put it in our truck."

"You bring the truck," Harry said. "I want to walk back there."

Harry stepped back into the sun with relief. It seemed cooler on the street now. He turned and walked down along the side of the building. A door near the back slid open and a head poked out. An adolescent male. As Harry approached, the face scowled and withdrew. It was replaced by the face of an agitated elephant printed on a case of Pachyderm beer. Harry grabbed at the beer as Mouse drove up. As he dropped it into the bed of the pickup, he saw the boy, smiling and bowing gracefully at Mouse.

You're just too cute, Mouse, Harry thought as he stepped away from the truck and collided with the old shopkeeper. The old man thrust the fly swatter at Harry, who flinched before he realized that the old man was only warning off a pair of flies hovering indecisively over his shoulder. Before the flies or Harry could react, the old man pushed out his other hand. It held a card. As Harry grabbed it, the old man said a single word.

"Excuse me," Harry said, to apologize for seizing the card the way he did, and also for missing what the man had said. The

man repeated it. A single word in English: "Dinner." At least
that was what Harry understood. He looked down at the card.
It was in English and nicely printed.

"What a Small World!
For Lunch
For Dinner
For High Tea
And always serving Pachyderm Beer.
It's Tasty; It's Strong! It's Pachyderm Beer!
Strong as a Pachyderm!"

"Mouse," Harry said, "Mouse, come here quick." When she
hurried to him, he said, "Talk to this guy. Debrief him. Find out
where this place is."

The directions Mouse got from the old man pointed them up
into the hills beyond the town. Their destination, he said, was
no more than a dozen kilometers off, set in a small valley surrounded by hills.

They drove in the way the old man said, and the farther they
got from the village, the nicer the world became. They started to
see trees that looked like trees, and grass and bushes that were
green. The sun shone as brightly as it did in the village, but the
air here was cool and fresh. Harry was thinking how good he
felt, better than he had in days, when Mouse interrupted his
thoughts. "The old man said that when we get close, we will see
signs for the parking lot."

"Parking lot?" Harry said. "This is the edge of the world. Who
needs a parking lot?"

Mouse shrugged. "If it is a good restaurant, it should have a
parking lot. Isn't that normal?"

"Yeah, it's normal. In Bangkok, even Rangoon. But here at
the edge of the world? I'd say that's anything but normal."

"You worry too much, Harry."

The road narrowed as the brush to either side grew thicker.
They bumped their way through a curve and found a huge sign
in a clearing that said: "What a Small World! Free Parking! 3

Km." They passed two more signs like it, the first painted in Chinese characters; the second in Burmese. As far as Mouse could make out, they said the same thing the first sign did: Free parking was just ahead. Harry shook his head in disbelief.

When they first saw it in the distance, "What a Small World" looked big. Closer to it, they saw that it was indeed big, a compound of many buildings contained within a great log stockade. It looked like a set from an American Indian war saga. An arrow pointed though an open gate: "What a Small World! Free Parking!"

The parking area contained a dozen of the usual battered white pickups and a few small sedans in two neat rows. Harry looked at his watch; it was a little after four in the afternoon.

"Business is good," he said. "Must be tea time."

They parked the truck, and from where he stood Harry could see numerous wooden structures, the biggest right in front of him. It was a large open building, a kind of grand pavilion. The entire structure was raised at least ten feet above the ground on massive wooden poles. A broad staircase led up to the entrance, over which a multi-colored carved sign said:

"What a Small World!"

Harry and Mouse stopped at the top of the staircase to take in the interior of the pavilion, a vast single room open to the daylight. The floor of highly polished teak planks gleamed as if sheathed in honey-colored gold. Their eyes followed the great wood pillars that rose from the floor up to an intricate latticework of wood beams that supported the roof and glowed softly in reflected light.

Harry swiveled his head trying to take it all in. "There's a forest in here. A fortune in teak."

"All of this is teak?" Mouse remarked with awe in her voice.

"It's all teak. Beautiful, isn't it?"

"Please. Walk this way." The shrill voice seemed to come out of nowhere. Harry turned completely around, but he saw no one. That was strange. Inspired, he looked down. Looking up at him was a distinguished face. It was attached to a very small person wearing flowing white pantaloons. Above the pantaloons was a white shirt with billowing sleeves under a scarlet waist-coat. It took Harry a moment to interpret what he was seeing. It was a miniature English butler. A miniature gentleman's gentle-man who had been conned into playing a part in a children's Arabian Nights fantasy.

The little gentleman bowed and said, "Please, walk this way." When Harry did not immediately respond, the gentleman looked back over his shoulder and frowned.

Mouse tugged at Harry's sleeve to get him moving. They fol-lowed the little gentleman toward the center of the room and a cluster of tables. Perhaps a third of the tables were occupied by groups of men, mostly young and mostly tough-looking. On each table stood a collection of Pachyderm beer bottles, but there was no sign of food. The buzz of conversation that Harry noted when they entered the room had ceased. By the time they reached their table there was silence.

"Nice place," Harry said, looking back at some of the eyes looking at him. "Seems to be a guy hangout."

"There are ladies over there," Mouse said. Harry looked and saw that there were indeed eight or ten ladies, sitting around a pair of coffee tables. As in many Asian social settings, the sexes had segregated themselves.

The little gentleman left them briefly and then reappeared. He did not bring the menus Harry had expected, but a silver tray with two large bottles of Pachyderm. The strong aftertaste of the beer he had at lunch still lingered in his memory.

"Look," he said to the little gentleman, "neither of us is up to beer right now. Could we have coke or an iced tea to start? Then we'll probably want high tea. We'll need a menu."

The little gentleman watched Harry intently as he said this, then stared at him even more intently after he finished speaking.

Mouse broke what was becoming an awkward silence. "Harry, I think you speak too quickly. He is not able to follow what you say." She turned to the little gentleman and said some-thing melodious that Harry did not understand. The little gentle-man opened his hands with a smile. He said words that Harry again could not understand, except for 'high tea'.

Mouse turned back to Harry. "Harry," she said, "this is high tea. High tea in this place is Pachyderm beer."

"Mouse, you must have misunderstood him. I can't drink that swill. I need something more benign. And I'm hungry."

Mouse turned to the little gentleman and, in the language they shared, tried to explain. The man looked back at Harry, and by the time Mouse finished, he was positively glowering at him. Harry had started to think that this could well turn into something awkward when the little gentleman suddenly turned on his heel and walked off.

Harry looked at Mouse. She shrugged. Harry leaned back in his chair and looked up at the ceiling. Lost in his thoughts he saw little of the beauty of its construction. Not much time had passed when Mouse cleared her throat in warning.

Harry looked up to see, marching directly at them, another little gentleman. This one was no taller than the miniature butler, but he was a man of a different cut, muscular and tough-looking – despite his pantaloons that were a shocking pink. Harry glanced at the pantaloons, then looked at the big chest and shoulders that filled a short navy blue jacket that had large gold buttons and gold braid. Gold sergeant's stripes were mounted high on each sleeve. All this finery was topped off by a peaked red hat with a gold braided visor. Harry and Mouse looked on in awe. The man stopped directly in front of them and saluted smartly.

Trying not to look intimidated, Harry said to Mouse out the side of his mouth, "They've brought up some rank. Could you explain to the mini-sergeant here that we need to order something more substantial and drinkable than this Pachyderm swill....?"

"No need for that, suh. We can converse directly." The sergeant's voice was deep and properly English.

"Oh," said Harry, taken aback by this unexpected development. "Well, Sergeant, perhaps you can...."

"Not Sergeant, suh. It is P.C. Jumbo here to serve you, suh."

Harry smiled despite an effort not to. "P.C. Jumbo, is it? A good name, Jumbo. But the rank is unfamiliar. What exactly is a P.C?"

"Pocket Commander, suh."

"Ah, yes, Pocket Commander, of course. And what are your duties here, P.C. Jumbo?"

"I'm the small chap who takes care of the small problems, suh, so the big boss can take care of the big problems."

That sounded almost ominous, thought Harry. "And who is the big boss?" he asked.

"The Raj, suh. We call him the Raj."

Harry's mind tumbled as it tried to come to grips with this distortion of time and place. Before he could say anything, P.C. Jumbo spoke again. "But on to our business, suh. You are not pleased with our selections for high tea?"

"No, no," Harry said. "Whatever your selections for high tea, I'm sure they would be fine. It's just that your man served us beer and called it high tea."

"We won't quibble, suh."

"Quibble! There's a hell of a difference between beer and tea."

"Suh! If you would come with me please. I'm sure we can find a way to fix this problem." Emphasis was on the word 'fix'.

For the first time since P.C. Jumbo had appeared, Harry took a quick look around the room. The silence was absolute. No one looked his way. It seemed every person in the room was intent on whatever his or her glass contained. When Harry looked back at him, P.C. Jumbo was waiting patiently. Harry looked at Mouse. On her face was a small Mona Lisa smile. She shrugged. "You worry too much," she said. There was no support there.

"Lead on, P.C. Jumbo," Harry said and got to his feet. "Lead on."

P.C. Jumbo led him across the wide floor to a door at the far end. They entered a long narrow space that seemed to be a hallway. Halfway down this passage, they passed windows, and Harry saw that they were above ground level, probably in a kind of enclosed bridge that connected the pavilion to wherever it was they were going. They passed through another door and entered a dimly lit corridor. This smelled different. Not the fresh-cut wood smell of the pavilion, but the musty odor of a big old house. They turned a corner and walked up to an entrance guarded by two huge and ornately carved doors. With some effort, P.C. Jumbo pushed one of the doors open, and Harry stepped into a book-lined room that he had seen countless times in old British movies.

"Where the hell are we, Jumbo?"

"Please wait here, suh." With that, P.C. Jumbo stepped back into the corridor.

Harry took the opportunity to explore. It was a time warp. He was in a classic Victorian study, completely intact, and furnished with the best of what the era produced. Portraits on the walls showed serious-looking gentlemen with serious whiskers, and beautiful ladies in beautiful gowns. There was a framed collection of early photographs, children and family groups, all in traditional British country settings. He glanced down at the highly polished desk that dominated the room and saw pens, an elegant cut glass inkwell, and a stack of expensive paper, all waiting for the British gentleman with the curved mustache and the high white collar who had trotted off to the W.C. just before he and P.C. arrived. This had to be one of the grand old houses that the British had built when this place was a part of the empire. It had probably housed a Colonial Administrator, a District Officer, or maybe a trader who had milked the wealth out of the area for the glory of the empire.

Harry whistled under his breath to contain his excitement. Old stuff did that to him sometimes. Old stuff, saleable stuff. It was the merchant in him reacting. And this was saleable stuff. All of it, and some of it looked pretty good. God save whatever remains of the British Empire, he thought, at least until we can find a way to ship this stuff out of here. It was at that moment that P.C. Jumbo reappeared.

"If you will come with me, suh. We're off to see the Raj."

It was an opportunity to see more of the house and Harry welcomed it. He had already forgotten whatever concern he had about meeting "the Raj." They went up a grand stairway that curved toward a domed ceiling high above. On the first landing they turned down a long wide corridor to another large set of doors. Each of the huge doors appeared to be cut from a single plank of an enormous ancient tree and then finely carved with scenes of entwined gods and goddesses doing things that would make a Victorian housewife blush. With his attention fully on the doors, Harry hardly noticed the two uniformed men standing alongside them. The fact that they were no bigger than P.C. Jumbo made little impression on him.

Chapter 3

hey went through the doors and into a large room that stretched out before them. Long mirrors on the side walls reflected Harry and P.C. Jumbo as they marched down its length. Once this was a ballroom, Harry thought, a hundred years ago when the British gentry gathered together here on a Saturday night to dance and drink and dull the loneliness at the edge of the empire – at the edge of the world. There were no furnishings in the room now, not a chair, not a vase, not a picture on the wall. A small area at the very end of the room was raised above the floor, a small stage. In the center of the stage was a great beautifully carved wooden chair. Harry recognized it as a preaching chair on which the abbot of some Buddhist monastery would sit when he addressed the faithful. As Harry and P.C. Jumbo approached the stage, a door in the wall behind it opened.

Out they marched, two by two, four little men. All were dressed in the white pantaloons and the shirt with billowing sleeves of the mini English butler in the dining pavilion. Each carried an oversized spear. With a small shock, Harry recognized that one of them was the mini English butler, and the pair at the rear might well have been the two guarding the door to the ballroom, but he could not be sure. They did look a bit winded. The four spearmen positioned themselves on either side of the big chair and stood at attention, spears upright before them.

25

There was nothing but silence for a moment, then through the door stepped two more small men. Both wore kilts and the other regalia that would have made them at home in Scotland. One carried a drum, the other a bagpipe. They marched into position before the big chair. The drummer beat a long drum roll and the piper started puffing into his pipe and produced an assortment of hisses, shrieks, and howls. Through the din Harry started to pick out a tune. He knew it had to be a British colonial air, but it sure sounded very much like *A Yellow Rose of Texas*.

When the steam engine sounds of the bagpiper eventually subsided, there was a silence that Harry found pleasing. Then a voice came through the door. It was loud and familiar. "Well, well, Harry Ross. What a small world!"

And through the door stepped Aloysious P. Grant, dreamer, schemer, and fugitive. This meeting was inevitable, Harry thought. In anything he did or probably would ever do in Asia, his fate linked him to Aloysious. As Harry looked on, he saw that nothing about Aloysious had changed in the two years since he had last seen him. He was as tall as Harry remembered, and the terrible eating and drinking habits that would have inflated the girth of anyone else seemed not to have affected him. Above his frayed and faded khakis, he wore a T-shirt emblazoned with a trumpeting red elephant. Scrolled on the border circling the beast's great head were the words "Walk the way of the elephant."

Aloysious dropped off the stage to floor level and walked the few feet to where Harry stood. He put his hand on Harry's shoulder. It was as great a sign of regard as Harry had ever received from Aloysious.

"Really great to see you, Harry. What's it been, two years? I wondered how long it would take you to get your ass up here." He turned to the little people who stood watching. "Guys, bring out the refreshments. Harry and I need to talk."

There was a flurry of movement on the stage while a table and two chairs were dragged through the door. For a moment Harry was engulfed by the sense of unreality that had been growing in him. Here was Aloysious standing right in front of him, while swarming in the background was a rowdy gang of little people in outlandish clothes. It was almost too much for his mind to accept. Running into Aloysious had been a remote possibility, one that he had viewed with mixed feelings. Now that the meeting had occurred, he realized that he was glad to see his old friend. Life would be different again.

Perhaps sensing some of what Harry was feeling, Aloysious said in a very conversational tone, "How do you like the house?" He waved his hand in a gesture that took in the ballroom and all that lay beyond.

"It's all quite grand. It's a great house from what I've seen of it. I hope I get the full tour."

"It's not so grand. Just old. Actually, I don't usually live in such splendor," he said, gesturing toward the little people. "I wanted the guys to put on a bit of a show when you got here. They're just wearing their restaurant clothes."

"And they don't usually call you 'the Raj'?"

"No, they don't. That was a little touch that P.C. threw in when he heard you were an old friend of mine."

Aloysious's statement prompted the question that had been niggling at his brain. "You knew I was coming up the river?"

"No, Harry, I didn't know you were on the river. But I knew as soon as you were off the river."

"I should have known. If you were anywhere in this part of the world, there would be someone to tip you off. It was the ugly kid at the restaurant, wasn't it? It didn't strike me at the time. I must be getting old."

Aloysious laughed and said, "That was just Jock. That's him over there with the bagpipe. He does make a hell of an ugly kid, doesn't he? It's his talent. But don't feel bad. My guys are good, and you had no reason to think anybody up here was running spies. This is my home now. The river is the way visitors get into my neighborhood. I'd be remiss if I wasn't prepared when a friend dropped by. I'd be even more remiss if it wasn't a friend." Aloysious looked at Harry's face closely for a moment before continuing.

"Speaking of friends, Harry, I understand you brought a couple along. By the description I got from Jock, the young lady must be your friend from Sato's operation. What was her name? Little Mouse?" Harry nodded. "I understand your other companion is a gentleman with boating proclivities. That wouldn't be our old friend and boatman, Wit, would it?" Harry admitted that it was.

Aloysious shook his head. "It's just like old times! All we need is Ting-Tong."

"Ting and Tong are on standby. They'll be here if we need them."

P.C. Jumbo stepped up on a stool to better position himself to pour a beer into the two glasses on the table. The bottle he held bore the label of a premium Thai beer. A bowl of what could only be good old American potato chips rested between the two glasses. Aloysious grabbed a handful of the chips and pushed the bowl toward Harry. As Harry picked up his beer glass, he looked at it closely and said, "Your restaurant serves nothing but Pachyderm beer, and you're drinking Thai beer?"

"I can't drink that stuff," Aloysious said a little sheepishly. "Come on, have some of the Thai beer. It's good, and it cost me a fortune to get up here." Aloysious turned to P.C. Jumbo. "Hey, P.C., fill one of the Pachyderm bottles with Thai beer and take it out to Miss Mouse. And don't let anybody see that Thai beer bottle. Get Mouse a big bowl of chips. Or anything else she wants. Tell her Harry will be back in a few minutes."

Aloysious turned back to Harry. "She'll be all right by herself out there. P.C and his troops will keep an eye on her. I wanted a chance to talk with you. What do you think of my operation here?"

"Well, for a guy who I last saw on an elephant galloping away from civilization as we know it, I'd say you've done quite well for yourself."

"Up here it's easy if you have a bit of cash. I had a money belt under my shirt when I went riding off on that elephant. You'd be surprised at how far a good old American dollar goes up here. Take this compound. The old house was here, but a local guy built the rest of it, and then didn't know what to do with it. It looks grand, but it's all local labor and local material. Up here, all that beautiful teak is not worth the price of a second–hand motor scooter. I have a ten–year lease on the entire compound for less than a couple of months rent on my old apartment in Bangkok. It gives me a place to live, a base of operations. The guy who built the place started the restaurant. It didn't go any-where until I introduced Pachyderm beer. Now the restaurant is our showcase for Pachyderm. We're starting to cut a pretty wide swath."

"You know, maybe I got a bad batch, but I can't say I much cared for the taste of Pachyderm beer."

"Yeah, well…anyway, it's not the taste. I'll show you our pro-duction facilities tomorrow. Tonight, you and Mouse can stay here. You can stay as long as you want. Our guest facilities aren't grand. We'll have a nice hotel here one day, but for now we make do. Did you get a look at the house, Harry?"

"I saw the library. It's wonderful – a time capsule. If the rest of the house is like that…."

"It's not, unfortunately. The rest of the house is a shell. That's all the library was when I first saw it. I put out the word that I was looking for old furniture, books, whatever. It took a while, but I collected a few nice things. Then I had to set up a restora-tion shop – most of the pieces were in bad shape – and the shop made copies of stuff too. A lot of what's in the library is stuff my guys made from photos in magazines. You probably didn't look closely at any of the books, but they're not old. A lot of them are Chinese. There's an old bookbinder up here the British taught. He'll put a cover with whatever title you want on any book. Anyway, the house needs a lot of work, but it has potential."

"Looks like you got yourself a good collection of people. Where did you get all the little guys? I can't believe P.C. Jumbo had his name or his rank before you came along."

"Pocket Commander? I can't think of a better rank for P.C. He's like the old pocket battleships: a lot of firepower in a small package." Aloysious smiled and looked toward the ceiling as if the rest of the answer was written there. "I guess I was probably the one who first called him 'Jumbo'. You know, he's a lot older than he looks. Somewhere along the line he was trained by the British S.A.S. or some such elite military bunch. He got in trouble in Hong Kong – over a woman, he said. Hong Kong was still British then, and he escaped jail time by running off to China. Then he made his way across China – god knows how – he's hardly inconspicuous, and he got as far as this place just as I was coming from the other way. We sort of teamed up. I made him a shareholder in Small World. I guess he gave me the idea for the name – after he got our team of little people together."

"And you like the little guys."

"They're smart, they're loyal, they work hard. Until P.C. came along and worked them into our operation they never had much of a life. P.C. showed them how they could have a real life and a good time too."

"So, now you guys fill a real need up here."

"Pachyderm beer fills a need; we just purvey the beer. Actually, now that I have this place sort of up and running, life's getting kind of boring. P.C. was really pleased when he heard that some kind of foreigner had arrived in the area. He figured that at least it meant entertainment of some kind. When I told him I knew you, he was even more excited. It got so that even I was looking forward to seeing you. I figured you must be up to something. Something big maybe, something that could bring all of us a little excitement. I know you didn't come all this way just to see me, Harry. So are you going to tell me what you are up to? Or do I have to turn you over to P.C.? He does a mean interrogation."

"I'm treasure hunting, Aloysious, that's all, treasure hunting. Just like the old days."

Aloysious shook his head. "You came all the way up here to look for antiques? You must know something I don't know. The only things I ever found up here are dilapidated odds and ends. No treasures. Up here everything is used up – or made into something else. I'll tell you, Harry, there are better places to look for real antiques."

"Well, maybe, but the kind of antique I'm looking for can't be found at the Sunday Market in Bangkok. I'm looking for some old airplanes."

"Old airplanes?" Aloysious looked at him as if he had not heard right. "Airplanes? You did say airplanes? Well, you always were a little queer for airplanes, Harry."

Aloysious sat and pondered this for a while. "You know," he said, "the nearest airport is probably 300 kilometers from here. The airplanes the local airlines bring in there sure are old, and they are beat up, but I can't imagine anybody would find them desirable."

"That's not the kind of airplanes I'm looking for. Ever hear of the Flying Tigers?"

"The Flying Tigers? Yeah, sure. That was a John Wayne movie." As he said that, Aloysious leaned well back and held out both hands as if to fend off a blow that he knew would come. "Easy, Harry, I'm just yanking your chain. Of course I know the Flying Tigers. They were a famous bunch of pilots in World War II. Weren't they?"

"They were one of the most effective combat units in the history of air warfare. And they flew in this area." Harry paused, realizing that he was not really sure where he was, and shrugged. "Anyway, they were based in Burma and southern China. We're talking 1941 and 1942. They started in Burma in mid–1941 with 100 Curtis P–40 Tomahawk fighters, and went into combat after the Japanese attack on Pearl Harbor on 7 December 1941 with many less than that number of operational airplanes. By 4 July 1942 when they were disbanded, the Flying Tigers had destroyed 298 Japanese aircraft in the air and many more on the ground. They lost a few airplanes in combat and others in accidents. And they got some fresh airplanes to replace some of the ones they lost. What I'm looking for are the original B–model P–40s, the 100 airplanes they started with. Well, make that 99. One was dropped into the water when it was being unloaded from the ship at Rangoon."

Aloysious sat well forward in his chair now. There was something he wanted to say so badly that he hardly let Harry finish. "Harry, you're talking over 60 years ago. You're looking for airplanes that went to war 60 years ago, and you expect to find some of them now? Harry, you of all people…you know this part of the world. If any of those airplanes escaped the war, they were turned into pots and pans a long time ago. And if you did find one, so what? Who would want it?"

"Plenty of people, Aloysious. I guess being up here in the hills you wouldn't be aware of what they call the Warbird Movement. Guys who restore and fly old airplanes, mostly from World War II. It's picked up a lot of steam in recent years, in the U.S., in Europe – in Asia for that matter. Australia has got a lot of people involved. Thailand next door has an air museum with dozens of old airplanes that still fly. A lot of people love the old airplanes. And some of them – the ones with a lot of money – have become collectors."

Aloysious's face lit up. "Ah, now I understand. The magic word, and you have said it. 'Collectors'! We're talking collectors. We're talking airplanes that are artifacts. We're talking big bucks. Collectors always mean big bucks. Don't they, Harry?"

"We're talking big bucks if I find what I'm looking for."

"You sound a little uncertain. You sound like you're going to need my help. And you certainly will need my help if you plan to work anywhere within a couple of hundred miles of here."

"I'm sure I'll need your help. There are a lot of things I need to do in this area, and I'm pretty well flying blind. You help, and if we find what I'm looking for, there's enough money for everybody."

"Okay, partner!" Aloysious pushed his hand out at Harry to shake on the deal. "But I have one question: Why are you are so sure that some of these Flying Tiger airplanes still exist?"

"Because I've seen the evidence," Harry said, and told Aloysious about his meeting with Riley and described the photographs Riley had shown him. By the time he finished, Aloysious was not looking particularly impressed.

"Neat. So you saw some old photographs."

"But they were not old photographs. That's the point. These photos were taken a couple of months before Riley showed them to me."

"I'm not sure I follow you. You got photos of old airplanes on an old airstrip, but the photos were taken yesterday, not 60 years ago. That's some kind of time warp. How could the pictures have been taken so recently?"

"Because they were. There were things on that airfield that could not have been there 60 years ago." Harry waited a moment to let this sink in. "In the background on some of the photos was a small airplane, an L-19, that wasn't built until the 1960s. There are still a lot of those around. A couple of the photos also had all or part of a car showing in the background, a Mercedes model that could not have been there until the year 2002 at the earliest, 60 years after the Flying Tigers were already history."

Aloysious pondered this. "You know, Harry, you accuse me of being out of touch up here in the hills. And you're right, I can't even get e-mail up here. But I do know that this is the age of computer enhancements. You can put any image you want into any photograph. I would be awfully suspicious of anybody trying to sell me a pig by showing me a photo of the poke it's in."

"You're right. But, the guys who own the photos are so sure that they are real, that they gave me real money – up front – to see if I can find those airplanes."

Aloysious was making restless movements in his chair. He started scratching his hip. "Harry, a last question. What's a nice guy like you, a simple dealer in ancient artifacts doing in the middle of some kind of international airplane scam? Why did these guys contact you?"

"An old airplane is simply an artifact of another kind. You accused me a little while ago of being queer for airplanes, and that's true. I've always liked airplanes, especially the old ones. Over the years I've learned a bit about old airplanes, and I've met a lot of people involved with them. They know me as a guy who deals in old artifacts and likes airplanes. But in fact it was my Asia experience that got me the job, not anything I know about airplanes."

"You got Mouse with you, so I guess you must have cut Sato in on the deal?"

"I told Sato about the deal. It's not his kind of thing, but I needed him to know. If I do find any airplanes, I'm going to need lots of help getting them out. Beyond what you can do for me. Sato has airplanes, helicopters, and ships. And he has people everywhere. Mouse was the first installment."

"Listen, Harry, nothing against Mouse.... I know she's a sweet girl and a smart one, but what you're really going to need when you're up against it, is a half dozen guys like P.C."

"Mouse is a half dozen guys like P.C."

Aloysious looked at Harry as if he had said something that both of them knew was silly, but chose not to make an issue of. "Okay, Harry," he said, "We can talk more about this tomorrow. I want to sleep on it. I know I'm going to have a lot more questions when I get up. In the meantime, let's go see what's happening with Mouse and the guys."

Chapter 4

H arry. Harry, get up!"

Harry raised his head. For a moment he was not sure where he was or who he was. Then he saw Aloysious in the doorway and he knew. "I'm up. I'm up," he said and dropped his head back on the pillow.

"No screwing around," Aloysious said. "There's somebody here you need to meet."

"Meat," Harry said, and drifted back into a dream of tribal dancing. "Oh shit," he said and jolted awake. Dancing. He was dancing to the wild beat of tribal drums, and then he tripped over something. A small animal, maybe. No, it was a child. The ugliest child he had ever seen! Enough to wake anybody. He sat up and looked around the room. It was small and bare except for the bed. His clothes were in a pile near the door. All of them. No wonder he had been cold. Memories of how he got to be there came back in snatches.

"Harry, goddamn it! Let's go!" Aloysious voice was from far away. He was getting restless.

Harry started to recall the big night at the edge of the world. It seemed like everyone for hundreds of miles around had joined them at the Small World pavilion. Despite the condition of his stomach and his brain he was pretty sure he drank no Pachyderm. Nothing but fine Thai beer had passed his lips, although it was all in Pachyderm bottles. He rubbed the back of his neck. It was stiff, and hurt when he tried to turn his head. It was not the beer. It was the scotch and cognac that Aloysious brought out.

Everybody drank it from water glasses and ate potato chips and peanuts. And there was music. Tribal guys with flutes, and drums and fiddles with odd numbers of strings. The music had led to singing, and the singing to dancing. Big people and little people. Harry had never been a dancer. Not until last night. And there had been fights. Not serious ones – no one was in shape for that. Ordinary fights. Harry ran his fingers over his face. Everything seemed to be in the right place. At least he had probably not joined any of the fights.

"Harry, let's go." It was Aloysious again, but Harry was dressed by now and making his way down the corridor. He was not sure where he was in the big old house – he had no recollection of getting to his bedroom – but he walked down a long dark corridor toward light. He found a staircase, and below, looking up, was Aloysious.

"Come on, Harry. There's coffee here, but you won't have time for it. We got to get out to the gazebo."

When he reached the bottom of the stairs, Aloysious was already out the door, and Harry hurried after. They walked through a garden behind the old house and into a heavy growth of trees and shrubs. They followed a brick walk through a mass of dense vegetation and came to a snow white Victorian folly concealed at its center – the gazebo, an open–sided octagonal structure with an elaborate gabled roof and gingerbread overhangs. A banister at waist height ran around its outside edge.

Inside, cushioned rattan chairs and small bamboo tables were set in little groupings. At one sat a slightly built man. His hair was white and cut short, and he had a trim white mustache. He was dressed in a tan linen suit, white shirt, and dark necktie that he wore like a uniform. Leaning against his chair was a walking stick, highly polished wood and a worn silver handle shaped into the head of a tiger. As they entered, the man rose and extended his hand to Harry.

"Good to meet you," he said. "Please call me Reggie." Behind them, Aloysious made a formal introduction. "Harry, I would like you to meet Captain Reginald Farthingale, M.C., D.S.O."

As they shook hands, Harry noted the man's serious look.

"I told Harry that you know this area, Reggie, both sides of the China–Burma border, better than any other man alive."

"You're forgetting some of the tribal chaps...," Reggie started to say.

"You're entirely too modest, Reggie," Aloysious said and turned to Harry. "Harry, this guy knew all the biggies here during World War II. He soldiered with Orde Wingate, knew General Stillwell, knew Field Marshal Viscount Slim. Hell, he even knew Mountbatten."

"You were with Wingate!" Harry was genuinely impressed that the man before him had known and served with General Orde Wingate, Britain's master of unconventional warfare who had disrupted the Japanese military push through Southeast Asia. "Wingate was quite a man, quite a soldier."

Reggie started to respond but was cut off by Aloysious. "He's too modest to tell you, Harry, but Reggie was one of Britain's top spies." In a most proper British accent, Aloysious added, "He did dashing things behind the lines."

Reggie took Harry by the elbow and urged him to sit down. They all three sat down around the table.

"I did get to know Wingate, slightly," he said, "and some of the others. The fact is, I was a youngster then. I did one or two things that a youngster can do and get away with. Nothing very significant."

"To me, Wingate was one of the most fascinating characters in the history of this area," Harry said. "I envy you your relationship."

"It was not much of a relationship. It was brief. It was the relationship that a youngster could have with a demanding and preoccupied teacher. And, as you know, Wingate could be demanding."

"You were very young then."

"I was in my teens. I appealed to Wingate because he wanted someone to 'go native' behind the lines. Well, I was native. I didn't have the burden of pretending." A flicker of surprise crossed Harry's face. With the faintest trace of a smile, Reggie continued.

"I was a lot browner then. My hair, of course, was black. Mother was part Arakanese and part Burmese with a touch of Karen. Father was very British. He was a district officer down near Mandalay. I traveled with him through the countryside a great deal when I was quite young. I was good with the local languages and I was more Burma native than the darkest of my dark–skinned chums. What I did for Wingate was what any native youngster might have done." He sat for a while, lost in his thoughts, before going on. "In any case, Aloysious has given me some background on your search for vintage aircraft. I understand you don't know the specific location of the airstrip you would like to find, but your research has given you some idea of where it might be."

"Reggie, let me show you what I have." From a case Harry pulled a large map which he unfolded and spread out over the table. On top of the map he laid out a half dozen photographs.

"The photos are of the aircraft and the airfield we are interested in. It all looks very vintage, but the photos were taken about nine months ago.

Reggie picked up the photos one by one and examined each one very carefully. When he finished, he looked up thoughtfully. "The airfield in the photos could be any of a number of airstrips I saw during the war." He picked up one of the photos to look at it again. "It does look very much like 1942, doesn't it? There is one thing I find troubling, and I'm sure you have considered it. Almost nothing of a military nature that existed in 1942 in this area would exist today. Airfields, in particular, were subject to destruction. The British and the Japanese destroyed anything in the way as they in turn advanced and retreated. And then the Americans came in. When the war was over, Burma got its independence and the civil war started. That assured the destruction of anything that still stood."

Reggie held the photo up to where Harry and Aloysious could easily see it. "Nothing as complete as this 1942–looking airfield could have survived. Everything in the photos looks too much like 1942 to be genuine."

Aloysious looked at Harry. "A good point, Reggie. Harry, what do you think?"

"It's an important point," Harry said. "And I'm not sure what the answer is. There are several possibilities, but I'd like to put aside any discussions of this question until we have a better idea where the airfield is located. In the meantime, let me tell you about the research I've done."

Harry sat back in his chair and closed his eyes for a long moment to collect his thoughts. Then he began, "I worked with old records and called on experts in the military history of Southeast Asia. First we located all British airstrips that existed in Burma when the war started in 1941. Then we looked for airstrips that might have been added during the war years by the Japanese, the Americans, or the British. There were few of those, so that was relatively easy. We identified airstrips cut into the jungle after the war by the Burmese government or by companies doing logging or mineral exploration. This again was easy. But there was a fourth category: airstrips built by the drug lords and drug traffickers in more recent times. With all the poppy fields and the heroin production that goes on in this area, that was no small job. And those airstrips were intended to be hidden. Anyway, I think we have most of that sorted out."

Harry took a drink and went on. "We did an elimination process. We did this with the help of overhead photos taken in recent years, including satellite shots. We crossed off any airfield that obviously would not serve our vintage friends. That included those converted into civil airports and used regularly, or even jungle airstrips where we could confirm regular use. A lot of minor wartime strips were eliminated because they were overrun by jungle."

"When we finished, we had about a dozen possibilities. About a month ago, with the help of our friend Sato...." Harry paused to look at Aloysious. "I'll get back to Sato later. For your background, Reggie, Sato is an old friend, a former Japanese Imperial Army officer who served in Burma during the war. Now he's a businessman with a big operation based in Thailand.... Anyway, with Sato's help we did photo flights over these areas to see what our targeted airstrips look like now. I have those photos here." He pulled an envelope from his bag.

"Before you look at these," he said to Reggie, "let me just add a couple of things. As you will see, our overflight photos let us eliminate all but four possibilities. And none of those four exactly matches the airfield we're looking for, although all four have hangars that look similar to the ones we have on the ground photos. I'm interested in your comments on two of the photos in particular, Reggie. Although we can't be sure from the overheads, we think both sites are too close to populated areas to make their use by our vintage friends practical."

Harry and Aloysious sat back quietly while Reggie studied each of the photos very carefully. After he reviewed each photo, he selected two and turned to Harry. "I assume these are the two questionable sites. I know both of these places, and I would say neither is suitable for hiding your vintage airplanes. This one," he held up one photo, "is very close to a small town. The town does not show either on the map or the photo, but it is there," he said and pointed at a spot on the map. "This one, although I can not make it out with my eyes...I know there is a large tribal village built among the trees on the perimeter of the airfield."

"Thank you, Reggie." Harry bent over the map. "That leaves only two good possibilities," he said and pointed to a spot on the map that showed a small lake. "On the map, there's one airfield here, right on the shore of the lake." He moved his finger across the map, perhaps an inch beyond the lake. "Across the lake and several miles inland is a second airfield. As you can see from the map, there is nothing for miles and miles around but the two airstrips. There are no towns, no roads, and civilization is a long way away."

Harry placed two photographs directly in front of Reggie. "But now look at the photos of the same area. There have been great changes made to the airfield on the lake. Have a look, Reggie. Maybe you can tell me what's going on."

Reggie looked back at the map to locate himself, then examined the photograph. "I see what you mean. The airfield has obviously been improved. Considerably."

For both Reggie's and Aloysious's benefit, Harry said: "The airstrip is a lot longer than it was in photos taken about five years ago. Also in the interval between our photos and the old ones, a couple of big hangars were added, and everything was paved. If you look at the apron to the left of the two hangars you can see two twin–engine jet aircraft."

"Now look at this area," Harry continued, showing where he meant with his finger. "Here, near the top of the photo."

Reggie studied the photo for a while and said, "Yes, isn't that interesting? These buildings are very substantial, nothing like what one would expect to find up in this neck of the woods. Very large and modern. Almost like a resort hotel. The heart-shaped area here – it's probably a swimming pool. And there's something back here that looks like a barracks area." He moved the photo closer to his eyes. "There's a cleared area that seems to enclose the entire area. Could that be a security perimeter?"

"I think that's exactly what it is. Also, it's hard to make out...." Harry fumbled around the inside his briefcase and pulled out what looked like a jeweler's loupe. "Here's a magnifier. It you look beyond the far side of the largest building, you can see among the trees large individual structures that look like houses. It's hard to see detail, but the look of the houses is not what you would expect to find here. They look more like Western houses. Most have swimming pools."

Reggie bent over the photo with the magnifier. After examining it, he turned back to the map and studied that for a while. Finally he said, "I know this area. I was there during the war. There was only the airstrip. It was an auxiliary field. With the exception of a few huts out on the perimeter and a cache of gasoline in steel drums, there was nothing. It's a remote area. Someone had to put a great deal of effort into bringing in the materials and machines to put those buildings up. It must have been a tremendous project."

"Do you have any idea what the complex might be?" Harry asked.

"Oh, yes, I know what it is."

Harry was completely taken aback. He had studied that photo for hours and thought about it for days. He had not one clue that might help explain what he was looking at. He watched Reggie, hoping for an explanation, but Reggie sat quietly, looking at the photo. Finally, he had to ask. "Reggie, what is it?"

Reggie lifted an eyebrow at Harry. "You know what it is. If you think about it."

"I have thought about it – a great deal, and I don't have a clue."

"You're an Asian expert, Harry. Tell me, what's more Asian than eating rice?"

"Gambling!" Harry said, without a moment's hesitation. "Of course." The light had been turned on. "It's a casino!"

"Yes, it's a casino. I have not been there, but I've heard reports of a gambling den in the jungle."

Aloysious had been quietly listening to this exchange with skepticism growing on his face. "Hey guys, nobody puts a casino out in the middle of the jungle. How the hell do you get the customers to go there?"

"It would seem an unlikely place, deep in the jungle, and yet it's a most obvious place," Reggie said. "Did not the Americans do something similar in Las Vegas, deep in the desert? Here in our jungle, the casino becomes a place where the very rich Asians can go and play with large sums of money, out of the sight of wives, shareholders, and tax collectors."

"And the media," Harry added. "Let's not forget the media."

"Well, Harry," Reggie said as he put the photo back on the table, "you have discovered a hidden casino. From what you have told me, the airfield in this complex is entirely too modern to be associated with your mysterious vintage aircraft chaps."

"It is," Harry answered, "but now that you have thrown light on the problem, the modern airfield starts to make sense. This is how the customers that Aloysious is so concerned about get to the casino. That's what those twin–engine jets are for."

"There's one photo I haven't shown you yet," Harry added, and reached down for his bag. As he put the photo on the table, he said, "This photo is the reason for my interest in the casino and its airfield. It shows the other airstrip, the one on the other side of the lake and a few kilometers inland. This airfield has not been improved. The runway is gravel and not very long. And you will note the old–style hangars. There are no aircraft visible, but it certainly looks like the airstrip we see from another perspective on the ground photos. The fact that these two airstrips are so close together left me feeling that there must be a connection. That's why I became interested in the casino."

Reggie looked at the final photo for a long time before he set it down. "What a curious business," he said. "I think you have found your vintage airfield, Harry. I also think you must be right in seeing a connection between the two airfields. The vintage field could not be there without the knowledge of the people who put a lot of money into the casino and its airport. Perhaps the vintage aircraft are simply a tourist attraction. Vintage fighter aircraft for the punters to look at when they tire of the blackjack table and the roulette wheel. Take them over to the vintage airfield in buses, eh?"

Aloysious tried to follow this conversation despite his growing distraction with sounds coming from somewhere near the main house. There were shouts and bursts of loud laughter. He finally got up from his chair and walked to the side of the gazebo where he craned his neck to see what was going on, but with no luck. He walked back to the table. He did not sit down, but hovered over Reggie. "Reggie, if you think that's a casino, I'll buy that. I'll also buy whatever you think is happening there. But, without more facts, whatever you think is just speculation. Our next step has to be the obvious one. We need to get a look at what's actually going on there, on the ground, and in real time. We need to make a reconnaissance. Isn't that what Wingate would do, Reggie?"

"Indeed, Wingate would send a small intelligence team to look things over. I don't disagree."

"Harry?"

"I agree. We need to know more. I assume you have some thoughts about how this should be done."

"I think it's a job for P.C. Look, let's hold any more talk about this until later. There's something going on over by the house that I don't know about. Let's go have a look."

"I say, Aloysious, if you don't mind, I'd like to stay here and go over the maps and photos."

"Good idea, Reggie. You're the man to brief P.C. on how to get in there. You may as well get your briefing together now."

Harry and Aloysious walked over to the side of the house where dozens of people had gathered in a loose circle on the lawn. They were men mostly, but there were also a fair number of women. When Aloysious appeared, many in the crowd stepped up to him to say hello and shake hands. "Clients," Aloysious said out the side of his mouth to Harry, "restaurant clients, but damned if I know what they're doing here."

"They're too happy to be a lynch mob," Harry said. There was a feeling of expectation in the air. He noted much glancing at watches and looking around. From the way eyes regularly turned toward it, the center of interest was a door at the rear of the house, where two of P.C.'s little guys stood like guards. Although he was not able to understand the mixture of languages being spoken, the hand movements of the speakers and fingers waved in the air convinced Harry that wagers were being made, although he had no idea what was being wagered on. It was like being at a cock fight with no chickens in sight.

The loud background buzz of the crowd suddenly ceased. Harry looked to see where everyone else was looking. There was a flurry of movement at the rear door. The two guards stepped aside, the door opened – and out strode Mouse. She wore loose fitting black trousers and an oversized warm–up jacket made of shiny black material. Harry did not recognize any of the clothes she wore. Her hair was pulled back from her face and tied up in a ponytail. She was barefoot.

There were cheers from the crowd. Mouse clasped her hands over her head and waved at the crowd like a sports champion. Whatever it meant, the crowd loved it. There was applause and a lot more cheers. A side of the circle opened for her, and Mouse walked to the center. She saw Harry and winked.

The miniature butler was on the perimeter of the crowd, trying to see beyond the edge and looking very agitated. When Aloysious noticed him, he called, "Bunster, over here." Bunster pushed his way over to Aloysious, and the two of them huddled in conversation. It was very one-sided. Aloysious knelt on one knee and leaned forward to let Bunster talk direrctly into his ear. Aloysious nodded his head occasionally. When Bunster had said his piece, Aloysious patted him on the back, then got back on his feet, very slowly. He looked puzzled as he turned to Harry.

"There's going to be a fight," he said. "Mouse and P.C. They had a disagreement last night about martial arts, and Mouse challenged P.C. Some of our guests heard about it. They demanded a formal match this morning. P.C. said nothing to me, probably because he was ashamed to be fighting a girl. Bunster says the smart money is on P.C., but there's a lot of sympathy riding with Miss Mouse. What do you think they're going to do? Wrestle?"

Harry shook his head. "No, Mouse won't wrestle."

There was a commotion near the door as P.C. stepped out. He wore gray sweat pants and a tight-fitting T-shirt that showed off his large muscular chest. There were hisses from the crowd, and boos and only a few cheers. He waved as he walked to the center of the circle and stood next to Mouse.

Jock, the ugly-child impersonator, was next. He waved at the crowd too, but got no reaction except for some giggles from the ladies. He had to push his way through the crowd to get near Mouse and P.C. Once there, Jock looked up at the crowd that towered around him. He waved his hands and called for silence.

"Ladies and gentlemans!" he shouted. His voice was high pitched and loud. "I introduce, first in English, later in everybody's language...." He pointed toward her. "Miss Mouse! Our visiting champion!" Mouse held up a hand to loud cheers. Jock turned and pointed at P.C. "And our Mr. P.C! Champion of Small World!"

A boo, a hiss, and a loud "No!" Some in the crowd obviously understood Jock's English. Unfazed, Jock continued, "Now they fight! Why? Because Mr. P.C. say 'No woman can fight him. And win!' And Miss Mouse say: 'Piss on that!'"

Great cheers now drowned out Jock completely. English speakers in the crowd translated for their friends. Jock waved the crowd to silence and began a local language version of his introduction. He was drowned out by shouts of "No, No! Fight! Fight!" Jock turned to the two fighters, took two steps back, and said, "And now...begin!"

P.C. made the first move. He waved at the crowd, then crouched low and started to dance a small circle around Mouse. He seemed not at all embarrassed by the situation. Poor guy, Harry thought, he thinks he knows how to handle this. P.C. continued his dance. Nothing happened. P.C. stopped. He threw his arms out to his sides, inviting Mouse to throw a punch at his unprotected body.

Mouse was quite relaxed, obviously not at all intimidated by P.C.'s dance. She took a step closer to P.C. and bowed to him. As she straightened up, she made a small gesture with her hand as if to say, "After you." P.C. shook his head derisively and repeated Mouse's gesture: "You first." With that, P.C. dropped back into his defensive crouch. His arms out in front, loose but ready. Mouse looked at P.C. for a long moment. She smiled prettily and shrugged her shoulders.

Her next move was so sudden, and the rest happened so quickly, that afterwards no one could completely describe it. Everyone agreed that after she shrugged her shoulders, Mouse suddenly whirled, like a dervish. Then, for just an instant, time stood still. Later everyone could recall that one scene clearly: Mouse balanced on one leg like a dancer. Her other leg gracefully extended toward P.C.'s head, a dainty foot aimed at a point directly between his eyes.

Whaap!

The little tableau exploded in a blur of motion. No one actually saw Mouse's foot touch P.C. Everyone saw his head snap back, his body hurl backwards across the well–trimmed lawn to land in a crumpled heap at the feet of the crowd. His eyes were open, but he never saw Mouse as she brought her heels together and bowed respectfully to him. Then she turned. Without a word or sign to the crowd, she walked slowly back to the house.

The crowd was stunned speechless. Whatever expectations had been, no one could have foreseen the speed of P.C.'s downfall. They stared at the defeated man who had been the cock of the walk. Someone gave a loud gasp. Squeals of concern arose from the ladies whose minds had finally caught up with the image of P.C. flung across the lawn like a discarded sack of rice. P.C. stirred and tried to sit up, but slumped back down again. This provoked giggles of relief and, moments later, general laughter. P.C. had survived after all, and the lucky ones in the crowd were now free to collect their winnings. Losers and winners met and settled up. Everyone wanted to discuss the presumptuousness of this man P.C., who thought he could outsmart a woman.

A phrase was coined that day. Not as alliterative in the local languages as in its English translation, it was henceforth used, here at the edge of the world, when anyone discussed the superiority of the sexes: "Don't mess with Miss Mouse!"

Harry and Aloysious stood side by side as they watched the whole thing unfold. Like the others, Aloysious quietly looked down at the fallen P.C. When the laughter reminded him that even when the mighty fall, the world goes on, he said to Harry in voice quieter than usual, "I saw it. I don't believe it. P.C. is not only tough, he's sneaky. How in the world did he let himself get suckered like that? Where did that pretty little girl learn to do that?"

It looked like the crowd was going to break up, but it did not. Everyone watched while P.C. was helped off the lawn by Bunster and Jock. Aloysious had quietly told Bunster to get P.C. over to the gazebo. Once they got P.C. on his way, the crowd moved in a single mass across the lawn and into the restaurant pavilion. Aloysious watched them, and when the last one was inside, said, "I was going to buy you breakfast, Harry, but I think the service is going to be terrible. P.C. will need some time to get himself together. Why don't I show you the Pachyderm production facility?"

Chapter 5

"Aloysious, I can't believe anybody would do that!"

Harry was absolutely appalled. Aloysious had just shown him the Pachyderm beer production facility. The secret process that made Pachyderm so popular here at the edge of the world was suddenly made clear to him.

"I can't believe you would do that!" Harry said again.

"It's just alcohol. You got to understand, we're providing something that cheers the local people and makes their life more agreeable...."

"Gives them monster hangovers, you mean. The screaming shakes. And worse."

"Oh, Harry, it's just alcohol."

"But you're selling it as beer. You just showed me that Pachyderm stuff is just a mix of some kind of no-name watery beer mixed with pure alcohol."

They stood among great wooden tubs under a massive banyan tree. Aloysious sighed. "It's not pure alcohol," he explained. "I mean, we do mix it with the beer. And we even dump some water in it. And we can sell it at a price people can afford. They love the stuff."

"Of course they love it. It gives them the biggest buzz they've ever had. A buzz that starts when they put the bottle to their mouth. What I don't understand, Aloysious, is why don't you just sell it as booze. Why dilute it with that crappy beer? It just makes it smell bad."

48

"It's the market," Aloysious said. "The people here don't drink booze. They think it's bad for them. They want to drink beer and that's what we give them. And they like it. There's a snappy little jingle they sing in the restaurant." Aloysious cleared his throat and started to sing:

> Pachyderm beer.
> So good! So strong!
> Strong like an elephant!
> La! La!
> And healthy too!

"It's something like that. I forget some of the words. They sing it in the local languages, so it does sound better than that," Aloysious explained.

Harry leaned back against the old tree. He really wanted to understand. "Tell me again, how this works."

Aloysious sighed. He wanted Harry to understand. "Okay, it's simple when you think about it. We get this cheap beer that comes out of China. Nobody wants it, so Pachyderm gets it at a good price. Then we have to hot-rod it up to sell it. P.C. had a source in south China for this cheap 200–proof alcohol. They run a boatload down here for us every couple of weeks. What we do then is dump a lot of the alcohol into that watery Chinese beer – using our secret formula, of course – and then that beer ain't so watery any more. And the local people love it. I think it's what the people in industry call an 'elegant solution'."

"Elegant? Jesus, Aloysious, you're selling 150–proof beer."

"I don't think it's that high. There's a lot of water. One–ten, one–twenty proof, maybe."

Harry shook his head sadly. "I find this all very hard to comprehend."

"I didn't mention, we also got a great deal on Chinese beer bottles. They were cheap because they were old stock and used. We reuse them too. We have a team of local kids to collect old Pachyderm bottles. This is a cooperative venture, Harry. And we have a great promotion program. We give each new customer a full week of free beer. They can drink all they want for a week. It's a great program. I've seen a lot of our customers make a big face when they drink their first bottle. Let me tell you, by the end of the week they are ready to give up their first-born – in a manner of speaking – to get on our regular customer list. This promotion costs us money, Harry, but over time it's worth it."

Harry shook his head. "It's the Japanese cigarette scam all over again," he said.

"What cigarette scam?"

"Something I read somewhere. In the 1930s, before the Japanese army moved into Manchuria, they sent in traders with cigarettes that were laced with opium. They were a big hit and soon everybody wanted them. When their Chinese customers got so they were willing to do anything to get their cigarettes, the Japanese used their opium cravings to benefit the empire."

"Harry, I think you're making too much of this. It's good alcohol we use, not the stuff that will make you blind."

"You're going to have everyone up here pissing their livers away.... Hey, Wit!"

As he shouted the name, Harry got to his feet. "Wit!" he shouted again, "what the hell are you doing there?" Wit was crouching near one of the brewing vats. He got to his feet slowly, looking guilty.

"Oh, hallo, Mr. Harry," Wit said in English and brought his hands together in front of his face in a *wai* to Aloysious, the traditional Thai greeting. "Oh, Khun Alo-wichit," he said speaking now in Thai and using the Thai pronunciation of Aloysious's name. "It is so good to see you again. I often remember the good times in the mountains of Thailand when we shared spaghetti and Spam, and good Thai beer." Wit turned to look at the vats with interest. "I knew one day you would make your own beer and it would be excellent."

Harry waited until Wit and Aloysious finished shaking hands and patting each other on the back. Then he said, "Wit, I want you to stay away from that beer. If you need a drink, Aloysious has some good Thai beer." Looking meaningfully at Aloysious, he added, "And I'm sure Aloysious will be happy to let you have all the real Thai beer you want."

"Yeah," Aloysious quickly agreed. This was no time to argue with Harry. "Whenever you want, Wit. Good Thai beer, just like we drank on the mountain. Just ask. But remember, drink it out of Pachyderm bottles!"

Wit was more than a little puzzled, but he also recognized Harry's serious manner. This was no time to challenge anything he said. "Okay," Wit replied in English. "Okay," he said again to assure that everyone understood.

"Hey, Wit," Harry said in a more normal tone, "what's Mouse up to?"

"Oh, Miss Mouse. She wants to go to the river. To get things from the boat." Now that the issue was raised, Wit went on. "Miss Mouse is a great fighter, but her heart is too soft. She is sad that she knocked the little man down before his friends and made him lose face. When I am a great fighter I will not worry about such things."

"Listen, Wit, why don't you go over to the pavilion and have a beer? Harry and I need to talk with Reggie and P.C. We can all get together later and have a Pachyderm high tea."

Back at the gazebo they found Reggie was still bent over the table. He was peering so intently at his maps that he never noticed them approach. P.C. was sprawled in a chair nearby, looking a bit shopworn. When he saw them, P.C. started to get up, but Aloysious waved him back down, then walked over and leaned close to get a better look at his face. The center of P.C.'s forehead was a big red lump. The top of his nose looked bruised, and his right eye was puffy and half closed.

"God, P.C., she got you good," Aloysious said. "Her aim was a little off to one side, though. What kind of shape are you in? Can you do the recon?"

"Yes, suh," P.C. replied, pulling himself into as much a position of 'attention' while staying seated. "Major Reggie briefed us. We will set out in the morning, suh."

"Good. I don't know who is in your team. Will you take Miss Mouse?"

"No, suh. Mr. Jock will be the young lady."

"Just kidding, P.C. Reggie, how do the maps look? Is this going to be a rough one?"

"Piece of cake, I think. The maps show roads and jungle tracks from here almost to our target. It would be difficult in the rainy season, but with luck I think most of it can be navigated. What I see on the photos confirms that. There is a village perhaps a few kilometers from the target compound. If P.C. can reach the village, he'll be almost within mortar range of the compound."

"Don't give him ideas, Reggie. How long will all this take?"

"Theoretically P.C. should be able to drive right to the village. It's less than a hundred kilometers from here. Hard to say what problems he might encounter, though. I would give him several days to do the job."

"P.C., get some rest. I'll see you in the morning. Harry, Reggie, let's go get lunch."

Harry, Aloysious, and Reggie strolled over to the pavilion. As they got near, they saw Mouse and Wit drive off in a white pickup truck. Off to the river to get stuff from the boat, Harry thought, and that reminded him. "Reggie, there's something I had almost forgotten about. Down at the river yesterday, I saw something I thought I never would, a C–46, just flying along, looking like it was going someplace. You know anything about that?"

"A C–46, is it? Never saw it myself. Heard there was a World War II transport that flew down the river once or twice a week. Assumed it was a C–47, what we called a Dakota. I understand there are a good many Dakotas still in service."

"The old Gooney Bird, your Dakota, it's still going strong. A lot of them are flying. But the C–46 is a rare bird. I knew of only one still flying until we saw your local one go by."

"I know nothing about it, except that it's apparently been flying up the river on an irregular schedule for several months. People have been talking about it. I have no idea where it comes from or where it's going."

Harry heard Aloysious say, "Bring us three Pachyderm high teas, Bunster."

"Aloysious, if that's what I think it is, I'll pass," Harry said.

"Don't worry. They know to bring Thai beer."

"I need something other than beer."

"They'll bring some local biscuits and nuts too."

"How about coffee? How about lunch?"

It took Aloysious a moment to answer. "I'll have Bunster fry something up. We don't have a regular menu." He got up and headed toward the pavilion. "Nobody comes here looking for food."

Harry looked at Reggie and chuckled. "Reggie, I have to ask, where are we? I can't seem to get anybody to tell me. What's this place called?"

"Sparrowfart."

"I'm sorry, Reggie, my ears are screwed up from days of listening to that boat engine. What did you say the name of this place is?"

"Sparrowfart."

Harry looked at Reggie hard. "Sparrowfart?"

"You seem to think it strange that a place is named Sparrowfart. It's rather appropriate, really. There's a time of night – the early morning hours before dawn, actually – when the world is completely still. If you wake then, you feel alone, like you are the only being on earth. Nothing stirs then, nothing happens. The locals call that time 'sparrowfart'. It's so quiet, a sparrow fart is all you might hear."

The explanation brought a grin to Harry's face. "What a great name," he said, and rolled it over in his mind. What better name could there be for a place at the edge of the world? After a while he asked, "But where are we, Reggie? In China? In Burma?"

"Somewhere between, perhaps. Does it matter?"

Harry thought it did, until he considered it. "No, Reggie, it doesn't. It doesn't matter at all."

*   *   *

Early the next morning all activity in the compound ceased so that the Small World staff could send P.C. and Jock off on their "secret" recon mission. Next to a battered white pickup truck stood P.C., jaunty in a camouflage shirt and shorts, matching floppy hat pushed to one side of his head, and high canvas jungle boots. Jock was nowhere to be seen, but on the other side of the truck, a young, slim–waisted girl in a sarong walked gracefully back and forth. Harry saw her, noted how she used a parasol to artfully conceal her face, and he knew. Jock.

By now Small World's other employees, small ones and full–sized ones were gathering around P.C., shaking hands and wishing him good luck. When several of the little guys advanced on Jock, he hiked up his sarong and fled among shrieks of laughter. Minutes later, Jock was back, dressed like P.C. in a camouflage shirt and shorts, his girlish sarong around his neck like a scarf. Bunster came carrying a woven picnic basket. He pushed it into the truck's cab, then fussily moved it around until it looked proper there. He gave Jock meticulous instructions on when and how to deploy it.

Harry walked around the truck and did his own inspection. He noted the license plate was so tattered and discolored that no one would be able to read the numbers. Everything else was pretty basic. This was no high–tech expedition. He had earlier seen P.C. swing a pair of expensive looking binoculars into the truck's cab, but there seemed to be no other equipment. Even Bunster's picnic lunch hardly looked out of place, packed in a locally made basket. And there were no weapons, thank goodness, at least as far as he could see. Carrying weapons while traveling in this region would not be uncommon, but without weapons it was less likely that P.C.'s secret mission would turn into a catastrophe if things started going bad. Harry looked at the faces gathered around the truck. Everyone seemed to be there, even Wit, off by himself, watching the proceedings. Everyone but Mouse.

Reggie completed his inspection of the truck and its two–man reconnaissance team. P.C. and Jock stood at attention, two small burly commandos.

"Gentlemen," Reggie said, "stand easy. I believe you are ready to go forth. Your mission is important. Not to the cause of world freedom, perhaps. But certainly to our own commercial interests and our personal fortunes. Gentlemen, good hunting!"

P.C. and Jock saluted. There was brief scattered applause from the onlookers. Reggie shook hands with both. Aloysious saluted them and shook hands. Then they clambered into the truck, drove through the gates of Small World and were gone.

Harry told Reggie how much he had liked his brief comments. "There's nothing like a reminder of personal interest to motivate a man," he said, just as Mouse appeared.

"Mouse, where have you been?" he asked.

"I have been setting up our communications so we can be in contact with Sato-san."

"Is everything up and running?"

"I spoke with his assistants at his company, Black Lion. I told them we expected to have a report for them in a few days."

"Good. What are you going to do now?"

"Maybe go shopping. Some of the food here is not great. The cooks tell me there are places to find good food. Some farms near the village."

"Tell me, have you been avoiding people?"

"A little bit." Mouse looked down at the ground. "I feel bad for P.C. He lost much face. I did not intend that. I thought he was a very experienced fighter. When I aimed the kick of the flying stallion, I thought he would duck. Then we would fight in a friendly way until we both decided to stop. I did not expect to win so easily."

"You know, Mouse, I think P.C. believed so strongly that no woman could beat him, that the kick of the flying stallion was a complete surprise. If he saw it coming he would not have believed it. If he believed it, he wouldn't have stepped out of the way. It was how P.C.'s mind worked. Now you changed that for him. You did him a favor."

Mouse looked up at him now and smiled. "Your words sound like wisdom, Harry, but I think they are only to make me feel good." She raised up on her toes and kissed his cheek.

Chapter 6

The first two days after P.C. and Jock left passed quickly enough. Aloysious was preoccupied with the restaurant, Wit with his boat, and Harry and Mouse drove around the countryside hunting for better sources of food. In time they found attractive vegetables, plump chickens, and pigs that were too expensive. They enlisted Wit, a fisherman of great experience, and he did not disappoint them. In short order, Small World's kitchen was filled with the sound of sizzling woks and delicious smells. Mouse showed Bunster and two very inexperienced cooks how to prepare some simple but tasty dishes. Under Aloysious's and P.C.'s management, the food served at Small World to staff and customers alike had been very much like the military rations P.C. had labeled them. While no one had starved, the thought of eating had not put a smile on anyone's face. Mouse was changing that.

It was the evening of the second day. The restaurant customers had left, having sampled the new Small World cuisine and been pleased by it. Now Aloysious, Mouse, and Harry sat with the little guys over a midnight snack of chicken sate, salad, and Thai beer. Bunster allowed that it was excellent, and it was too bad P.C. and Jock were not there to see it. Everyone fell silent. No one had been worried really, but individually, everyone had calculated that P.C. and Jock would complete their 'secret' mission and be back before dark on that second day. Now it was well after dark, and they had not arrived.

The third day passed, and by noon of the fourth day there was real concern. Noon of the fifth day had come and gone when the first sounds of their return were heard in the distance – the roar of an unmuffled engine.

Harry and Aloysious were sitting in the pavilion, enjoying the real coffee Mouse had found when they heard it. It could have been any truck, but somehow they both knew. They were already out of their chairs when the white pickup drove into the Small World parking lot. Like all the local pickups, it had always been battered. Now it carried distinctive battle damage.

"Look at that thing," Aloysious said. "It got run over by a tank."

By the time Harry and Aloysious reached the truck, P.C. had half–fallen, half-crawled out of it. He was wearing shorts, but no shirt. On the other side, Jock extracted himself out of the cab very slowly, very carefully. He was wearing neither sarong nor shorts, but had the remains of a tattered shirt wrapped around his middle. Their faces were colorful. PC's was more yellow and blue. Jock had some black on his face, but a lot of it was an almost orange–red. His nose was swollen larger than it usually was. Both had great scratches on their arms and legs, and from the way they moved, it was obvious they were stiff and sore.

"Good lord," Aloysious said, "what have you guys been doing? Bunster, get some cold water. Are we going to need a doctor, P.C.?"

"I don't think so, suh. No broken bones. Just cuts and contusions."

"Harry, let's help these guys get over to the gazebo. We'll have to send someone for Reggie."

The tried to make the two of them comfortable. Bunster brought Geoffrey, one of the little guys who had been a medical student, to check them out. When he finished he turned to Aloysious. "Nothing major. They both need rest – and a very good bath."

"Did you find out what happened?" Aloysious asked. "Did they get beat up?"

"Looks more like someone rolled them both through a bramble patch while beating them with a big stick."

"I'll have Bunster help them get off to the bath and then get them something to eat. Aloysious said to Harry. "Later, if they're up to it, we can debrief them. I've sent somebody for Reggie."

Reggie showed up within minutes, and the three of them sat in the gazebo and waited for Jock and P.C. to complete their ablutions. Finally, the two tattered commandos limped into the gazebo. Aloysious got to his feet quickly. "Reggie will handle the debriefing," he said. "But, to satisfy my own burning curiosity, I gots to know. Did you guys make it to the target?"

"Yes, suh," P.C. responded.

"Other question: Did you get away clean? Or can we expect the people you pissed off to come here and batter down our door while we're asleep?"

"Clean, suh. We got away clean."

Aloysious sighed his relief. "Okay, Reggie," he said, "It's yours."

Reggie started at the beginning as Harry expected he would, and very thoroughly took P.C. and Jock through all they did and all that anyone did to them after they departed Small World five days ago.

"The mission," as they all referred to it, also went more or less the way Harry had expected. Getting to the target was not quite the "piece of cake" that Reggie had thought it might be, but nor was it particularly difficult. There were problems. The roads were not always good, at times more like jungle track. In several places what road there was had been washed out and never repaired. Once they came to a Y in the road and took the wrong fork. They drove on until that track ended and they had to return, backwards for a good part of the way, until they found a place wide enough to turn around. They reached the outskirts of the village early the next day. To P.C., it had the look of a place where visitors rarely set foot. He wisely entered the village alone, leaving Jock hunkered down in the bush a short distance outside of town.

P.C.'s appearance created a small sensation in the village. Every resident in earshot looked up when they heard the sound of his pickup truck approach. They stopped whatever it was they were doing to watch the truck go by. P.C. drove slowly down the main street, the only street. At the end, he pulled up at the town's premier tea shop, a small unpainted shed, with two tables inside, and two tables outside under an overhanging roof. By the time P.C. got his tea and carried it to the less wobbly of the two outside tables, a small crowd had gathered on the street in front of the shop.

It was not an unfriendly crowd, just very curious. P.C. had found himself in similar situations in other places. He knew it was something he could handle. From the start he made no pretense about not noticing the crowd, but quickly acknowledged it. He raised his tea cup to the people gathered in front of the shop and then waved at them. This opening gesture got him no more than cold stares, but he smiled and shouted greetings in several different languages. This brought him a good number of greetings in return.

It was evident that P.C. had no one language in common with the residents of the village, but he soon found he shared bits of several languages with them. In a very short time he and the villagers were engaged in a lively conversation in which a mixture of phrases in different languages were interspersed with a good deal of laughter. It was not long before P.C. shared his table with new friends, three men of assorted ages, and two women, both of whom were very old and probably very wise.

P.C. knew that these bolder members of the community now sharing his table were likely to be among the leaders of the village. Instinctively, he knew that as the day progressed and many cups of tea were drunk, he would learn all that went on in the village. With a little luck and a lot of tea he would get some insight into what the village knew about the compound at the nearby lake and the village's relationship with the compound.

As the tea flowed, P.C. regaled his new friends with stories. He told them of his days as a soldier of the British queen. He had stood tall then – as tall as he could – in a red uniform with a fur hat almost as tall as he was. He spoke of training with the Gurkhas for "secret missions," but no one knew what a Gurkha was, and "secret missions" had no meaning. But when he added that he specialized in missions of "small" secrets, everyone laughed. When he talked of travel in the countries of Europe, everyone listened politely, but said nothing. The places he spoke of were unknown. Then he spoke of China and the great stone wall that he had walked along for days and never saw its end. Everyone listened carefully to that. They knew China was a neighbor, and as he told of the wall there was much nodding of heads. A good thing, a wall, everyone seemed to agree, and looks of great meaning were exchanged. One of the men, the oldest one, said that walls were good things. Not to keeps things out, but to keep things in. He told P.C. that he could speak of this, not because of much experience with stone walls – indeed he had none – but because he had some small experience with fences of steel. P.C agreed that yes, fences, like walls could be good things.

And so a long and pleasant afternoon was passed. Many, many cups of tea were consumed as were the mounds of sweets made of egg yolk and coconut by one of the old ladies. By then P.C. knew the village. He knew how many people it contained (133 women, 97 men, 13 boy children, and 11 girl children); the number of good people (the five at the table were in that number); and the number of bad ones (none of those still lived in the village, although there were a few slackers).

P.C. learned the village's economy was based on growing rice and raising chickens, and that the economy was sound and growing. This latter fact was attributed to purchases made by those who lived behind the fence in the compound near the lake. This new commerce was good for the village, although there had been great disappointment earlier, when the residents realized they were not wanted to assist in the construction of the compound. An even greater disappointment came afterward, when no villagers had been asked to work on the compound when the construction work was completed. Did not the maintenance of a place so big require the labor of people like the good souls in the village?

And this compound, which P.C. admitted he had never seen, what was in there, he asked them. A hotel, the villagers told him, just a hotel for rich people from another place on the earth. Perhaps, one old lady suggested, people from strange places like the Europe P.C. had spoken of. There was much laughter at that. When the laughter ended, the old man, who had not said much for a while, spoke. "Yes, walls and fences are good things." P.C. noted that the old man shivered a little as he said that.

After a respectful pause, P.C. asked what went on in the compound. Did any of them visit there? No one knew what happened in the compound. No villagers actually had visited the compound since the steel fence went up. But the village's sale of rice and chickens was good. Sellers were paid top price. On the spot! In cash! Chickens and rice were delivered to a small hut that had been built on the road that led from the village to the compound. The shed was outside the gate of the compound. In fact, from the shed you could not see the gate. Residents of the compound, whoever they were, never visited the village. All transactions took place at the roadside shed. Chickens (live) and rice (in 10-kilo bags) were dropped at the shed, and cash paid on delivery. Usually the same two men were at the shed on delivery days. They were not local men. They had round faces. Maybe they were from China. Except for some words, mostly to do with rice and chickens and money, they spoke no language any villager knew.

How did the villagers know there was a hotel in the compound? Well, it looked like a hotel, like the pictures of hotels they had seen in the few magazines that found their way into the village. At least that's how it looked when it was being built, before the fence went up. What else could it be? Some of it still looks like a hotel, the youngest of the three men said. If you climb one of the big trees you can see the hotel. But there are other buildings too, he added, many smaller buildings.

And how do the people in the compound come and go, P.C. asked. Do they not pass through the road of the village? No, he was told. They come in airplanes and they go in airplanes. Some day there is much noise, and many airplanes come and go. And boats, maybe they go by boats, one of the old women said. There are boats on the lake. But the lake goes nowhere, another said. It just goes round and round. Or that was what P.C. understood her to say.

Is there just one place where the airplanes gather, or are there many places? Only one place, everyone agreed. Then the youngest man, who spoke of climbing trees, said there was another place. It was distant from the lake, and the airplanes that landed there were smaller, he thought. Yet there was a fence around this place too, and sometimes other people walked in the jungle, but they were noisy and the villagers avoided them easily.

Yes, the old man offered, the compound was new and the village had always been here, probably long before there was a China or even a Europe. Everyone here lived in peace. It was because of the fence. The fence kept whatever was in the compound inside. It let the village continue its ways. The village people and the village spirits were not disturbed by strange foreign influences. The village people could put up with a lot, but the village spirits were more sensitive. There were spirits contained inside the fence, and if it were not for the fence they would be free. There are spirits that are evil and spirits that are good. If we find an evil spirit we must drive it back behind the fence, the old man said.

It was almost evening when P.C. was escorted to his truck by his five new friends. The old lady who made the sweets put some in a plastic bag and laid them on the seat. The other old ladies wanted P.C. to stay for dinner, but he said he had to be on his way before dark. He would stop here again if he could in the next few days.

When he got to the place where he had left Jock, he had to hunt around for a while. He finally found Jock wedged in the crook of a tree, sound asleep. Jock had not expected to be left alone for so long. P.C. told him all he had learned about the village and the compound. Jock didn't think it was very much at all, so P.C. explained the important things for him. The compound could not be entered from the village; they could forget about that. Maybe they would to sneak under the fence to have a quick look, but that was all. They would get a good night's sleep and in the morning go into the forest and look at the fence, and maybe climb some trees.

At first light P.C. got up quietly so as to not disturb Jock, and then walked a wide circle around their little camp. Last night P.C. had driven the pickup off the road and into a small stand of stubby banana trees, but had taken no pains to conceal it. Now, as he walked around the truck, he could see it was well hidden from view at almost any angle until one all but stumbled over it. The few flaws in its natural concealment could be supplemented by tactfully placing a few banana tree leaves in the gaps. He walked back to the camp and had coffee ready before waking Jock.

P.C. had a good innate sense of his surroundings. He knew where the sun was even when jungle leaves were thick over- head and hid the sky. He also had a compass mounted on his watchband. It was small, but it was all that he needed. As Jock drank his coffee and ate the old lady's sweets, P.C. briefed him on the day's plan. "We'll walk to the fence, then we'll walk it all around. We'll not find any weak points, but we need to look. Once we walk all the fence, we look for high ground and tall trees. We need a look into the compound. Questions?"

"A lot of damned walking," was all Jock said.

And so they started. They got to the fence easily enough, and then walked alongside it, staying well within the cover of the brush. As P.C. had suspected, there was little to be seen inside the fence, just more heavy brush. Here and there they saw signs that others had trod small paths, and then they walked more carefully still. Eventually the fence led them to the shore of the lake, where it extended out into the water for a good distance.

"Far as we go," Jock stated the obvious. "If we could get out on the lake...."

P.C was ahead of him. He had thought it through. "They'd have us right away. No place to hide out there."

Maybe after dark, P.C. thought, and maybe not. Whoever had taken the trouble to extend the fence way out into the water to foil any obvious incursions from the shore had probably taken care of the lake itself. P.C. knew a bit about night vision devices, and knew there were other ways of detecting intruders in an area as exposed as the lake.

"Well," he said, "let's follow the fence back the way we came and walk down the other side."

They turned around and walked back the way they came. After a while they met the road that ran between the compound and the village. Before crossing it, they followed it to the compound's main gate, making sure to keep well inside the tree line where the brush was heavy. The gate was closed. On the other side they could see a guard shack. Dark glass in the shack's windows prevented them from seeing inside, but P.C. looked at Jock and nodded. Jock watched the shack for a time. Then he caught P.C.'s eye and nodded back. They could not see him, but each was sure there was someone inside. Then they saw the TV cameras, two of them, mounted in the trees outside the fence. They pointed back at the gate. There were probably others they could not see. They watched for a while, and when nothing happened they moved farther into the trees and started back. They finally crossed the road only after they went beyond a curve, where the cameras could not track them.

They walked along the fence again until they came to the end and were again at the lake. They had walked along the entire fence now, except for the ends that extended out over the water. They saw nothing in the fence that they recognized as a weakness. P.C. was sure there was no way to broach it without risking immediate discovery. As they walked, P.C. examined it with his binoculars. And to confirm what he thought he was seeing, P.C. picked a place where the brush was particularly thick, and crawled on his belly up to where he could touch the fence – had he dared. He kept his hands to himself, for now he saw, just inches away, the fine wires and miniature insulators that confirmed the fence was fitted with intrusion alarms. P.C. crawled back to where Jock lay hidden under a bush and shook his head.

"What now?" Jock asked.

"The high ground. We need a tall tree."

"Lunch," Jock said. "Lunch is what we need."

"Later. We'll do our work. Then we'll eat. Come on, let's find our tree."

They turned away from the fence and walked a perpendicular route deep into the jungle. Jock was lost within minutes and followed closely behind P.C., whose determined stride showed that he knew the way. After a while P.C. said, "The ground rises here. At the top we'll find our tree."

Jock was glad P.C. told him. The jungle was thick. He had no sense of the ground rising where he walked, and no sense of east or west. The sun could rise and it could set, but walking through the brush in the shadows cast by the thick canopy of trees overhead, he could not see the sun or even point to where it was in the sky. The walking seemed to get more difficult, and Jock had started to tire when P.C. said, "We've made the top. Now let's find our tree."

There were trees everywhere, short ones, tall ones, stubby ones, spindly ones. But among the more puny examples stood massive trunks like pillars supporting the great dome of a temple. To Jock, each one of these giants looked like the others; none looked like it could be climbed.

"This is it," P.C. said and patted one of the great columns of wood that thrust up into the green canopy far above. "This is it. This is our tree," he said and sat beneath it. He leaned back and took off his boots. Barefoot, P.C. went up the tree, binoculars strung over his neck and swinging behind. He went up straight, like a monkey trained to pick coconuts. In less than a minute he was gone among the leaves and lost to sight. He made almost no sound, but for a small rustle of leaves. Then, although Jock listened carefully, the only sound that broke the silence was the call of birds and the buzz of insects. It was some time before the sound of P.C.'s voice came as if from a great distance. "What a view! I can see it, Jock. I can see the whole damned thing." For a time Jock was left with his own thoughts. Then P.C.'s voice again: "I've got to get higher." And then: "Damn!"

A crack like a gunshot, a series of thumps and grunts and just once, P.C.'s voice saying, "Oh, shit!" This was followed by a whirlwind that thrashed down through the leaves. A great final thunk! And silence.

Jock waited a long while before calling quietly, "P.C., P.C., are you there?"

There was no answer. Jock walked backward away from the tree, keeping his eye on it as he went. If he got far enough back, maybe he could see up into the leaves. But all he could see was the leaves, the bottom-most ones, the underside of the great green canopy.

"P.C.!" he said, louder now. "Are you all right, man?" The answer was silence and Jock knew P.C. was not all right. "Goddamn it," he muttered and kicked at the jungle floor. He did not know what to do. He did not even know where he was. Without P.C. he would never find his way back to the truck. "Goddamn it," he said again, and then shouted at the top of his lungs: "P.C.! P.C.!"

This time there was an answer. It was faint, but it was unmistakably P.C.

"Jock, what the hell? Where are you?"

"Here, here man, under the tree," Jock answered and waved his hands until he realized that P.C. could no more see him than he could see P.C. "What's happening, P.C.?" he asked.

There was a long silence before P.C. spoke again. "Knocked myself silly. Fell. I'm crammed in the crook of the tree. There are leaves, nothing but leaves. I'm getting up now." Jock could hear P.C. moving. Then he saw a bare foot burst through the leaves, quickly followed by a leg, and then immediately by the rest of P.C., all coming very quickly.

"Oh shit!" P.C. yelled, and the yell followed him halfway down, until he impacted the top of another tree – a huge plant with broad leaves and a pulpy trunk that looked like a fat banana tree. P.C. demolished it, completely, in a kind of slow motion as he hurtled through layers of leaves and branches, each layer slowing him as it collapsed and dropped him to the layer below. With each drop P.C. grunted and Jock winced. Finally, with a "Whoompf!" P.C. arrived in a shower of debris on solid ground. All Jock could think was, "He completely destroyed that tree."

"My head, Jock, my back. I'm broken in pieces."

Jock looked him over. P.C. looked beat up, terribly beat up, but not broken. "You're okay," Jock said. "Nothing is broken. We need to get out of here, back to the truck. Can you get up?"

Slowly, with Jock's help, P.C. raised up and got to his feet. Then he quickly sat down again. One of his feet would not take any weight. Most of him had come through the ordeal relatively intact, but some damage had been done to one of his ankles. He massaged his foot while Jock cut him a walking stick. Then, holding on to each other, the two little commandos stumbled through the jungle. Progress was slow, and before long P.C. said, "Wait, we're going the wrong way. Let's head over there." This was a good sign, Jock thought. P.C. still had his sense of direction. Thank god, or they would never get out of here. They stumbled along until P.C. stopped again and said, "We don't have to follow the fence now. We can go directly to the road. It will be shorter, easier." Jock supported P.C. and followed his painfully slow lead.

They came to the road that led from the village to the compound and turned in the direction of the village. They had not gone far when they reached a bend in the road and saw beyond it a little building that was probably the place where the villagers brought their rice and chickens for sale to the compound. Behind the building, partially hidden by a stand of trees, was a small open–sided shed where the day's business seemed to be taking place.

Jock helped P.C. to a shady place under a tree. P.C. sat and massaged his leg before taking up his binoculars and watching the business being conducted in the shed. It was chicken day, it seemed. Some of them were being held by their feet by men engaged in a discussion of some kind. Others were in baskets of woven bamboo. Some, tied together by their feet, were in bundles on the floor. A man sitting at a table seemed to be in charge of the proceedings. P.C. shifted his binoculars outside the shed, where there were a few men and women, but nothing seemed to be happening. On the far side of the building were half a dozen bicycles, two motorbikes, and one white pickup truck. The pickup truck was unmarked. It had no dents that he could see. It was obviously the property of the compound. P.C. passed the binoculars to Jock.

"Nice to have a motorbike now," Jock mused as he swept the area with the binoculars.

"It would," P.C. agreed. "I know what you're thinking. With my bad leg, I would never get close enough. They probably beat thieves to death here."

"I can do it myself. I'll get one of the motorbikes and come fetch you."

"Too chancy. When you start the motor they'll have you."

"I'll go behind, pull one into the trees. Walk it away from them, then start it. They will just hear another motor. Won't even notice."

"They'll notice. Then you will be in deep trouble."

"I'll be the child. No one notices the child."

Jock went to the small back pack he had carried all this time and pulled out his sarong and the parasol. P.C. thought about stopping him, but it was a long way to their truck. Jock was right: nobody paid much attention to a child. Jock had done this a hundred times. He could do it once more. It was worth trying.

In a little while Jock was on his way, skipping down the road, well off to one side, He was playing with a ball, tossing it in the air, and letting it hit the ground sometimes. When it did, he used the closed parasol to bat it along. All the while he was moving closer to the market and the parked motorbikes.

Jock knew that anyone glancing his way would see a child and never give him another thought. That was his experience – until now. He had not considered the possibility that some situations might be different, and that while his child guise would protect him anywhere else, it might not work here. The main problem was that he was coming from the direction of the compound rather than from the village. No one ever came from the compound, except for the two men who were now in the shed buying chickens. And they did not count; they had a pickup truck. They never walked.

Instead of being the inconspicuous and harmless child he usually was, Jock became the center of attention as soon as his presence was noted. Which was almost immediately. As he drew closer to the little shed, Jock noticed that first one person, then another and then everyone was looking at him. As a defensive reaction he unfurled his parasol to hide his face. He was not quick enough though, and someone noticed what Harry had seen a few days earlier. "What an ugly child," this person said. It was said in a language that Jock did not understand, but he knew from the speaker's tone of voice what it meant.

"That is no child," someone else said.

"No. It is not." This third speaker was the old man who yesterday had shared P.C.'s table at the tea house, and he said the word first: "It is a demon! It is a Nat. That is where they come from." The old man pointed down the road toward the compound. "The steel fence cannot keep them in!" With this the old man picked up a stone and threw it. His strength and accuracy were surprising. The stone whistled by Jock's ear, but only because he jerked his head aside at the last moment. At the same time he lowered his parasol to see where it had come from. And that was an unfortunate move. All the villagers staring at Jock now saw a face that was not the face of a child.

"Nat! Nat!" they cried and started running toward him, throwing stones as they came.

Jock may not have shared much of the local language, but he knew the word Nat. Everyone in this part of the world did. A Nat is a spirit. Some Nats are spirits of nature, the guardians of places or of trees. Other Nats are the spirits of people who were not pleasant to begin with and had died in particularly disagreeable ways.

Jock was not too concerned when he first heard himself being called a Nat. Nats, he knew, were not attacked by humans. It simply was not done. What Jock did not know was that for years, the town had been plagued by Nats. With the advent of the compound, it had been virtually overrun by particularly wicked ones. Rice withered in the fields; chickens went mad; old women were tormented by things that made them itch. Expensive ceremonies to placate the Nats had not been successful. A great accumulation of resentment had built up in the village. Jock was right: humans did not attack Nats – but it was not often that a Nat manifested itself where humans could deal with it. Every villager now confronting Jock recognized an opportunity.

Villagers bent over searching for the perfect stone. In their excitement they grabbed at whatever came to hand. Some of the rocks they threw at Jock were too small. Some never even reached him. Those that did, stung, but did not have enough weight to do real damage. The second and third volleys were more serious. Bigger stones were being cast. This required more strength than some of the older villagers had. But more and more of the bigger stones that could cause real damage fell near Jock. The villagers were moving closer. Jock danced around trying to avoid the stones as he came at him. He knew it was just a matter of time. Sooner or later he would be hit by something big enough to stun him. Once that happened, the villagers would be on him and it would be all over.

"Did they get you, Jock?" Aloysious interrupted Reggie's debriefing. He could not resist. "You look like they tore you limb from limb."

"I was down on one knee, sir," Jock said. "A projectile caught me on the temple. I was dazed. Then... I heard the motor. It was a hell of a ruckus, that motor, the chickens squawking, people screaming...." He shuddered as he had a brief but vivid flashback.

"And where exactly did the sound of the motor come from?" Reggie took over the debriefing again after with a hard look at Aloysious.

"It was P.C. He attacked with a motorbike. While everybody was stoning me, P.C. crept in and stole a motorbike."

"P.C.?" Reggie said, and every eye in the gazebo turned to the second little commando.

"No choice, suh. They were killing Jock. No one was looking at me. I crawled to the machine. I had to improvise, suh. Needed surprise. There were chickens tied on the back of the motorbike. There was an empty gunny sack. I pulled the sack over my head and shoulders. Looked like a brown lump, I did, suh. There were more chickens tied together by their feet. I threw some of these over my back. Then I accelerated right at the villagers. I thought the noise of the engine, the chickens, and them not seeing a man driving the motorbike might disconcert them, suh."

"Terrified them, it did," Jock jumped in. "It was like a huge demon coming down on us. No P.C. on the bike. Looked like a great vegetable driving. Or maybe a chicken, a giant one with nothing above his shoulders. It was a sight, sir. Wings flapping, feathers flying, everyone screaming. It terrified the shit out of me. I can tell you that, sir."

"And so you both made it back to the truck?" Reggie asked.

"We did, suh," P.C. said. "Stayed overnight. Too battered to leave that day, suh."

"Did you leave in the morning?" Reggie again, leading them along.

"We tried, suh. The villagers found us. They were on us at first light. They had staves. Beat the truck. Beat us. When we got the truck moving it was easier for us. They ambushed us, suh. Along the road. They were up high. In the banks along the road; in the trees. Dropping things. Throwing things. Smashed our vehicle something awful."

"And then you made it back here?"

"Took time, suh. Truck was damaged. We were damaged."

Aloysious took over at this point. "Reggie," he said, "it looks like the guys are getting tired, and I think we know enough for now. P.C., Jock, you guys did great work. We'll want to get back to you later for more details. In the meantime I think we have enough to think about. Bunster, get these two cripples out of here. Reggie, Harry, you stay here. We need to talk."

After everyone else left the gazebo, Aloysious turned to Reggie. "What do you think?" he asked.

"Well, it's not good, is it? The village is not our way in to the target. There is no intercourse between the village and the compound at all. Nothing to take advantage of. Even the fence. By P.C.'s description, there's no way to get through it without becoming very conspicuous very quickly. I don't like saying this, but it doesn't look like there is a way in for us."

Aloysious shook his head a couple of times as if to clear it. Then he turned to Harry. "What's your reading, guy?"

"The same. Except for the lake, maybe. It might be worth taking a harder look at that. Frankly, though, I have little hope for getting in by the lake."

Aloysious shrugged and lowered his head, the picture of disappointment. The three of them sat in silence, listening to the sounds of the night closing in around them. Aloysious got up, paced back and forth for a while, then sat down again. When Harry looked over at him, his eyes were closed. Dozing off, probably, Harry thought. The next time he looked, Aloysious's eyes were open, wide open, and full of fire. When he caught Harry looking at him he exclaimed, "I know!" It was almost a shout. "I know how to do it!" He slapped his open palm down on the table with a crack that sounded like a rocket launcher being fired.

"Reggie!" he said loud enough to startle the old gentleman. "Do you remember what Wingate did? He hit them from the sky. That's what we're going to do! We'll hit them from the sky!" He leaned toward Harry, eyes wide. "You said Mouse has commo with Sato. I need to speak with Sato. Right away. Is Mouse's commo encrypted?"

Harry had not really thought about it. He shrugged. "I think it is."

"Okay, let's get Mouse cranked up."

It took Harry only minutes to find Mouse. She led him and Aloysious to the small room in the old house where she had set up her communications equipment. Computer–like things stood on a small table. Wires were strung along the floor and over the window sill. Mouse's contact with Sato's office was almost instantaneous. Then they waited almost 15 minutes until Sato himself was available. Aloysious said he would speak with no one else. Mouse said a few quiet words into the handset, then passed it to Aloysious.

"Sato, that you?" Aloysious shouted into the mouthpiece. "Good! Listen, I know how to fix your problem. What? Okay,

Harry's problem. Whatever. Bottom line is that we need an airplane. A big one." Aloysious turned to Harry. "Hang on a second," he said into the phone. To Harry he said, "Listen, guy, I need to talk to Sato. Alone. No offense." Harry shrugged and left the room. The last thing he heard Aloysious say was "We'll need two pilots, good ones. Yeah, your personal ones will do. And here's what else...."

Later, after Aloysious finished, Harry found Mouse closing down the communications room.

"Harry," she said. "Sato–san wants you to go to Bangkok right away."

"Fine. How am I supposed to get there?"

"Sato will send someone to pick you up. Wit will take you to the pickup point by boat. You will need to take a GPS. I have coordinates where you must wait. You must be there before 6 o'clock tonight." She looked at her watch. "You must leave right away."

Chapter 7

H arry left with Wit within a few hours. Wit got the boat out on the river and then it was grand confusion while Harry directed Wit downstream, then upstream, then back downstream again.

"I'm sorry, Wit, I don't have a lot of experience with this GPS. I had to see which way the coordinates rolled."

Wit had no experience with a GPS at all. He said quietly, "I hope we go only one way now."

They moved down the river, and after watching the GPS for a while Harry was sure they were headed the right way. As they got closer to the pickup point, Harry started to get concerned. According to Mouse's instructions, Wit was to drop Harry at the pickup point and then leave there immediately. It was starting to look like the pickup point was in the middle of the river. That was not good. Harry watched the GPS put him closer and closer to the position, then he looked out at the river and saw it. Practically in mid–stream was a small island, or maybe sandbar was a better description. It was all but covered by the swiftly moving river. Wit got the boat as close as he could and cut the engine.

"Shit," Harry said as he gingerly put one foot on the island and felt cold water seep through his sock. "Shit," he said again as his second shoe started filling with water. Wit let the boat drift well away from the island before he started the engine again. Then he steered it in a wide circle, all the while looking greatly concerned. When he started a second circle, Harry shouted, "It's okay, Wit. Go home."

Wit shrugged. He waved once and swung the tiller around. Harry watched the boat move slowly back upriver until it was finally out of sight. He looked around for a dry place to sit down. There was not much room for him at all, and none of it was dry. He looked up at the sky and hoped it would not rain. He looked at his watch and knew that in 20 minutes it would be dark.

I did it again, he thought. Here I am, stranded on a submerged island in the middle of a river. And I just sent away the only person who could help me. He laughed. It was actually funny.

"Sato, you old devil!" He said aloud. "You got me to do this." If Aloysious had talked him into it, Harry would be really worried now. With Sato there was always a good chance for survival. In fact, with Sato, there was really no question that he would be picked up. In minutes a speedboat would appear, or a submarine. Whatever. He shivered. It was starting to get cold.

Distracted by the cold and the roar of water rushing by all around him, Harry never heard the helicopter until a dark cloud settled down on him. The chopper was painted dull black. It never really touched down, just hovered inches above the river. A rear door opened, and a grizzled old man in black coveralls gestured for him to hurry. Harry jumped and felt himself grabbed and then dragged aboard by the man, who said "*Kombawa*," as Harry went by him.

As the helicopter ascended, the old man strapped Harry into one of the two well–padded VIP seats mounted in the center of the cabin. Then he went to a small cabinet and brought a glass and an unopened bottle of Black Label. He broke the seal and poured Harry a big scotch. He added a dribble of cold water, but no ice, just like Harry liked it. Where they flew above the river gorge it was still daylight. Soon it would be dark here too. He settled back and relaxed.

He was not sure how long the chopper flight lasted. He dozed off and on, and woke when the chopper started down. Outside there was nothing to see. They were moving through a pool of black ink. Then a flash of light and jungle below lit up. Twin lines of light outlined a paved runway cut into the jungle. The chopper flew down the center of the runway until it alighted on an apron at the end. The old man helped Harry get out the door. Across the apron was a small Lear jet, its engines running.

Harry was inside the Lear in less than a minute, strapped into a leather seat by a young Japanese stewardess as the Lear was starting its takeoff run. In moments they were in the air and the young lady handed him a whiskey, with a dribble of cold water and no ice. He sat back to enjoy the flight.

Harry woke when the Lear's wheels chirped as they touched down on the runway. From the window he could see the terminal at Bangkok's International Airport. They taxied to the Domestic Terminal, where a black Mercedes waited. A black–uniformed Japanese driver saluted and opened the rear door as Harry stepped from the airplane.

They took the superhighway into Bangkok and turned into a residential area with narrow winding streets, lined with high walls and steel gates. A gate opened for them, and they drove into a compound and parked under the portico at the side of a big house. Harry recognized it as Sato's formal residence, but not the place where Sato preferred to live. He stepped out of the car, and a guard walked him to the path that led through the garden to the little Japanese house at its center. The old man waited by the open door.

"Welcome, Ha–Lee," Sato said and bowed. "I hope your journey was not too tiring. Please," he said, gesturing with his hand, inviting Harry into the house. They moved to a small room that opened on the garden and sat on mats at a small wooden table.

Sato carefully poured the tea. It was well over a year since Harry had last seen the old man. He did not look much older, but he was smaller than Harry remembered. If one knew nothing of Sato, it would be difficult to imagine that this old man was in control of something as vast as Black Lion Enterprises, with its planes in the air, its ships at sea, and its own people everywhere. When Harry once asked what Black Lion did, Sato said, "We make things happen." And, as Harry learned, Sato indeed did make things happen.

When he looked up and invited Harry to drink, there was just the trace of a smile on Sato's face. His eyes were alert and full of interest. Sato's comprehension of English was excellent, but he spoke it infrequently. With Harry he preferred to speak Thai, a language in which they were both fluent.

Harry took a sip of tea. He put down the cup and said, "It's a great pleasure to see you, Sato–san, as always. You look well. The world must agree with you."

"Ha–Lee," Sato said, pronouncing Harry's name in his Asian fashion. "The world does not always agree with me. But it still piques my interest. Like your project, which now is becoming interesting. Your friend, Alo–wichit...."

"Our friend, Alo–wichit, " Harry interrupted. He emphasized 'our' and, like Sato, he used the Thai pronunciation of Aloysious's name. He wanted to remind Sato that he remembered the private relationship that Sato had maintained with Aloysious in the past.

"Ah, yes. Our friend...the one who has presented me with certain requests."

"He would not tell me what they were. I know he needs an airplane. A big one. He said we would 'strike from the sky', so I expect he has some other requests that may be interesting. I hope they are not too unreasonable."

"Not unreasonable. Except perhaps for wanting to change the color of my airplane to a brilliant red. No, Alo–wichit's requests are simple ones. I will let him use my airplane, the Gulfstream. We will not paint it red, but we will put new markings on it." Sato saw the question on Harry's face. He added, "The markings of a corporation that we will create in Hong Kong. A new corporation, but Alo–wichit insists that it must look like it has been there for years. His other requests are more modest: A new wardrobe. Bright shirts. Italian shoes."

This brought a smile to Harry's face. "Italian shoes! I'm confused, Sato–san. I thought Alo–wichit was planning an aerial invasion. What the hell does he want with fancy clothing?"

"It is an aerial invasion. It is...how do you say it in English? 'State of the art'."

"We're going high tech?"

"Alo-wichit's plan is to descend on your casino from the air – in my airplane. It will bear the markings of his new corporation, 'PRIC'."

"PRIC. What the hell is that?"

"Pacific Rim Investment Company. The corporation we will form in Hong Kong. Alo-wichit will be its president. He will have a new name."

"Alo-wichit! A new name? I don't believe it. No one has ever dared call him anything but Alo-wichit. I mean Aloysious."

"He said he is willing to make – how do you say it in English? – 'Sack-lee-fice'. He will be an international investment 'hot-shot'. A 'big boss'." Sato said these last words in English, then continued in Thai. "His story will be that he is looking for invest-ment opportunities all over Asia. He believes that if he can use my Gulfstream, everyone will believe he is the big boss."

Harry listened to these comments with a bemused smile. "Sato-san," he said, "I really appreciate you doing all this. My project needs a breakthrough. If anyone can find a way into that com-pound and get us closer to the airplanes, it's Alo-wichit. At the same time I don't want to lose your airplane. Or have the scheme blow back on you and Black Lion Enterprises. I don't know about you, but I'm still trying to recover from Alo-wichit's last scheme."

The small smile came back to Sato's lips now. He turned his eyes down toward the top of the table. "I thank you for your concern, Ha-Lee. There is always risk with Alo-wichit. But this scheme is clever. And I do have some interest in knowing more about the casino and the people behind it. If it is drug money? Or money from smuggled jade or rubies? Big money is involved. And big money always requires washing clothes."

"Washing clothes?" Harry repeated before realizing that Sato had used the Thai phrase for 'laundering' literally. "Somebody's washing something for sure, but it's not clothes. It's money."

"So," Sato went on, "if Alo-wichit appears from the sky as a finance 'hot shot' he will draw the interest of many people. They will want to listen to what he has to say. You will be there. You will meet people. It is a good scheme."

"Perhaps you are right, Sato–san. I hope so. We'll be flying into that place blind. I hope they wait until we land and listen to what he has to say – before they react."

"There are other things Alo–wichit requires. He wants to take along an old British army officer, and someone he calls 'P.C.' And two young ladies we must fly from Chiang Mai. He said he needs an entourage. You will take Mouse? She will be an asset."

"Mouse will go with us. The two Chiang Mai ladies are Ting and Tong. Alo–wichit's former business associates."

"One more thing, Ha–Lee. Alo–wichit did not ask, but a 'hot shot ' financier needs cash money to visit the casino. When you return to the airport, the driver will give you a briefcase. It will be full of dollars. There will be enough for Alo–wichit to play 'hot shot' at the casino."

Harry studied Sato's face. "Why are you doing this, Sato–san?" he asked. "It can't be the money. Even if the project succeeds, all we will have is some old airplanes. Airplanes that are 'artifacts'. In the past you told me you do not deal in artifacts. They are individual things, and not much money can be made from dealing in individual things."

Sato closed his eyes for a long moment. When he opened them he looked at Harry and said, "It is not money. Alo–wichit's scheme is interesting. If it succeeds or if it does not succeed. Sometimes, just to do a thing is important. In a long life there are not always enough things to hold one's interest."

Sato turned his eyes from Harry and looked into the garden. "There is another thing that is important to me. The airplanes you are hunting are part of my life. I fought in Burma during World War II. I remember the Flying Tigers. Their airplanes kept our column from entering China. They almost destroyed us. They caught us when we tried to cross the gorge at the Salween River. They killed many of my men. Many of my friends. I hated those airplanes with their shark teeth. The men who flew them were brave. They did their duty. If you find one of the airplanes, it will be a memorial to the Flying Tigers. It will speak of what they were." Sato paused then and shifted his eyes to look directly at Harry before continuing. "It will speak of what I was then. If you find an airplane, or if you don't find it, your effort will stir up the past. It will make people examine the past. Perhaps that will be the real success of your effort."

Sato reached over for the cognac bottle. "Enough of such talk. I will save it for my poetry." Sato poured two glasses and said, "There are practical matters. I know that Alo–wichit will be the big boss on this operation. There must be a big boss, and it is Alo–wichit's scheme. But you, Ha–Lee, must bring balance to his impulsiveness. At times he moves too quickly. In too grand a way."

"I will try, Sato, but as you know...."

"You must try."

Harry raised his glass. "I will try, Sato–san. I will try."

Chapter 8

T
he chatter in the airport VIP lounge where Harry had gathered what he thought of as the 'assault team' ceased when the door swung open and Aloysious strode into the room. Above khaki trousers with a knife–edge crease he wore a Hawaiian shirt crowded with banana trees and blue parrots on a background of brilliant red. Wow, he is taking this incognito stuff seriously, Harry thought.

Aloysious headed for the center front of the lounge, then turned to face them. Despite the smile on his face, he managed to look serious. He started to raise his hand to call for silence, but dropped it when it struck him that the room was already quiet. He cleared his throat loudly as if checking the acoustics. He started to speak, and sounded very formal.

"Good morning, guys. And ladies. In a few minutes we'll be on our way. I know Harry has briefed you on the background to where we are going. So you probably know as much about that as I do. Who we will meet there is the big question. We need to make some assumptions. We need to take a few precautions. First off, I won't be Aloysious while we're there. I'll have a new name. My name will be Sunny Bright. That's right: Sunny Bright." He said the name slowly, savoring it. The smile on his face grew bigger as he added, "My mama called me Sunny because I was so bright." He paused for possible laughter. A muffled giggle came from Ting's direction. He stole a glance at Harry, winked, and went on.

"So, from here on in, Sunny is my name, and investment's my game. I will be the man from PRIC, the Pacific Rim Investment Company. Is that a great name or what? I'll be the PRIC biggie, the chairman of the company. You all should know that PRIC is based in Hong Kong, but it does business all over Asia. Sunny Bright has a motto that you should all know: 'You've got dreams and I've got schemes. I'm here to make your money grow.' Well, gang, that's who Sunny Bright is. And that's who I'm going to be while we work this scheme. Your job will be to support me while I spread the PRIC gospel of investment."

Aloysious paused, and looked from face to face before going on. "Now, you understand that what I've been talking about is just our cover. We are not really selling investments. But we want people to be interested in us. We want them to watch me." Aloysious stopped talking. He looked directly at Harry and pointed a finger at him. "I want people to watch me so that Harry over there can quietly go about finding his airplanes." After a moment he added, "Does anyone have questions?"

No questions were asked. But some of the faces before him had questions written all over them. He turned to Harry. "What do you think, Harry? Do I sound like a hot shot Hong Kong financier?"

Before Harry could respond, Reggie raised his hand. "Sunny?" he said. "Bright?" He looked a bit uncertain.

"A nice touch, don't you think? A name with a good old boy sound. Makes it benign. Makes people want to trust me." Aloysious's eye caught a flutter at the back of the room. "Ting-Tong," he said to the two young ladies, old friends he had not seen in a long while. There had been no chance to talk since they arrived from north Thailand earlier that day. "It's great to see you. I'm glad you're going with us. Tong, you had your hand raised. Do you have a question?"

"Aloysious...," Tong said and started to giggle. She quickly caught herself and went on. "Excuse me, I mean Mister Sunny. Can we have new names too?"

There was a flurry of comments from the others. Aloysious held up his hand for silence. "Okay, here's the deal. I'm making it easy for everybody. You guys have to learn to call me Sunny, but that's all you have to learn. You all get to keep your own names."

"Wait a minute," Harry said. "We don't know who we're dealing with – you just said that yourself. What if we don't want these guys to know our real names?"

"The guys we'll be dealing with, Harry, they won't care about your name. They will want to deal with the principal. And that's 'Sunny Bright'. Besides, if you all changed your names, how the hell would I know who's who? The fact is, international financiers like Sunny Bright got a lot on their minds. They don't remember names. Of clients or staff. What if Sunny Bright just calls everybody 'Booger'? That way they won't get to know your name."

"Booger?" Harry asked.

"Yeah," Aloysious said, looking a little surprised. "If you come from America's deep south – where Sunny Bright would have his origins – that's what you call your buddies, don't you? An international financier like Sunny would call everybody 'Booger' when he's got a lot on his mind. Wouldn't he?"

"Jesus, Aloysious," Harry said, "not Booger. Bubba! If you grew up in the American South you call your pals Bubba."

"Bubba!" Aloysious looked even more surprised. "Is that right?"

"It's been a long time since you've been in the States."

"Whatever. Anyway, it's only names. More important in the international finance arena is positions and titles. And I got a good one for you, Harry: 'Art Investment Advisor to the Chairman'. You're the artifact man. You advise the chairman – that's me. Everybody else you just tell how much money they can make from buying and selling artifacts – through PRIC artifact–based venture fund derivatives. And by artifacts I mean anything – anything from a bronze Sukhothai Buddha to a rare World War Two airplane. That puts you right in the driver's seat, Harry. Right next to all that big money."

"A title," Harry said, doing his best to sound sarcastic. "I'm really overwhelmed."

Aloysious was looking quite pleased with himself. "You know," he said, "I think we'll call them the 'PRIC Ad–Venture Funds'. Doesn't that sound neat? Get it? Adventure funds?" The questions were rhetorical. Before Harry could say what he wanted to, Aloysious turned to Reggie and started to brief him.

"Reggie. You're the 'Southeast Asia Advisor to the Chairman'. In your role you know everything about Southeast Asia: the history, the politics, the strange beliefs, and customs of the whole region."

"Righto," Reggie said, sounding confident now.

Aloysious looked around the room. He was not finding what he was looking for. He looked straight down. "Ah, P.C., there you are. You're going to be my man Friday as usual. But now you have a new title. You will be 'Bodyguard of the Chairman'. The bodyguard part is what I want you to concentrate on. Hot–shot financiers always have a bodyguard. It's a status thing."

"Miss Mouse," he said, turning to her, "you're the PA, the 'Personal Assistant to the Chairman'. When we get where we're going, you stay close. There's a big black notebook in our baggage that you will always need to carry. Take notes when I talk with anyone. Doesn't matter what you write. Just take notes."

Aloysious walked over to Ting and Tong and shook hands with both. Ting leaned forward, raised up on her toes, and kissed him lightly on his cheek. He looked surprised, but pleased.

"Ting–Tong," he said. "Great to have you guys along. I know you both have gained a lot of business experience in the past few years. But on this trip you have to be the fancy ladies."

"Fancy ladies?" Ting looked at Tong. Tong looked at Ting. "Fancy ladies? What is a fancy lady?" Both looked puzzled.

Aloysious looked down at his hands, suddenly preoccupied with something else. Finally he said, "Every entourage has fancy ladies. Harry, you explain it to them." He looked toward the door. "Where are the pilots? Come on, Harry, we gotta brief the pilots."

With the help of a security guard, they found their way out to the apron where Sato's Gulfstream waited. All gleaming white and gold, a beautiful long–winged airplane, perched on slim landing gear like an elegant bird. Harry recognized the aircraft, as he had flown in it before. The Black Lion symbol of Sato's corporation was no longer on the tail. In its place was something greenish that looked vaguely like a dollar bill with the letters P R I C stamped across it in red.

As they walked to the aircraft, Harry glanced at Aloysious and shook his head. "Jesus, Aloysious. Fancy ladies! You got those two kids totally confused. You need to tell them something better than that."

"An entourage has got to have fancy ladies," Aloysious said with conviction. "I mean it's only for show, Harry. You know that." Harry shook his head again.

At the open door near the front of the aircraft stood the three-man flight crew. They came to attention as Aloysious and Harry approached. The elder of the three, with the four stripes of a captain on his epaulets, saluted and introduced himself as the pilot. He introduced the other two as the co-pilot and the steward. All three were Japanese. The captain said that the weather was good and the flight would be pleasant. It would take just over two hours.

Aloysious waited until the pilot finished speaking. "Captain," he said, "I want to talk about the profile of the flight. I know you've been told that this is a special flight. When we get about 100 miles out from our destination, I want you to drop the airplane down on the deck. Get us as low as you can. If those guys have a radar out there, I want to be under it. I want to be down and landed before anybody even knows we're coming. On the way, you can monitor whatever radio frequencies you need to, but don't talk to anybody. I don't want anybody telling us we can't land. If anybody says 'don't land', don't hear them! If we have a problem, we'll deal with it after we land."

Harry watched the captain's eyebrows rise as he listened. When Aloysious finished, the captain stood silently for a moment, thinking. Then he nodded and said, "In that case, Mr. Bright, I think we should make a straight-in approach, and not fly a regular landing pattern."

"That's right, Captain, just plop it down. Once we're on the ground, they'll have to invite us to dinner."

The inside of the airplane was what Harry remembered. It looked and smelled like his idea of what a fine car custom-built for a very wealthy man should be – all creamy leather and exotic wood.

They boarded like kids getting on a bus that would take them on a holiday to the seashore. Aloysious set the tone. He found a floppy hat somewhere, and red and green elephants now marched across his brow. He toted a heavy-looking rattan picnic hamper. Bunster's work, Harry thought. Behind him came P.C., all but hidden by the heavy cooler he carried. Harry helped him get into the plane.

Seating in the main aircraft cabin was arranged in intimate groupings of leather chairs and settees separated by small tables. Aloysious quickly determined that the center of the cabin could be arranged in conference seating and swiveled all the seats around until they faced one another. He took his place at the center and assigned seats to the others as they came aboard.

The picnic basket and cooler were popped open. Before the aircraft door was closed, everyone had a beer in hand. Potato chips in dainty ceramic bowls were strategically placed on the tables and the plush carpeting that covered the aircraft floor.

Aloysious took the opportunity to get reacquainted with Ting-Tong, the matched pair, as he referred to his old friends. He listened with interest to their recent adventures with their tour company in north Thailand. From time to time he interrupted to tell a funny story when he was reminded of past adventures he had shared with the two. After a while the aircraft cabin reverberated with Aloysious's wit, some shouts, and much loud laughter.

"Aloysious," Ting spoke up during a brief lull in the conversation and asked the question that had been on everyone's mind. "When we get there," she asked, "will they shoot us down? Or will they grab us when we land? And put us in jail?"

"No," Aloysious said, "no. No one will hurt us." He stood up and raised his hand until he had everyone's attention.

"Listen, everybody. Ting asked a good question. I want everybody to hear the answer. Ting asked if anybody will try to hurt us when we get to where we're going. The answer is no. I'll tell you why. Where we're going they're used to dealing with the snooties. The high rollers. The rich and the super rich. When we drop in on them, they won't have a clue about who we are. But they will notice us – I'll guarantee you that. And they will have to assume that we are clients – the super rich who are used to doing things their own way. They'll try to check us out real quick. And they will learn some things about Sunny Bright and PRIC."

Aloysious paused here, and raised his hand, showing half an inch of air separating the tip of his thumb from his index finger. "They will learn only this much," he said, and paused again to look at their faces before he went on. "The super rich are super private. Those guys know that. When they don't learn much about us, they will stop worrying and we'll all be friends. So, when we get there, don't worry. Do what you want to do. That's what they will expect. Be demanding. They will cater to you. Be arrogant. They will kowtow to you. It's what they expect." He finished and looked at Harry.

"Good speech, Sunny," Harry said and raised his beer to him. The others raised their beers to Aloysious and they all drank. The group needed that, Harry thought. A little cockiness would help ease them into their roles.

The party went on until the captain's voice came over the aircraft's PA system. "Mister Bright. We are just a little over 100 miles from our destination. We have started our descent and ask everyone to take their seats and fasten their seat belts."

A series of clicks as everyone buckled up. Looking out the window, Harry saw that they were already well below their cruising altitude. Just above the trees, they leveled off and for a while skimmed over the treetops. Then flaps and landing gear went down. Moments later they dipped below the trees and the Gulfstream's wheels gently touched the concrete runway. Harry knew they were on the ground only because he was looking out the window.

The Gulfstream rolled down to the end of the runway, then turned around and started back. There were buildings at the far end of the airfield that looked like hangars and a small passenger terminal. Harry kept his eyes on that area, expecting at any moment to see the beginnings of frantic activity triggered by the Gulfstream's unannounced arrival. The buildings grew bigger as they taxied closer, but there was no movement. No sign of life.

"Please stay in your seats," the aircraft PA system announced. "Please keep seat belts fastened. Vehicles are approaching us. We may have to brake suddenly."

Immediately after this announcement, the aircraft lurched two or three times and came to a halt.

"Please stay in your seats. We have been requested to follow a vehicle to the terminal."

When the aircraft moved forward again, Harry craned his neck to see what was happening beyond the nose of the airplane. He could see nothing but more runway. From across the aisle he heard Aloysious say, "Now goddamn it, Harry, isn't that class?" Harry swiveled to look directly out his side of the aircraft. Just ahead of the wing was a white sedan keeping pace with the Gulfstream.

"Mercedes S–class, Harry. New ones."

Harry turned to look at Aloysious who was looking out the window on his side of the aircraft, where a second Mercedes kept pace with them.

"I was expecting jeeps and guys with machine guns," Aloysious said.

When the aircraft reached the apron at the front of the terminal, Aloysious got up and walked to the aircraft door. "I'll go first, Harry. I want to talk to the reception committee. Keep everybody inside the airplane for one minute, exactly. Then go outside, mill around and look pissed off. P.C., you come with me. Look threatening, but don't do anything."

Aloysious helped the steward open the door, then walked down the stairs to the ramp with P.C. right behind. Harry watched from inside the doorway as three young men in dark suits exited one of the Mercedes and walked briskly to intercept Aloysious. When they reached him, Aloysious stuck his hand out to the man in the lead, probably the man in charge. The two shook hands and started to talk. P.C. stood nearby and watched the other two young men while they watched him.

Harry was too far away from the group to catch any of the conversation, but when he saw Aloysious wave his hands in the air to emphasize something he was saying, he decided to move. He started through the door just as Aloysious turned in his direction and shouted, "Hey, Harry! Was it the prime minister who told us about this place? Or was it the foreign minister?" Aloysious turned back to the man he had been talking to without waiting for an answer. "And then there were all these generals. They said that...."

Harry never did learn what the generals said, or whose government Aloysious was tarnishing to establish Sunny Bright's credentials. But it was a good choice. In moments Aloysious turned back toward Harry and waved him over, a big smile on his face. When Harry reached him, Aloysious pointed to one of the white Mercedes. "The closest car is for you, me, and Reggie," he said to Harry. Then he turned to P.C. "Hey, P.C., the Mercedes over there is for the ladies. Take them and follow us to our villas."

The Mercedes came with a driver. Aloysious glanced at Harry and winked. They got in and stayed quiet during their short drive out of the airport and through a well-kept jungle. On both sides of the ribbon of smooth concrete on which they drove, was lush foliage, great broad-leafed plants in all imaginable shades of green. After a minute or two they turned into a gated compound. A blue lake of a swimming pool separated two villas that were mirror images of one another. The villas were big, single-story buildings with pale yellow walls and brown tiled roofs that extended out over verandas fronting the pool. It all looked cool despite the glare of the tropical sun.

Aloysious stepped from the car and headed directly for an umbrella that shaded a chaise longue near the pool. He flopped into the chaise and somehow managed to look completely ex-

hausted. Just then another Mercedes drove into the compound.
It brought the three young men in suits. They got out of the car.
Two remained by it, while the third walked to Aloysious,
sprawled in the chaise with his eyes closed, and stood stiffly before him.

"Excuse me, Mr. Bright," he said, "I am William, the front
office manager. I can handle your check–in right here. May I
have everyone's passport please." As he said this, William studied the official–looking forms that he held in his hand.

Aloysious opened his eyes slowly and turned his head until he
was looking directly into William's eyes. "No, William," he said
very softly. "You may not have my passport. You may not have
the passport of anybody in my party. I no more want my visit
here to be a matter of record than would the prime minister of
Shangri–La."

Then he sat up in his chair and leaned toward William. "Son,"
he said, "you know all that. You can fill out your forms without
our passports. Write me down as John Smith, or Fu Wang Lee,
or whatever name you choose. What I choose is that Sunny Bright
is officially not here. None of us is here." Aloysious paused to
scratch an armpit. Then he yawned and said, "William, I've had
a long and tiring journey. Maybe you can find us some whiskey.
And some ice."

Harry stood close enough to see William's eyes widen as
Aloysious spoke to him. William inclined his head in a bow and
all but clicked his heels. "Of course, Mr. Bright. I will see to it
immediately, sir." He turned and walked back to the car, looking like he was in a great hurry.

Aloysious clasped his hands behind his neck and watched him
walk away. "Well, that's the formalities taken care of, Harry.
We'll have us a whiskey and then go scout out this place. Oh,
look, here come the girls."

Ting and Tong flung open the rear doors of their Mercedes
and jumped out before the car was even stopped. They headed
toward the swimming pool to check it out, leaving Mouse and
P.C. to deal with all the baggage that had been unloaded from
the airplane. Aloysious decided that the ladies would be housed

– officially, at least – in the second villa. The 'Villa of the Left' he called it. The men got the 'Villa of the Right', which happened to be closer to where Aloysious sat in his chaise when he made that decision. It made little difference really. Each villa had more suites and rooms than all of them put together could use.

Aloysious selected the largest room in the 'Villa of the Right' for his own use, and told P.C. to take the room closest to him. He designated a large sitting room as 'the PRIC on-site office', and asked Mouse to see to getting four or five additional telephone lines installed. To Harry he whispered, "If we need them, we can get a lot of telephone calls for Sunny Bright. Sato can generate as many as we need. It will make us look busy." Aloysious stood in the center of the living room and scanned the walls and then studied the ceiling. "You know, Harry, I think we should take a walk in the garden," he said.

They walked into the garden behind the two villas. When he was satisfied that they were well away from anything that might be used to conceal an instrument capable of prying, Aloysious spoke, his voice unusually quiet, almost a whisper. "Tell the troops, Harry – quietly – that there will be no talking about any real stuff anywhere in the house. I don't know who we're dealing with, but if they're doing their job, they will have these nice little houses all wired up. And that goes for the pool area too. I don't want to hear any talk in the house – or on the verandas – that isn't PRIC business. Or just frivolous. The only real talk should be between you and me. We'll do it all out here, where there's nothing but grass. I guess now we should get cleaned up and see what the rest of this place looks like."

They walked back into the 'Villa of the Right' to find both sides of the entrance hallway lined with staff. Each of the villas, it seemed, came equipped with a cook, a butler, and three maids, and now the ten faces assigned to the two villas looked expectantly at Aloysious, awaiting their marching orders from the big boss. Although not inclined to do so, with Harry's prompting, Aloysious addressed this multitude. "Greetings." There was a long pause while he looked from face to face. "I tell all my staffs that I expect three things: Stay alert. Be prepared." He looked at them at them for another long moment. "Do that," he said, "and we'll get along fine."

As they walked away, Harry said quietly, "You told them only two things."

"Wondering what the third one is will keep them awake."

From their new butler they learned that one got from the villas to the casino via a track that started at the bottom of the garden and meandered off through the trees. The proper way to negotiate the track was by cart, which the butler said he would fetch.

"Cart?" Aloysious said, and then patiently waited with Harry until a golf cart with a fringed top silently glided up to them. "Follow the track, sir," the butler said. "Just follow the track."

Harry drove. Dense vegetation on either side of them was a screen through which they occasionally glimpsed other villas and gardens, and an industrial–looking area. A barracks compound for staff, Aloysious suggested. They wound their way through a grove of tall teak trees and found themselves rolling onto a broad well–trimmed lawn. On the far side they could see a large building, probably the casino.

"A juke box," Aloysious said.

They sat and looked at it for a while. Shielded by a barrier of trees, the building glowed in reflected sunlight. Three stories of cream–colored marble. Pillars of a dark brown stone flanked the entrance, two on each side. There were no straight lines in the building's design. Where walls met they were rounded and flowed into each other. The windows were round too, and ringed in chrome like great portholes. The wide steps that led up to the entrance were layered curves cut from the same dark stone as the pillars. Broad chrome handrails led up the steps up to the large glass doors of the entrance, which were also framed in chrome.

"Art deco," Harry said. "Not classic. More art deco nouveau."

"Why the hell would they build something like that out here in the jungle?" Aloysious asked. When there was no answer from Harry, he added, "Well, it is kind of classy."

They parked the cart at the bottom of the steps and walked up. When they reached the top, one of the large glass and chrome doors swung open of its own accord. A cool breeze brushed their faces.

"Ah, Mr. Bright! How excellent!" The voice was followed by a big man who bustled through the door. A friendly face under an unruly mass of black hair. Burmese, Harry thought, or maybe Indian. "I am Peter, sir, the general manager. Welcome to our establishment! Think of our club as your own."

All three shook hands and walked into the building side–by–side, like old friends. When Peter asked if the gentlemen would like refreshment, Aloysious waved the suggestion aside and got down to business. "We don't have much time, Peter, just a few days. I want to relax. I also want action. There will be action here, won't there, Peter?"

"Oh, of course, sir...if you mean games of chance. We do have roulette wheels. And we have craps and cards. All of that is in our private rooms, sir. We have many other styles of wagering also. Chickens if you like, sir. We have a pit in back for the fighting of cocks. Or crickets, if you prefer. We have fighting crickets by request. And we have special events. When elections take place in neighboring countries, the wagering can be quite exciting. Especially if guests are contending in the same election. We do employ extra security then, of course, sir."

"Of course, Peter. Everything sounds quite adequate." Aloysious looked quietly around the large domed foyer in which they stood. "But, besides the wagering...."

"Ah, yes, sir. Forgive me, sir. It escaped me that you are not totally familiar with our establishment. We will do a tour." Peter led them on a tour that consumed the better part of half an hour. They saw private game rooms, some empty and some full of cigarette smoke and players; visited the library and the smoking room; made a minor detour to peer into the cockfighting pit; and quietly stuck their heads into the 'Club Room', where two members dozed in leather chairs near a fireplace.

"Many of the members are British school 'old boys'," Peter explained their lethargy.

Aloysious walked along muttering "capital, capital," and "good show," but finally ran out of patience. "Peter," he said, "I appreciate your fine facilities. But there is one additional thing I require. I am a businessman. I look for opportunities. I would like to allow my fellow guests to avail themselves of my special knowledge of finance." He paused to let this sink in, then asked, "Do you get my drift, Peter?"

"Oh, indeed, sir, I do. You wish to do sales pitches."

"Now you're cooking, Peter," Aloysious said, rubbing his hands together.

"But that is not permitted, sir."

"Not permitted, Peter? All I want is a place where I am in proximity to my fellow guests and – possibly – can meet the more qualified."

Peter looked a bit uncertain. "Meet them, sir?"

"A venue, Peter. We will need a venue."

Evidencing some uneasiness, Peter said, "The Rudyard Room, I think. It is named for Mister Kipling, the Great Imperialist. With that, Peter led them up a curving flight of marble stairs. At the top was the entrance to a 1930s era art deco dining room. They could see a bandstand and small polished dance floor at the far end. With dinner still hours off, the dining room was quite empty.

"We have our own big band, sir. The Dorsey sound. On certain evenings we have two bands, actually. Then we have the battle of the bands."

They entered and walked among the empty tables toward the bandstand. Aloysious ambled along, looking right and left with considerable interest. Harry assumed he was evaluating the seating arrangements in relation to their distance from the band, the stars, the kitchen, and other factors that would have great meaning only to Aloysious. When they completed their tour of the dining room, Aloysious said, "This looks great, Peter. But we have to get it right. I will want to observe as many of the other guests as I can. Then I want to meet the best of the lot. And there's where I need your help, Peter."

"Sir," Peter said quickly, "we do not introduce our guests. They generally prefer not to know the others who dine here. Frequently our guests are heads of state and others of global importance. They value their privacy, sir."

"Exactly the class of person who needs the services of Sunny Bright – wouldn't you say, Harry? Now, Peter, I'm not asking for state secrets, only the name of someone seated nearby. It can easily be whispered in my ear."

"Please, sir...."

It was time for action, Harry decided. "Peter, old chap, join me behind the potted palm if you will." As he said this, he took Peter by the elbow and moved him gently away from Aloysious, who, with raised eyebrows, watched them walk off. He heard Harry say, "My boss needs to know who breaks bread in the same room. It's a cultural thing." Then Aloysious shrugged and turned away to meander slowly back through the restaurant to its elaborate entry way. He stood there deep in contemplation of a troupe of life-sized bronzes, lean female dancers with small breasts and short hair, when he was rejoined by Harry and Peter. The two were smiling and chatting like old friends. With a big, warm smile, Harry patted Peter's back.

"Okay, Peter. We'll see you at dinner. If I need anything, I'll give you the high sign."

"The high sign, Mister Harry!" Peter said enthusiastically.

They all shook hands again and left Peter there to find their own way back outside. As the big glass door shut behind them, Aloysious turned to Harry. "What the hell is the high sign?"

"I have no idea," Harry said. "He said it first. It must be some art deco thing."

"How did you two get to be pals?"

Harry pulled his fist from his pocket. He opened it to display a fat roll of American dollars. "I had a lot more before I met Peter. Sato's driver gave me a briefcase. It's full of hundred–dollar bills. You will get answers to your questions tonight, sire. I assure you."

"You were that generous? Well, if it works....How did you like the smoke screen I laid?"

"A little heavy. But Peter should be convinced that Sunny Bright is a determined and persistent salesman. I hope he shares that with his boss. Whoever he is."

"He will. Never fear. Just remember, Harry, what I'm doing is only the smokescreen. Behind it you will have to ferret out the airplanes. I don't know how you're planning to do that, but I got a couple of ideas there, too."

Harry waited. Aloysious said nothing more. "Want to share?" Harry finally asked.

Aloysious pondered the question for a while. Finally he said, "You know, Harry, it's hard to explain the dynamics of a good scheme. It's better if I let you see it in action."

"Whatever," Harry said.

Chapter 9

T hey arrived at seven, a half hour before most of the other guests. Peter had arranged a large round table in the most 'propitious' area of the dining room. From there Aloysious would have an unimpeded view of almost every other person dining that evening.

As the 'fancy ladies', Ting got to sit alongside Aloysious, and Tong next to Harry. It was like old times. Mouse sat next to Reggie, and P.C. seated himself off to one side, ensconced on two cushions with his back wedged against the wall. His eyes roamed the room and fixed on anyone who even glanced in their direction.

Waiters in long black coats, white trousers, and white turbans were plentiful. The tables were heavy with crystal and silver. There were more knives, forks, and other silver instruments in front of Harry than he knew what to do with. The menu was totally Western. Dishes were elegantly, if not clearly, named, and the words 'Monte Carlo' appeared in at least a half a dozen entrees. Other delights purported to be the specialties of Europe's premier chefs. The Maitre'd glided up to advise that Asian food, or indeed any food they might desire, was probably available in the Rudyard Room's ample larder – or would be flown in from Hong Kong or Singapore for tomorrow's lunch if not.

While they contemplated their choices, the big band played *Sentimental Journey* in the background. It sounded good. Harry turned to watch the band for a while. In this setting it was not necessary to close his eyes to imagine that he was sitting in one of the great American ballrooms of the 1930s. It was as if their journey in the Gulfstream had brought them not just to another place, but to another time.

"Hey, Booger!" The words snapped Harry right back to the present. He looked up to see Aloysious grinning over the top of his menu. "Want to share some Louisiana crayfish? Some hush puppies? We could have them flown in for lunch tomorrow." Harry smiled, but shook his head. With the slightest provocation, Aloysious would do just that. Harry was sure that there would be things to explain to Sato before this was over. Crayfish and hush puppies need not be among them.

The food was delicious. The service was excellent. Otherwise it was an ordinary meal. All through dinner, Aloysious was preoccupied with the other guests. His eyes roved around the room and he had little to add to the dinner conversation.

The other guests in the Rudyard Room that evening were mostly men, as could be expected in an establishment of this kind. There were no obvious family groups and a disappointingly small assortment of 'fancy ladies'. Those that were there were dressed very fashionably. The men were a mixed collection. Rough-looking for the most part, with bad haircuts, and expensive, ill-fitting clothes. They sat in bunches and tore into their food with gusto, drank a lot, and smoked through the whole meal. They were having a great time. They might have been hard-working rice farmers on a rare night out on the town, but when their hands moved, gold flashed and diamonds glittered.

There were men of another sort, but relatively few. These were dressed stylishly, but casually, and looked quite at home in their clothes. Some sat together in small groups, a few with ladies. For the most part they showed not the slightest interest in the other guests, but seemed preoccupied with their female companions if they had them, their food, or themselves. They might have been alone in the room. Unlike the farmer types, they wore little or no jewelry, but almost to a man they wore glasses. That made them look very intellectual, like professors. Or writers.

After ordering dessert, the ladies departed for the powder room. Aloysious slid into a chair between Harry and Reggie. "What do you think, guys?" he asked them

Reggie looked from Aloysious to Harry and back again before he spoke. "A preponderance of drug lords. Garden variety, for the most part. Except, perhaps, for the chappie presiding over the three tables in the corner. He may be one of the majors. There are a few elegant gentlemen scattered about who probably would be more lucrative. I recognize none of them, unfortunately."

Aloysious turned to Harry. "How do you see it?"

"Like Reggie. You can write off everybody, except maybe two or three. A couple of faces I think I've seen in the newspapers, but I'm not sure. Peter might be able to confirm that. My candidates are the two guys with their ladies up near the band. And then that guy getting up to dance now. Whoops, he's a little unsteady on his feet."

Harry and Aloysious watched the gentleman stumble along and all but bring down his dancing partner, a rather elegant young lady. She helped the man steady himself, and then supported him as they proceeded to the dance floor. As they watched, Harry added, "There are four guys two tables over from him. The ones with the military haircuts. They're with him. Probably his keepers."

When dessert arrived, so did Peter. Harry saw him on the far side of the room, making his way toward them. It was a slow passage as he obviously felt obliged to pause at each table and say good evening. Where guests knew him, he was required to engage in exchanges of some length. Despite this, he was very much in control – until he reached the enclave of three tables presided over by the largest and roughest of all the rough–looking men there. This was a man with immense girth, unruly hair, and a great capacity for food, drink, and loudness. There was no question that he was enjoying himself.

Harry watched the big man as he insisted that Peter join his group in a toast. He poured brandy into Peter's glass and then over Peter's shoe when the glass was full. Glasses were raised high while the big man made a speech. Finally, when glasses were tipped to mouths, Peter did his best, but that was simply not good enough. He did not have the capacity of the others. He coughed and sputtered and tried, but he looked near drowned when the big man mercifully released him with a shout and a slap on the back. Laughter from all three tables followed a bedraggled Peter as he headed for the safety of the PRIC table. The big man watched him go, and when he caught Aloysious looking his way, he smiled and waved, and yelled something. Caught off guard, Aloysious raised his hand just off the top of the table and returned a weak, noncommittal wave.

"You do smell nice, Peter," Aloysious said when Peter reached their table. "Like 50–year–old brandy."

"Good brandy, indeed, Mister Bright. The best brandy in the house for Mr. Piggy."

Reggie looked up. "Mr. Piggy," he said, "is he the big chap? The one in charge over there?"

"Indeed, sir. That is Mister Piggy. It's the name he prefers. He was 'Piggy' as a child, and he's 'Mr. Piggy' today." Peter turned to Aloysious and said more quietly, "He is the one to meet, sir. He has already asked that you come by his table for a drink."

As if hearing Peter's remarks, Mr. Piggy picked that moment to wave a brandy bottle in their direction.

Aloysious raised his hand and gave another small wave in return. "Not my type." He said to Peter, "Maybe Harry can meet Mr. Piggy. But tell me about the guys over there," pointing with his chin. Peter turned slowly and stole a glance at the tables that Harry had pointed out earlier. He leaned toward Aloysious and said something that no one else could hear. Then he was back up and smiling at everyone. "I really must go now," he said, bowed several times, and moved on to the next table.

Aloysious was obviously pleased. He looked over at Harry. "The guy you fingered, the dancer, he's it tonight. Peter said he would make it happen. You're going to have to do the honors with Mr. Piggy. He's starting to get frantic."

Harry turned to look. Now Mr. Piggy was waving a very large brandy bottle at them with one hand and pointing at it with the other. There were at least two dozen people seated at the three tables where Mr. Piggy presided, and all faces were turned in Harry's direction. Some shouted and waved. Things were getting raucous.

"Wonderful," Harry said as he turned back to Aloysious, who was staring at a dark alcove across the room. Harry could just make out Peter standing there, his body twisted like he was trying to scratch his back.

"That's it, Harry," Aloysious said, "the high sign! I gotta go. You take care of Mr. Piggy."

With a sinking feeling Harry watched Aloysious, with P.C. in tow, head across the room. He turned to the others at the table. Ting, Tong, and Reggie were huddled in serious conversation. Mouse was watching the action at Mr. Piggy's table. In Harry's mind, it was up to the remaining male members of the 'assault team' to take on Mr. Piggy and company.

"Harry. Harry."

Caught up in his own concerns, Harry missed Reggie's attempts to get his attention. "I'm sorry, Reggie. I thought maybe you and I ...."

Now that he had Harry's attention, Reggie laid out his own agenda. "Ting and Tong have asked me to escort them to see the cockpit. Seems they are both very fond of chickens. With luck we'll see them perform. Would you care to join us?"

"No. You go ahead, Reggie. You guys have fun," he said to Ting and Tong. As they walked away his spirits sank further. He turned to the last person at the table. "Mouse, I need help," he said. "We need to meet Mr. Piggy."

"Poor Harry," she said. "Now you must face the tiger."

"It's not the tiger I fear, Mouse," he said as he took her arm. "It's my stomach I'm afraid of." As they walked over he thought, it's always cognac with these guys, good cognac that you had to gulp down. And then they fill your glass and you gulp it down again. A shiver rippled over his ribs just as they reached Mr. Piggy's table.

"Ah, Mr. Piggy, what a great pleasure to meet you, sir." Harry said all this in English with a smile as big as he could manage. He was not sure what languages Mr. Piggy spoke, but he knew from experience that it did not really matter. Not at this stage. Mr. Piggy would get the tone of what he was saying, and read his body language. He would know more or less what Harry intended, and that it was benign.

Mr. Piggy took Harry's hand and shook it vigorously. He held on to the hand and used it to steer Harry to the center of the table, where he turned him to face the other guests. They were all on their feet now. Still holding Harry's right hand tightly in his own, Mr. Piggy used his left hand to pat Harry's shoulder as he started to address the crowd.

Harry could not understand a word, but he knew Mr. Piggy was praising his character, his judgment, his life of virtue, and probably his sexual prowess. The fact that Mr. Piggy knew nothing at all of Harry's existence until a few minutes ago did not hamper his orations. Mr. Piggy spoke on while waiters moved around filling glasses with cognac for the toast. Harry got a glimpse of Mouse, inconspicuous at the edge of the crowd. From the smile lighting up her face it was evident that she understood at least some of what Mr. Piggy had to say. All the other faces crowded in front of him were hard faces with hard eyes that were intently focused on Mr. Piggy. Harry wondered what it took to hold the attention of all these thugs. Mr. Piggy must be quite a guy.

Suddenly everyone started to clap. Mr. Piggy had stopped talking and was looking fondly at Harry. He still held Harry's right hand, and a waiter pushed a tumbler of cognac into Harry's left. When the clapping stopped, the silence in the Rudyard Room was absolute. Mr. Piggy raised his glass. All the other glasses shot toward the ceiling. It was a solemn moment.

Mr. Piggy moved his head and looked toward the band. Its members were on their feet, their instruments poised. They were ready. Mr. Piggy nodded. The music began. It was a familiar strain. Even Harry knew the tune. Mr. Piggy started to sing and everyone joined in. Everyone.

> *Oh, Susanna, don't you cry for me*
> *Oh, I come from Alabama*

With a banjo on my knee.
Oh, Susanna.....

Those were all the words Harry knew. Mr. Piggy knew all the words, all the verses. So did the others. They were singing in English, or what they took for English. Harry faked it.

The song ended to thunderous applause. Everyone clapped until Mr. Piggy raised his hand. He turned to Harry, raised his glass to him, then tossed the cognac down. Everybody did the same. What a shame, Harry thought and gulped. As he looked in wonderment at his empty glass, a waiter started refilling it. He could feel the cognac taking effect. He felt relaxed. Then stunned. Everyone was looking at him. He turned to Mr. Piggy and with some difficulty said, "I really don't know how to express my feelings."

Which was true, and it was as far as his oratory took him. His mind went totally blank. Every face was turned to him, expectantly – except Mouse and a young man she was talking to. A good looking young man, thought Harry, not a thug.

In the end it did not matter. It was not what Harry said – no one understood him in any case – but the obvious sincerity with which he said it. Everyone recognized that, and everyone came to accept that Harry's words were a simple, direct, and truly exceptional response to Mr. Piggy's toast.

Mr. Piggy stepped back, smiling and nodding his head, to let the other guests crowd around Harry. They all seemed to want to touch him, clap him on the back, or shout unintelligible words into his ear. His cognac glass was filled again – by Mr. Piggy personally. He was feeling panicked when he heard a familiar voice. "Mr. Harry, Mr. Harry." It was Peter.

"Mr. Harry, sir. Mr. Sunny Bright needs you, immediately, sir. In the Club Room, sir."

Harry handed his full cognac glass to the nearest guest, and screwed up his face in disappointment. "I am truly sorry, Mr Pitty, er...Piggy. Duty calls. I must...go." He started to bow, but stopped when he felt his head start to swim.

Mr. Piggy looked quizzically at him. And then at Peter, who said something. Mr. Piggy turned to Harry, slapped him on the back, and gave him a big thumbs up. Harry shook Mr. Piggy's hand, and the hands of a few others, then he walked off, a little unsteadily, as everyone cheered.

He stopped on the staircase and took some deep breaths before proceeding to the Club Room. He found P.C. and two men in military haircuts in chairs just outside. The only two people in the Club Room were Aloysious and the man Harry recognized as the unsteady dancer.

"Ah, Mr. Defense Minister," Aloysious said to the man, loudly, when Harry entered. He looked directly at Harry as he continued, "I would like you to meet my advisor on art and artifacts. Mr. Harry. He is the expert. He has the answers."

The Defense Minister looked up at Harry, his eyes glassy. He held a large glass balloon of a brandy snifter in front of his face with both hands. It was full. The only expression on his face was a trace of what was probably confusion.

"Harry, I was telling the Defense Minister here about our new investment instrument, the PRIC Adventure Funds. I explained the tremendous potential for capital appreciation and the total absence of downside risk." Aloysious turned to look at the minister.

"That, sir, is because you do not buy shares in the hypothetical profits of some company. You buy actual, real property. Things you can touch and see. Antiques, Mr. Minister! Ancient artifacts! Objects that have grown in value over the millennia. Objects that can only increase in value when they are collected into a PRIC Adventure Fund. You, Mister Minister, will share in the grand profits that these objects will command at international auctions. Premier auctions, stage–managed for maximum financial impact, Mister Minister!" Aloysious swung around and pointed right at Harry. "By my own advisor for art and antiquities, Mr. Harry!"

To make the concept perfectly clear for the minister, Aloysious shouted these last words at him. The minister reacted by looking frantically around the room. Seeing no escape, he took a big gulp of brandy. When he finished, he looked up at Aloysious with curiosity.

Aloysious saw this as an invitation to proceed. He looked at Harry, then turned back to the minister.

"Sir, as Minister of Defense, there is a PRIC investment vehicle that should fit you well: the PRIC War Adventure Fund. Here we bundle old artifacts of war, particularly objects from World War II. We package them for maximum sales advantage. Airplanes, Mr. Minister. PRIC is now seeking old warplanes. If you have any, PRIC will get you top dollar. If you know any government that has old warplanes – or any individual who does – PRIC will pay you the top finder's fee."

The Defense Minister's eyes grew unfocused. As Aloysious reached the end of his pitch, the minister started to his feet, taking care to balance his brandy snifter. Upright, he said, "My good man...," and peered at Aloysious, as if trying to see him more clearly. Then, like a felled tree he slowly toppled over and struck the floor with a dull thud. The brandy snifter rolled across the rug. It lay there unbroken, the spilled brandy around it slowly soaking into the rug.

"Is he dead?" Aloysious asked Harry.

"I don't think so," Harry said. Just then the minister emitted a choking sound. And then a snarl.

Aloysious prodded the minister with his shoe. "Good god," he said.

"It's okay," Harry said. Another snarl came from the minister. "I think he's snoring. The booze must have just knocked him on his ass."

Aloysious shuddered. He looked down on the minister with no pity. "Demon rum, Harry," he said. "That's what it does to a man." He turned and looked Harry straight in the eye. "Let that be a lesson to you, Harry."

*   *   *

Afterwards they sat in the grass behind the villas. The only light came from the stars and a half moon partially hidden by a cloud. It was postmortem time. Time to review success. And failure.

"What do you think, Harry?' Aloysious asked. "What did we learn today? What did we accomplish?"

Harry watched the bug swimming in his coffee. "You know," he said, "I think we went backward."

"It's not that bad, Harry. We did meet the Defense Minister. If he's not a prospect himself, maybe he'll tell friends."

"I doubt he heard much of what you said. Or understood it. His brain was in his brandy glass."

"Yeah," Aloysious said. There was great resignation in his voice. "I guess you're right. We won't get another crack at the minister. They'll be pouring him into his airplane this morning and flying him back home. He won't remember it, but he had a good time here. Too bad." Aloysious quietly watched the moon for a while as it struggled to throw off the cloud that clung like a tangled shawl. "You know," he said, "the damnedest thing happened last night. I was sitting there with the minister, and I could have sworn I heard a male chorus singing *Oh Susanna*. It was like background music in a Hollywood epic. And there I was, ready to make an epic pitch on the Defense Minister. I took it as an omen, a good sign." He shook his head to clear it. "Christ, sometimes I think I drink too much."

Harry had the swimming bug on his finger now, and flicked it off into the bushes.

"Susanna?" he said.

"How did you make out with Piggy?" Aloysious asked. "Did you learn anything?"

Harry took a big drink of coffee and felt better. "Did I learn anything? I don't think so. I was only with him for a few minutes. He's a real godfather type."

"Godfather," Aloysious said, not really listening.

"You know what I mean." Harry went on, "It's the guy we meet in every village. The big guy. Not the mayor, but the one who really runs the place. The guy who controls the local commodity. The loan shark. The drug lord."

"Drug lord?" Aloysious said, picking up the tag end of what Harry had said.

"He probably is. The commodity of the place he comes from is probably opium. He's cornered the market and tapped into the distribution system. Reggie thought he might be one of the majors. I doubt that. He's shrewd, I'm sure. But I doubt that Piggy's a biggie." Harry smiled; he liked the sound of that. He added, "He just doesn't look bright enough, Sunny."

"Anything there for us?"

"No, nothing."

They finished their coffee and walked back around the house to the veranda. Things were lively there. Ting and Tong were splashing in the pool. Reggie was stretched on the chaise having a nightcap. But something was missing.

"Hey, Reggie," Harry asked, "where's Mouse?"

"Don't know, old man. Probably still at the casino, winning at poker."

Harry looked out over the pool. "Hey, Ting–Tong!" he shouted. "Where's Mouse?"

The girls stopped splashing long enough to look at each other. He could see Tong shrug her shoulders. Ting shouted back, "I think she is with her new boyfriend!"

Just then P.C. came out of the house. Harry yelled and got his attention. Then he yelled again, "Where's Mouse?"

Chapter 10

U rrrfff," Harry mumbled, and burrowed deeper into the sheets. This was followed by the muffled tap, tap, tap of someone walking across the highly polished teak planks of his bedroom floor. That sound pulled Harry from the depths of sleep and left him bobbing just below the surface of consciousness. "Bluurff," he grunted now to the giant cognac bottle that was asking him to dance. The bottle burst in an explosion of light. "Fuuuuh," Harry said and sat up.

The girl was dressed in a kind of red bellboy outfit, a pill box hat cocked on top of her short black hair at a jaunty angle. Was he really awake, he wondered, as he stared at her. She gave a great tug on the drapes and the room filled with the drab gray light of dawn. When she turned, she saw he was sitting up in bed. She was very pretty

"Good morning, sir. Your breakfast is here," she said as she stepped to the small table near the window. "I'll bring your coffee," she said.

While she poured it, Harry shook his head and used his index finger to poke at some morning crud in the corner of his eye. Why was he awake he wondered? He had just gotten into bed. The girl set the coffee on the nightstand. "What time is it?" he asked.

"Five-fifteen, sir."

He took a sip of coffee. What a pretty girl, he thought. What a nice way to wake up. Even if it was the middle of the night. But why was he awake?

"Why am I awake?" he asked her. "What time did I leave my wake-up call for?"

"Miss Mouse left the wake-up call for you, sir. She said she would join you for breakfast. Would you like more coffee?"

"Yes. Please." A flash of memory returned with a jolt. Mouse! He must have really been asleep. Last night was just starting to seep back into his head. He remembered being almost frantic about not finding Mouse. After laughing at him, Aloysious joined him in the hunt. But back at the casino there was no Mouse. No one had seen her. She had disappeared. Near desperation, Harry asked Peter, the general manager, if there were any big animals in the jungle that surrounded them. Peter said, "Yes," but that was all he knew. He had not heard of any workers being taken by tigers. But then again, he would not, would he? He was much too busy to be bothered with reports of workers being eaten. So maybe there were tigers.

That did it. Harry was almost sick with worry. There was nothing more to do but pace back and forth on the veranda, until Ting and Tong convinced him to get some sleep. They even walked him to his room. He glanced at the clock on the end table. That was not more than two hours ago. But he had really slept. The cognac had probably helped. Dead to the world and forgotten Mouse completely. He was wondering whether he should feel guilty about that when there was a light tap on the door.

The bell girl put another full cup of coffee next to him and went to answer the door.

"Harry?" It was Mouse's voice, very quiet. "Are you doing something you shouldn't be?" The girl opened the door. Mouse gave her an appraising look as she stepped through the door. "Hope I'm not disturbing anything?"

"Come on, Mouse. Have some breakfast."

Mouse was in a khaki safari suit, a designer job. It seemed a little tight, and the shorts were cut high and showed off her legs. She looked fresh and perky. She seemed not to be lacking sleep or anything else.

Mouse helped the girl finish laying out the breakfast table. When the girl left the room, Harry threw back the covers to get out of bed.

"Stay there, Harry. I'll bring everything to you. It's very early and you haven't had much rest." Mouse set a bowl of fruit on the end table, and a basket of bread and rolls on the bed next to him. She sat down on the edge.

"It is early," Harry said. "Why are we having breakfast at this hour? And what about you? Where were you last night?" That sounded kind of testy, he thought. He hoped Mouse did not notice.

Mouse patted his arm. "I was working, Harry. I was very busy."

"No one knew where you were and...."

"Poor Harry," she said. She gently touched his arm again. "You didn't have to worry. I was with Tommy."

"Tommy?" The reaction was immediate. He went to full alert. "And who is Tommy?"

"I met him after dinner. When we went to Mr. Piggy's table."

A face flashed through Harry's mind, a young, handsome face. "Tommy," he said reflectively. "You were talking with him at Mr. Piggy's table. The young guy. A handsome kid."

"Yes," Mouse said, "that's Tommy. He's very nice. But," she added, after a moment's reflection, "he's not handsome. Just very cute."

"Cute?" Harry said. "Did you two have a good time?" That sounded a bit testy, too. He hoped he was not starting to sound like a father.

"We talked for a long time," she said, then raised her hand to look at her wristwatch. "Harry," she said, "I don't want to hurry you, but we have to leave here in ten minutes."

He looked at her in surprise. "What happened? Is Aloysious pulling us out? Are we going back to Bangkok?"

"No, Aloysious is still asleep. Everybody else is asleep. Just you, Harry. I have a surprise for you."

He did not much care for surprises, not at that time of morning anyway. He tried to get Mouse to tell him what was going on, but she refused to say anything. "You must wait and see," she said. He gave up trying and took his coffee into the shower with him. After the hot water beat on his back for a while he felt a lot better. When he finished dressing he said, "Okay, Mouse. What now?"

"Okay," she said. "Now we will meet Tommy in the driveway."

As they stepped out onto the veranda, Harry saw the jeep parked nearby. It was an old thing and, although he knew nothing about jeeps, he would have called it 'vintage'. It struck him how rare it was to see a jeep in this part of the world. The great love of the pickup truck did not seem to extend to the fabled jeep.

"Good morning, Tommy," Mouse said very quietly as if not wanting to disturb the others still asleep in the house. Harry had not noticed Tommy until that moment. He was standing off to one side of the jeep looking toward the sun that was climbing up over the trees.

"Good morning, Miss Mouse," he said, and then turned to Harry. "Good morning, Mr. Harry." He walked over and extended his hand.

"Good to see you," Harry said, and gave Tommy a long, hard, evaluating look as they shook hands. About Mouse's age, he thought, maybe a year or two older. Good looking. Or maybe 'cute' did suit him better. Whatever. Pleasant looking in any case. Not much taller than Mouse. Compact and healthy looking in jeans and a long-sleeved work shirt. Good eyes, bright, alert, and intelligent. Nice teeth, a disarming smile. Chinese? Burmese? Shan? A mixture of all those and probably more. Nice looking kid.

"We have to go, eh," Tommy said, looking at the sun. "Before it gets hot." His English sounded good, like he learned it from an expensive teacher.

They climbed into the jeep. Mouse beside Tommy; Harry on what felt like a very thin leather-padded shelf in the back, which he shared with a big rattan chest. Once the engine started to rumble, he felt like General Patton being driven off to war. It was a great time of the day. Over the sound of the jeep he heard the chirp of the birds greeting the morning.

Apropos of nothing, Tommy looked back at him, grinned, and said, "You like airplanes, Mr. Harry?"

The question was so unexpected it made Harry grin. "I do, Tommy," he said. "Why do you ask?"

Tommy's answer was just another smile.

They drove through the compound and passed by the casino at an unfamiliar angle. After a while they came to the front gate and drove right through it. It was open when they got there. Two uniformed guards, one on each side, saluted as they went by.

They drove up the road, and Harry knew this had to where P.C. and Jock had their encounter with the villagers. They went right by the shack where the chickens were sold. At this hour it was closed, even if it was a chicken day. After another 100 meters Tommy turned right and plunged into the jungle. They had cut through what was just a fringe of brush growing alongside the road. When Harry looked over his shoulder most of it had already popped back up.

They were on an overgrown trail. It must have been cut out of the dense growth that surrounded it a long time ago. There were a lot of plants growing on the trail itself, but all of them were young and all were low, just fender high. Someone was keeping it cut back. Although Harry doubted that P.C. and Jock had walked up this far, if they had, they could have crossed this trail and never noticed it was there.

They spoke very little while they drove. With the noise and the bouncing around it was difficult. Harry got the worst of it in the back. He needed one hand to keep himself in the jeep, the other to hold on to the bouncing rattan chest. Tommy was driving faster than he needed to. Just what you would expect from a kid, Harry thought, more critically than usual.

They suddenly broke out into the open, a wide, flat field of gravel and low-growing grasses. There was not a tree to be seen. Just ahead was a small flat-roofed wooden structure. It was completely open at the front with wide windows cut into the walls on the other three sides. The shed would offer protection from the sun, but not much else. Tommy parked the jeep in front of it.

Tommy and Mouse hopped out as soon as the jeep stopped. Harry got out a little more carefully. His right knee was a little sore where it had banged repeatedly against the unpadded side of the jeep. Tommy was already tugging at the rattan chest, and Harry helped him get it out of the jeep and carry it into the shed. Despite being stuck in the middle of nowhere, the shed looked cared for. Inside were two wooden tables and a half dozen chairs.

They set the chest down on one of the tables. Mouse opened it and pulled out a couple of large stainless steel thermos flasks. Harry could smell the coffee. That was followed by Danish and breakfast rolls, and dishes of cut-up fruit. Very nice, he thought, but a hell of a long way to come for a second breakfast.

He stepped out of the shed, yawned and stretched his arms. It was turning into a beautiful day. The sun was much higher now, but it was still cool. He turned to survey his surroundings and looked out across the field. In that very same instant he knew exactly where he was.

On the far side of the field were several buildings, bigger than the shed right behind him. At least two were airplane hangars. He recognized them. He had seen them in Riley's photos and, from a different angle, in the overheads. He scanned the rest of the area. He was certain of it. He was standing on the perimeter of the second airfield that the overhead photos showed near the casino, the same World War II British auxiliary airfield that Reggie remembered visiting 60 years ago. He had known the airfield was only a few miles from the casino, but he had not expected to find himself suddenly standing on it.

"Mr. Harry," Tommy's voice snapped him out of his reverie. "See you in a little while." Tommy was already seated in the jeep. With a small wave of his hand he drove off while Harry was still getting his thoughts together. He stepped back into the shed where Mouse was pouring coffee. She looked up and caught him watching her. "Do you know where we are?" she asked.

He nodded. "Yeah, I know where we are. It's the airfield in the photos. The same one Reggie thought he visited during the war. We got so fixated on the casino complex that I forgot that this was really the place I wanted to go. It just didn't seem possible. I don't know how you did it, Mouse. It's a hell of a surprise."

He knew there was much more to say, but he had to get back out there and look at it all. He was probably the first Westerner to set foot on this field since the British abandoned it 60 years ago. The shock of finding himself here was starting to wear off. He could feel the excitement building up. "Mouse, forget the coffee. Let's get across the field. I want to see the hangars and all the other stuff over there."

"We must wait for Tommy. He will be here soon. Come, have something to eat."

Harry did not feel like eating. History was pulling at him. Where the hell had Tommy gone? He stood and looked at the field and at the buildings across the way. He tried to imagine what it would have been like on a morning in 1942. Exactly like this, probably! Nothing here would have changed much over the years. The field would have looked just like this. From what he could see of the hangars and the other buildings across the way, somebody was taking care of them. But they probably looked like they did when they were built. Mouse put a cup of coffee in his hand, which he really did not notice, but he sipped at it as he stood and looked out across the airstrip and wondered.

It sounded a long way off. Just a cough, but something in Harry's head clicked and he knew exactly what it was. He looked toward the hangars, and he heard the cough again, a couple of times now. Then the roar. An Allison V-12! It had to be. The engine that powered the P-40. A wisp of smoke drifted up from behind one of the hangars. There was movement and the airplane came into view. He saw it from the side as it taxied across the apron and onto the runway, its long, pointed nose stuck high in the air. The airplane turned slowly until it faced him. Head on, it looked small and was harder to see.

It sat there for maybe half a minute, its engine just ticking over. Then the engine was brought to full power. A full-throated roar and a geyser of smoke and dust rose up behind it. It started moving, slowly at first, wings bobbing and rocking as it picked up speed. The tail went up and the airplane moved faster. It was still a good distance from Harry when it rose above the field.

The airplane stayed close to the ground as it came toward him. He watched with interest as the landing gear retracted. Much slower than he expected, and looking ungainly as first one wheel twisted and folded up into the wing, and then the other. Once the landing gear disappeared, the clumsiness was gone. The airplane was sleek and powerful.

When it passed him it was not much higher than his head. Maybe 20 feet to his right, but so close that he felt he could stretch out his arm and touch it. He twisted on his heel to watch it go by, so fast that he felt dizzy. He was enveloped in sound and blasted by the wind flung back over its tail. His eyes tried to absorb it all. The color was the green and brown camouflage he had expected, but the markings were a blur, except for the shark teeth on its nose that his eyes fixed on.

The airplane pointed its nose at the sky and climbed. At the top of its climb it banked sharply to the left. With one wing high it twisted around, back in his direction, and hurtled down toward him. He had the target's view, the dove's last look at the hawk plunging down. God, it was wonderful!

The airplane pulled up well above him and slowly rolled over as it climbed back into the sky. The aerobatics continued for a time. The P-40 banked and rolled and dived. Then it flew down low over the runway one more time, and at the end pulled up in long climbing graceful turn. Landing gear dropped and the P-40 positioned itself for its landing.

Mouse stood alongside him as he watched the P-40 approach the far side of the field and gently touch down. Once the airplane was rolling down the runway, he turned to look at her. Her hair was wind-blown and tangled, but her face glowed with excitement. "Do you like your surprise?" she asked. There was laughter in her voice.

"Did you know the airplane was here?" he asked.

She nodded.

"You made a miracle, Mouse. I don't know how you did it,

but you did." He kissed her nose. "We'll have to talk about all this later."

As the P-40 neared the end of the runway, it turned onto the grass and started rolling toward them. "The pilot's bringing it over here," Harry said. "We'll get a good look at it." When the P-40 got closer, Harry could see the pilot through the windscreen, his face hidden by his goggles and leather helmet. The airplane rolled up to the shed and came to a halt. A last burst of power and the engine was shut down. There was silence now, except for the ticking and crackling noises from the hot engine.

The canopy was rolled back, and the pilot took off his goggles, helmet, and gloves. It was not who the pilot was that surprised Harry, but that this "kid" possessed the skill to throw this old fighter plane around the sky the way he had. The big grin on Harry's face reflected both surprise and the unique pleasure the pilot and this old warbird had just given him. He shouted up at the pilot, "Great show, Tommy!"

Tommy responded with a wave and a thumbs up, and started pulling himself out of the cockpit. Harry walked slowly past the nose of the airplane and around the wing, seeing things he had not noticed from farther away. The guns had not been removed; the barrels still protruded from the nose and wings. The paint was scuffed and worn, some of the metal panels were dented and warped. On the fuselage just forward of the canopy he could make out a cartoon panda bear, partially rubbed away and almost hidden by oil that had caked over it. He ran his hand along the top of the wing. It came away oily and rough with grit. This was a working airplane, not a rich man's pampered pet.

Tommy stood on the wing. With his big boyish smile and his battered leather jacket he could have been one of the AVG pilots just returned from a mission against the Japanese Air Force. It was 1942 again.

"Great airplane!" Harry said, and he meant it. "Is it yours?"

"I wish, Mr. Harry. No, I am only the pilot." Tommy had cocked his head slightly toward him. He was probably having a little trouble hearing after his session in the cockpit. Harry waited until Tommy hopped off the wing and was only a couple feet away from him.

"I know it's an early P-40. Is it a 'B' model?" Harry asked. He was pretty sure he knew the answer, but he was curious to see how Tommy would respond.

"Some people call it a 'B' model. I'm not sure what to call it. On the aircraft identification plate on the fuselage it says Hawk 81. Hawk 81-A-2. You know that model, Mr. Harry?"

"I know it," he said. Under his breath he said to himself, "Incredible." He repeated the designator, "Hawk 81-A-2," loud enough for Tommy to hear, then added, "That was the export version. The P-40 Tomahawks they sent to the Chinese and Chennault.

"Yes sir! The P-40 Tomahawk. They came to Burma in 1941, before Pearl Harbor. The airplane of the AVG." Tommy patted the wing. "The American Volunteer Group. The Flying Tigers. And this one is one of their airplanes."

"Hard to believe," Harry said. His mind told him it really couldn't be, but the evidence was parked right there. He was touching it. "Where did you guys get this thing?"

"I'm not sure, Mr. Harry. My uncle, you must ask him. He is a great collector. He knows a lot about airplanes - just like you. He has many airplanes. After World War II there were many airplanes in Burma and in southern China. I think that's when he found them. A long time ago. He had them for many years. No one flew them."

"How much of this aircraft has been restored? Rebuilt?"

"Only the engine, sir. We had to do an overhaul when we were ready to fly it. We also did many small repairs. We replaced parts like the wiring and hydraulic hoses, and some of the instruments. We tried to keep everything original. All the new parts we put in are original."

"You didn't copy parts? You didn't have to make new ones?"

"No, sir. We didn't have to. My uncle has a big warehouse. He collected many things after the war. A lot of aircraft parts were stored in Rangoon and at some airfields upcountry."

With Tommy alongside, he walked slowly around the airplane.

It sure was a tired-looking old bird, all faded and worn. Most of the markings were still visible. On the tips of each wing was the 12-pointed white star on a blue roundel, the insignia of the Nationalist Chinese Air Force. He stopped to examine the tail where he saw just a shadow of a number a few inches high. It looked like it had been stenciled on the metal skin a half century ago. He could not quite make out all of it, but just enough. He could tell there were four digits and, preceding them, the letter 'P'. And that's exactly what was supposed to be painted in that spot: the original Chinese Air Force serial number. If this airplane was not original, somebody who knew a lot about the AVG airplanes took great pains to make it look that way. On the side of the fuselage, the white number '36' looked too good, as did the Walt Disney tiger jumping through a Victory 'V'. Those were AVG markings all right, but the number looked like a repaint; the tiger was probably added when the AVG was already history.

Harry stepped up on the wing and stuck his head in the cockpit. There were a lot of shiny places on the drab metal inside, wear spots, and in all the right places, where hands and feet and knees had rubbed or rested. The smell of old airplane was intense: a mix of hot metal and paint, oil and gasoline, rubber, leather, and sweat. Harry hopped off the wing and walked back some distance. He turned around to look at the whole airplane. It was incredible! Fantastic! And the most fantastic thing was that the airplane was so totally original. It was as if the Flying Tiger pilot who last flew it had just landed it, shut down the engine, and walked away. And ten minutes later – not 60 years later – along comes Harry and says, "What a neat airplane!"

"A good one, Mr. Harry?"

He looked at Tommy. "A good one. It really is. I've looked at a lot of old airplanes. I've never seen one that looked so…so real. It actually looks like it's been through the war – spent the best years of its life in combat. Then it was left alone. Nobody came along to make it look better than new. Nobody rubbed it down and polished it. It could not be better. It looks like a real honest-to-god warplane. You just don't find old warbirds like that."

"Do you think it's worth a lot of money?"

"I would say it is. I don't know how you put a value on something like this. In a way it's priceless. If it did come on the market, there are collectors and museums that would probably fight each other for it."

"That sounds very good. You must tell my uncle. He will be very happy."

"I'd love to talk with your uncle," Harry said. Tommy's comment helped snap him back to reality. This was exactly where he should be taking the conversation. "You said your uncle has other airplanes. Are they as good as this?"

"Some are as good, some maybe better."

"Tommy, I'll be here for a couple more days, probably. Do you think I might get a chance to meet your uncle?"

"You already met my uncle, Mr. Harry."

"I did?"

"You did. Last night. You had a drink with him. My uncle is Mr. Piggy."

Chapter 11

"Mr. Piggy! I don't believe it!"

Aloysious was taking the revelation a lot better than Harry had expected. He had waited until the two of them reached the center of the lawn behind the villas where Aloysious felt they could talk freely. Aloysious sat there now, on the grass, staring at the sky and pondering what Harry had just told him. After a long while he spoke. There was a hollow echo of defeat in his voice.

"Life is cruel, Harry. I've always considered myself a good judge of character. Even of character types. But Mr. Piggy wasn't even on my short list. I doubt he would have been even if I had met him last night." He sighed heavily. "It's ironic, isn't it? Here I am hustling the obvious suspect, a Minister of Defense for god's sake, and this kid, this Mouse - my own 'Personal Assistant' - uncovers the real target. How did she do that? I feel like a total failure."

Total failure was not Aloysious. Things needed to be set right. "Actually," Harry said, "You did exactly what you set out to do. You blew the smoke screen. That let me and Mouse poke around. She found the target, but you set up the situation. Mouse could never have done it on her own."

That lightened Aloysious's mood. "I think you're right, Harry. My scheme was pretty good, wasn't it? But that Mouse is something else. How did she find out about Mr. Piggy?"

"I took her along when you sent me over to meet Mr. Piggy. Piggy and I exchanged toasts and she talked with Tommy. His English is pretty good, and he was really the only one there she could communicate with. It was Tommy who approached her. He wanted to know who I was. Mouse told him I was your advisor on artifacts, and emphasized the old airplanes aspect. Tommy picked up on that right away. He was trying to impress a pretty girl, I guess, and he told Mouse he was a pilot. In fact, he said, he sometimes flew an old airplane right over the casino. He probably figured that not one woman in a million would do anything but look at him wide-eyed and say, 'Well, shut my mouth'. And be greatly impressed. But not Mouse. She asked him straight away, 'What kind of old airplane?' And right off he says, 'P-40'."

"Great!" Aloysious interrupted as the story began to unfold in his head faster than Harry could tell it. "So then she set a date to see the airplane?"

"Not so simple." Harry went on. "She tried, but Tommy said no way. He was just the pilot. Only the boss could authorize somebody taking a look at the airplane. Mouse had already figured Tommy was concerned that he had gone too far by telling her all this, and that he wasn't about to take her request up with his boss. That would only highlight his indiscretion."

A smile was growing on Aloysious's face. He could appreciate the problem Mouse faced. "Go on, Harry," he prompted.

"She had to work out a plan. On our boat trip upriver we had a lot of time to talk. I told her all about the Flying Tigers and their P-40s. She knew enough about my project to put together a plan in her head. She got Tommy to tell her more about his boss's interest in aviation. As expected, because he had a P-40, the boss had a pretty big interest in the Flying Tigers. Up here in nowhere land an interest like that is a little hard to pursue. The boss read a lot of books about the Flying Tigers, but he never met people who shared his interest. He certainly never met an expert."

Aloysious was stretched out on the lawn by now, head propped up on his wrist. He was listening intently, enjoying it. "And so you became the expert."

"You got it – I became the expert. Mouse convinced Tommy that his boss would love to meet me. All Tommy had to do was to present it as his own idea. So Tommy went and told Mr. Piggy. Mr. Piggy got thoroughly excited. He really wanted to talk airplanes with an expert. He got Tommy to introduce Mouse. Then he personally asked Mouse to set up this meeting. Mouse said she would try, but she voiced a little concern. She told Mr. Piggy that I had been looking on my stay here as a holiday, and that I might not want to talk about airplanes. That just got Mr. Piggy more excited. He really wanted to meet me now. So Mouse suggested he might want to sweeten the pot by showing off his airplane. And that's how the air show came about."

Aloysious shook his head in approval. "The old hard-to-get approach. Works every time. Smart girl, that Mouse. Okay, now she has everything set up. You've seen the airplane. What's the next step?"

"Next step is we meet Mr. Piggy. In fact, we're invited to tea. Tommy will come by at four to pick us up. You, me, and Mouse."

"Great!" Aloysious said. Harry could see he was still thinking about Mouse's coup. "You know, that Mouse has natural talent. With a little more experience and some training, she could work some world class schemes. I could teach her a lot." From Aloysious, this was high praise.

*   *   *

One of the casino's Mercedes picked them up and delivered them to Mr. Piggy's villa. They arrived in a setting that was more European forest than Asian jungle, although some of the bigger trees were teak and not chestnut. The main building was a dazzling white French chateau, with a sloping roof and a peaked tower. It had a familiar look and left Harry feeling that he had seen it regularly in French travel guides.

Aloysious, Harry, and Mouse had spent the early afternoon discussing different scenarios that might evolve during their meeting with Mr. Piggy, and the roles they would assume in various circumstances. It was agreed that, as the airplane expert, Harry would necessarily handle all substantive discussions relating to airplanes. Aloysious would jump in if the talk turned to money. Mouse would take a passive role that would let her observe and try to interpret the nuances of what was going on. Mr. Piggy's English was not good, and Mouse felt that Tommy would probably serve as his translator.

Tommy was there to greet them as their car pulled into the driveway. He led them down a path through a garden at the side of the house. In a clearing among the trees and alongside the small lake of a swimming pool were several round tables. Tommy led them to one of the tables and seated them on one side. He said Mr. Piggy would sit across from them. Tommy would sit on Mr. Piggy's left, next to his better ear, and serve as his translator.

They had no sooner seated themselves than Mr. Piggy himself appeared. He was all smiles. He shook hands and, then waving them back into their seats, stood before them and made a short speech. It was his welcome. That was obvious even before Tommy translated. Mr. Piggy spoke of his humble dwelling and the honor his guests paid him by their visit. Once Tommy finished translating these comments, Mr. Piggy signaled for an elaborate drinks cart to be pushed to the table by two burly men in the black trousers and white shirts of waiters. The cart had sandwiches and pastries, scotch and cognac, and wine and beer. All was the best, the whiskey was premium, and the beer was European.

They chose sandwiches and cakes, and Mr. Piggy encouraged them to start drinking seriously. When everything was just so, Mr. Piggy started to speak. He said a sentence or two, and then paused while Tommy translated what he said into English. It was evident that the two of them had had practice with this technique; they worked easily together. It was so effective, in fact, that as it went on, Harry quickly forgot that Tommy was in the middle of their dialogue and felt he was talking directly with Mr. Piggy.

Mr. Piggy began by saying, "Mr. Harry, I am greatly honored to meet someone who has studied the history of aviation in this

region. Particularly the history of the famous Flying Tigers. It is
a time that interests me greatly. When I was young, I was fortunate to witness some of that history being made. Now I am old,
and I am fortunate to have the means to become a collector of
the airplanes that made that history. My dream is one day to
share my good fortune with others.

Harry was taken with Mr. Piggy's apparent eloquence. Before
answering, he glanced at Aloysious and saw the glint in his eye,
probably provoked by Mr. Piggy's comment on sharing. Harry
decided to start his questions with the beginning: "How did your
interest in aviation begin, Mr. Piggy?"

"When I was a boy, the war started. My family lived in
Rangoon. Mother, father, brothers, and sisters. My father had a
business. He bought and sold things for the British companies.
We lived in a comfortable house. We had a garden. We had ser-
vants and cooks. Life was good. It was peaceful and happy. In
my second year of school the Japanese came. In our school they
told us that Japanese soldiers were coming to steal our country.
We were young and it meant nothing to us. Then the Japanese
airplanes came to bomb. It was very terrifying. For the grownups.
For a child it was exciting! I was like a young animal, very curious about the world. I had to see everything, to know everything. When the Japanese airplanes came, everybody ran to hide
in ditches or under the houses. I ran to where I could see the
airplanes better. Sometimes my friend and I would sneak away
from school to a place on the river where we could watch the
Japanese airplanes bomb the docks. We saw the bombs fall and
watched them explode. It was very exciting.

Harry tried to fit this into what he remembered of history.
"That must have been when the Japanese began their march
into Burma, in late 1941, early 1942."

"Yes, it was about that time. For me it started at Christmas, in
1941. My family was not Christian, but my father had close deal-
ings with the British, and we all knew Christmas. The first time
I saw the bombing was near Christmas day. The Japanese airplanes came and we hid under the house. We could hear the
bombs. Bang! Bang! Bang! I crawled out to look at the sky. I

heard my mother scream my name. I pretended not to hear and ran into the garden. I saw the Japanese airplanes fly over our house. They flew together – like this!" Mr. Piggy used his hands to form a 'V'. Harry nodded; he knew that was the way the Japanese airplanes flew in formation. Mr. Piggy continued, "They were all together, the Japanese airplanes. Then I saw others, small airplanes, drop from the sky above the Japanese. We could hear the guns. Some of the Japanese airplanes fell from the sky in flames. We did not know what we were seeing. Later the grownups said it was the British airplanes who chased the Japanese away. Others said no, it was Americans. We were children. We did not know."

Mr. Piggy paused to take a long pull at his scotch. Then he turned and quietly said one sentence to Tommy. Tommy looked across at Harry and said, "Mr. Piggy would like to tell you a story of the Flying Tigers." He turned back to Mr. Piggy and nodded.

"One day my father visited a British plantation where he had business. He took me with him because it was more dangerous to stay in Rangoon. When we got to the plantation we found American pilots staying there. There was a small airfield nearby where they kept their airplanes. It was hard for the Japanese to find them there. When my father went to look at teak trees with his British, I went on a bicycle to look for the airplanes. I found the field. It was not very big. A British soldier in short pants came to chase me away. I turned to run, but a big American stood in my way. He was one of the pilots who stayed at the plantation of the British. Maybe he saw me there. I don't know. He asked if I wanted to see the airplanes. Yes, of course I wanted to see them! We went in his jeep to where the airplanes were parked among the trees, hidden from the Japanese. He lifted me on to the wing. Then I saw it – on the nose. The painted shark teeth. The American showed me the guns. Then he sat me in the cockpit and showed me how to aim the guns. We laughed. He held me up so I could rub the shark teeth. He said it was good luck. Then he took me to a small house nearby. There were other pilots there. This was where they sat and waited for the Japanese to come. I sat with them and we all had tea. Just as we are doing now." Mr. Piggy gestured at the table as he said this.

Before Harry could respond, Mr. Piggy added, "Those pilots, they were the Flying Tigers of the American Volunteer Group. AVG! You saw my P-40, Mr. Harry. Do you think it is a good one? Do you think it is AVG?"

"I think it is an excellent P-40. I would have to confirm the serial number, but I'm almost positive it is an AVG Tomahawk."

"Tommy said you think it is...." Mr. Piggy paused and turned to Tommy. After a brief discussion, Tommy turned to Harry. "I think the word Mr. Piggy wants me to say is 'authentic'."

"Yes," Harry said, "it looks authentic. It looks like it must have looked during the war."

When Tommy translated this, Mr. Piggy was very pleased. "Yes, yes," he said, excitedly, "that's how it looks. Like it looked when I saw it. When I was a boy. That's how I remember it."

"How did you find that airplane? The one Tommy flew?" Harry asked.

"When the war was finished many things were left behind. They were abandoned by the British, by the Japanese, and by the Americans. It meant nothing to me. I was too young. I was sent to China to school. But my father gathered such things. He put them in warehouses where they would not be seen. He thought that one day the war and all the things left behind would be forgotten. Then these things could be sold. If only for the value of the metal."

"Your father," Harry said, "was he a collector of airplanes?"

"No. My father knew how to survive. He knew how to get money. He knew how to make our family prosper. But he spent no money on himself. Even if he wanted something, he would not spend money. No, my father was not a collector. I became the collector. I did not want an empty life like my father. My father died, and one day I went to one of his warehouses. There I found boxes of airplane parts and other things he preserved. I found this airplane. That was the beginning."

"Your father found the P-40 after the war...."

"I think my father found it on the plantation of the British. I think it was left behind by the Americans when they fled Burma. Maybe because it was damaged. I think my father found it and hid it. First from the Japanese. Later from the British and then the Burmese. He feared they would take these things from him."

"You said that was the beginning. You found other airplanes. Where did you find them?"

"As I already told you, when the war ended, many things were left behind. In Burma and in China. Some airplanes were left in fields where they crashed. Others were abandoned at airfields. When the Americans left, the farmers fell on these airplanes like locusts. They chopped them into pieces for the metal. To make tools. To make pots. In some places a big man in the village might take an airplane and hide it. One day it will be worth more he thought. But that was rare. Sometimes airplanes landed or crashed in remote places. For years they were hidden. No one knew they were there. Then a man came, maybe a hunter, and found it. He would not tell anyone, but keep it for himself. For these reasons some airplanes survived. When I became a collector, I went to the villagers. I told everyone that I would pay much money for old airplanes. Even wreckages. I would buy them not as a pile of scrap metal, but as a thing of history. For those who believed me, it was the opportunity they knew that one day would come."

"So you found a lot of airplanes?"

"No, not a lot, but I found some. I found one here. One there. Sometimes just an engine. Once in a remote place in China I found a warlord. He had brought together the wreckages of six airplanes. From those we could make three. It took a long time. Now I have many airplanes. Most of them are kept together. In a safe place."

"The airplanes you found. Were they like the P-40? Do you have others like it?

"There are other P-40s." Mr. Piggy laughed. "The P-40 is the star of my collection. I have more than six. But there are other airplanes too. American and Japanese. Even two British."

"Where are these airplanes now?"

"In a safe place, Mr. Harry. In a place of which I never speak. If I spoke of it, it would not be safe."

"I saw the P-40 fly. Do you have other warplanes that fly?"

"One day all my airplanes will fly. We have other airplanes that fly now, but not all. For a long time none of the airplanes flew. I had no pilots. One day I knew I needed my own pilots. Tommy is the son of my brother. He is very bright. I knew he could be a pilot."

Tommy already looked very uncomfortable as he translated this. Then Mr. Piggy said something to him, and he turned to Harry looking flustered. "Mr. Harry," he said, "Mr. Piggy asked me to talk about myself. About my flying." Tommy looked as though doing this was not in good taste.

"Please," Harry said, "tell us about yourself. It will help us understand what your uncle is trying to do."

Tommy looked down at the table and started. His words were softer than they had been when he translated Mr. Piggy's comments. "Mr. Piggy first sent me to Thailand. He had a friend there who had an airplane. A Cessna. That was my introduction to flight. To see if I liked it, if I could do it. I loved it." He looked up at them with a big smile. Then he looked down at the table and continued. "There were political reasons why I could not train there. So Mr. Piggy sent me to America. To the state of Florida. I did all my commercial flight training there, from basic flight school to business jets. When I qualified I could be the chief pilot for Mr. Piggy's personal Lear jet. When I finished in Florida, I went to Texas to do a special course on piston airplanes. Finally I flew some of the old warbirds there. I flew a P-40. Then I was ready to come home and fly for Mr. Piggy."

"So, you're the chief pilot," Harry said. "You fly Mr. Piggy's Lear, and you fly the warbirds. That's a big job, Tommy."

"Mr. Piggy believes it is very important that a member of his family is his chief pilot. I'm sure you know, Mr. Harry, that life here is very political."

"Yeah," Harry said, "I know it's all politics. But tell me, where are we going with all this? Your uncle has what sounds like an incredible collection of airplanes. All very valuable. Some of them fly, and it sounds like one day he wants them all to fly. This is a huge operation, an expensive operation. Where does he see it all going?"

As Tommy translated this for Mr. Piggy, Harry glanced at Aloysious, who was sitting on the edge of his chair. His eyebrows were up, and he was struggling to hold back something he wanted to say. Harry winked at him and said, "Hang on."

Tommy turned back to Harry and began translating Mr. Piggy's answer. "I have many airplanes now. Enough to fill a museum. And that is what I want to do one day. I want to build a museum where all these airplanes can be preserved and seen by anyone who has an interest in them. You said, Mr. Harry, that this is a big, expensive operation. Yes, it requires a lot of money. But money is not a problem. The problem is a political one. Where to build the museum? We must have a place where people from everywhere can visit easily. I love this place," Mr. Piggy said with a wide gesture of his arm that encompassed his villa, the casino, and the jungle that surrounded them. "Here there are no political problems, but this place is too far, too remote. But in other places there are problems."

"What kind of problems?" Harry asked.

Mr. Piggy laughed when Tommy translated the question. "Political problems," he answered, "always political problems."

"Well," Harry said, "I don't know what your political problems are, but it strikes me that your museum would be a great asset to any area. It would bring in tourists. It would...."

"You know, Harry," Aloysious suddenly piped up. "You said asset, and I'd like to emphasize to Mr. Piggy what a tremendous asset he has in these airplanes." He turned to Mr. Piggy and leaned toward him. "Yes, Mr. Piggy, these airplanes represent a wonderful opportunity. What Mr. Harry and I call our War Adventure Fund would be a wonderful place to shelter your aircraft. Under the ownership of the Pacific Rim Investment Company, your airplanes would not only be preserved, but pay you a handsome dividend. Alternatively, if you sold to PRIC only six P-40s, you could have enough money to build a museum to house all the rest of your airplanes. If you wanted to do an outright sale of all your airplanes, we could put you in contact with collector-buyers, and handle all negotiations. Our fees for transactions of this kind are most reasonable, sir."

Mr. Piggy sat back in his chair and watched with great interest as Aloysious spoke. He waited for a time after Tommy had translated everything before responding. "My dear Mr. Sunny Bright," he said, "I have heard you are a man of genius with money. And I appreciate your proposal. But I have no need of more money. My concern is for my airplanes. And for my project to put them in a museum. I also have a proposal: I propose that the three of you come and work with me. Mr. Harry, you are the airplane expert. You can become the general manager of the museum. Mr. Sunny Bright, you are the expert on money. I would give you a lot of money to manage for my company, and more money to create the museum. Miss Mouse, you are an expert with people. You can manage the public relations for the museum, for my business, and for me. Together we will find away to solve all the political problems. Or to work around them."

"Mr. Piggy," Aloysious said, "what is the cause of your political problems?"

Mr. Piggy thought about this for a moment. "My business," he said. "Always my business. I make money easily. It upsets people."

"What is your business, Mr. Piggy?"

Tommy translated this, and Mr. Piggy looked at him quizzically. He thought for a moment, then leaned forward to say something to Tommy. Tommy rose, walked to a chair nearby, and picked up a black leather briefcase. He brought the briefcase over and held it while Mr. Piggy poked about. Finally Mr. Piggy withdrew a packet of business cards. With small bows, he gave one to Aloysious, one to Harry, and one to Mouse. The cards were full of Chinese characters.

"There," Mr. Piggy said. "My card. It has telephone numbers where I can be reached anytime, from anywhere in the world. The offer I made to you is sincere. I know you all have great responsibilities, and that you may not be able to make any decisions immediately. But when you do, please let me know. I look forward to working with you."

They were all very taken by Mr. Piggy's offer of employment. Suddenly being handed this simple business card made the offer somehow more real. Mouse looked at Mr. Piggy's card and a small puzzled smile crossed her face. Aloysious looked at the card and visions of being a real Sunny Bright danced in his head. Harry looked at the card and saw a vivid scene in which he was 'the curator', striding down a polished marble floor lined on both sides with rare and wonderful airplanes, the master of all he surveyed. Just then Mr. Piggy stood up, ready to take his leave.

As Mr. Piggy shook his hand, saying words that Tommy was translating behind him, Harry felt a rush of gratitude toward this big, burly old man who given him a chance to see an AVG Tomahawk and who now offered him every airplane lover's dream job. With complete sincerity Harry said, "If ever there's anything I can do for you, Mr. Piggy, I would be honored."

Mr. Piggy's reply came via Tommy almost before Harry had finished. "Well, actually, yes, there is one thing. You are an expert, Mr. Harry, and you will understand. I have always had a great wish to meet the Flying Tigers. I would like to discuss with them their history, their airplanes, and the plans for my museum. It would be a great thing for me. I'm sure you can arrange to do this for me, Mr. Harry. Please stay in touch with Tommy."

"Yes, of course, I'll certainly try," Harry said, but Mr. Piggy had already turned to Aloysious. Over Tommy's translation of Mr. Piggy's parting words, he heard Aloysious say, "Now, Mr. Piggy, if you do decide to sell any of those P-40s – even if it's just one – just remember, 'Sunny Bright will do you right!'"

Chapter 12

T he following day it was tea back in Bangkok with Sato. Harry looked out over the garden, not really seeing it as he went back over his thoughts, trying to assure that he had missed nothing. He had told Sato all about Sunny Bright's "assault team" and their adventures at the jungle casino and how it all culminated in the meeting with Mr. Piggy. Although set deep inside the city of Bangkok, the old Japanese house where he and Sato had spent the afternoon talking and drinking was quite comfortable. There was none of Bangkok's heat, only a soft warm breeze that occasionally brushed their faces. There was no traffic noise, just the sounds of insects and the occasional chirp of a bird.

"So that's where it stands, Sato–san," Harry concluded. "Mr. Piggy's job offer may give us an opportunity to infiltrate his operation and get closer to the airplanes. Maybe it's not such a great idea for Aloysious to take a job handling Mr. Piggy's money, but being curator might work for me. Problem is we don't know much about Mr. Piggy. Or what he does. He comes across like a big businessman, but we don't even know what business he's in."

A stray recollection crossed Harry's mind and made him laugh aloud. "Sato–san," he said, "you should have been there. It was really funny. Piggy gave each of us his business card. It was all in Chinese, of course. Aloysious was completely beside himself. He knew he had the crown jewels. He carried his card all the

way back to the villa in his fist. We went out in the back yard
where he figured it was safe to talk. 'Ha!' he said, 'we got it all.
Mr. Piggy's business card will have everything! His name, the
name of his business, his address. The whole salami! All we have
to do is decipher it.' Well," Harry went on, "by this time Mouse
had already done that. So she read it out for him:

> Please remember your friend, Mr. Piggy
> He remembers you!
> If you need to call him
> Please dial the numbers below
> And leave a message
> Any time. Any language.

Harry handed Sato the card. "So, there wasn't any name.
There wasn't any address. There is nothing there we can use.
Some telephone numbers, but so far we can't even identify what
country they're in. What do you make of it? Who is this guy? Do
you know him?"

"Perhaps," Sato said. He looked at the card carefully, then set
it aside on the table. "Tell me again what you know of his early
years."

"Not much. He was born a few years before World War II.
Spent his childhood in Burma. His father was a businessman
who dealt with the British before the war. His father must have
been a big success. Mr. Piggy spoke of warehouses that were full
of things. Soon after the war Mr. Piggy was sent to school in
China. And that's about it."

Sato nodded his head just once. He seemed deep in thought.
After a while he looked up and said, "Your Mr. Piggy is Chinese. His family name is Wang. I do not recall his given name.
He has a Christian name too. Michael, I think. Because his father did business with the British it was good to have a Christian
name. His father came to Burma from China in the 1920s. He
made his fortune in Burma."

"That's pretty good, Sato. Your memory never fails to astound
me. So anyway, if Mr. Piggy's father was a successful businessman...."

"His father was a thief." Sato said it quietly.

Business in Asia can get rambunctious at times, but Harry had never heard Sato call another businessman a thief. With some surprise he repeated, "A thief?'

"A thief. A very big thief. Before Burma fell he stole from the British. After Burma fell he stole from the Japanese. Then the war ended and he stole from the Burmese, from the British again, from the Americans, and from anyone else who passed by."

"And what about our Mr. Piggy?"

Sato looked at Harry with a twinkle in his eye. "There is an American phrase," he said, "what you call, I think" – and he said the words in English – "hitting the jukebox."

Harry held Sato's eyes for a long quiet moment while he thought about it. Then it struck him. "Oh, yeah," he said, "hitting the jackpot." Harry smiled to himself and took a sip of his cognac. "So you think our Mr. Piggy is the jackpot? A big deal?"

"Yes," Sato said. "Mr. Piggy is a big deal. A real jackpot."

"Well, who is he? What does he do?"

"He is a very big..... Again, it is best described with an English word. How do you say it in English?" He thought for a moment and then pronounced very successfully, "Narco–terrorist."

"Oh, shit," Harry said. He looked at Sato, speechless for a moment. Then, a small smile playing on his lips, he said, "Well, there goes my curator job."

"A narco–terrorist of the first order," Sato added, reverting to Thai. "Perhaps the biggest narco–terrorist in Southeast Asia."

Harry just shook his head. "We figured he must be into some kind of hanky–panky. That would be par. But nothing really big time. He doesn't come across like that. How do you know all this stuff about him, Sato? Do you know this guy?"

"I do not know him. I know of him. I think every big business in Asia knows of Mr. Piggy. Perhaps not under that name. Do you know how he got his name 'Piggy'?" Harry shook his head. "He was a very clever student. In China, as you said. But whenever he became engrossed in studying from his books he grunted like a pig. And all the other students called him Piggy. A pig is an intelligent creature, so he liked the name. And he kept it. I am told he is in some ways a humble man. He has a sense of humor. But he can be viscous. He is dangerous. There is no question of that."

"What qualifies this guy as a 'narco–terrorist'?"

"He controls the production and distribution of certain narcotics. He controls the hills where the opium grows, the refineries where it is processed, and the networks that get the product to the consumer. He also has laboratories that produce designer drugs. To protect all his assets he has an army, a sizable one, with weapons more modern than the government forces where he operates."

"That makes him a drug lord all right. But that's still a few notches below your narco–terrorist."

Sato's brow wrinkled; he spoke with intensity. "For Mr. Piggy drugs provide money, but money is only the means. Mr. Piggy is a clever man. A man with aspirations. He has a dream of controlling whole regions of Asia. He is not satisfied with just an organization that produces and distributes drugs. He wants to create 'institutions' that are substitutes for government. I said that almost all big businesses in this part of Asia know of Mr. Piggy. That is because when a business expands into some areas they find themselves dealing with Mr. Piggy's licensing agents – or his tax collectors. And if they do not buy a license, or do not pay the tax, bad things happen. Mr. Piggy is a throwback. He is a Chinese warlord who has survived into modern times. He already governs wide areas through force and terror."

"Well," Harry said, "that's pretty heavy stuff. I guess that's the end of my project. It's too bad. I thought we had really accomplished something with this trip. At least enough to get us to the next step. But I guess that's all over now."

"Why must your project be over?"

"Well, if Mr. Piggy is what you say he is – and I have no doubt that he is – then the whole business becomes too dangerous. Shake hands with Mr. Piggy and get caught in the crossfire between his army and a dozen different governments. Just to help set up his museum would probably cost me my passport. I can't afford to do that. I might never be able to go home again. It's not about just airplanes anymore."

Sato looked down at the table. He would not meet Harry's eye. "You don't agree, Sato–san?" Harry asked.

"I don't agree," Sato said simply.

"What would you do?"

"I would not abandon the project. It is still about airplanes. Nothing has changed. The risk you see now seems greater than before because you know more about Mr. Piggy. Before, you suspected he was involved in hanky–panky, but you were enthusiastic. All I did was confirm the kind of hanky–panky it is. The point is, the project is about airplanes. It must be. All you need to focus on is your objective, the airplanes. Your job is to deal with Mr. Piggy as a collector of airplanes, not as a 'narco–terrorist'. You don't need to get on his payroll. And you don't need to fight him. All you need is to find a way to maintain the dialogue about airplanes that has already started."

"And if I piss this guy off?"

"Your incentive not to do that has increased considerably."

"You may be right, Sato–san. I'm meeting Aloysious this afternoon, to bring him up to date. I'm curious to see what he has to say about it. If I do get on the wrong side of Mr. Piggy, I'll be living at the edge of the world with Aloysious."

*   *   *

"Well, that puts a fine edge on it," Aloysious said. "A project worth doing should have a certain risk. That's what makes it worth doing. Besides that, it's your ass, Harry." The emphasis was on 'your'.

Harry had just told Aloysious what Sato had said about Mr. Piggy. He turned to the window and watched a rice barge being towed down the river, and thought about what Aloysious had just said. The two of them were in the sitting room of Aloysious's suite at the Oriental Hotel on the bank of the Chao Phya, the river that flows down along one side of Bangkok. Aloysious, wearing one of the hotel's elegant bathrobes, was busy sampling

a large collection of European beers he had ordered from somewhere outside. He kept opening bottles and tasting them while
Harry talked. It was evident that Aloysious had enjoyed the
luxury of recent days and now clung to what was still left to
him. The suite at the Oriental was booked through the weekend
– courtesy of Sato's Black Lion Enterprises – but his return to
Sparrowfart and the edge of the world was drawing near.

"My ass?" Harry finally said, turning his eyes back to Aloysious.
"I'm not just thinking about myself. I'm thinking about you and
Mouse and anybody else who gets involved in this thing."

"It is your ass, Harry," Aloysious said, examining the label on
a bottle. He looked up. "Think about it, Harry. You're the one
who has to lead the charge. I'll back you up, but I'm not the one
who can go to work for Piggy. I have other responsibilities. Come
to think of it, I don't think you should work for Mr. Piggy either.
Sato was right when he said that you're not going off to fight
Piggy. You're just going to talk him out of some of his old airplanes. The fact that Piggy is a world–class narco–terrorist becomes significant only if you screw it up." He picked another
bottle, glanced at the label, and took a small testing sip. "So don't
screw it up."

Harry turned to look back at the river. He thought about it for
a moment, then said, "You and Sato seem to be together on that,
so I guess you must be right. I think my problem is that I was
focusing on infiltrating Piggy's operation by becoming the curator of his museum. That's a very tempting job offer. But now I
don't see doing that, and neither you nor Sato seem to think it's
a good idea either. So where the hell does that leave me? Do we
all go back to the casino and play pinochle with Mr. Piggy? I
really don't see a way to move this forward."

"Harry, all you have to do is take a single step. You don't want
to join Piggy's operation, but you don't need to tell him that right
now. He's not expecting a quick answer anyway. I was thinking
more along the line of you getting in touch to ask more questions
about the job, his airplanes, or whatever. Just find a natural way
to do it."

"A natural way?" Harry said a little skeptically. "I'm not sure I can look on Mr. Piggy in a natural way anymore."

"You know, Harry, I was only half listening at the end of our meeting with Piggy, but wasn't there something he wanted you to do? Find him a Flying Tiger or something? What are chances of that? Are any of those guys still around?

"He did ask me that, didn't he?" Harry said, thinking back. "Are any of those guys still around? You bet they are. They were a tough bunch of guys when they signed up to go to China. And they stayed a tough bunch over the years. There's a number of them still around. But where do I find a Flying Tiger – one who wants to go off to some remote area of the Golden Triangle? To have high tea with the local warlord?"

"Well, hell, Harry, I wouldn't worry about it. They're probably used to that. Probably did it every afternoon back in the old days. Speaking of the old days, Harry, you want to try some of this beer. I need to get the flavor just right when we start upgrading Pachyderm beer. I'm sure I can do that at a better price than this German swill."

Harry was not really listening. He looked at his watch. "I need to use your phone. It's early morning in the U.S. I need to call Riley – the guy who started me on this project – and tell him that we found his P–40. Maybe he can find us a Flying Tiger."

"Good idea, Harry. Order us up a Flying Tiger."

Chapter 13

"R. 'Hawk' Herrington? He's no Flying Tiger!"

"He is, Harry!" Riley was adamant. He was shouting into the phone. "He damned well is a Flying Tiger! And you better be nice to him. He's on his way."

Harry held the phone a couple of inches away from his ear until he was sure that Riley was finished. When he put the phone back to his face and spoke into it, he tried to stay controlled. "Riley," he said, "I'm not trying to argue with you. All I said was that I checked the roster of the American Volunteer Group Flying Tigers and there's no pilot by the name of R. 'Hawk' Herrington. Check it yourself. Any good history of the AVG will have a roster of the group's members in the appendix."

"Well, he is!" Riley said a little breathlessly, and Harry hoped he was close to exhausting himself. This was about the fifteenth telephone conversation they had in the last two days, and Riley seemed to get louder and more upset with each call. Harry was getting upset, too. He was starting to feel he had a right to be upset. "Riley...." He started to say – and then he blurted it out - what he had been thinking all along, before he could stop it, "The man's a fraud, Riley!"

"He's not a fraud," Riley answered quietly and went on, carefully pronouncing each word. "He was there, in Burma and China. He got himself in trouble. Pissed off the 'Old Man' – Chennault – and got himself fired. He was the best I could do on short notice, but he won't disappoint you. He's on his way now. You'll see. You'll like him."

Harry thought about that for a moment. "You say he's on the way?" If R. 'Hawk' Herrington was going to be here in a couple of days he might as well meet him. "Listen, Riley," he added, "I'll meet the guy, but if I think he's not up to the job, I'll send him right back to you."

There was silence on the line, then a large relieved sigh. "Okay, Harry. Fine. You do what you want, but meet Hawk first. You'll see. He's up to the job."

"Okay, then we're agreed. You might as well give me his flight number. I'll pick him up at the airport."

"Good," Riley said. "He'll be getting into Rangoon...." Harry did not hear the rest.

"Riley, did you say Rangoon?"

"Yeah, Rangoon. That's in Burma."

"I know it's in Burma. But I'm in Bangkok. That's in Thailand."

"I know that, Harry." Riley was sounding testy again. "You didn't let me finish. Hawk is on his way to Rangoon. That's what he wanted to do. You don't have to meet him at any airport. You'll meet him right at his hotel in Rangoon, The Strand. It's where some of the AVG stayed in 1941, when they first got to Burma. I've already booked a room for you there. All you have to do is to get to Rangoon in the next couple of days." Then Riley added, unkindly, "That's only an hour away by air, Harry. I'll book you a flight from here. If that's difficult where you're at."

*   *   *

Harry liked Burma. It was an exotic land, lost somewhere in the backwaters of history. Nothing much had changed there in the last 60 years. Such lack of progress was wonderful for tourists, the few who had visited in recent years. It was not quite so wonderful for those who lived there, the Burmese. They were a patient and tolerant lot, too tolerant perhaps, of their leaders, who had taken the country down a lonely path to isolation and economic ruin. Burma was locked into a distant and decaying past, but the people remained proud and welcoming.

The Strand Hotel had a car waiting for him at the airport. There was no traffic, and the ride through town was an easy one. He got to the hotel in short order. He checked in, sent his bag up to his room, and went off to explore the hotel. The Strand felt like history. Built in 1901, it was Rangoon's version of a grand hotel, like the Raffles in Singapore, or the Oriental in Bangkok. It may have been grand in its early days, but its glamour had already worn thin when the Flying Tigers got there in the summer of 1941. By the time of Burma's independence it was positively run down. In the early 1990s it was taken over by an investment group and restored to what it had been in its days of glory, and made even nicer than that.

The lobby was all marble, cool and quiet. There was no sign of other guests, no one to be seen but a uniformed clerk at the reception desk. Harry walked over and asked for Mr. R. Herrington. "Ah, yes," the clerk responded without hesitation. 'Mr. Hawk' had been in the lobby just a moment ago, looking for a newspaper. He had been sent off to the small shopping arcade through the door at the far corner of the lobby. Harry slumped into a nearby armchair to wait for Herrington to reappear. He did not wait long. A man came out of the shopping area and walked across the lobby, a small tabloid newspaper in hand. Just looking at him, Harry knew it had to be R. 'Hawk' Herrington.

He was average size, compact-looking in a navy blue blazer and gray trousers. Harry figured that he had to be in his early eighties at least, but he did not look it. He could easily have been 15 years younger. He had most of his hair, all silver and neatly brushed down, and a face that showed signs of wear, but was tanned and healthy looking. His walk was brisk, if a little stiff and military. There was little about him that said 'old man'. He was in the latter part of the prime of his life. He carried a walking stick, although he didn't seem to need it, and wore a pair of aviator sunglasses with dark gray lenses.

"Mr. Herrington?"

He turned to face Harry and reached up to take off his sunglasses. His eyes were pale blue and clear. "You must be Ross," he said. "I wasn't expecting you until tomorrow or the day after."

"I got in a little early, Mr. Herrington. Just thought I'd say hello and tell you I was here. There's no hurry. We can get together whenever you want."

"Call me Hawk, son." His eyes studied Harry. After a moment he said, "I was going for a stroll. Care to join me?"

"Sure," Harry said. A minute later they stood out on the hotel's shaded steps that led down to the street. As the heat and humidity of the Burmese afternoon seeped through Harry's skin, a little tune echoed in his head:

> *Mad dogs and Englishmen*
> *go out in the noonday,*
> *out in the noonday,*
> *out in the noonday sun!*

"Over there," Hawk said, and waved his walking stick out in front of them, a little off to the right. "The docks, they're over there. That's where it all began. Where the P-40s were unloaded and the AVG personnel arrived. The summer of 1941." Harry looked toward the river, but could not see it. Buildings and trees were in the way. In the distance the long arm of a crane was silhouetted against the sky.

They walked down the steps to the sidewalk and turned right. Strand Road followed the course of the river here. No one else was walking, but there was a steady stream of vehicles on both sides of the road. Just ahead, on their side of the road, were buildings left over from the days of the British Empire, big brick and stone structures, aged and decrepit-looking, but still used as offices. Vines clung to the walls and up high weeds grew in old cracks. Hawk looked at them with great interest. "My god," he said, "the buildings were better kept then, but it looks just like it did 60 years ago. It's goddamned amazing."

Several long blocks later, they turned right again and walked down a busy street that seemed to be taking them toward the center of the city. There were many people around them now. Most were going somewhere, on foot, bicycle, or minibus. Others simply stood around, leaned against walls, or squatted on the sidewalk. There were fewer large buildings here, and most were well off the street, deliberately pushed into the background. At the far end of the street they could see the glittering gold roof of a pagoda, but where they walked were mostly small shop-houses of two or three stories with fronts open to the street.

Hawk Herrington just strolled along and seemed not bothered by the heat and noise. Harry could not see his eyes behind the dark lenses of his sunglasses, but he knew they were moving, taking in everything. From time to time Harry heard words the man muttered under his breath: "Damn!" or "Will you look at that!" or "Isn't that something!" Distracted by the intensity of Herrington's interest, Harry caught his toe on an upturned piece of sidewalk and stumbled. He might have fallen if Herrington had not grabbed his arm and steadied him. Nothing got by the old man. And he was still quick.

"Here," Hawk said, "let's go down here," and led Harry down an overgrown lane. "I may have my directions crossed," he said, "but somewhere around here was the Silver Grill. You've heard about the Silver Grill?"

"Yeah, I've heard about the Silver Grill. It was where the Flying Tigers spent a lot of their off-duty time."

"That's it. The Silver Grill was a good place. It was the best thing we had. It was comfortable. The food was okay, and there was dancing too."

Halfway down the lane they stopped to look over a two-story yellow-brown building that stood by itself in a large overgrown lot. It had an ornate facade with columns and a fancy portico. Other architectural details were hidden by sagging lines of wet laundry.

"I'm really not sure," Hawk said. "My instincts tell me it was here. And maybe it was, but there's nothing here I recognize."

He looked up and down the lane. "Well, let's head back to the hotel."

As they strolled along, Hawk mused, "The Strand's a nice hotel, isn't it? I don't remember that it was so nice in my day. I stayed there several times. The rooms were not great. I'd swear they weren't as big as they are now. And I don't recall the lobby being so full of shiny marble. Maybe it was, but you know, when you're very young, stuff like that – being in a nice hotel - is not so important. It could have been the nicest hotel in the world in 1941. I wouldn't have noticed."

By the time they got back into the cool, dry air of the lobby, Harry was weary and wet. His shirt stuck to his back, his trousers clung to his legs, and his hair was plastered down on his scalp. Beside him, Hawk looked as crisp and as dry as he had been before they stepped outside.

"Harry, what say we get a beer?"

"Sounds good, but I'll have to freshen up a bit first."

"You do that, Harry. I'll grab a table," Hawk said and walked on into the little restaurant off the lobby. When Harry stepped into the restaurant a few minutes later, it seemed like the entire hotel staff was clustered around the old man's table, smiling and giggling. They slowly drifted away as Harry approached.

"You seem to have achieved celebrity status," Harry said as he sat down.

"You mean the staff? That's not celebrity, Harry, that's old age. One of the young ladies wanted to know if I'd been here before. I told her I had, and that it had been over 60 years ago. It blew her mind. She told the others and they all wanted to get a look at me."

Within minutes of ordering, a waiter brought them two frosted bottles of the local beer. They tipped their glasses to one another and drank deeply. When he finished, Hawk held up his glass to look at it. "Not bad," he said and picked up the bottle to read the label. "Bottled in Myanmar, wherever the hell that is." He looked at Harry. "I know it's what the local ruling class calls Burma now, but that's not really its proper name, is it? You can't change things by changing names. That's silly. Burma was a good name, a proud name. That's what will be remembered."

"Hawk, what was it like back then?" Harry asked the old man. "The exotic East? Back when this was part of the British Empire?"

"I don't know, Harry." Hawk looked at him thoughtfully. "Like I said, we were young. I don't recall that we thought it was anything special. The British Empire, I mean. It was what it was. The 'exotic East' was something else. When I was a kid, I was fascinated by just the idea of it. And then here I was! And it was wonderful. Particularly in those last months of 1941. We were based at Toungoo then, about 170 miles north of here, at the airfield where we did our training."

Hawk stopped talking. He looked at Harry for a long moment. He was not seeing him, but something far away. His eyes got bright. He started to speak again and the words came in a rush. "Can you imagine what that was like?" he said. "We were young. We were paid princely salaries to fly these wonderful airplanes. And we did it all in this exotic tropical setting." He shook his head slowly, as if this was all hard to believe now. "We were always looking for reasons to come down here to Rangoon. This was where all the pretty girls were. And the prettiest ones were the British girls with a little bit of Burmese blood. They had silky black hair, great dark eyes, and skin like burnished bronze, but incredibly soft and smooth. And, my god, how they liked us! There were British RAF pilots here too. But we were special. We were the Americans. We were young and cocky. We had money. We were civilians, for god's sakes. To those exotic English-Burmese girls we were the exotic ones."

"It must have been wonderful." Harry agreed. They were both silent for a long while, looking into their beer glasses, lost in their own thoughts. After a while, Harry looked up and said, "You guys were civilians then, but you started in the military. As I remember, all the AVG pilots were recruited while they were on active duty with the Army or Navy. What were you doing when you first heard about the AVG?"

"I was a Navy pilot. I was flying dive bombers off the Saratoga when I heard somebody was looking for pilots to go to China and defend the Burma Road."

"That caught your attention?"

"It sure did. I spoke to the recruiter and learned that they would pay me a fabulous salary to fly fighter planes in the exotic East. Maybe even get in some combat time. It was a chance to fight and see how good I was. I couldn't imagine anything more interesting or more romantic."

"But you had to become a civilian to do that."

"That was the downside for some of us, but that was the deal. We had to become civilians. The AVG was the American Volunteer Group - of the Chinese Air Force. The Japanese had invaded China, but America wasn't at war with anybody. The idea was to help the Chinese. It was all worked out at the highest levels of our government. We were allowed to resign our commissions so that we could sign one-year contracts with the AVG. We were promised that when we completed our contracts we would get our commissions back. All of this came right out of the White House, right out of President Roosevelt's office. What we were doing didn't have a name then. Now they would call it a covert operation."

"And the job was to protect the Burma Road?"

"That was the job. The Japanese had seized all the Chinese ports. The only way China could get anything from the outside world was overland via the Burma Road. Supplies came by ship right here into Rangoon. They were unloaded down on the docks – right across the road from here – and trucked up into China. If the Japanese could cut that road, China would just wither away. The AVG's job was to keep the road open."

"And then Pearl Harbor happened."

"That's right. It came on 7 December 1941. Most of us weren't here but a few months. Pearl Harbor was attacked by the Japanese and America was dragged right into World War II. The AVG was still up at Toungoo. We had finished most of our training by then, and were ready to move up to what was to be our home base in China, at the city of Kunming. But then the war started and the 'Old Man', Colonel Claire Chennault, sent one of the AVG's three squadrons down here to help the Brits defend Rangoon. The other two squadrons were sent up to Kunming, to defend the city. The Japanese had started bombing Kunming. They were killing a lot of Chinese civilians."

"The AVG stopped the bombing at Kunming pretty quickly as I recall."

"They did that! The AVG had its first fight with the Japanese Air Force on 20 December 1941. The Japanese sent in ten bombers to hit Kunming. They had no fighter escort. They just weren't used to meeting any opposition. The AVG bounced them before they reached the city. When it was over, only one of the Japanese bombers got back to its base. And, I'm sure you know, the Japanese Air Force never did come back to Kunming while the AVG was in China."

"For a covert operation, that wasn't a bad start."

"Look at it that way, and the AVG was one of the most successful covert operations of all time. The AVG did some remarkable things. Now mind, Harry, I'm talking about the AVG – not myself. In the early days of World War II, the Japanese were advancing everywhere. We were losing in the Philippines. Malaya collapsed, Singapore fell, the Jap was in Thailand. Burma was next. Things were black, and the only spot of light was the AVG. The Flying Tigers were knocking down Japanese airplanes when everybody else thought the Jap was invincible. The AVG helped the British hold the line in Burma as long as they could, and then defended Kunming and other cities in China. They went after Japanese air bases in Thailand. The Flying Tigers destroyed almost 300 Jap airplanes in seven months."

"That's quite a record of achievement, but you're forgetting the Salween River."

"I guess that probably was the AVG's biggest accomplishment, stopping the Japanese Army at the Salween River gorge. The Japs had marched right through Burma and were up against the Chinese border. Once they crossed the Salween River they would be in China. And there was nothing to stop them from marching all the way to Kunming and grabbing control of China.

But the Flying Tigers caught them at the river. They chewed up the Jap Army there and turned it back. It gave the Chinese time to put a holding force on the river. The Japs never did get across the Salween."

"While all this was going on, did you guys – did the AVG know that what it was doing was something extraordinary?"

Hawk took a deep drink of beer before answering. "You know, Harry," he said, "I was at an air show a few years ago. The AVG were the honored guests. Everybody treated them like heroes. Somebody asked one of the Flying Tiger pilots that same question. The pilot replied, 'We were doing our job, that's all. We didn't feel we were doing anything but what we were expected to do. We didn't know we were heroes'."

Chapter 14

I
t was over dinner that night that Harry felt confident enough to ask. They had had drinks before dinner, and wine with their meal. They were both relaxed and even a little mellow.

"Hawk, I was a little puzzled by something," he said. He paused and then jumped in. "I've never come across your name on the AVG roster."

"That's because I'm not on the roster. I was taken off it."

"You were taken off it?"

"That's what I said, son."

Harry thought for a moment. How could he say this nicely? "I guess what I meant is, why were you taken off the roster?"

Hawk explained, "You got to understand about the rosters. The rosters you see in books have the names of those who served with the AVG for the length of their contracts. The contracts being for a year and expiring on 4 July 1942. There were some who joined the AVG who got removed from the roster. There were different reasons for why that happened. Some guys quit, some got tossed out. In my case, I had a falling out with the 'Old Man', Claire Lee Chennault, himself. That happened to others, even Pappy Boyington.

"As I recall, a couple guys got fired because they broke up some airplanes. Is that what happened to you?"

"Not exactly. I never busted up any airplanes. I was a pretty good pilot. And I wasn't reckless, not really. No sir, it was a simple matter in my case. The 'Old Man' and I didn't see eye to eye. On one thing in particular."

There was silence. A whole series of questions was working its way through Harry's mind. He decided to ask none of them, but just sit and wait, and keep his eyes on Hawk Herrington until the silence became too much.

"I've been 'Hawk' for a long time," Hawk Herrington finally said. "You know what they called me when I first came to the AVG? 'Red Rob'. That's what they called me. 'Red Rob'. I got that name about the same time Black Mac McGarry got his."

"I know about Black Mac," Harry said, "but I don't exactly recall how he got that name."

"Black Mac. He was drinking with some of his old Marine buddies before going off to join the AVG. They decided if Mac was going off to war, he needed a nom de guerre, a better name than just plain William, or Bill. Which was his real name – William McGarry. I mean plain old Bill is just not romantic enough for a fighter pilot. You know, the pilots back then, including the AVG guys, when they were boys they were brought up on the stories about World War I and the air aces. They knew all about the famous pilots like the 'Red Baron'. McGarry, well, he couldn't be a count or a baron, but he could be 'Black Mac.' That just sounded good. Well, in kind of the same way I got to be 'Red Rob'. That's what one of the guys decided."

"Rob. So that's the 'R' in R. 'Hawk' Harrington. What's the Rob for? Robert?"

Hawk was quiet for a while, looking deep into his beer as if an answer lay submerged there. It took a while. He was silent for so long that Harry thought maybe he forgot the question. Finally Hawk looked up. He looked Harry right in the eye and said, "No, sir, not Robert. Robin!"

"Robin?" Harry repeated the name with just the smallest smile.

"Yes, Robin. That's the name of a bird," Hawk said. He looked away, lifted his beer and took a deep swallow. Yeah, it's a bird's name, all right. A goddamn songbird."

"There's nothing wrong with that. Is there?"

"Criminey, son! There certainly is - if you're a fighter pilot. Well, we weren't called fighter pilots back then. We were pursuit pilots in those days. But it was the same thing. Just like now, all fighter jocks are big at grab ass. They joke about everything. Nothing is sacred. It wasn't long before my name became an issue. If you are named for a bird, it's okay. It's okay as long as the bird's name is 'Hawk', or 'Eagle', or some other kind of raptor. But not a songbird." Hawk looked Harry right in the eye. "Well, you can understand that, can't you, son?"

What Harry understood was that he could not let the small smile on his face get any bigger. "Well, hell, Hawk. What's a little name calling?"

Hawk did not respond to that, but went on. "I was a whistler, too, when I was young. That just made it worse. Some of the guys would get ideas, but they were careful what they called me. I already had my new moniker, 'Hawk', by the time I got up to Toungoo. That's what most people called me, and just about everybody forgot that the 'R' in my name stood for Robin. But not the 'Old Man'. Not Chennault. He remembered it was Robin. That was okay. I liked the 'Old Man'; he could call me whatever he wanted. And then he caught me whistling one day. After that he called me 'Tweetie'. Now that got my goat. I tried not to show it, but whenever the 'Old Man' saw me, he called me 'Tweetie'. A few others picked up on it, and I figured it was just a matter of time before everybody in the AVG was calling me 'Tweetie'. No way was I going to go down in the annals of aviation history as Tweetie Herrington. That's a terrible sounding name, isn't it?"

"It doesn't quite have the ring of Hawk Herrington," Harry agreed, and then he waited very patiently for Hawk to tell him the rest of the story. But Hawk just sat quietly, staring down at the table, saying nothing. For a long time neither man spoke. Finally, Harry had to ask, "Well, tell me, Hawk. What did happen in the end? Did you talk to the 'Old Man'? Did you tell him how you felt?"

"I couldn't talk to the 'Old Man' about it. The whole thing seemed so petty. Kind of silly. What could I do about it? Nothing! I figured, what the hell, let it ride. Then one of the pilots – who I will not name - made a real thing out of the Tweetie business. He made sure everybody knew about it. He briefed the local staff at Toungoo, the cooks and the dishwashers. Tried to get them to call me 'Mr. Tweetie'. Can you imagine? They kind of understood what was going on and were too polite to do that. It might have all ended right there, but that individual, that same pilot, he got to the Silver Grill. Before long it seemed that every girl in Rangoon – all the pretty ones, and even some not so pretty – they were all calling me Tweetie. And that was it. That was too much."

"So what did you do?"

"I quit. I resigned from the AVG."

"You quit! Did you talk with the 'Old Man', tell him how you felt? Did you tell him what was going on?"

"I did not! I did not want to upset him. He was a good guy. He had a lot of important things on his mind. Nope, I sent him a letter. A letter of resignation. For personal reasons, I said. I don't think he ever knew why I resigned, but he knew it was something personal. He never held it against me. Somebody told me much later that when he spoke of me, he spoke fondly." Hawk shook his head. "But he always remembered me as Tweetie Herrington."

Hawk looked at his watch and took a sip of his beer before looking up at Harry again. "Son, you haven't laughed once since we started this conversation. I think you understand. And I appreciate it."

"What happened after that, Hawk? You left the AVG. The war was going on. What did you do?"

"There wasn't much I could do. I stayed on in Burma. Hung around the airport at Mingaladon. The British Royal Air Force was having all kinds of problems, and I started to help out there. I was a reasonably good mechanic. They trusted my flying and I was able to take some of their aircraft on maintenance test flights.

They were short of everything, especially airplanes and pilots. I even flew a couple of combat missions for them. Some of my AVG friends were at Mingaladon too, and I hung out with them whenever I could. One way or another I stayed involved with the AVG and all of the stuff going on. Until the end came, and everybody evacuated Rangoon."

"What did you do then?"

"I got a flight to India with some of my RAF friends. I hung around Calcutta for a little while, and finally tied up with the U.S. Army Air Corps. Volunteered for a flying job and got one. They had me flying transports at first, out of India. I flew over the 'Hump', for a while, to China. The 'Hump'- that was the Himalayas, and what I was doing was flying supplies into Kunming for the Flying Tigers. So there you are. I had come full circle. I got to see some of the AVG guys regularly in Kunming, and once in a while when they got down to India. I kept in touch with what was going on with the AVG. Later on I got a job with a Fighter Squadron in China. By that time the Flying Tigers were gone. They were disbanded and absorbed into the U.S. Army Air Corps on 4 July 1942. But Chennault was still there. He was the big honcho of the 14th Air Force in China. He made Major General before it was over. Theoretically, he was my boss while I flew in China, but I rarely saw him. I did fly with a couple of the Flying Tigers who stayed on."

"So while you weren't always with the Flying Tigers, you got to see a good bit of their history."

"I saw it all, Harry. One way or another. What I didn't witness personally, I got first-hand from one of my AVG friends. I stayed in touch with a number of them, even long after the war was over. I flew with some of them in a couple of funny places in the world."

"What did you do when the war was over?"

"Like a lot of the other guys, I stayed in aviation. At one time or another I did it all, I guess. I was an instructor pilot, flew with a couple of small airlines. I had my own charter company for a while, a couple of times, in fact. I still have a small airplane company now. I even did aerial photography for a big real estate company once. But my best flying days came when adventure called. I did more of those covert operation things. I guess I was always drawn to the secret and the mysterious. I flew in the Congo. I flew in Vietnam. While the French were there I flew missions for them. I dropped paratroopers and supplies into Dien Bien Phu. Later I went the Air America route and flew in Vietnam, Laos, and Cambodia. But I never got back here to Burma, until now."

"You've had quite a life of adventure, Hawk. Are you ready for a bit more of that now?"

"Well, I think I am, Harry. You tell me what you need."

"I need a Flying Tiger, Hawk. Somebody who can talk about the old days, the glory days of the AVG, and do it convincingly. I need somebody who knows airplanes, really knows them, and can talk about them with passion. I need somebody who can go face to face with a world-class thug or two and not be intimidated. Somebody who can lie, cheat, and maybe steal from the same world-class thugs."

The smile on Hawk's face grew as he listened. "That's a pretty tall order, son."

"I don't know how much friend Riley told you about what I've been doing?"

"He said that you thought you found an old Flying Tiger airplane. He mentioned some Chinese warlord. I think he called the whole thing 'highly dangerous'."

"Riley is not far wrong about some things. I am about 100 percent convinced that I've seen an old AVG P-40, one of the original 'B' models. Unfortunately, the guy who holds the ownership title to the airplane is a kind of a warlord. He claims to have more airplanes, AVG P-40s and other types as well. As for it being dangerous, I think that depends on what we do. Nobody will mess with us so long as we play it straight - but god help anyone who tries to make some moves on those airplanes. Unfortunately, that's exactly where I think my game plan is taking us."

"Well, to be perfectly frank, Harry, this all sounds quite interesting. If you're willing to take me on, I think I would enjoy the job."

"I think you'll do fine, Hawk, but I'm not sure how much time you're going to have to enjoy it. When we get busy, I expect we're going to get very busy. You had better rehearse all your old war stories, because you're going to have to use them to mesmerize some people and open some doors. If we can do that, you'll have to help me identify what kind of airplanes we're dealing with, whether they're real or not. And if those P-40s are real, then we have to deal with the hard part: taking possession of some of those airplanes."

"Sounds like you have it pretty well worked out, Harry. I'm glad you feel that I might be able to help you. Riley said you would send me back if we didn't get on. Riley also said you had a whole infrastructure out here: people, communications, airplanes. Whatever you need, he said, you name it, Harry has it."

"What I have, Hawk, is some good friends. They're smart and they know how to do things. You'll get to meet them all before long."

"What's our present schedule?"

"Our present schedule is for you and me to enjoy the Strand Hotel and Rangoon for another day or two, or a week, or for however long it takes for my 'infrastructure' to make some contacts that will let us take the next step. Or, to put it another way, a young lady named Mouse is trying to telephone a man named Piggy to set up a meeting with a Flying Tiger named Hawk."

"Criminey, Harry! It sounds like you're running some kind of 'Zoo Parade' here."

Chapter 15

And it was of a caged zoo animal that Harry thought the next morning as he watched R. Hawk Herrington pace the small VIP section of the departure lounge at Rangoon's Mingaladon Airport. For Hawk, it was a return to glory, a chance to see the airfield where he had spent the most intense moments of his young life as the storm of World War II broke over Burma during the waning days of 1941.

"Goddamn it, Harry, I wish I could see something out of those windows. They parked that bus right out front, and I can't even see that little piece of the runway that I could see before. You know, back then, the Brits...."

"Yeah, Hawk." The Brits.... Harry tried to listen, but he could not keep tuned in. His plastic chair had one short leg and he had to sit still. That took concentration, which was difficult to maintain when his mind was churning out the different scenarios that might play out over the coming hours. When he forgot the short leg and shifted his weight, the chair lurched back as if to topple over, then stopped with a jolt when the short leg hit the floor. That snapped him instantly back to the present. Each time it happened, Hawk turned to give him a long look, and each time he said, "Harry, you're going to hurt yourself." It sounded very parental. And may have been why Harry refused to change chairs.

Harry had been on the telephone with Mouse for an hour the night before and another hour this morning. She had made contact with Mr. Piggy through Tommy, and word had come back: Mr. Piggy wanted to see them immediately. In Kunming, China. He wanted to see not just the Flying Tiger, R. Hawk Herrington, but all of them, Harry, Mouse, and Mr. Sunny Bright too. Mr. Piggy insisted that Sunny Bright's presence was necessary. And, if he came, well, then he could bring the others up to Kunming in his airplane.

Mouse had worked it all out. She got Sato to approve the use of his Gulfstream. It would come to Rangoon to pick up Harry and Herrington and fly them to Kunming. Mouse had also learned that – although he was not supposed to be there – Aloysious, in fact, was still in Bangkok. If she could locate him, she promised, he would be on the airplane as well.

"… And so their Buffaloes reached the intersection of the two runways just as the Tomahawks were getting airborne. It was a near thing."

Harry's mind sorted Buffaloes from Tomahawks and put them in context. Hawk was telling a story about AVG and the RAF aircraft taking off on Mingaladon's two intersecting runways when Japanese bombers were spotted on their way to bomb the city.

But Harry's mind drifted from Mingaladon to Kunming, which was only an hour away as the Gulfstream flew. Piggy said they would need two days in China at least. Mouse knew nothing more about any arrangements that Mr. Piggy had made.

"…And these things falling around me, they were shell casings from the guns the airplanes were firing as they zoomed over me. Those things were hot! Falling from a couple of hundred feet over my head, they could have done some damage. There was this one Japanese pilot…."

Harry's chair tipped back, and he again experienced a moment of free fall, very brief as the chair was grabbed from behind by a uniformed Burmese official. He had come to escort them to their flight. "Sir," he said to Harry, "you will hurt yourself," and an echo came from Hawk Herrington, "I told you so, Harry."

The uniformed official led them out onto the apron just as Sato's Gulfstream rolled down the tarmac toward them. It was still wearing its PRIC disguise. When it reached them, the aircraft turned slowly until it showed them its full left side. The noise it made diminished as the engine on that side wound down. The door opened and the airstair dropped. The steward appeared and waited at the top to help them aboard.

"Criminey, Harry," Hawk said, as he admired the aircraft. "You do have good friends. A Gulfstream! This is first class." Then he noticed the tail fin, where the red letters of PRIC were superimposed over a green banknote. "Quite a logo. Dollar Bill Airlines?"

Aloysious was no longer among the missing. He stood just inside the door, carefully keeping out of sight of anyone who might be watching from the apron or the terminal. As Herrington stepped aboard, Aloysious took him gently by the arm and led him into the cabin. There he shook the old man's hand. "So, you're Hawk, the Flying Tiger," he said. "I've heard a lot about you guys – mostly from Harry over there. Come on, Hawk, come sit over here. The steward will bring you a drink and we can talk. Just call me Sunny; it will be easier for you to remember."

Harry watched until the two sat down and strapped themselves in, then he walked to the back of the cabin where Mouse was seated. After chatting with her and then going forward to check in with the pilots, he returned to take a seat across from Aloysious. He closed his eyes for a moment to collect his thoughts. Aloysious had been briefed earlier about Herrington, and last night he briefed Herrington about Aloysious. He had done what he could. Across from him now, the two were already chatting like old friends. That was gratifying. With Aloysious one could never be sure. When someone new came on the scene, he could be totally charming – or lapse into an instant and chilly dislike – for no discernable reason. As Harry tuned in to their conversation, Herrington was saying to Aloysious, "Harry tells me you have a little homestead up in the hills, way up north of here. It sounds like a quiet place, almost a retirement home. You're not retired, are you, Sunny?"

"Well, you could almost say that, Hawk. In a way I'm retired, I guess. Temporarily, anyway." Aloysious looked into his glass and explained. "A while back I felt a need to leave the active life. To go off where I wouldn't have the distraction of dealing with people." He stirred an ice cube with his finger. "You know the kind of thing I mean. And it does free a man to try some new things."

"It's good to try new things, Sunny. Retirement is not for everyone. It's like marriage. Marriage cramps your style, but retirement can be worse. From what I've seen of it, retirement frequently ends with the expiration of the retiree."

Aloysious pondered this. "Well, I'm planning to avoid that part of it, Hawk. I'm just living up in the hills, relaxing, waiting until certain circumstances become a little more favorable."

"You sound like a man who has suffered a business setback."

"Yeah, you could say that. I did have a bit of a setback." He looked over at Harry and winked. "Harry too. But he came through it a little better than me." He turned back to Herrington. "You know, Hawk, Harry and I had a real interesting project going on."

Harry was starting to feel a little uncomfortable. Aloysious's projects – or 'schemes' as he usually called them – were not things that Aloysious readily shared with anyone, particularly if they were not enormously successful. And their last 'project' – the one he was referring to now, had been spectacularly unsuccessful. But Herrington's eyes were full of interest and invited confidence. "What kind of business were you boys doing?" he asked.

"Oh, we did antiques. A bit of art. A little bit of archaeology, you might say."

"Big–scale stuff? Was it high end?"

"Yes, it was that." Aloysious thought for a moment, then turned to Harry. "Harry, what was the colorful thing the newspapers said?" Without waiting for an answer he went on. "It was something like 'their footprints were found in the trampled ground around our national cultural treasures'. I don't recall the words exactly, Hawk, but it was something like that. That gives a sense of what we were dealing with." Harry squirmed in his plush leather seat, but no one noticed.

"You were selling? Distributing?" Hawk asked.

"We were selling. Or trying to. Distributing? Re–distributing might be a better way to put it. You could say that we had identified an imbalance in the accumulation of certain cultural treasures and were seeking ways to redistribute that accumulation." Aloysious thought that over and then added, "So that others might enjoy."

"Well, that's nice. I would think there would be big money in that."

"Yes, usually there is. But we never quite reached that stage in our project."

Hawk shrugged and turned to Aloysious a face full of experience. "So now you've got a nice little place up in the hills." Then he raised an eyebrow at Aloysious. "And keeping out of the sight of some people."

"Yeah," Aloysious admitted. "There's some people I wouldn't want to see right now." Looking up toward the ceiling he added, "Some organizations. Couple of governments...."

Hawk chuckled. "It must have been a super project, Sunny."

"It was, Hawk. You would have loved it. We had a great time, didn't we, Harry? It cost me quite a bit. It's still costing me. I just spent a few days in Bangkok. That's the first time I dared set foot in that city in almost two years. I did it because now I have a passport that says I'm 'Sunny Bright'. It doesn't mean I didn't keep looking over my shoulder." Aloysious looked over toward Harry. "Now, Harry there, he did a little better. They didn't want to see him in Bangkok for a while, but he can still travel around the region. Isn't that right, Harry? Harry's just smarter than most of us. He can talk his way out of almost anything when he needs to. Looking at him you might not think so, but he's a real glib, silver–tongued devil when he needs to be."

"Well, that's right handy," Hawk acknowledged with a nod at Harry. "But up there in the hills, Sunny, what have you been doing?"

"I've been making beer," he said a little defensively, with a quick glance at Harry. "It's a noble calling."

Hawk turned to look directly at Aloysious. "Now that is a noble calling. Are you selling all that beer?"

"All I can make. Right now, anyway. Don't know what the future holds. It's a competitive world, even up there in the hills."

Hawk leaned closer to Aloysious, his tone confidential now. "I've recently taken an interest in producers of alcohol. Beer, wine, or spirits. Surplus production can be turned into fuel, did you know that? They have new engines that will burn almost anything. Goat pee if you have it. I'll tell you, Sunny, you want to look into that. Start a subsidiary selling your excess hootch to your local petrol station." Hawk glanced over toward the window. "You know Sunny, we ought to talk more about that, but I wonder...I've never been in one of these Gulfstreams before. Do you think the pilots might let me take a look at the cockpit?"

Harry spoke up. "The pilots are waiting for you, Hawk. I told them you'd be coming up to see them." As Hawk unbuckled himself, Harry added, "Oh, Hawk...the crew, they're all Japanese."

Hawk paused and let a little frown slip across his face. "Flying from Mingaladon to Kunming with a Japanese crew. I could never have imagined that, son." Standing in the aisle, he turned to look down at Harry. "Peace makes for strange bedfellows," he said, and strode toward the flight deck. When he was safely through the door, Aloysious turned to Harry, "You don't think he's still pissed off at the Japanese about World War II?"

"Oh, I don't think so. He's a pretty level-headed fellow."

"He looks like a pretty good guy. He gave me a wonderful idea for improving Pachyderm beer sales." Aloysious looked pre-occupied and turned to stare out the window. After a while he looked back at Harry and said, "You know, I think I like that guy, Hawk. He seems real smart. Real simpatico." From Aloysious this was high praise indeed. It made Harry thoughtful.

Minutes later the Japanese co-pilot walked down the aisle and leaned down to speak to Harry. "The captain invites you both up to the flight deck," he said. "We will soon begin our descent into Kunming. It is a beautiful day. You will be able to see much of the area."

Up on the flight deck they found Hawk ensconced in the right–hand copilot seat, leaning forward, watching the captain point out the features on one of the half dozen brightly colored glass computer–like screens that made up the flight panel. The two looked up and nodded as Harry and Aloysious crowded into the small space behind them. When the captain finished, Hawk leaned back in his seat and half turned so that he could easily talk with them.

"Flew up this way to Kunming a half dozen times in the old days, but we never got this high. Just look!" he said, gesturing at the scene beyond the windscreen. "From up here you can see the Sittang River, and there's the Salween right over there. Back in my day, everybody was always getting lost. From up here it's like looking at a map. And, if it weren't such a nice day, we would still have that," he said pointing at the electronic map displayed on the glass screen in front of him, their position precisely indicated by an electronic airplane in the center.

The captain had already started their descent and they were gradually losing altitude. After a while the ground started looking more like rivers and hills and rice paddies than squiggles on a map. It was rugged country below them, with not much sign of civilization, except here and there in the deep river valleys where little clumps of villages could be made out.

"We have to stay fairly high," Hawk said. "Kunming is up at almost 6,000 feet. The way we're coming in, we should get a good look at the lake and the old airfield." He turned a bit more in his seat to address his comments directly to Aloysious. "Sunny, you'll like the city. Kunming was quite the place in my day. Quite important. It was the terminus of the Burma Road that supplied China in the early days of the war. Later, when the Japanese Army shut down the Burma Road, all the supplies for the Chinese and for the U.S. forces here in China were brought in by airplane from India. Those were the famous Hump Flights over the Himalayas. It was probably the most dangerous flying in the world. Did a little of that myself."

Ahead was a ridge of high hills. "There," Hawk said, pointing in their direction. "See that notch in the hills over there. The airport was on the other side of it, across the lake. We would take off over the lake and aim right at those hills. Sometimes we were too heavy and didn't have the altitude to go right over them, so we'd slide through that notch. It's like God cut a notch in those hills so we could fly right through."

The city slid into view and grew in the windscreen, big, sprawling, and nondescript. From their altitude it could have been almost any city anywhere. They watched silently until Hawk half rose in his seat and craned his neck to look off to their left.

"There's the lake," he said. As if following his gaze, the aircraft banked in that direction. "The airport is right there," Hawk pointed. "It's the same one we used. It looks so much bigger, though. I guess it's been updated. We'd come in this way sometimes, but not so high."

The aircraft leveled out, its new course taking it alongside the lake to its far side. There they would turn again and start on their final approach. As they passed the lake on their left, Hawk raised himself in his seat to watch it go by. "Good lord," he said, "I really knew this place once, but there's nothing down there now that I recognize. The lake doesn't even look the same. What the hell has happened? The contours of the shoreline have changed. It's all a different shape now."

Behind him, Harry said quietly, "It's 60 years, Hawk," but Hawk never heard. He sat back quietly and looked, not out the window, but at the computer screens in front of him as if seeking an answer in the display of brightly colored lights.

The captain turned to them and said quietly, "Gentlemen...." It was time to return to their seats in the cabin for their landing in Kunming.

Chapter 16

"Hey, Harry, there's a kid over there, waving at you. He looks frantic."

Chinese immigration officials had met them at the airplane and escorted them into the terminal building. They waited now for Mouse, who had accompanied one of the officials to a counter where their passports were being examined. Earlier she had told Harry that Sato had personally made the arrangements that would ease their entry into China. This was very reassuring, and Harry had been quite relaxed until Hawk started poking at him and pointing to the exit. The "kid" Hawk had spotted was Tommy, who waved again when Harry looked his way. Harry waved back and pointed toward Mouse. Tommy nodded.

Formalities out of the way, Tommy led them out to the curb where two black Mercedes waited in the diplomatic parking area. He directed Hawk and Sunny to the first car and Harry and Mouse to the one behind. He stuck his head into their car to advise that the ride would take about 20 minutes, then trotted up to join Sunny and Hawk in the lead car.

Once they exited the airport it was evident that they were driving away from the city rather than toward it. They stayed on a major road, but their surroundings changed quickly from city outskirts to a distinctly rural landscape. Before long they were out among rice paddies, Kunming well behind them.

Twenty minutes passed and another twenty. Harry had started to wonder, when the two cars turned off the road and pulled into a gravel courtyard hidden from view by a cluster of small buildings. Lunch, Harry thought, but that quickly proved wrong. Two large sports utility vehicles with mud-splattered camouflage paint pulled alongside them. Tommy hopped out and told everyone to change cars. The SUVs were for the last stage of their journey, another hour perhaps. Certainly less than two.

They headed south, moving fast. The countryside became rougher, and main roads were soon exchanged for secondary ones. Mouse and Harry sat back, quietly watching the passing scene. They spoke very little, not so much for lack of things to say, but because they had separately concluded that Aloysious's prior warnings about 'security' were probably not misplaced here. Their driver gave no sign that he understood any language but Chinese, but who could say? And a device to record their words could have been hidden anywhere in the vehicle.

Harry could tell that Mouse had something on her mind, and she finally broke the silence. "How do you like your Flying Tiger?" she asked.

"A good man," he said quietly. "He knows his stuff." He looked to the driver, who was obviously intent on the road ahead. "I think he has just the kind of personality we need."

"And the rest goes along well?"

This was coded, Harry knew. It meant: 'How did Mr. Sunny Bright take to Mr. Hawk?'

"Splendidly," he replied. "Everything goes well." After a moment, he added, "So well that it scares me."

Mouse looked at him thoughtfully, then reached over and patted his arm. "It was your choice," she said. "A good one."

He wanted to say there was no choice involved, but he did not. Instead, he looked at the driver, whose eyes were still fixed on the road ahead, then reached over and pinched Mouse's thigh. He got nothing but a raised eyebrow in reply. They fell back into silence.

The two vehicles slowed when they turned onto a lane deeply rutted by ancient oxcarts and more recently by SUVs. They went only a short distance before a heavy gate barred their way.

Tommy hopped out and walked to a guardhouse set off to one side. They seemed to be on the edge of a forest. There were a lot of trees ahead, big, mature ones, and out among them Harry could see soldiers. They were hunkered down in groups of two or three, as if they were manning some kind of positions, he thought, and watching. He could almost feel the intensity of their gaze through the darkened windows of the SUV. Their interest seemed more than idle curiosity.

Tommy trotted up to the lead car, spoke through the open window, then trotted back to Harry's car and got in next to the driver. The gate had been opened and the lead car was moving off. He turned in his seat to face Harry and Mouse.

"Just a couple of minutes now. Mr. Piggy will give us lunch. Then we will go on a little tour. I hope you will enjoy this place."

They moved along a smooth dirt road that took them up one side of a small wooded hill and down the other. Before them was a valley, like an oval dish that had been carefully scooped out of the surrounding hills. Its floor was perfectly flat and carpeted with short grass and scattered wildflowers. Down its center ran a long gravel strip. Harry immediately saw it for what it was: a runway! Primitive looking, but perfect for any World War II era aircraft. They had arrived.

Beyond the end of the airstrip, a cluster of wooden buildings stood in a grove of old trees. As they drove toward them, Harry asked the question that had been bothering him. "Tommy, what were all those troops doing up near the gate?"

"Troops, Mr. Harry?"

"The soldiers. In among the trees. A couple of squads, at least."

"Ah, the soldiers in the trees. Yes, I saw them too." Tommy thought for a moment. "They are what I think in America you call 're-enactors'."

"Re-enactors," Harry repeated. That was a new one. Before he could say anything else, Tommy added, "Maybe you noticed their uniforms. They were not PLA, not Chinese Liberation Army uniforms, but old ones. The uniforms of the Chiang Kai Chek soldiers."

There may have been something unusual about the uniforms, Harry thought, but he could not have said what it was. He was about to ask Tommy more when the car reached the largest of the wooden buildings and stopped.

Hawk and Aloysious had already left their car and, deep in conversation, had wandered off in the direction of the airstrip. "Gentlemen! This way, please," Tommy called out, just loud enough to get their attention. When they were all together, he led them toward the building, a long wooden structure that had a newly built look about it. Its roof of red tiles and graceful eaves looked very Chinese. A long covered porch ran along the front. On it were white wicker chairs and tables. All very inviting, but not very Chinese at all. As they reached the steps to the porch, Mr. Piggy appeared in the doorway above. He bowed low, greeting them with a short burst of Chinese.

"Welcome, honored guests," Tommy translated, "to Flying Tiger Land!"

Hawk glanced at Harry, a question written across his face. Harry shrugged.

A few quick words from Mr. Piggy, and Tommy invited everyone inside. They filed past Mr. Piggy with bows and handshakes. Harry looked around. The entire ground floor was a single room. A big round table set for lunch was at one end and a well-stocked bar at the other. In between was a gracefully curved wooden staircase that led to the floor above. The rest was empty space that had the look of a hotel lobby that was yet to be furnished.

Tommy got their attention and assigned seats at the table. Mr. Piggy on the far side, Hawk and Aloysious on his flanks, then Harry and Mouse, with Tommy in between. This put Tommy directly across from Mr. Piggy, in perfect position to handle the translation duties.

Within moments a half-dozen ladies in black trousers and white blouses appeared, balancing large plates of steaming hot Chinese food. There was little talk; everyone was hungry and preoccupied with the delicious-looking dishes before them, except Mr. Piggy, who showed less interest in his food than the in

the pleasure of his guests. A most gracious host, he was solicitous of everyone at the table, offering special foods and enticing
them with choice morsels he placed in their bowls. What little
talk there was centered on the food. There was an occasional
witticism from Sunny Bright. When everyone had eaten their fill
and was sitting back relaxed, Mr. Piggy rose to speak.

"I am honored to have you here as my guests," he said, and
bowed toward each in turn. "Mr. Hawk Herrington, the Flying
Tiger who came all the way from America; Mr. Sunny Bright,
the financial genius; Mr. Harry, the famous aviation expert; and
Miss Mouse, always charming and efficient. You are special
people. I hope I may call you friends. You have come here to
share my dream. My vision. With your help I will create a Flying
Tiger Land where those heroes of America and China will be
remembered and honored. Where their airplanes will fly again
and their story will live on. People from America and around
the world will be invited to come to Flying Tiger Land. To relive
those exciting times. My honored guests, my friends, your visit
here is the beginning of my dream becoming a reality."

When Tommy finished translating this statement, Mr. Piggy
raised his glass. They all stood. "To the Flying Tigers," he said.
"May they live always in the memories of the Chinese people."

They drank to that. Then Hawk responded. "Mr. Piggy," he
said, "that was a fine speech. A wonderful toast. The AVG Flying Tigers were a part of China's struggle against Japanese op-
pression. May that spirit of cooperation be kept alive in the realization of your dream. I drink to that, sir, and ask you all to join
me."

They drank again, and Harry feared the toasts yet to come,
but Mr. Piggy was eager to get underway. He nodded at Tommy,
who said, "Mr. Piggy will now take us on our tour."

As they moved away from the table, Hawk edged close to
Harry and said quietly, "He's putting us on, right? Relive those
exciting times? I tell you, Harry, it was fun once, but I wouldn't
go through those times again for anything."

Mr. Piggy led them out to the porch. He stepped up to the rail
and looked out over the valley, then turned to face them. His

voice, quiet at first, almost solemn, grew louder and more force-
ful as he spoke. Tommy's voice came from behind them with the
words in English.

"Before us, this pleasant valley. Quiet, peaceful. Listen…the
only sound you hear…the singing of birds. This valley is the center of my vision, my plan for Flying Tiger Land. In time, this
peaceful valley will come alive again. It will quake with the roar
of the Allison engine! It will echo the sound of the AVG P-40
Tomahawks…as they pursue their Japanese opponents across
the blue sky…over this beautiful place."

The words seemed heartfelt. Harry was sure they were. The
valley was a pretty place, and to some, the roar of a P-40 engine
at full throttle was a beautiful thing. As they turned to follow
Piggy down the porch steps, Mouse looked at Harry and wrinkled
her nose in disapproval. Harry shrugged and said quietly, "You
own the valley, you pick the sound track." Mouse showed him
her tongue.

They followed Piggy across the soft grass to the nearby cluster of buildings. The first was a low single-story structure of mud-
colored bricks and a few small windows. It might have been a
local farmhouse but for a small roofed entry that gave it a vaguely
Western look. "This house," Piggy explained, "is a copy of a villa
once used by General Claire Lee Chennault. The original is in
Kunming and is too precious to move. So we made a copy here.
Perhaps you remember this house, Mr. Hawk?"

Hawk smiled noncommittally and they moved on. He looked
back at the house, turned to Harry, and shrugged. Mr. Piggy
was well ahead, approaching the next building, a long three-
storied barracks-like structure. "This is a copy of the hostel where
some of the pilots lived. It was near the airport at Kunming. We
built it from photographs. In the future, guests of Flying Tiger
Land may stay here."

Next was a single-story "mess hall" and commissary. Tommy
said this would be a snack bar and gift shop when it was finished. There was another "barracks" like the first. When they
finished walking around the buildings, Mr. Piggy gestured at
the small hill behind them and spoke a few words. Tommy said,

"The museum hangars are behind the hill. We will go there in a few minutes to see the aircraft."

Then Mr. Piggy pointed across the airstrip to a distant hill. "There on top of that small mountain," Tommy translated, "will be the casino and a gentleman's club with an excellent view of the airstrip and all the airplanes here." Mr. Piggy pointed to the big building where they had lunch, and then turned and gestured toward a hill on the far side of the valley. Tommy translated his comments: "Our headquarters building – where we had lunch – will be the 'Officers Mess', the living quarters of special guests like yourselves. But one day a five-star hotel will be built across the hills on a beautiful lake. I hope you will all come to see it."

With that Mr. Piggy bowed to them and set off by himself back across the grass. Tommy led the rest of them to the small hill behind the buildings, and down a wide tree-lined lane that led to the hangars on the other side.

As they strolled along, Tommy told them about the valley's past. It had been an auxiliary airfield during World War II and later was used by the Chinese Air Force. The hangars were big wooden structures painted in the dull green and brown patterns of World War II that helped them blend into the small hills around them. The lane was the taxiway used to bring aircraft to the airstrip. "They could not hide the airstrip," Tommy said, "but the workshops and the airplanes were back here where they were difficult to see from above. During the war against the Japanese, decoy airplanes made of canvas and wood were parked around the airstrip. They were destroyed many times, but if a real airplane was struck by a Japanese bomb, it was an accident."

The two big doors on the first hangar were cracked open just a bit. They went through the small opening in single file. It was cooler inside and almost dark. As their eyes adjusted, airplanes took shape in front of them, indistinct forms, menacing in the gloom. Three long-nosed fighter planes could be made out, crouching on landing gear like panthers poised to spring. Three Chinese mechanics in blue coveralls rushed in from outside, put their shoulders to the big hangar doors and slowly rolled them back. Light streamed past the edge of the opening doors and washed over the airplanes, revealing tan and green camouflage, and great teeth in open shark mouths vivid on the long noses. Next to Harry, Hawk caught his breath, a small sound like a gasp. He just stood and looked. Aloysious, Mouse, and Tommy were somewhere behind. There was no other sound.

Hawk stepped up to the closest airplane, put his hand on the wing and rubbed it back and forth, then looked up at the cockpit. After a minute had passed, Harry said, "What do you think, Hawk?"

Hawk turned, his face blank, looking at Harry, but not really seeing him. "Oh, Harry...," he finally said. "This is something else, isn't it? I've seen P-40s over the years. But, coming up on these airplanes - with the taste of a Chinese lunch still in my mouth – it's, well...it's different, isn't it? Like stepping into the rabbit hole – and falling back 60 years. Christ!" He shook his head. He walked slowly along the side of the airplane, keeping his eyes on it. Then he stepped back until he was far enough away to take it all in. He looked long and hard, as if imprinting the airplane in his mind. He turned to its stable mate alongside and studied it in the same way. When he satisfied himself, he walked to the third P-40, the one that stood by itself behind the others.

The lights inside the hangar were turned on. With the overhead lights and daylight streaming through the open door, the hangar was now as bright as the day outside. Hawk climbed up on the wing of the third P-40 and peered through the glass canopy into the cockpit. Tommy made a small gesture and one of the mechanics got up on the wing and slid the canopy back. He helped Hawk climb in. Once he was seated, the elevators moved up and down as he pulled the stick back, then shoved it forward. Ailerons flapped up and down on the ends of the wings, and the rudder waved back and forth. With one hand on the stick, Hawk used the other to explore the movement of the throttle and the positions of switches. With one finger he tapped the round glass faces of the gauges on the instrument panel as if to assure that their readings were true. His checkout complete, Hawk sat and looked through the windshield at the sky beyond the hangar door. The others stood by quietly.

After a while, Hawk climbed out of the cockpit. The mechanic stood back, sensing that the old man did not want his help. Upright on the wing, Hawk looked down at them. "Fine airplane," he said. "She's ready to go."

He eased himself off the back of the wing, slowly and carefully. No springy jump like the old days. He brushed off his trousers as he walked to where they stood, a smile on his face.

"Squinting through that gunsight ring sure brought back memories." He turned to Tommy. "They're fine airplanes, Tommy, all three of them. They sure look right. I see they all have the double digit numbers of the AVG airplanes painted on their side. I don't remember their numbers now, or who was who, but they sure look like three old friends. You say you found all the P-40s in China?"

"My uncle will tell you, Mr. Hawk. Some were found in China, some in Burma. In the next building are two other P-40s. And two in the workshop."

Hawk went over the count in his head. "That's seven," he said. "My god."

"And one at the airstrip where Harry saw it fly."

"Eight," Hawk said simply. He shook his head in wonderment. "That's just incredible, son."

"Sir, if you would like to see the other aircraft...." Tommy gestured to a door at the side of the hangar. "We can walk through there."

The second hangar was more crowded. Coming through the side door, they saw the two P-40s at the rear of the building. But up front, near the main door, pride of place was given to an airplane that looked smaller and rounder than the P-40. It did not have the long shark nose. It was not as sleek, not as streamlined, but just as menacing.

Aloysious said it first. "A Zero. Is that a Zero?"

Hawk said nothing. Harry looked at Aloysious and, not wanting to break the spell, raised his hand to ask for quiet. Hawk walked up close to the airplane, looked up at the big round engine in front, then strolled around the wing, running his fingers along the leading edge until he got up near the rounded tip where the bright red disk was painted, the red rising sun of the Japanese Empire. "The meatball," he said, and touched it.

He continued around the wing, then stopped, and backed away from the airplane a good distance. "This is the angle I like to see it at. From maybe two hundred meters out. Through a gunsight." Still looking at the airplane, he responded to Aloysious's question.

"Yes, Sunny, it's what we called a Zero, but it wasn't really a Zero. The Zero was the Japanese Navy airplane. Mitsubishi built it and it looked a lot like this one. This one was a Japanese Army airplane. Early in the war, nobody on our side knew the difference. We called any single-seat airplane like this a Zero. Properly, this one's called a Hayabusa. I guess in English that means 'Falcon'."

"Mr. Hawk is right," Tommy said. "It's a Hayabusa, a Nakajima Ki-43. It was a Japanese Army airplane that fought the AVG in China. A very good airplane. The Flying Tigers destroyed many of them."

"It was a good airplane, all right. It was quick. It was nimble. Have you been flying this airplane, Tommy?"

"Just one time, Mr. Hawk."

"Well that's pretty good, Tommy. That's one more time than I've flown it. There are not many still around who had the chance to fly it."

As he was looking at Tommy, Hawk glanced beyond him and said, "What the hell is that?" He walked to the other side of the hangar, where a little silver airplane stood by itself.

"It's a Nate, Mr. Hawk, a Nakajima Ki-27.

"These were the beginning," Hawk said. "The first ones the AVG met in Burma. They buzzed around Rangoon like gnats. Talk about nimble, they were all over the sky.

"We have three more in sheds outside. Not such good condition."

Under his breath, Hawk said, "My god!"

"Come, let's go outside."

Behind the hangars were rows of smaller buildings, all different sizes. Most were sheds, open at the sides and the front. Two of the small Nakajima fighters were clearly visible in the first shed, and sections of wings and fuselage they saw in the second were probably parts of the third Ki-27. The other buildings had parts of aircraft, entire wings in some cases, or sections of wings and fuselages. There were bigger buildings behind them, and Tommy led them to one of these.

"You must see this one, Mr. Hawk. It is one of our prizes," he said. Tommy pulled back the door and there was an airplane, bigger than any they had seen so far. Most of it was in shadows. It was much bigger than the P-40s or the Hayabusa. It had an engine on each wing and a glass nose sectioned like a greenhouse. Atop the fuselage was another greenhouse, the long main canopy with a machine gun pointed out its back end. Far behind the gun was the rudder, a big one. The airplane lacked the fine lines and the grace of the P-40. It looked purposeful, a farm tractor rather than a sports car.

"It was called the 'Sally'," Tommy said. "Mitsubishi Ki -21. It was the Japanese Army bomber. It had a crew of seven, five machine guns, and carried twenty-two hundred pounds of bombs."

"I remember it," Hawk said. "I think it was the one we called the 'Flying Cigarette Lighter'. Or something like that. It was as easy to light up, easy to set on fire."

Tommy went on. "There are Japanese aircraft in the other buildings. Two bombers that were called the 'Betty'. And we have a fighter with two engines, the Ki-45. The Toryu." Harry knew of the Toryu, the 'Dragon Killer' from stories he had heard from a couple of pilots who had encountered it. They attacked what they thought was a bomber, an easy target, and then were surprised by its speed and agility – and the stinger in its tail.

"And we have...," Tommy said, but Harry no longer heard. There was too much to look at, too much to absorb. For a long while he just walked around and looked and did not even try to identify what he saw.

Chapter 17

They were assigned individual rooms on the second floor of the main building, the 'Officers Mess' where they had lunched. The rooms were large, bright, and comfortable, and no attempt had been made to create a 1940s atmosphere. Which was just as well, Harry thought. He silently agreed with Hawk: The 1940s were interesting to read about, but not a time to re-live. He was glad of his small comforts. After all, it had been a long day, interesting but mentally taxing. He had walked among aircraft that he had thought extinct. He had seen the treasure that had lured him here and it was richer than he could have imagined. But he was no closer to his goal to 'acquire' one or more of the Flying Tiger P-40s. This pretty little valley that held them was isolated and well protected. There was no way a P-40 would leave here unless Mr. Piggy decreed it. His imagination had roiled with effort all afternoon, but he could not conceive of a single reason why Mr. Piggy might willingly give up even one of his airplanes. He went down to dinner, feeling a little subdued.

He found Hawk out on the porch, staring into the darkness. Night had closed in around them and there was not much to see. It took a moment for Hawk to register Harry's presence.

"Oh, Harry, good evening." He glanced back inside. "I just ordered a scotch. A double." Harry caught the barman's eye and ordered the same for himself. When the barman brought the drinks, they raised their glasses to each other and drank deeply. Hawk was looking weary, Harry thought. As though reading his mind, Hawk turned to him and said, "A long day, Harry. I'm still trying to digest it." He shook his head slowly, and turned to look out at the night.

"Words fail me," he said. "The only word that even comes close to describing what we saw today is 'awesome'. Goddamn awesome. A treasure trove...." His voice trailed off. He took another drink of scotch and tried to explain. "One AVG P–40, one P–40 in the condition of the ones we saw today would be remarkable. But they've got a total of eight. That's absolutely astounding!" He stared off into the night. "But what I find totally unbelievable are the Japanese airplanes. You know, none of those exist. Anywhere! They were all destroyed after World War II ended. Even the blueprints they used to build those airplanes were burned. That was 60 years ago. There's only one real Japanese airplane of that era that still flies, as far as I know: a Zero that does an occasional air show. That's not counting a couple of collections of bits and pieces with new engines. And, of course, there are some replicas. Not very good ones. Beyond that, there's nothing. Nothing at all like the Nates and that big bomber. There's nothing like the Betty and the Toryu. It's totally unbelievable."

Aloysious had walked out on the porch while Hawk was speaking, and stood by quietly, listening. When Hawk finished, he said, "You say it's unbelievable, Hawk, but we saw all those airplanes. Right over there in those hangars."

"You're right, Sunny. I saw them. I touched them. But it's still unbelievable. Never before have I been near so many Japanese airplanes. I don't think I ever saw so many at one time." He took a long drink from his scotch. "Except maybe during those first few raids on Rangoon in December 1941."

He turned to Harry. "You know, Harry, it makes you think. You know the dollar value of old airplanes. Even the best of the ones you and I have seen, very few are totally original. Almost none have a combat record. Few were even part of a combat unit. Most of the old warbirds flying now still exist because they got diverted to some kind of duty that kept them out of combat. But the ones we're seeing here participated in the war as it was going on. They were part of history as it was being made. That sure adds a lot to the dollar value."

Aloysious started fidgeting. He looked over his shoulder, then turned back to them. "Hey, guys," he said. When he was sure both were looking at him, he cupped both hands over his ears, like headphones in a listening post. He raised his eyebrows. "You know, you guys should take a walk. Take a look at that old airstrip over there. See if it can really handle those airplanes."

"Great idea," Harry said. "Come on, Hawk. Let's walk on over there."

Hawk understood what Aloysious meant as well as Harry did. He appeared a little reluctant to stroll off into the night, but he followed Harry down the steps nevertheless.

They walked in the glow of light from the house, the grass a soft cushion under their feet. "Sunny always gets concerned that someone might hear us," Harry said in case Hawk did not understand.

"Yeah. Well, he's probably right. Walk will do us both good."

Harry stopped before they had walked too far. "Let's stay here in the light. We're far enough away from the house. Hawk, you were talking about the dollar value of those airplanes."

"It's like I said, Harry, it's a treasure trove. There are airplanes there that nobody knows still exist. In multiple copies. How do you put a value on something like that? It's priceless." He looked Harry right in the eye. "Translate those airplanes into dollars and there's a hell of a lot of money involved. A hell of a lot!"

"Hawk, this may sound like a silly question, but when there's so much money involved, it has to be asked: Are those airplanes real?"

"Hell, yes, Harry." Hawk answered with no hesitation. He had turned so that the light was behind him now and his face was in the shadows, but Harry could feel the intensity in his eyes. When Hawk spoke again, there was a slight hesitancy in his voice.

"What I mean is, I didn't examine every nut and bolt on those airplanes this afternoon, but they sure as hell look real to me. I know exactly what you're thinking, Harry. And it's a good way to think. The Japanese used to be the world masters at copying anything. In recent years I think the Chinese have outdone them. They're even better than the Japanese. But I'm not finished looking at those airplanes yet. I already asked Tommy to see if his uncle would mind if I spend a few hours tomorrow climbing over them again. The P–40s, I mean. I know the P–40. If there's something wrong with them, I expect I'll spot it. I can't say the same for the Japanese airplanes. I just don't know them well enough. In fact I don't know them at all. I don't know anybody who does."

"Okay, Hawk, we're on the same wavelength. Those P–40s look good to me too, but we have to be as sure as we can. I find the Japanese airplanes fascinating, but the P–40s are the ones we came for. Which brings me right around to my next big question. If those P–40s are as good as they look, how are we going to grab some for ourselves?"

Hawk stayed quiet until Harry started to think that maybe he had gone too far, that he had shocked the old man with his directness. But Hawk was just trying to phrase his answer. Finally he said, "I've thought about it a lot today, Harry, and I don't know. This place is a little remote and I would say fairly well protected. Once we drive out of here, I don't know how the hell we would ever get back in without somebody noticing. I didn't see them, but I understand from Sunny that you saw a bunch of soldiers up near the gate. With all the trees covering the hills around us, there could be a whole army in here." After a pause he added, "And there probably is."

Harry thought he heard something and looked back toward the house. He could see Mouse at the edge of the porch, waving at them. "Come on, Hawk," he said, "time for dinner."

Mr. Piggy was waiting at the big round table. When everyone was seated, the food was brought in, and he encouraged them to eat and drink. He was most solicitous of Hawk, seeing to it that Hawk got a taste of every dish and that his glass was always full. He said that he had many questions to ask about the Flying Tigers but that would wait until dinner was finished. He did not want Hawk distracted from the pleasures of the table.

And he was true to his word. It was only at the end, when everyone was relaxed and just picking at the enormous dishes of a dozen varieties of fruit that capped the meal, that Mr. Piggy started asking his questions. They were basic questions, mostly, about the history of the AVG Flying Tigers. Harry knew the answers to most of them, but Hawk's responses were informative and well spoken. He found himself listening as attentively as Piggy and enjoying himself as much.

"What was the greatest victory, the greatest achievement of the Flying Tigers?" Mr. Piggy finally asked.

Hawk did not have to think about it. "As you know, Mr. Piggy, the Flying Tigers had many victories. They helped the British Royal Air Force hold the line in Burma. They cleared the skies of Japanese bombers over Kunming and Kweilien. But their greatest achievement came at the gorge of the Salween River. You know the Salween River, Mr. Piggy?"

"I know the river well. It is to the south, not far from here. It is a natural border between Burma and China."

"Then you know how deep the gorge is, how difficult the river is to cross. I don't know what's there now, but in 1942 there was a suspension bridge that carried the Burma Road over the river into China. It was the only place the river could be crossed for a hundred miles. At that time, the war in Burma was going very badly. The Japanese were pushing north and the British, with the help of Chinese units, were trying to hold them back. In early May the Japanese broke through. Their tanks headed straight up the Burma Road, right for China. What was left of the Chinese forces got across the bridge. Then they blew it up. That stopped the Japs. But not for long. Their engineers started building a pontoon bridge. If they could get across the Salween, there was nothing to stop the Japanese Army from rolling all the way to Kunming. There was nothing in front of them but a few disorganized Chinese units that were trying to get out of the way." There was long pause before Hawk added, "And the AVG Flying Tigers."

Hawk turned to Mr. Piggy. "You know the gorge on the Salween. On the Burmese side, it's miles down to the river on a road that twists and turns like a drunken snake. There are 18 big switchbacks before you get to the bridge. That was where the AVG caught the Jap Army. All stretched out. Tanks and trucks backed up for 20 miles, all waiting for the Jap engineers to finish the pontoon bridge. Chennault said that when the AVG P–40s caught them there, the Japs were like 'flies on flypaper'."

Hawk sipped from his drink before going on. "Chennault picked some of his best pilots, Second Squadron guys mostly. The Second Squadron – they called themselves the 'Panda Bears'. They picked that name for themselves because it fit with the Chinese theme. We called them the 'water boys'. They were mostly ex–Navy dive bomber pilots. Tex Hill was Second Squadron Leader then. He led the flight to the Salween. There were eight of them, four to dive bomb, four for top cover. Tex went in first, dove his P-40 down and dropped his bomb on the rock walls above the road. That brought tons of rock crashing down on the Japs. And it blocked the road. The Japs couldn't retreat then. They were trapped. Tex's guys worked them over, bombing and strafing. By the time they finished, the Japanese column was in total chaos. Burning tanks and burning trucks. Smoke and fire and dead Japanese troops scattered all over the road. Other AVG flights came back to mop up, but after Tex's first attack, it was all over. What was left of the Japanese finally got turned around and moved out of there. They were last seen headed south! The Japanese Army never tried to cross the Salween River again."

"Mr. Hawk," Mr, Piggy said in a solemn tone, "we sit here now, very comfortable, in Yunnan Province. Not far from Kunming, not far from the Salween River. Not far from the bridge. What would have happened if the Japanese Army had crossed the Salween?"

Hawk shrugged. "Who can say? It seems to me, that if the Japanese had crossed the Salween, nothing would have stood in their way to keep them from reaching Kunming. Back then, Kunming was the terminus of the 'Hump' flights over the Himalayas from India. If Kunming had fallen, China would have lost its last major supply point. That would have removed China from the war. With China out of the war, the Japanese would have been free to throw their military might against the British in India. What would that have meant? I don't know. But I suggest it's possible, Mr. Piggy, that if the Japanese had crossed the Salween, the Burmese and the Indians, who now speak English, would be speaking Japanese. And maybe, Mr. Piggy, even you would be speaking Japanese."

Piggy laughed. But when he stopped, his face became serious. He nodded. "Yes," Tommy translated, "I know that was one of the most dangerous times for China. I know that if the Flying Tigers had not helped us, China might now be a province of Japan. This is why the Flying Tigers airplanes are so important. These airplanes remain long after the Flying Tigers returned to their own country. It is these airplanes that will keep the memories of the Flying Tigers alive in the minds of the Chinese people. For a long time. Maybe forever."

Chapter 18

Early the next morning, Mouse quietly opened the door and slipped into Harry's room. Standing by the window, he didn't notice. The room was dark except for some dull gray light that spilled through the small opening he made by parting the heavy drapes just a little bit. He was leaning forward, peering intently at something outside. Becoming aware of Mouse's presence, he spared her just a quick glance before turning his eyes back outside again. Mouse sat down on the bed. It felt warm. "What's going on, Harry?" she asked.

"Have you looked outside?"

"It was still dark when I looked," she said and got up to stand next to him at the window. He held the drape open a little wider for her. There was not much she could see.

"Well it's light now," he said, and pulled the drape back a bit more to give her a better view. "Look at that! What the hell is going on?"

Mouse stuck her face up against the window. Out on the grass between the house and the runway were 50 women in black pajamas. Five rows of ten, all facing Harry's window, all gesturing menacingly. The group moved as one, slowly up on their toes like weary dancers, a long pause, then slowly, 50 right hands were raised face high and drawn back. A shifting of feet, and 50 hands were thrust forward, slowly, slowly pushing the air at Harry's window.

"Oh, it's 'Repulsing the Monkey'," Mouse said.

"What?"

"'Repulsing the Monkey'. You know, it's T'ai Chi. The ladies are doing their exercise."

Harry looked out again and watched for a while. "You're right." he said, "it is T'ai Chi." He stepped back, looking relieved. He had witnessed Chinese exercise groups doing their T'ai Chi drills before. It must have been the extreme hour that kept him from recognizing what these women were doing. Looking out your window in the half light of dawn to find 50 old women making threatening gestures at you was enough to put anyone off his breakfast. "Hell of a thing to wake up to," he commented.

Still watching the scene outside, Mouse said, "Look, Harry, now they are doing 'Golden Cock Stands on One Leg'."

"Yeah, well, I hope nobody topples over. Where the hell did all those women come from?"

"I see some who serve the food and work in the kitchen. They are probably staff here, and maybe wives of staff."

"Just goes to show you how many people they have around this place. There're probably dozens of other women who are not doing T'ai Chi now."

"You worry too much, Harry," Mouse said. "Come on, let's go to breakfast."

Breakfast was served on the porch, the best place for it. It was the nicest time of day. The sun was not yet far above the hills and the air was fresh. There was still dew on the grass, and no sign of the T'ai Chi corps. The ladies must have completed their drills and disbanded. Harry and Mouse looked over the breakfast choices and ordered toast, marmalade, and coffee. Neither was very hungry after all the food of yesterday. Harry had just poured the coffee when Hawk joined them.

"I've already had some coffee," he said. "I had it in my room. There were a bunch of ladies out here, marching on the grass or something, and I didn't want to interfere. Tommy said he'd meet me out here and we'd walk over to the hangars together."

"Going to take another look at the airplanes?" Harry said. "That's good. I'll probably walk over there later." But Hawk did not seem to be listening. He was looking up at the sky. "There he is," he said. Harry followed his eyes. The sky was clear; there was nothing to see. "What do you have, Hawk?" he asked.

"Can't tell yet, but it's got piston engines," he said, just as Harry's ears picked up a distant drone. "I think he's coming here."

Mouse saw him then, and a moment later so did Harry. The airplane was low over the hills, on a course that would take it right over the house. When it crossed the last hill beyond the valley, it dipped toward the runway. "C–47," Hawk said. "He's going to land right here." At the same time a half dozen pickup trucks in a single line cut across the grass and drove to the airstrip.

"It's one of my uncle's airplanes." Tommy had arrived on the porch without them noticing. "It's an old C–47, but he still uses it to carry cargo between his companies. It should be here overnight. Maybe we can take it for a ride."

The C–47 landed and taxied onto the grass. The pickup trucks drove up next to the C–47, and soon a dozen men were busily unloading it. It seemed to be all cardboard boxes and what looked like sacks of rice. From the perspective of the porch it was hard to tell. Within minutes, the workers were finished, and the pickup trucks drove off. The C–47 stood by itself on the grass.

"Well, let's go over and look at it," Hawk said. "Harry, you just started breakfast. You stay here and keep the young lady company. Tommy, how about you?"

"I can't go with you, "Tommy said. "My uncle will have breakfast with Mr. Sunny inside. They will want to talk. He will need me."

"I guess I'm the Lone Ranger," Hawk said. "I'm just going to walk over to the hangars. I'll see you all later."

Tommy went off to attend to the linguistic needs of Mr. Piggy, leaving Harry and Mouse alone on the porch. They sat quietly for a time, enjoying the stillness and the warming sun. "Well," Harry said after a while, "the first part of the morning was eventful. I wonder what comes next?"

"Hey, Harry!" Aloysious strode out on the porch, waving a whiskey glass in the air. Mr. Piggy and Tommy were right behind. "Harry," he said, "there's something here you might be interested in. In fact....," he paused to look at Harry meaningfully, "there's something I might need your help with." He slid into the chair next to Harry. Mr. Piggy and Tommy sat down across from them.

"Mr. Piggy and I were talking financials," Aloysious said in his formal Sunny Bright voice, "and he mentioned something that just might be mutually beneficial." He turned to Tommy. "Now you correct me, Tommy, if I've misunderstood something. I want Harry to hear this just the way I did." He turned back to Harry and went on:

"We were talking financials. All hypothetical. All esoteric stuff. I asked Mr. Piggy if he was having any problems in the international arena – you know, things like hedging foreign exchange trades. Mr. Piggy said he had only a single problem: all the countries where he does business have restrictions on the amount of money he can take out. It's a moot point in a way, because his companies deal in local currencies and there never is any foreign exchange. The bottom line is, he's short on hard currency to buy stuff overseas. That's no big deal right now, but it will be when his air museum gets rolling. There will be a lot of stuff to buy overseas, and he won't have the money to pay for it. It's not simply a question of not having money. He's got money coming out of his ears, he says, but it's not the right money. It's Burmese kyat, or Thai baht, or whatever, but no hard currency, no dollars. And even if he had dollars, he'd have no way of getting them out of the country in any quantity."

Here we go, Harry thought, Aloysious loves being Sunny Bright and he's going to get us caught up in some crazy smuggling scheme. We'll all be neighbors in Sparrowfart before it's over. If Aloysious had not winked at that precise moment, Harry would have ended the discussion right there. The wink made him hesitate. Was something more subtle at work here? "Yeah," Harry said, "I see the problem." That was as far as he was willing to commit himself.

"And it's a tough problem, Harry. I told Mr. Piggy that there are several possible solutions to something like this, and I suggested the solution that I thought was the most elegant one." Aloysious thrust a finger in the air. He spoke slowly and deliberately. "Mr. Piggy has a surplus of warplanes." A second finger went up next to the first. "Our Pacific Rim Investment Corporation has established the PRIC War Adventure Fund." The third finger joined the other two. "Mr. Piggy will shift his excess inventory to PRIC in exchange for hard currency funds delivered in the country of his choice." Aloysious waved the three fingers in their faces for a moment before dropping them.

Seeing where this was leading, Harry prepared himself to rise to the occasion. He sat up and thoughtfully considered the Sunny Bright recommendation. After an appropriate interval he said, "Very interesting, Mr. Bright. An elegant solution indeed! But I believe a lot would depend on the specific items of excess inventory that Mr. Piggy might make available in such a venture."

"Ah, and there's the rub," Aloysious said. "Regrettably Mr. Piggy is a true collector. He does not want to give up anything. I felt that as he has a total of eight P-40s, he could easily consign as many as half to PRIC. But Mr. Piggy said that a P-40 is the last thing he would give up. He is willing to let us have a couple of those cute little Nakajima Nates. I would have to defer to your knowledge of market values, Harry, but my feeling is that those two airplanes would not raise the kind of money he needs. So, Harry, I'd like your feelings about the requirements of Mr. Piggy's air museum, and a few of your thoughts, as to how Mr. Piggy's aircraft might fit into the PRIC War Adventure Fund portfolio."

Harry carefully considered all of this. "You are right, Mr. Bright. The two Nates are handsome aircraft and would undoubtedly bring in a nice price at auction, but as I don't know Mr. Piggy's precise monetary requirements...."

Tommy had been quietly translating Harry's comments into Chinese for Mr. Piggy. Before Harry could finish this thought, Mr. Piggy said something in Chinese and gestured impatiently at Harry. Tommy turned to Harry and said, "My uncle asked me to say that the amount he needs in hard currency in Switzerland is no less that ten million US dollars."

Harry let that figure slide past him as though such amounts were the stuff of his daily life. Not one muscle in his face twitched. Aloysious, totally immersed in his Sunny Bright character, wore a poker face that would not have winced at a figure ten times that amount.

"Well, even such an amount," Aloysious said, his tone implying that this amount was no great matter, "would probably not be met by the liquidation of a few Nates, right, Harry?"

"You're right again, Mr. Bright. To raise even that amount, I think it would be necessary to dip into the P-40 pool."

Listening to Tommy's translation, Mr. Piggy looked distinctly unhappy. It was time, Harry thought, to become the sympathetic version of the expert in aviation history that Mr. Piggy believed him to be. "Mr. Piggy," he said, "I know we've discussed this at length, but could you go over again your plans for the P-40?"

"Yes, yes," Mr. Piggy said, visibly agitated. "As you know, the P-40 is the core, the centerpiece of my collection. The P-40 will be the star of Flying Tiger Land. I need all eight P-40s. I need a dozen! I need all I can have!"

"And these P-40s will all fly?" Harry asked calmly.

"Of course they will fly. Most of them can fly now. They will all fly over this beautiful valley. They will fly in pairs. In flights of four. In squadrons! That is what I visualize. People will come from every land to see them fly." Mr. Piggy all but shouted his last words.

"Admirable," Harry said, no emotion in his voice as he went on. "I can see the P-40s flying now, even as you see them. People will come from around the world to see the Flying Tiger P-40s fly again. I agree. And it is these people we must consider. It is exceptionally important that we think of their safety." Harry paused to let Tommy translate this. When Tommy finished, he knew he had Mr. Piggy's full attention. Mr. Piggy looked at him and uttered a single word. Tommy translated it as "Safety?"

"Yes, Mr. Piggy, safety. The people who come here to walk through this beautiful valley will be spectators. Innocent spectators. They will look up to the sky and see Flying Tiger airplanes roar past overhead. It would not do for these spectators to see a P-40 fall out of the sky. Worse still would be for a P-40 to fall from the sky and strike a spectator. That would not do at all."

Harry took a sip of his drink while Tommy translated this. Mr. Piggy looked more puzzled now. Harry nodded and went on. "We must recognize the fact that these P-40s are old aircraft. They are over 60 years old. They were designed only for short lives in combat. There was no expectation that any of these airplanes would still be flying over a half century later. Because of that, there are many problems of safety related to flying them. This is an increasingly great concern for every museum, for every collector who flies these airplanes where there are people for them to fall on."

Harry paused again. He hoped he had not overdone it. But, as Tommy translated, he watched Mr. Piggy's face fall. It was obvious that this was something Mr. Piggy had never considered. A problem that he did not know he had until Harry pointed it out for him. It was the beginning of Mr. Piggy's enlightenment. Harry could see the recognition of his predicament written on Piggy's face, and the realization that, without help, his vision for Flying Tiger Land would be shattered while his precious P-40s fell out of the sky like over–ripe apples. When Tommy finished his translation, Piggy looked at Harry and threw out his hands as if to say, 'What can I do?'

Harry was in control. In a reassuring tone he said, "You can still have your Flying Tiger Land, Mr. Piggy. You can still have your Flying Tiger P-40s flying overhead. The answer is replicas: brand new airplanes that look like the old ones, but are built with modern materials and state–of–the–art technology. You can easily have P-40 replicas that will be completely safe and reliable."

Of course, this was the answer. He could see it in Mr. Piggy's eyes. "I have people," Mr. Piggy said, "who can build such airplanes." Obvious relief washed over him.

"Yes, Mr. Piggy," Harry said. "I'm sure you have the people with skills to do exactly that. They can use one of the original P-

40s as a model. They can copy all the pieces of that plane and build replicas. All the replicas you want. The original aircraft will still be important, but their importance will be as static displays, as pieces of history preserved in a museum where people can see the airplane exactly as it was when it flew with the Flying Tigers. And no spectators will be endangered.

Mr. Piggy uttered the Chinese equivalent of 'splendid', which was the way Tommy translated it. "A wonderful idea, Mr. Harry," he added.

Harry was not finished. "Now," he went on, "the other good news that derives from this approach is that you will not need a squadron of authentic P-40s. A squadron of replicas will do that job nicely. It means, Mr. Piggy, that you can easily divest yourself of as many as six of your P-40s. Two should be enough for static display and as exemplars for the replicas."

"Wonderful!" Mr. Piggy said at first. But as he thought about it he added, "I still cannot believe that I could bring myself to give you six P-40s. Why do you use that number, Mr. Harry?"

"For a very practical reason. Six P-40s would give you the ten million dollars that you require. I don't think there's a combination of your other aircraft that would accomplish that."

Mr. Piggy fell back in his chair. A load that he had not been aware of until now had been lifted from his shoulders. He stood up, bowed to Harry, and then to Aloysious. "Thank you, gentlemen," he said. "Thank you for showing me a way to solve my problem. It will be difficult for me to give up any of my airplanes, particularly the P-40s, but obviously it is something I must face. I will go now and think about this." He bowed once more, then turned and walked out of the room. Tommy paused before following his uncle out the door. "I too want to thank you both for your help," he said. "The airplanes are very important to me too, and I'm happy you showed my uncle a way to keep them – or most of them at least." Tommy awkwardly reached over and shook Harry's hand.

As Harry watched him walk away, he felt a little guilty. He turned to Aloysious. "I need a drink."

"Come on. Let's go take a walk down the runway. Exercise will do you good."

When they had walked far enough away from the house, Aloysious clapped Harry on the back. "That was totally brilliant, Harry," he said. "You played him like a banjo. I could see the whole thing in his face. Let him stew over it a bit and he'll be begging us to take those airplanes. I was a little surprised, though, that you went for six. Do you think your investors are going to want that many?"

"Ten million for six original AVG P-40s is a bargain. Somebody will want them. My feeling was that even if Piggy didn't want to give us six P-40s, he would see the wisdom of giving up at least some of them."

"Well, I think you got some of them, probably all six. Hey, was that true what you were telling him about replicas and P-40s falling out of the sky?"

"Well...not exactly."

"Anyway, it sure sounded good. I would never have thought of that approach." Aloysious looked at Harry with something like affection. It was the look of an artist regarding a protégé not previously suspected of brilliance. "There will be a lot of details to work out if Piggy goes along with this," he added. "That we can do as we go along. There's no real risk for us until money changes hands. Anyway, you did real good, Harry. I wish Hawk had been there for that. Come to think of it, where is Hawk?"

"He's over in the hangars, poking around the airplanes."

"You find him and brief him on this. He will be surprised and – I expect – gratified by what we pulled off here today."

Chapter 19

If Hawk was surprised and gratified, he failed to show it. Harry caught up with him as he was walking back from the hangars and briefed him on what Aloysious – still in his Sunny Bright mode – was now calling their "pivotal" meeting with Mr. Piggy. When he finished, if anything, Hawk looked a little worried.

"What's the matter, Hawk? Something troubling you?"

"I don't know, Harry. I'm not sure."

"Something wrong with the P-40s? Something you didn't like?"

"I don't know." He shook his head. "I spent all morning with those birds, went over them with a fine-tooth comb. They look absolutely perfect. I found numbers where they're supposed to be. The few numbers that I could match up, matched up. I looked at the airframes. I looked at the engines. I looked at individual components in the electrical system, in the hydraulics. Everything looks the way it should, or at least the way I think it should. Nope, they look absolutely perfect, Harry."

Harry smiled. "What can I say? If they look good to you, Hawk, everything looks good. In fact, it looks like we may pull this off. Get a few of those P-40s for ourselves."

Hawk nodded, but his eyes were far away.

"Hawk, there is something bothering you?" Harry asked.

"Okay. I don't how to say this, but it's the 'patina'."

"Patina?"

"Yeah. You're in antiques, Harry. You know about patina." Harry looked a little uncertain, so Hawk explained. "Look," he said, "I know 'patina' is not a word used with airplanes very much, and maybe it's the wrong word for it. The way I understand patina, it's what time does to something. Like with people. When you're old you have scars, and age spots and wrinkles. An old chair has scars too, and cigarette burns and scuff marks. The wood on a chair can have a soft glow from being used a lot. And that's part of the patina too. What I mean is, when things are around a long time, they get a certain look. It's what time does as it passes by. It's patina. You understand what I'm saying, Harry?"

"I know exactly what you're saying, Hawk. An old airplane like an old chair should have a patina. It's the story of the life it's led."

"And isn't it true that with some things…I mean it's your trade, Harry, but can't you make a new thing look old?"

"Absolutely. Some people are very good at that. I've known a few myself. Are you saying those airplanes are made to look old?"

"I don't know, Harry. I really don't know. They look old, just the way they should. It's more like they don't feel right."

"Is it just the P-40s that bother you?" Harry asked. Hawk nodded. "What about the Japanese airplanes in the hangars. How do you feel about them, Hawk?"

"Well, that's the funny part. I don't know much about the Jap airplanes, but I feel very comfortable around them. It's like there's no pretense involved. But I have no reason for saying that. I look at them, and I don't really know if what I'm looking at is the way it should be. I just don't have the experience with them. With the P-40s I look at them, and everything I see is exactly the way it should be. But then I step back and I look and I feel sort of uncomfortable. It's a gut feeling, Harry, that's all it is. And I've never had any use for anybody else's gut feelings."

"I understand what you're saying, Hawk, and I don't know how to resolve it. Right now, it's not critical. Mr. Piggy hasn't agreed to do anything yet. But if he does, it will be critical."

Hawk nodded. "I'm planning to take another look at the airplanes after lunch. The mechanics are used to seeing me there now, and nobody said that I can't go back."

"Sounds good to me, Hawk. Get a real good look. If we have to make the big decision, I want to be ready."

*   *   *

About an hour before dinner Harry met Hawk on the porch for a drink. With big scotches, they strolled across the grass to look at the parked C-47.

"Nice airplane, isn't it, Harry? I have a lot of hours on the C-47. I first flew it here in China. Over 'The Hump' from Kunming to India. Flew it in Africa later, and in Vietnam when the French were still there. The same old C-47s I flew then are probably still flying now. This may be one of them. It's a hell of an airplane."

Harry grunted, but his mind was not on C-47s. "How did it go this afternoon?" he asked.

"It went good, but I'm still not a hundred percent. After all the time I spent looking at those P-40s, most of me says they're okay. But something is still niggling at me. I don't know, Harry, I'd say that right now I'm about 93 percent sure that those airplanes are real."

"Well," Harry said, looking up at the sky, "maybe 93 percent is as good as it gets. With the kind of antiques that I usually look at, 93 percent would not be bad at all." They stood silently looking at the C-47. "Let me ask you something, Hawk. If you were doing this same thing back in the States, and you could have anything you needed, would there be a test? Would there be any other thing you would want to do?"

Hawk thought about that. "I don't think so, Harry. There's no test I know of....Well, maybe we could strap Piggy down on a lie detector. No, as far as the airplanes go, maybe there is something technical you could do, but I don't know what it is. Hell, I'm no scientist."

"I understand that, Hawk. Anyway, the way I see it, our job is to do the best we can." He smiled and added, "And hope that our best is good enough."

Hawk rocked back and forth on his heels. Still looking up at the C-47, he said, "You know, Harry, maybe there is one thing....I remember you telling me about Tommy flying that P-40 at that jungle airstrip down by the casino. Number 36, you said it was. That was one of the Panda Bears. It was Ed Rector's airplane, did you know that? When I listened to you describe old Number 36, how it looked, and how it sounded – and even how it smelled – I knew you were talking about an honest-to-god AVG airplane. I just knew that, Harry. Maybe it was just your powers of description, but it sure sounded right."

Harry waited for him to go on. Hawk had turned to look at him, but seemed reluctant to say more. "Yeah, go on, Hawk."

"Well, I guess what I'm saying is…it might be interesting, sort of as a basis for comparison….I know this sounds silly, but when you talked about it, Number 36 sounded so good, that if I saw it, it might give me some perspective on what we're seeing here. Know what I mean?"

"Yeah, I see what you're saying, Hawk, but we don't know that Number 36 is any more real than the airplanes we have right here. How would we know that?"

"Yeah, you're right, Harry." Hawk shrugged. "Well, it was just a thought. I guess I figured I would feel more comfortable if I saw all of Piggy's P-40s. All eight of them."

A silly idea? Maybe, but it got Harry thinking. He could see himself standing on that little airstrip in the jungle and feel the P-40 as Tommy flew it by, almost close enough to touch. There had been no question in his mind then that it had been real.

"Hawk, maybe you have something," he said. "It just might be worthwhile to have you look at that airplane. At least that way we could tell Riley you saw them all." There would be complications, he knew that. "I'm not sure how easy it will be. We're supposed to leave here tomorrow. I doubt they can fly Number 36 up here by then, but maybe we can go there. Let me talk to

Tommy. He'll be able to tell us how difficult it would be to set it up."

*   *   *

"I have to ask my uncle," was all Tommy said when Harry asked him the question. As Tommy walked off to find Mr. Piggy, Harry thought he'd better have a quick talk with Aloysious.

"Whatever," Aloysious said after Harry explained the situation. "It's your show, Harry. If you think it's worth doing, go ahead and do it. But you better talk to Mouse. She's in charge of our airplane."

'Our airplane', Sato's Gulfstream, would be in Kunming to pick them up in the morning. Harry needed to talk with Mouse. Maybe the Gulfstream could be routed via the casino on its way back to Bangkok.

"I think it will be all right, Harry," Mouse said, "if it takes only a few hours. But I will have to confirm it with the captain."

Harry sat on the porch and had another drink. He had done what he could. Now it was in the hands of Mr. Piggy. He sipped his scotch and looked at the old C-47 parked on the grass. It looked like it belonged there, sitting by itself against a background of small hills. A fugitive from history. A sudden feeling of loneliness washed over him as the daylight faded and darkness crept into Mr. Piggy's pretty little valley.

Dinner was a more relaxed affair now that Mr. Piggy knew their ways. They all enjoyed Chinese food, had no peculiar dining habits, and required little encouragement – except to drink his brandy. It made Mr. Piggy's job easier. He could be a perfect host and not have to work so hard at it. As usual, conversation during the meal was kept light. Harry avoided any mention of Number 36, knowing that when the time was right the subject would be raised. The table was being cleared for dessert when Mr. Piggy turned to Harry.

"Tommy said Mr. Hawk would like to see the airplane that you call Number 36. That is a problem. We cannot bring Number 36 here. The distance is too great; it would take too much time. And you cannot go there. The airstrip in the jungle is small and not paved. Mr. Sunny Bright's airplane cannot land there."

Harry was prepared for that possibility. "We can take Mr. Bright's Gulfstream to the big airfield at the casino, where we landed before. From there, we could drive to the jungle airstrip. We did that when Tommy flew the P-40. It's a ten-minute ride."

Tommy looked at his uncle, then back at Harry. There was a frown on his face. "It's not possible to do that now," Tommy said. "There are problems at the casino."

"What kind of problems?" Harry asked, knowing that it was probably none of his business.

Tommy translated the question. Mr. Piggy considered it and then spoke to Tommy at some length. Tommy nodded and turned back to Harry. "My uncle said it is a problem of superstition. It is very complicated. When my uncle decided to build the casino, he chose that place because it was quiet and peaceful. Very few people lived there. Only the people in one village. He knew those people are very backward. And very superstitious. But they were peaceful and my uncle built the casino. They never bothered us. They stayed in their village. We helped their economy. We built a market to buy chickens and rice. They were happy. They never came close to the fence. There was no problem."

Mr. Piggy spoke again. Tommy listened carefully, then turned back to Harry and translated. "Recently, strange things happened. The villagers became bold. They demanded more money for their chickens. They came close to the fence. Some days ago many villagers gathered at the gate. They shouted and threw stones. Finally, some rushed past the guards and ran through the compound. Windows were broken, things were smashed. The guards tried to stop them and villagers were injured. Guards were injured too. My uncle said it is fortunate that there were not many guests. The casino is closed now. For renovations."

"Gee, I'm sorry to hear that," Harry said. "What about the jungle airstrip...and the P-40?" he added very quickly.

Tommy shook his head. "The jungle airstrip is not a problem. It has been there as long as the oldest villagers. To them it is like a thing of nature. They accept it, like a tree or a mountain. The villagers will not disturb it. But now they roam freely through the forest. In the past they did not. My uncle fears that if we drive through the forest to the airstrip now - as we did before - we could meet the villagers. And that would not be good."

"Do you have any idea of what caused this uprising?" Harry asked. 'Uprising' may have been an unfortunate choice of a word, but Tommy did not seem to notice.

"We know only that it comes from the villagers' superstitions."

"What kind of superstitions?" Harry asked. His interest was more than academic. Spirits were still an important part of everyday life in many parts of Asia. They were not to be discounted.

Mr. Piggy nodded, and Tommy translated as he spoke. "The villagers in places like that can be very backward. I'm sure you know that, Mr. Harry. These people believe in spirits – spirits of all kinds. Good ones and bad ones. They believe strongly in Nats. Maybe you know about Nats, Mr. Harry? They are spirits too, and many of them are not good. They are like demons. They hate people. Some of them were people themselves once, bad people. The worst Nats are people who led bad lives and died in horrible ways. Such Nats torment people and torture them."

Mr. Piggy refreshed himself with a big drink of brandy, before going on. "Recently, we learned that the villagers believe that Nats live behind the fence of our compound. That was why they dare not make problems for us. At our chicken market, some villagers told our staff that they met the Nats. And defeated them in a great battle!"

Piggy chuckled when he said that. He shook his head as he continued. The whole idea of Nats was beyond belief. "The villagers even described the Nats they met. A Nat is small, they said, just so high. A Nat can take any form. It can be a young child one moment. In the next, it becomes an ugly old man." Piggy paused to laugh. He tried to speak, but his words were choked off by laughter. "They said...they said...." He got that far and broke up completely. He tried to hold it back, but when it came, the laughter shook his body and doubled him over in his chair. He slapped his knee and then grasped it tightly with his hand as he spoke through clenched teeth.

"They said...that the Chief of the Nats had chickens growing out of his shoulders...and he drove a motorcycle!" With that Piggy exploded in a gale of laughter that shook his body until it seemed he would tear apart.

And then Harry saw it - P.C. hanging on to the motorbike, gunny sack pulled over his head, bundles of chickens flung over his shoulder, accelerating at the villagers who were stoning Jock. And then, Jock's voice, describing the scene: "Terrified them it did. It was like a huge demon coming down on us. Looked like a giant vegetable driving. Or maybe a chicken, a giant one with nothing above his shoulders. It was a sight, sir. Wings flapping, feathers flying. Everyone screaming. It terrified the shit out of me. I can tell you that, sir."

Harry glanced at Aloysious, who had been watching Piggy with a bemused smile. When he caught Harry looking at him, Aloysious grinned. His face lit up, but he quickly looked away. Like Harry, he was right on the edge, and a smirk from either of them would send them both over, to join Piggy in wild laughter.

Mr. Piggy finally composed himself. He said to Harry, "So, you see the problems we have: backwardness and superstition." He shook his head. "For now it is not good to drive in the jungle."

"It's really too bad," Harry said, "but...."

Hawk spoke up just then and a little wistfully said, "Well, that is too bad. I was really looking forward to seeing old Number 36 again."

Mr. Piggy was wiping his brow with a napkin. He paused to ask, "You knew that airplane, Mr. Hawk?"

"Maybe. Maybe I did. It was Eddie Rector's airplane. I may even have flown it a couple of times."

Mr. Piggy looked at Hawk thoughtfully. He said something in Chinese. "Too bad" Tommy translated. Then Tommy said something to Mr. Piggy. Mr. Piggy listened carefully. He nodded and then turned to Harry. "Tommy reminded me that we may send the C-47 to the casino. So, it may be possible to see the P-40. If the C-47 goes to the casino, Tommy will be the pilot. He can land the C-47 at the jungle airstrip. Mr. Hawk can see the P-40, and then Tommy can fly the C-47 to the casino. It will take two

minutes and you will not have to drive. Mr. Sunny Bright's airplane will come tomorrow. On his way home, Mr. Sunny can
land at the casino and pick up you and Mr. Hawk. Do you think
this is a good idea, Mr. Harry?"

Harry looked at his companions. Aloysious shrugged and nodded. He was okay with the idea. Mouse inclined her head slightly.
Using the Gulfstream was probably okay, but the captain would
still have to agree. Hawk smiled and said, "It sounds like a plan."

Harry looked directly at Mr. Piggy. "I think that if we can do
that, Mr. Piggy, we should."

"Good. It will be done. There is one small thing. Other passengers. The C-47 flight will take some passengers to the casino...."

"I don't see a problem," Harry said. "Who are the other passengers?"

Tommy answered after glancing at his uncle, "They will be
some of our re-enactors."

"Oh," Harry said and tried to hide his surprise. "Oh, yes, the
re-enactors. Why are they going to the casino?"

"For experience." Tommy said. "When tourists come to Flying Tiger Land they will be the re-enactors. They will play the
role of World War II Chinese Nationalist soldiers who defended
the Flying Tiger airstrips. But they are peasants with no experience. How will they get experience to be like soldiers of World
War II?"

"So you will take them to the casino and they will pretend to
be soldiers?"

"They will have the experience of flying in the C-47, like the
soldiers of World War II. At the casino they will live like soldiers.
They will patrol. If the villagers come, they will act like soldiers
and protect the casino. It will be a good experience."

When Tommy finished, Mr. Piggy stood up. He was wearing
his formal face, as if he were about to make an announcement –
or a speech. Tommy got up and stood beside him.

"I will not make a speech," Mr. Piggy said, "but I again want
to say my thanks to all of you. Your visit here has honored me. I
have some souvenirs that will remind you of your first visit to
Flying Tiger Land. The first visit of many, I hope."

With that, Mr. Piggy looked toward the door through which all the good food had come, and four serving ladies appeared. They carried not steaming dishes of food this time, but four neatly folded bundles of cloth. The first lady presented her bundle to Mr. Piggy. He held it at arms length, and with an exaggerated motion shook it out. It was drab green, a coverall that World War II flight crew might have worn. Sewn over the right breast pocket was an embroidered tag that said 'Flying Tiger Land'. Over the left pocket a similar tag said 'Major Hawk'. Mr. Piggy held the coverall up for all to see. "There is one for each of you," he said with a smile.

He looked again at the door, and his look made another lady appear, carrying in her hand a finely made leather box. Piggy took it and opened it, and stepped over to Mouse. With a small bow he presented the box to her. "For the charming Miss Mouse," he said. She looked in the box and then at Mr. Piggy, surprise on her face. "It's beautiful," she said, "but I can't...."

"You must take it, Miss Mouse," Tommy said, as Piggy tilted the box for the others to see. "Or Mr. Piggy will be very hurt." It was a brooch, a jeweled tiger leaping through a victory 'V', the famed mascot of the AVG Flying Tigers. It sparkled with the brilliance of the rubies, sapphires, and other colored stones that were set into its golden body.

While they admired the tiger, another lady appeared with a souvenir for Harry. Mr. Piggy presented him an elaborately framed photo of a P-40, the number 36 visible on its side. "We have many airplanes," Mr. Piggy said, "but Tommy thought you would like this one most of all." Harry was touched. It would have been his choice.

Next was Aloysious. Mr. Piggy gave him a handsome brief-case of glowing black leather, the richest, blackest leather they had ever seen. It was his own design, Mr. Piggy said, and demonstrated how, with hidden folds, the half-inch-thick briefcase could be expanded as large as a shopping bag. As Mr. Piggy explained, "This is a 'black bag', Mr. Sunny. You know the 'black bag', I think. To carry secret money. I know for your business you have a great need for it."

Watching Aloysious, Harry knew that he had also been touched by his gift. Aloysious, who had never owned a briefcase in his life, now accepted this very special briefcase in his role as Sunny Bright. To Aloysious, this was an affirmation of what Sunny Bright was, and that in fact Aloysious was Sunny Bright. Aloysious loved his Sunny Bright persona, Harry knew. This presentation could make him even more difficult to live with.

They all watched for the next lady. She appeared carrying a long cylindrical object. Piggy held it high, for a dramatic moment. The he started to unroll a large scroll painting. "My uncle is a painter," Tommy said, "and a poet. He has made this painting for Mr. Hawk."

With Tommy's help, Piggy lifted the scroll up where everybody could see it. The background was craggy black and white mountains, the kind often seen in Chinese paintings. Around the mountains were gracefully shaped clouds. You could almost feel them gliding by. Near the top of the highest peak was a tiger, a tiger in all its glorious form and color, leaping toward the clouds. One side of the painting had a short column of Chinese characters, to which Mr. Piggy now drew their eyes with a small gesture of his hand.

"My uncle's poem," Tommy said. "He will recite it for you."

The poem was short. A few phrases that Mr. Piggy spoke with reverence, as if he were saying a prayer. All but the last words. They boomed out into the room. Everyone turned to Tommy, eager to hear him put the words into English:

> *When Tigers fly,*
> *The heavens quake,*
> *At their thunder!*

A small shiver rippled down Harry's spine. It was just a few words, but they evoked something of what he had sensed in the P-40s and what he felt when he listened to the stories that Hawk told. Just then Hawk stood up and cleared his throat. He carefully put on a pair of spectacles that Harry had not seen before, and peered intently at the scroll. His face looked as if the flag had just been paraded by.

"Why, what a wonderful thought," he said. "And how well it is expressed. It's a beautiful painting, Mr. Piggy. I shall treasure it always."

They all started to clap their hands at that point. Somehow it seemed appropriate. In the Chinese fashion, Mr. Piggy joined in, clapping with the rest of them, a very pleased look on his face. Somehow, Harry thought, their visit to Flying Tiger Land could not have had a better ending.

As the applause died down, Tommy leaned toward Harry and quietly said, "My uncle appreciates your advice. He said that it is difficult to give up any airplane, but the money is important now. He will inform Mr. Sunny."

The smile Harry had on his face was now frozen there. He was stunned. Whatever next move he might have expected, this was not it. Or, at least, this was not the time for it. Piggy was accepting his 'offer'. And he was not ready. He quickly looked to where Aloysious was now standing next to Hawk, both admiring the scroll and the tiger that was trying to fly. If the tiger's luck was like Harry's, its bold leap toward the heavens would not take it there, but send it tumbling down the mountain. He would have to warn Aloysious before Mr. Piggy got to him.

But that was not to be. Mr. Piggy invited everybody to the big bar for brandy. As they were walking there, Harry heard Mr. Piggy said something that Tommy translated for Aloysious. "Mr. Sunny Bright, I am ready to give you six P-40s for ten million US dollars. We can talk about it now or whenever you wish."

Harry had never seen Aloysious speechless. He was not speechless now, but it did take him a long moment to devise the appropriate Sunny Bright response: "Ah, very good, sir. My board of directors…they will have to be advised. Just a courtesy, of course. We will discuss…."

But Mr. Piggy was not a man to dwell on detail. "No problem, Mr. Sunny. Tommy will work with you. To collect the airplanes. And to bank the money, of course."

As Mr. Piggy elbowed the barman aside to pour everyone a large brandy, Aloysious turned to Harry and said, "Well, Harry, it looks like you got your airplanes. Are you sure you want them?"

Harry reached for one of the brandy glasses. "You know, Aloysious," he said, "I wish you were asking me that tomorrow."

Chapter 20

Tomorrow came too quickly for Harry, as it often did. The grass was heavy and wet with dew. He could feel it seeping into his shoes as he walked toward the C-47. He thought he was the first, but as he came closer to the old airplane, he noticed the open side door. Then he saw Hawk and Tommy standing on the other side of the aircraft, staring up at the nose. Hawk pointed a finger and said something and Tommy laughed. Then they walked on, slowly, looking up at the aircraft as they went, doing their preflight inspection.

The 're-enactors' had also arrived. About a dozen were sprawled on the airstrip behind the C-47. When Harry got closer he saw that they had laid out bamboo mats that kept them off the wet grass. They were chatting among themselves and showed absolutely no interest in him.

The previous evening, before things broke up, Aloysious and Mouse agreed that Harry would join Hawk and Tommy on the flight to the jungle airstrip. Aloysious and Mouse would return to Kunming and meet the Gulfstream. They would all join up again later that day at the casino airfield. If Mouse had a problem diverting the Gulfstream there on its way back to Bangkok, Harry and Hawk would fly back to Kunming with Tommy in the C-47, and then go on to Bangkok on a commercial flight. Hopefully, that would not be necessary.

The pre-flight was taking longer than it should have. From time to time Hawk and Tommy stopped to talk. There would be a burst of laughter from Tommy, and then Hawk would join in. Hawk was telling war stories again.

It was a good opportunity to give the re-enactors the once over. Harry walked back toward the tail where he could get a better look. He counted an even dozen, all in rough uniforms of faded green. The uniforms did look old fashioned, like something you might expect to find on a World War II re-enactor, but maybe they were just cheap.

The re-enactors stopped talking when Harry got closer, and turned to look at him. A rough-looking bunch, they might have been peasants, but they did not have the look of inexperienced soldiers. Each had a rifle; two squatted next to a light machine gun. When they moved and handled their weapons, they did it with an easy familiarity. And, unlike the eyes of any peasant he had ever met, the eyes that watched Harry showed him no deference.

Hawk and Tommy, still chatting, climbed aboard the aircraft. They were too engrossed in their talk to notice Harry. A man in green coveralls appeared in the C-47's door after they went through. Probably the crew chief, Harry thought. He shouted something in Chinese, and the re-enactors – or 'the troops', as Harry now thought of them - responded. They got to their feet, stretched and yawned, and then stopped to watch and to advise two of their comrades who rolled up the mats. Gradually they formed themselves into a ragged line at the back end of the aircraft. The crew chief stuck his head out the door again and started making hurry-up motions. The troops slowly clambered aboard the C-47.

When the crew chief noticed Harry, he motioned, 'hurry-up', and then helped him through the door. The inside of the airplane was bare, except for small folding seats that dropped from the side of the fuselage. Because the aircraft sat with its tail down on the ground and its nose poked up in the air, the floor sloped to the rear. The 'troops' were in their seats, feet braced on the floor. The crew chief led Harry up the slope toward the cockpit, and pointed to a seat intended for him near the front.

The door to the cockpit was open, and Harry stuck his head in. Hawk sat in the left seat. He would be the pilot in command. His sleeves were rolled up and a pair of silver-rimmed spectacles perched on his nose. His left hand held a checklist of some kind, while he used his right to flip switches, set gauges, and do all the other things he needed to make the aircraft ready for flight. He noticed Harry, nodded a greeting, and went right back to work. He was the totally professional airman this morning.

Tommy noticed Harry then, and turned around in his seat. "Hey, Mr. Harry. Sorry you have no better seat." He gestured at Hawk. "Mr. Hawk will be the pilot today. He has many hours in the C-47, many more than I have. He will be my instructor pilot today," he added with a smile.

"I'll let you guys do your work," Harry said. He gave them a thumbs-up and went back to his seat.

It was not long before one engine coughed a couple of times and started. Then the other engine started and joined its mate in a noisy rumble. After flying in the Gulfstream, Harry had forgotten how loud the inside of an airplane can be. They taxied across the grass and the engine noise was joined by creaks and groans from the fuselage and thumps from the landing gear as it found bumps in the smooth grass. They held at the edge of the field for a few moments while the engines were brought to full power. Then they started to roll, slowly at first, the airplane shaking and rattling like an old pickup truck. Then faster and faster. The tail lifted, and for a moment the floor was level. The nose came up and the shaking stopped. They rose smoothly in the air.

It was a smooth flight. It took about two hours, but seemed not that long at all. They passed over the same terrain they had flown over in the Gulfstream, but they were much lower than in the jet. Miles lower. When they leveled out, Tommy caught Harry's eye and gestured, 'come up here', and, when he did, shouted in his ear, "We stay where it's smooth, Mr. Harry. When we cross the border from China, there's no radar, no air control. We can fly where we want."

Hawk's hand was on the control wheel, flying the airplane. He turned to Harry from time to time, and his lips moved with words that the engines promptly drowned out. With conversation difficult, they quietly watched the geography go by. This was still one of the most remote areas of the world, and one that had always interested Harry greatly. They were low enough for him to make out details. He was content to just look out the windows and watch.

Hawk was the first to spot the airfield that was their destination. He pointed out the runway at the casino first and, while Harry was still looking at that, he pointed to the small area of light green that was the grass of the airfield. It was barely visible against the deeper green of the jungle itself.

Hawk said something. Tommy nodded and Hawk started a steep descent with the airplane's nose aimed at the airfield. He leveled out just short of it, down low over the jungle, and stayed low. With engines roaring at full throttle they flew across the airstrip, the grass rippling in the wind they left behind. Out over the jungle again, Hawk pulled the airplane up in a steep banked climb from where he and Tommy could survey the airfield that he kept under their left wing tip. After two tight circuits, Hawk straightened the aircraft out, then started a long sweeping turn that would line them up with the end of the runway on their final approach.

When Hawk throttled back, Tommy smiled at Harry and shrugged. "No villagers, no staff," he said. "If anyone was there, our low pass would scare them. Make them run." From what Harry saw, no one was running on the airfield, but he would not take bets on what might be lurking in the fringes of the jungle.

The C-47 touched down lightly at the end of the grass strip. Hawk let it roll to almost a stop, and then taxied close to the hangars. He braked to a stop and shut down the engines. Tommy unbuckled himself and said to Harry, "I have to make sure the crew chief does not let the re-enactors leave the aircraft. If any villagers are near, I don't want them to see anything different. To them, this is a special place of the past. I don't want them to change their minds."

Harry and Hawk followed Tommy to the nearest hangar, then waited while Tommy went around the side to a little shed. He went inside, and moments later an engine started. "Diesel generator," he said when he came out. "We need a lot of power here. For lights and other things."

They went in through a small door that Tommy fumbled with for a while before he got it open. Inside, only a small area of the hangar was illuminated by the single light bulb right over the door.

"Please wait a moment," Tommy said. "I need to make some light."

A glint of metal in the corner caught Harry's eye. As he walked over, he could make out the form of an automobile, an automobile he had seen before - or at least its fender. This undoubtedly was the Mercedes in the photo Riley had shown him at that first lunch, which now seemed so long ago. At least his identification had been right. It was an SL500. In fact, as he looked closer he saw it was the 'hopped-up', up-market model, what the buffs called a "55". It was something he would like to own. Hawk would probably love the thing. He called to him. "Hey, Hawk, come look at this."

"Whatcha got, Harry?"

"A car. It's really neat."

"Ferrari?"

"No," Harry replied and turned to look at Hawk, who was poking around at tools on a work bench. He seemed to have little interest in what Harry had found. "You want it to be a Ferrari?" Harry asked. "You have rich taste in cars."

Hawk held some kind of a tool he had found up to the light. "Son," he said, "it's not a matter of taste. A car is transport. A Ferrari is something else." He laid the tool back down on the table and walked to where Harry stood. "I always say a thing is what it is," he continued. "But sometimes a thing is more than what it is. A P-40 is like that. It's an airplane, but it's more. It's a legend. A Ferrari is like that."

A dozen bright lights in the ceiling came on all at once, flooding the inside of the hangar with light, making it look as bright and as clean as an operating theater. "Whoa," Hawk said, "this is some fine working area. Drop a screw on the floor here and you're going to find it. Well, that is a pretty car, Harry."

Harry was no longer looking at the Mercedes. In front of him, glittering like a multi-colored gemstone despite its dull camouflage paint, was AVG P-40 Number 36. It looked more beautiful than any car he could imagine. Hawk walked up to it, eyes bright.

"Now look at this," he said. "It's just like I said, Harry. A thing is what it is. But sometimes it's more." And silently Harry agreed.

"My uncle's favorite," Tommy said, walking up from behind. "This is one you can't buy, Mr. Hawk. My uncle would never sell it. It's his favorite."

Hawk was up on the wing. He started bending down to look in the cockpit, then straightened up again and looked around the hangar. Something had caught his eye. "Tommy," he finally said, "what the hell is this building made of? Those walls aren't wood."

Harry started looking around at that point. The walls were white and reflected the bright overhead lights right back in his eyes. They were almost hard to look at.

"It's metal. It's like steel," Tommy said. "Only the outside of the hangar is wood. It's like a wooden shell that covers a steel box. All the hangars here are made like this one. It makes my uncle feel that his things are safe. He says the hangars are like a bank vault. No robbers can get in."

"Criminey!" Hawk said.

"I thought the villagers will not come here, Tommy."

"It's not the villagers, Mr. Harry. It is others. People who do not like my uncle because of politics. And robbers. There are many robbers here."

Hawk was already back to examining the airplane. "Tommy, would you mind if I got in the cockpit?"

"Whatever you like to do, Mr. Hawk. Would you like to hear the engine?"

Total silence. Tommy's question had stopped Hawk in his tracks. Harry could see the smile starting to light up his face. "Can we do that?" Hawk asked.

"Sure can, Mr. Hawk. We have to open the door first and take the airplane outside. You want to do that?"

"You bet! Let's do it!" Hawk jumped off the wing, ready to go. He would push the airplane out himself if he had to.

"Okay," was all Tommy said. He walked up front and pressed a big black button set in the wall near the main overhead door. A whir of electric motors and the hangar door slowly lifted. From where he stood some distance away, Harry could see that this was not a door he would expect to find on any other hangar. It looked armored. Thick steel plates hinged together to form the door.

As the door went up, Tommy walked to the back of the hangar. Soon the muffled sound of a small engine came from there, and Tommy drove up on what looked a small golf cart. It was a miniature aircraft-tug to tow the P-40 out of the hangar.

Within minutes, Tommy was doing just that. Hawk and Harry stood along the sides of the hangar to help guide the P-40 through the door. It was not a problem. The hangar was wide and there was plenty of room on either side. Once he had it outside, Tommy pulled the airplane away from the hangar and sideways to it, so that the prop blast would not blow through the open door. The airplane was ready to start.

"It's a one-man operation," Tommy said as he rejoined them. "My uncle never wanted to have too many people here. Only our chief mechanic comes when we need him." He turned to Hawk. "The airplane is ready to go, Mr. Hawk. I think you know where the self-starter is. Come on, I will help you get organized in the cockpit."

Harry walked with them to the airplane, but once alongside, he turned to look back at the hangar and its surroundings. There was no question that this was where Riley's photos were taken. He had known that from the first time he had visited the field, when he watched Tommy fly. But now he was looking at things from the same angle that Riley's photographer had. He wondered if the photographer had also walked over here to look at an airplane. Like he had just done. Then he thought of what might have happened to the photographer, and little shiver went down his back. He turned completely around to look at the C-47 that brought them here. It was parked just a short distance away and looked like it belonged. Except for the inside walls and doors of the hangars that were made of steel, this airstrip in the jungle probably was just the way it was 60 years ago.

The P-40's great 12-cylinder Allison suddenly burst to life. Harry was close enough to feel the engine's thump in his chest. It had the sound of a race car, one of Hawk's Ferrari legends. Even if it could not achieve the Ferrari's distinctive high-pitched wail, it sounded more like that than the rumble of the big round engines on the C-47. He moved back a few paces to get completely out of the wind blast that the spinning propeller created. He saw Hawk, wearing his spectacles, staring intently at the gauges on the panel in front of him.

Tommy held his thumb up in the air and, when Hawk looked at him, brought his hand down and pointed straight ahead. Hawk snapped a small salute back at him and released the brakes. The P-40 lurched forward and Hawk taxied it out on the grass for about a hundred meters. There he turned it around and taxied back toward them, blipping the throttle as he came, making the engine roar. Harry waited for one of those roars to become a full-throttled rush across the grass that would lift Number 36 and Hawk into the sky. But Hawk was on his best behavior. He taxied up in front of them and cut the engine.

When it was quiet again, Hawk said, "I never thought I would do that again, not in an AVG P-40." And that was all. For the rest of the time, while they helped Tommy get the airplane back in the hangar, Hawk never said a word. Harry helped Tommy wipe grass off the landing gear and underside of the wings and fuselage. Hawk seemed preoccupied. He wandered around the hangar, just looking at things, just going through the motions. After a while he came back to the P-40.

"Well, I guess I won't have this chance again," he said. "Tommy, I'd like to spend a little time with this airplane. Just looking at it."

"No problem, Mr. Hawk. We have plenty of time."

Harry and Tommy walked out and sat on the grass in the shade of the hangar and gave Hawk some quiet time with the old airplane.

Chapter 21

"Okay, so both you guys got a good look at that airplane," Aloysious said. "What do you think we have?"

Aloysious got out of his seat right after the Gulfstream lifted off from the casino runway, and stood in the aisle. He had arranged the seats in the Gulfstream's main cabin so that Hawk, Harry, and Mouse were seated more or less in a row. All three were looking up at him.

"Well, Harry?" he added when the answer did not come quickly enough.

I think you should hear it from Hawk."

"Okay," Aloysious said, just a bit impatient now. "Hawk, what do you think? That airplane you guys just saw. Is it real?"

"It's real," Hawk said, nodding his head. "As real as I am."

"And it's an AVG airplane?"

Hawk nodded.

"You're sure of that?"

"I'm sure, Sunny." He turned to look at Harry. "Harry, you saw me. I crawled all over that airplane, especially when you and Tommy went outside. Everything looked good. And, when I got in the in the cockpit and cranked up that engine, I knew it was real. That was Eddie Rector's airplane; I don't question that. Eddie was a great pilot. He was a no-nonsense guy. He wouldn't have carved his initials in one of his airplanes, or scratched his name on its panel. There's nothing like that. But I know that was his airplane. I know I sat in it before. It was all so familiar. It

214

was like I was remembering it. The scuff marks, the dents in the metal, the wear on the seat. Its marks that I might have left. I sat in that seat, and I knew I sat there before."

Hawk watched Aloysious as he spoke. Sensing he had not said enough, he added, "That's all I can say, Sunny. The airplane looks real. It feels real. It's like an old friend. But I really can't prove that."

Hawk, Harry, and Aloysious looked at each other. Finally, Harry said it. "It had the patina, Hawk." It was a statement, not a question.

"It did. It had a fine patina."

"Okay," Aloysious said, "okay, you're telling me Number 36 is real. Fine. Now let me just review real quick where we stand. Harry has made an offer – ten million dollars for six P-40s – and Piggy has accepted that offer. Our concern is that the goods Mr. Piggy is offering are not genuine, that the airplanes are not real. Am I right so far?"

"You are right, Sunny," Harry said.

"Now, you're telling me that Number 36 is real. Okay, I'll buy that. But Number 36 is not part of the deal. Now, what about the other P-40s, the ones we saw at Flying Tiger Land. Those are the ones Piggy is offering to sell. Are they real or what? If they're real, we don't have a problem. If they're not real, we do. Hawk, what do you think?"

"I don't know how I could ever be completely sure. After seeing Number 36, my instincts tell me that the other P-40s are not real. I would have to say that they are copies. They are good copies, excellent copies. I don't know if they were built from scratch or from pieces of real airplanes. I don't know if you should call them copies, replicas, or forgeries. Whatever they are, they look great. They just don't feel right."

Aloysious sighed, loudly. "And that's a problem. Harry, what are your thoughts?"

"When I first saw Number 36, I felt just like Hawk. There was no question in my mind that it was a real AVG airplane. Now that I've seen it again, I still feel that way."

Harry shrugged and continued. "The other P-40s are more of a problem for me. I've looked at a lot of old airplanes over the years. I've listened to a lot of experts tell me what's good and what's bad. It's like any antique. After years of looking at old things, you get to know what you're seeing. You know what's real; you know what's not real. Nobody has to tell you. It's hard to explain this to somebody else. When I look at Piggy's airplanes, they all look good to me. All of them. If they're not real, they're great forgeries. They're great pieces of work. Even as copies they would just about be worth the money we're offering for real ones."

Harry stopped there for a second, letting all this sink in. Then he went on again. "But I don't have Hawk's experience. I never sat in an airplane that I knew for sure was a real AVG P-40. I never flew Ed Rector's Number 36 in 1942. Hawk did all of that. If he says that Piggy's P-40s at Flying Tiger Land are not real, I would have to go along with that."

"Well, then we do have a problem," Aloysious said. He sounded a little morose. "We're being offered six P-40s that we don't think are real. What the hell do we do?"

"Actually, we don't have to do anything," Harry said. "We haven't given Piggy any money. We can just walk away from the deal. Piggy won't ever know what happened to us. Let him look for Sunny Bright in Hong Kong. He won't find anything."

Aloysious looked at Harry, thinking. Finally, he said, "That's sort of defeatist, Harry. We can't just give up on this project. If there is one real P-40, that's the one we want. And both of you are telling me there is one."

"And that's the one Piggy won't sell," Hawk said, "which just convinces me that we're right. It's the one he wants to keep. That's the real airplane. It means we have one real P-40, and the rest are copies."

"That's a good point, Hawk," Aloysious said. "Let me ask both of you – and you too, Mouse – what the hell is going on. What is Piggy trying to pull?"

"He's trying to scam us," Hawk said.

Aloysious turned to Mouse. "Mouse," he said, "you've been very quiet, but I know nothing gets by you. What do you think is happening?"

Mouse looked first at Aloysious and then at Harry. She smiled a sweet smile. "You two should know," she said. "You are the experts of scam. But you ask me. I think Mr. Piggy always does the same thing. He gives people what they want and he gets as much money for it as he can. But in this case, I think there is more. He has a great respect for the Flying Tigers. I think more than money is involved."

Aloysious turned back to Harry. "What do you think?"

"Mouse has a good point. The airplanes really do mean something to Piggy. I'm sure it's really hard for him to give them up, replicas or not. But I can't say I know what's going on. It involves money for sure. But any worthwhile scam is about more than money." He looked up at Aloysious. "You know that."

Aloysious laughed. "You got me there, Harry. We've both done things that never brought us the big bucks we expected. And that was never the important thing, was it? You're right about that, Harry. But what I'm also hearing is that you guys are not sure what's going on. Well, I'm not either, but let me tell you what Sunny Bright thinks."

"I'm all ears, Sunny."

"Okay. Sunny Bright thinks Mouse is right. A Piggy cannot change his spots. Piggy is out to make money. On a substantial scale. That's what's happening. You are all looking for something more than that. I think that's all there is. Piggy said that he has a lot of money, but it's the wrong kind. He needs dollars, the stuff that buys you a good time anywhere in the world. You can't do that with Burmese kyat or Thai baht. Mr. Piggy needs dollars. That's his motivation. And I think that's all there is."

Harry thought about that. He shrugged his shoulders. "Okay," he said, "let's say you're right. Does that move us ahead? Does Sunny Bright say 'buy' or does he say 'pull out'?" This time when there was no quick answer, Harry looked at Aloysious and said, "Well?"

"I don't know, Harry. I don't have all the answers." He turned to Mouse. "Mouse, do you think the steward would fix us all a drink?"

For a while they all just sat, looked out the windows, and sipped their drinks. Hawk was the one to break their contemplation. "Boys," he said, "let me tell you what I have concluded," and that got their attention right away. "What I think is that Mr. Piggy is ready to take our money for questionable goods. Well, I don't think we should buy those goods." Aloysious started to interject at that point. Hawk stopped him with a raised finger. "Now, just hold on, Sunny. What I said is simple fact. I'm not being defeatist. But I see both of you drifting away from our goal. There is one airplane that both Harry and I think is real. Number 36. If any one of Piggy's airplanes is real, that's the one. Now, hold on, Sunny, I'm not finished. All I want to say is that Number 36 is the airplane that we want."

Aloysious was eager to jump in. "Right, Hawk, I agree. That's the one we want, but that's the one we won't get. It's not on offer. You both told me that's Piggy's favorite. It's the one we can't buy. Isn't that right?"

Harry nodded in agreement, while Hawk said, "I didn't say anything about buying that airplane."

Aloysious took a long look at him. "You're suggesting we 'acquire' that airplane by other means. Extra-legal means, perhaps?"

"Well, if you want to call it that," Hawk replied.

"Okay, you're suggesting we steal it."

"Yes, I am," Hawk answered, forthrightly. "I've been thinking about that a lot. When I met Harry's friend Riley, you know what he said? He said that Harry is one single-minded fellow. Harry would follow the trail until he found those airplanes. And then if nobody offered to sell them, well, Harry would just find a way to steal them. And that's what I've been thinking about."

"My pal, Riley." Harry said. He shook his head.

"No offense, Harry," Hawk said. "I didn't mean it in a bad way. I just wanted to illustrate that the only way we will get what we want is to take it. When we're dealing with somebody like Piggy, that doesn't count as stealing. That's what I'm trying to say. It's a matter of liberating."

Aloysious looked from one to the other. "I don't have much problem with that," he said. "But from what Harry told me, that airplane is locked in a steel box. How the hell do we go to steal it? I'm just looking at the practical side now, Hawk."

"I haven't figured that out yet," Hawk said, "but if you get me another double scotch, Sunny, I'll start working on it." As Aloysious started up, he added, "Oh, and there's something else I need – a map. The pilot should have one, or...Miss Mouse. Miss Mouse, didn't I see you with a map a little while ago? The scale of it doesn't matter."

Mouse had several very good maps of the area, and within minutes Hawk was contentedly sipping at his scotch and studying a map through the spectacles perched on his nose. After a while he looked up and asked, "Sunny, what is the name of your home town, that place up in the hills where you have your little retreat?"

"Sparrowfart, Hawk."

"Sparrowfart," Hawk repeated. The map rustled as he unfolded another section. "Well, I'm sure it's a place well named," he said. "Can you show me where it is on this map?"

"I'm not good with maps, Hawk. It's all that small print."

"I think I can," Mouse said. "Approximately."

"Approximately is fine, dear."

Mouse sat down next to him and pointed out features on the map while Hawk asked questions and jotted notes on the back of an envelope. Then he did some calculations. Mouse brought him a small writing pad which made it easier. Finally he put the map aside, sat back, took a big drink of scotch, and said, "Okay, I think I see how to do this, but I need to know a few things first. Harry, can you fly an airplane?"

"I can't fly a P-40, Hawk."

"No, that's not what I asked, Harry," Hawk said very carefully. "Can you fly a small single-engine airplane? Fixed landing gear, high wing, something like a Cessna or Piper?"

"I can handle that, I think."

"Good. Now, Miss Mouse, you seem to be in charge of this wonderful airplane we're riding on. I understand the captain is flying us into Bangkok." Hawk looked at his wristwatch. "We should be starting our descent in a few minutes. Do you think you can get him to divert to Chiang Mai in north Thailand? We're probably no more than 30 minutes from there."

Mouse made a little bow, stood up, and headed for the cockpit. Hawk turned to Aloysious. "Do you have an airstrip up there in Sparrowfart, Sunny?"

"We got nothing like that up there, Hawk. Nearest airport is a hundred miles away."

"Well, do you have any friends in Sparrowfart who can build you an airstrip? I don't mean anything fancy. No terminal buildings or anything. Just an airstrip, a short one? Doesn't need to be big enough for a P-40, just for a small plane."

"Maybe," Aloysious said, and immediately started seeing possibilities. "Yeah, we can do that." He thought about it. "Yeah, I think we can. We got a guy who could do that." He looked at Harry. "P.C. can do it. He was in the S.A.S or something like that."

"There's Reggie too," Harry offered. "He was with Wingate and the Chindits."

"Why, that's just perfect," Hawk said, looking up at them from his notes. "A man who was with the Chindits would know exactly what I want." Just then Mouse appeared. She nodded and said, "The captain said it would be no problem, Mr. Hawk. He expects to get his clearances and start his turn in a few minutes."

"Thank you, Miss Mouse. I have something else I need you to do." He passed her a pen and the writing pad. "Please write down for...what was his name? Reggie? Please write down for Reggie that, quote, 'Reggie will supervise the construction of an airstrip suitable for handling liaison-type airplanes, of the L-4 or L-5 class'. End quote. That's it, Miss Mouse. You get that to Mr. Reggie and he will know exactly what to do."

Hawk sat back and thought some more. "Now, I'm going to need some equipment, specifically some radio gear."

Harry caught Mouse's eye and nodded at her. "Mouse can help you with that."

Hawk turned to her. "So you're the logistician, dear. Well, here's what I will need.... Maybe you better take some notes."

Aloysious leaned toward Harry and quietly said, "Major Hawk is turning into a general. Right in front of our eyes."

Harry smiled and shrugged. "He's got something in mind. Let him run with it."

"I hope he tells us what it is."

Mouse filled up three pages of the writing pad with notes that Hawk dictated. "Well, I think that's all of it, young lady," he finally said. He looked around, caught the steward's eye and said, "Friend, could you freshen this up, please," and handed him his whiskey glass. Then he turned to Harry and Aloysious.

"Well, boys, I have done as much planning as I can. Now we have to do. What I would like is that when we get to Chiang Mai, you boys and Miss Mouse carry on to Sparrowfart. Miss Mouse tells me there will be a helicopter waiting to take you there. At Sparrowfart, Miss Mouse will give Reggie my note to build the airstrip. I added a comment on how I want it marked so it can be identified from the air. Then you all will have to wait for me. Miss Mouse is arranging communications gear. When I finish what I have to do, I'll be on the radio to tell you I'm on my way."

"And what are you going to do while we're building airfields at Sparrowfart, Hawk?" Aloysious asked.

"I'll be getting an airplane to get me up to Sparrowfart."

"Why don't you just come up to Sparrowfart with us in the chopper?"

"No, you don't understand. We're going to need the airplane that I will bring to Sparrowfart. Once I join you there, Harry and I will do some flying. I don't want to go into details now, but I will say this: 'We will strike from the sky!'"

"Now where have I heard that before?" Harry mumbled to himself.

"Now, that sounds like a real plan," Aloysious said with great enthusiasm.

Chapter 22

Fiesta!

Fiesta was not what they called it at Sparrowfart, but Fiesta was what it became. Although the night was black when the helicopter set them down quietly in an isolated clearing far from the nearest house, somebody in Sparrowfart saw something or heard something, or maybe just sensed something. Somebody on that dark night sat up in bed and said, "Aha! They are back."

By morning, the word was out. Aloysious – 'The Master of Small World' – had returned. Maybe even more exciting was the reputed re-appearance of little – 'Don't mess with'- Miss Mouse, who now enjoyed greater celebrity in Sparrowfart than any visitor in over half a century. By early morning, the parking lot at Small World was crowded with horn-tooting battered white pickup trucks jockeying for parking spaces, even as more trucks could be seen coming down the road. Adding to the parking frenzy was a rumor of a tribal group approaching from the west on a dozen elephants.

It was not simply the return of these 'celebrities' that caused such excitement. It was the expectation of things that would now happen. The return of any traveler meant new things, novel things, glimpses of things never seen or even considered before. It was generally assumed, for example, that on his travels Aloysious must have discovered secrets that would allow an improved version of Pachyderm – a tastier, more potent, and less expensive beer. There might even be a completely new product. Wine! There was much talk of wine. Wine was a good possibility. An excellent one! Were there not vineyards springing up everywhere in Asia? In China. In Vietnam. Even in neighboring Thailand! Why not Sparrowfart? Why not, indeed! Was Sparrowfart's earth not good enough? Was it not rich and fertile? Surely, in time the vineyards of Sparrowfart would rival those of Europe.

And what of Miss Mouse? Ah, now there was a mystery! Speculation was endless. Why would that capable, modern, and very beautiful young Miss Mouse return to this godforsaken corner of the earth that was Sparrowfart – unless...unless her return was somehow related to a project of great social and economic consequence!

One man recalled a traveler's recent remarks that Thailand's kickboxing champions had signed on to some kind of a 'World Tour'. Someone else remembered that the kickboxing impresario was a woman! Now that had to be Miss Mouse! Surely there could not be two like her. The kickboxers were probably on their way to Sparrowfart even now. And there were probably Japanese sumo wrestlers and Korean tae kwon do masters coming as well.

And that, of course, explained 'The Great Construction Project'! Everyone knew there was a construction project. No one claimed to know exactly what it was. The world's tallest TV tower, some thought. A dam to rival the one in China's Three Gorges, said others. But if Miss Mouse was brought into the equation, why – it was obvious! The project was a modern-day coliseum that would make Sparrowfart the world center for kickboxing, sumo, tae kwon do, and god knows what other Asian martial arts.

In the Small World restaurant toasts were made and many celebratory beers were consumed. The 'Miss Mouse Theory' explained all. It was comforting to know the answer and to be able to look into a future that was bright with promise. A promise that had nothing at all to do with economic ramifications or financial implications for Sparrowfart or its residents. It was a promise of entertainment, of things that would happen in Sparrowfart now, things that could be watched and marveled over. Things that could be talked about for days and weeks and months to come.

Despite all the revelry, the talk and the music and the periodic gunshot noises that emanated from unmuffled pickup trucks, Harry slept past noon. His room in the big old house was so far removed from the restaurant and its sounds that all he heard was a distant murmur. It was only when he stepped through the side door and onto the lawn that he was overwhelmed by the uproar produced by a hundred loud voices, laughter and music, and the grunts of trucks and animals. It was a country fair brought to life in the instant he stepped through the door. He could not see what was happening at the restaurant. Nor did he want to. He remembered the gazebo hidden among the dense vegetation to the rear and quickly turned in that direction.

"Good day, sir."

Harry looked down to see Bunster beaming up at him. "Bunster,' he said, "good to see you." They shook hands and Harry asked, "What the hell is going on out there?" The question was essentially rhetorical. Bunster's grasp of English was tenuous at best, and Harry got only a bigger smile as his answer. But from somewhere behind came the voice of Aloysious:

"Harry, over here."

Aloysious and P.C. sat at a small table on the far side of the gazebo. When he saw Harry, P.C. slid off his chair, stood at attention, and snapped a salute. Harry made a vague salute-like gesture with one hand while he grabbed a chair with the other and pushed it up to the table.

"What the hell is going on?" he asked again as he sat down.

Aloysious just shook his head and went back to buttering a piece of toast. P.C. answered, "Everyone from the region is here. Everyone pleased to see the 'Master of Small World' back, suh," he said, and bowed toward Aloysious. "It is a grand occasion. At Sparrowfart any occasion is an excuse for revelry."

As if to underline P.C.'s statement there was a thump of drums and a tinkle of bells that rose above the distant murmur of a hundred people talking all at once.

Aloysious looked up from his coffee. "It's because we came back. I don't know how the hell they find out so quickly, but they always do. Now they're excited. And it's great expectations time."

"Great expectations time?" Harry repeated.

"Yeah, you know. Great expectation of entertainment. And I mean entertainment beyond all the singing and dancing that will go on here. It's the way kids think. If somebody is back from somewhere, they must have something new. Or they know something. Something to astound and amaze."

The music coming from the restaurant got louder. They listened for a while. "Tonight there will be singing and dancing," Aloysious said. "And worse...." He looked at P.C. "What do you think, P.C.? Is there anything special we need to do? Maybe you and Mouse could put on another boxing exhibit. That would give them something to talk about."

P.C. ignored the last remark. "A few words from 'The Master' on his return would be appropriate, suh. A suggestion of great things to come. Perhaps comments on the construction project, suh."

"Construction project?" Aloysious said. "You mean the airstrip? How the hell did they find out about that?"

"They don't know it's an airstrip, suh," P.C. said, and then paused to consider this. "It might be best not to tell them what it is. We could say it's a polo field."

"Polo? I don't know anything about polo."

"They will know even less about polo than we do, suh."

"Do we need to hire some of them?"

"We can use a dozen. We will be lucky to find that many. Few will want to work. Everyone will want to watch.

Aloysious nodded. "Whatever you think, P.C. Hire who you need." The music was all tribal now, flutes and gongs, and getting louder. They listened for a while. "Do we have enough

Pachyderm to keep them happy for the next 24 hours or so?" Aloysious asked.

"I think so, suh," P.C. said. "Jock has the brewmeister duty. I think we're in good shape....Even with the elephants." It was evident from the casual way he slipped into 'the elephants', that this was an issue P.C preferred not to address. Aloysious's love-hate relationship with the big animals was well known, even in Sparrowfart. Just the word 'elephant' put him on immediate alert.

"Elephants," he said, and then he said "elephants" again. "Why?" he asked. P.C. was about to try to answer the question that had no answer for Aloysious, but Aloysious went on. "Useless beasts," he said. "They eat. They shit. They will crud up the parking lot. I guarantee it."

"No problem, suh. We'll keep them behind the hill. I think we can employ them in the construction project. They have great entertainment value."

Aloysious shook his head sadly and looked at his watch. "Speaking of construction, I hoped Reggie would come today. We need to talk."

"Suh," P.C. spoke up briskly, glad that the conversation was back to something manageable, "Reggie is already up on the hill across the road. He's surveying our new airstrip."

"He's there already?" Aloysious shook his head again, looking even sadder. "He knows too? Everybody does. They know what I'm doing before I even know that I'm going to do it." He turned to Harry with a look of resignation. "Come on, let's go across the road and see if we can find out what's going on."

Reggie was wearing a bush jacket and a broad-brimmed hat that kept the sun off his face. He was standing atop the small hill right across the road from the parking lot. It was not much of a hill, just tall enough to hide a view of the old rice fields that stretched from its foot to the small hills beyond. The rice fields long ago had fallen into disuse. The land was generally flat, but the fields themselves were divided into separate plots by small earthen dikes that controlled the flow of water when they were still in use many years ago. Now everything was brown and dried out.

"Good afternoon, Aloysious, Harry. Welcome back." Reggie nodded his greeting as they approached. They all shook hands and then turned to look across the fields.

"I have done just a preliminary survey," Reggie said, "but I think this is the best place for an airstrip. It's certainly level enough. We need to knock down some dikes, move a few big rocks and cut a bit of vegetation. Not much to it. From what your Major Hawk says, we don't really need much. Just enough length for liaison-type aircraft. I've marked off fifteen hundred feet. It's probably more than he needs, but it gives a bit of margin."

"What's Mouse doing out there?" Harry asked. She was standing out in the fields all by herself.

"She just paced off fifteen hundred feet," Reggie said. "You see where she is. It's not very far."

Just then Mouse turned, saw them, and waved. They all waved back.

Aloysious put his hand to his eyes, to shade them. "Reggie," he said, looking off in the distance, "one thing does bother me. We don't want our little airport here to be too easy to identify by somebody just passing by. Or flying overhead." He put down his hand and looked at Harry. "Just in case Piggy starts hunting us," he said. His eyes widened as he added, "Which is not unthinkable."

Harry could not disagree with that. It was something to ponder. They both turned to Reggie. "I think very few people will see an airfield here," Reggie said. "When we finish, it will appear much as it does now. From above it will all look like rice fields. To anyone passing on the road, it will also look like rice fields. The surface will be smoother. A few small sections of dike will be knocked down. But when the operation is complete, we can rebuild the dikes and no one will be the wiser."

"Yeah, but what about all these people?" Aloysious asked, throwing a glance over his shoulder. Even as he spoke, several happy family groups came walking up to join them on the hill, to see what was going on. "They all know about the big construction project," he went on. "And look, these people coming up here now. I'm sure they've already decided it's here. How long before the whole world knows about our airfield?"

"I don't think it's a problem," Reggie said. "This is a very exciting event in their lives. They will all come and watch – whether we allow it or not. Once they understand that what we are doing is 'quite illegal' – which we must make an effort to point out to them – they will tell no one. No one outside Sparrowfart will ever hear of it. It may surprise you, Aloysious, but they're very protective of you, Small World, and Pachyderm beer. You've made a big difference in their lives."

Aloysious looked a little skeptical, but said nothing. P.C. had joined them, and now added, "They need to watch, suh. We owe them a bit of spectacle. The elephants will be grand. We can use them as the earth levelers."

"Ah, I see," Aloysious said. "I figured all this softening up was leading somewhere. It's those goddamned elephants, isn't it? Okay, you guys want elephant road graders, go right ahead. Just don't call me when it's time to clean up the elephant shit."

*   *   *

As it turned out, the elephants stole the show. Or maybe they were the show. Reggie used them to move rocks, to pull up scraggy trees that were in the way, and to kick down the small earthen dikes. The hill was crowded with people every day. They came at sun-up, spread their mats, and opened their modest 'picnic hampers' which were really just the ordinary woven and lacquered food containers they used every day. But out here, with the elephants to watch, it was all very special, all very grand. They realized now, for the first time, that their simple food containers were useful and beautiful, and that the ordinary food they brought from their homes was quite delicious. When darkness fell, they packed up, left the hill, and walked across the road to the welcoming lights of Small World. Then the music would start, and the singing and the dancing.

The construction of the runway took two days. It could have been done in as many hours. Reggie and P.C. kept the beasts working at a slow and steady pace, with many water breaks, when the beasts were at their best. Great vats were borrowed from the Pachyderm brewery and filled with all the water the beasts could want. To drink, to splash, to fill their great long trunks and blow back on the spectators sitting on the hill, like a sudden, warm midsummer shower. It made the nearest spectators scatter and brought gales of laughter from the rest.

Elephants are not only among the most intelligent of creatures, but a fair percentage of them are born actors. It was not long before the elephants figured out that their job was to entertain and that the 'work' part of the contract was incidental. When the work on the runway was extended well beyond any reasonable time, P.C. remembered that he had once said that the project could be called a polo field. It was an inspired thought. All elephants love playing polo.

In this way the best part of a week passed. While the elephants entertained themselves and the inhabitants of Sparrowfart, Mouse was at work. She set up the communications gear that would let them talk with Hawk, when he eventually appeared. The gear itself was not much. A small black box-like thing with a dangling microphone. Mouse put it on one of the small tables in the gazebo and explained its workings to Harry, Aloysious, and all the staff. She manned it herself mornings and early evenings, the time when it was most likely that Hawk would appear. In between, someone from the Small World staff was assigned to be within earshot, waiting for that first crackle of static that would announce that Hawk was nearby. Before anyone much noticed, a week had passed.

At breakfast on the eighth day, Aloysious observed, "What the hell is going on, Harry? I thought Hawk was going to rent an airplane in Thailand and come right up here. It's been over a week now."

"I think what Hawk was planning to do was more complicated than that," Harry said, although he was not really sure.

"Maybe when he had a chance to look over his plan, he saw it wasn't worth much. You know, he's not a young man, Harry." Not quite sure how the two statements fit together, Harry said nothing. Finally, Aloysious asked, "Do you think he's pulled out on us?"

"No, I don't think so," Harry said with as much conviction as he could muster. "Give him another day or two."

On the ninth day, Harry and Aloysious were having a late afternoon beer, talking about this and that, when Bunster interrupted, "Sir, sir." He was obviously very agitated, and his English would not take him beyond that. Finally he added a frustrated, "Miss Mouse, Miss Mouse," and pointed to the table where the small communications device rested. "What's up, Bunster?" Aloysious asked. "Mouse is over on the hill with Reggie," he added. By then Harry had grasped what was happening and was on his feet, but Bunster beat him to the table and turned up the volume.

"Mouse, Mouse, Mouse Base," the radio said. "Hawk Flight calling Mouse Base. Mouse Base, do you read me? Over." The radio repeated, "Mouse Base, this is Hawk Flight. Do you read me? Do you read me? Over."

Harry finally got around Bunster and grabbed the microphone. "Hawk Flight, Hawk Flight," he repeated. "This is Mouse Base. We read you loud and clear. Over."

"Hey, Harry!" Hawk's voice was loud now. "I must be right over your location. Do you hear my engine?"

So much for radio protocols, Harry thought. "Hang on, Hawk," he said into the microphone. "We have some loud music here. I have to shut it down." He turned to Bunster. "Tell those guys to knock off the music for a few minutes." Bunster hurried down the path toward the restaurant. In the background, Hawk's voice could be heard. "Well, I'm glad you boys are having a good time."

Mouse came jogging down the path, almost running over Bunster heading the other way. When she saw Harry, she pointed straight up and shouted, "Airplane!"

Harry did not wait for Mouse to reach him. "Hawk, we have you right overhead. Do you see the runway?"

There was silence for a couple of seconds and then, "Harry, all I see is what looks like an animal preserve. There's a whole gang of elephants chasing each other around. Probably some kind of mating thing."

"That's the runway, Hawk. The elephants are friendlies. We'll have them make room for you. When you land, don't let them get too friendly."

Again, there was a quiet interval before Hawk responded, "You're kidding, right, Harry? Listen, I told Mouse how to mark the airstrip. Could you ask her...."

Mouse was nodding as she turned and started to run back to the airstrip.

"Okay, Hawk. The runway will be marked in a minute. Stand by."

The scene was surreal, like something a movie director would work on all day to get just right. Spectators stood and sat and squatted all over the top and sides of the hill, everyone talking excitedly. Below them, the elephants were now grouped close together, their huge bodies swaying restlessly. People and elephants looked out over the rice fields toward the hills where the sun was settling in. Watching, waiting for something to happen. A single figure, a featureless silhouette against the sun, walked back from the fields where she had just formed an 'X' with strips of white cloth. From somewhere behind them came a small silver airplane that glittered in the waning sun and glided quietly toward the 'X'. Chatter ceased. Silence was complete. Then a single elephant lifted his trunk toward the sky and trumpeted a welcome.

When the airplane's wheels touched down, P.C., Bunster, and Jock ran out to meet it. They stood back while the pilot climbed out, then walked over to help him unload whatever the airplane carried. The pilot pointed to two big boxes and some small bags. P.C. and Jock each took a box, flung it up on a shoulder, and started carrying it away.

"That's the plastique, boys," Hawk said. "The explosives. Oh, that's all right," he added, when Jock reacted with a little hop. "You don't have to worry, son. It won't go off without the detonators." He turned around to Bunster, who was balancing a small wooden box in one hand while tugging a bag out of the airplane with the other.

"Now those are the detonators," Hawk said, pointing at the little wooden box. "Don't you drop that box, young fellow. If you do, it will blow your ass right over that hill over there."

Bunster did not understand all the words, but he certainly got the gist of what Hawk meant. He might have been walking on eggs as he carried the small box across the road.

Chapter 23

Crack!

A muscle in Aloysious' neck twitched in response, but otherwise he ignored the sound. "Okay, Harry," he said, "so you guys went flying this morning. And you're going to do it again tomorrow?"

Blap!

Aloysious flinched.

"Yeah, Hawk wants me to get familiar enough with the airplane," Harry said. "It's no big deal flying it. It's just that I haven't flown anything in years."

"P.C. said he helped you scrape all the identification off the airplane. Even took some number plates off the engine."

"Yeah, if anything goes wrong, Hawk doesn't want it to blow back on his friend in Thailand who loaned him the airplane."

Kerploww! Blooom!

That brought both of them upright in their chairs. Off in the distance they heard cheers and what sounded like applause. Aloysious frowned and shook his head. He stood up, stepped to the edge of the gazebo, and stared up through the trees at a small visible patch of sky. There he could see a column of smoke and dust rising.

"Damn," he said, "I wish P.C. and Hawk would find someplace else to blow things up."

"P.C. thought they may as well do it where everybody could

watch. You can't set off explosives anywhere around here and try to hide it. Doing that would cause more of a fuss."

"Yeah, I guess. But what the hell are they doing? Practicing?"

"Well, not exactly. It's more like R&D. Hawk needs to blow out a door, and they're trying to get the charge just right."

"Do they know what the hell they're doing?"

"P.C. is pretty good with explosives. He's bringing Hawk up to speed."

"How long will this go on?"

"Till they get it right, I guess."

"Wonderful. Has Hawk told you any more about his plan?"

"No. He promised to brief us as soon as he works out what he calls the 'technical' details. I think the main hang-up right now is sorting out the bomb plan. We're going to have to blow our way into the hangar."

"This is starting to get complicated," Aloysious said. "You're taking flying lessons. P.C. is blowing shit up. Mouse has become a communicator and administrative assistant. What next?"

Harry was about to say that Hawk was considering Aloysious for the project historian slot, when Hawk himself strolled into the gazebo and sat down at their table. Bunster poured a Thai beer disguised as a bottle of Pachyderm while Aloysious rubbed the back of his neck. "Hot work," he said and took a big drink.

He put the glass down carefully and looked up at them. "Gentlemen," he said, "you may have noticed some bangs out there this morning. That was just me and P.C. We were practicing blowing down the hangar door. Not the main door, you understand, just the little one on the side."

He turned to face Harry. "I think you know what I'm talking about, Harry. When we were up there, you and Tommy were sitting out on the grass, I was inside that hangar, looking at the doors and the walls. Looking for a way in. The only weak point in that steel box is that side door where we first went in." He swiveled around so he could address Aloysious as well as Harry and went on:

"The main hangar door is too big and heavy," he explained. "It's all steel. If we try to blow it and don't get it exactly right, it could get stuck in place. We would never be able to move it then. We could never get the airplane out." He stopped to take another drink of beer before continuing.

"That small side door is made like the door on a bank vault. A cheap bank vault, fortunately. Whoever did it didn't have his heart in the job. The craftsmanship is very poor. The locking bolts that go into the frame are short, and there's only half as many as there should be. I really examined that thing. I even sketched it. I have a friend in Thailand – the same one who loaned me that little silver airplane out there. We ran some computer simulations. If we punch that lock the right way with the plastique, the pressure will snatch those locking pins right out of the door frame. P.C. has a lot of practical experience blapping stuff with plastique. He agrees that's the way to do it."

Aloysious listened carefully, interest showing on his face. His eyebrows rose high on his forehead when Hawk mentioned 'computer simulations'. When Hawk finished, Aloysious nodded and said, "Okay, so you blow your way into the hangar. Then what?"

"The rest is easy. Harry knows the layout. There's a generator in a shed outside the hangar. We have to get that turned on. That will lift the main door for us. Then we just wheel the airplane out, and off we go. The airplane has got a self-starter. Thanks to Tommy, I remember how it works. When you guys were out on the grass, I checked the fuel tanks. They're full, except for the little I burned off when I taxied the airplane around. There's enough fuel to make it to Thailand."

Aloysious looked puzzled. "Thailand? I thought you're bringing it back here. Isn't that what we built the airstrip for?"

"Nope," Hawk said. Another swallow of beer and he added, "When we go into that hangar, it will be like kicking over a hornet's nest. There's an alarm system that I'm sure is connected right back to the casino and god knows where else. When it goes off, I expect the first reaction will be from those 'troops' we took up there in the C-47." He looked at Harry. "You know more about how long it will take them to get by road from the casino to the airstrip, Harry. I figure we safely have about 15 minutes to do our thing and get out of there."

"I didn't know there was an alarm," Harry said.

"I would not have either," Hawk said, "if I had not been so interested in the lock on that side door. That's how I found it. Anyway, the alarm means that Piggy will know pretty quick that somebody is messing with his airplane. We want to get that P-40 as far away as we can – as quick as we can. Once I land it in Thailand, the airplane will disappear. Nobody will ever find it."

"Wait a minute, Hawk," Aloysious said. "Hang on. You're going to take the airplane and fly it to Thailand? Then you're going to make it disappear? That raises a few questions. And what is Harry's job in all this?"

"Harry's job is to fly me and P.C. up to the jungle airstrip and then bring himself, P.C., and the little silver airplane back here."

"P.C. is going with you to the airstrip?"

"I need P.C. up there. He's awfully good with the plastique. The charge has got to be set just right to get that lock open. If it gets screwed up, the door will jam, and we'd never get to the airplane. I don't want to risk trying it by myself. I just don't have the experience P.C. has."

"Okay, I understand that. But why do you want Harry to come back here? Why can't he follow you to Thailand?"

"Having Harry follow me to Thailand just isn't practical, Sunny. Here, let me see if I can explain that." He looked around, caught Bunster's eye, and gestured. When Bunster came over, he said to him, "Young fellow, could you find Miss Mouse and ask her to bring us those aeronautical charts? Tell her it's the ones we marked up."

The incomprehension on Bunster's face turned to distress. "I'll help Bunster get the charts," Harry said getting to his feet. "Come on, Bunster."

As he and Bunster started down the path to the big house, he heard Hawk say to Aloysious, "You know, this won't be the first time that old Number 36 pays a visit to Thailand. It went there way back in March of 1942. That's when the Flying Tigers attacked the Jap air base at Chiang Mai. The AVG lost Jack Newkirk that day. And Black Mac McGarry."

Harry did not hear the rest. But he knew the story that Hawk went on to tell Aloysious.

"Claire Chennault saw the need to strike back at the Japanese. Their infantry had pushed up through Burma; the Jap air force shot up the airfields. The AVG was hit really hard. They lost some people and a bunch of airplanes on the ground. The AVG had to pull back to Kunming. The 'Old Man' wanted to hit them at Chiang Mai where they had a major air base. The Japanese felt safe there. North Thailand was well beyond the range of the P-40s operating out of China. But the Japanese did not realize how determined the AVG was, and that they would stage the P-40s to Chiang Mai via a couple of small airstrips in Burma that were still in British hands. The Japanese were not expecting the Flying Tigers when six P-40s appeared in the sky early that morning on 24 March 1942. I remember that date well; it was a great victory for the Flying Tigers."

Hawk took a drink from his beer and continued. "Japanese airplanes were lined up in rows along the runway, about 40 in all. Four of the P-40s dove down on them and started shooting. Ed Rector – he was in Number 36 – and Black Mac McGarry in Number 69, those two boys stayed up on top, just in case any of the Japanese fighters were already in the air. Well, they were not; the Flying Tigers just got there too early for them. So, Rector and McGarry dove down to join the fray. By now the Japanese anti-aircraft gunners were well stirred up. Rector and McGarry both made one pass over the field. Then Black Mac turned back to make a second one. That was not a good idea. His airplane got hit by ground fire, but he joined up with the rest, and the boys started back to Burma. Black Mac had trouble keeping up. It's rough country there, and between them and Burma were mountains. Ahead was a ridge that Black Mac just couldn't get over. So he rolled his airplane on its back, unfastened his straps, and dropped out. Rector saw Black Mac land in his parachute in a little clearing. He dropped him a map and a chocolate bar, and waved goodbye."

Harry was hurrying back down the path with Mouse in tow when he heard Hawk ask, "Do you know what happened to

Black Mac?" Aloysious shook his head, and so Hawk told him, "That jungle is thick up there. Black Mac wandered around for three weeks. Nothing to eat but the chocolate bar that Ed Rector dropped him. He about reached the end of his rope when the Thai police found him. They had to turn him over to the Japs, who were occupying their country. The Japs took him down to Bangkok. They kept him locked up there until the Thai guerrillas broke him out in 1945."

As Harry and Mouse stepped into the gazebo, Hawk asked, "Do you know that story, Harry? How Chennault learned that Black Mac was alive? How the Free Thai got him out?" He did not wait for Harry's answer.

"Chennault heard that Black Mac was a POW in Bangkok. The OSS was operating there. The Office of Strategic Services. They were an like an early-day CIA, and Chennault probably heard about Black Mac from them. He told OSS he wanted Black Mac out, wanted him brought back to Kunming." Hawk took a big swallow of beer to help finish the story.

"Well, OSS turned the job over to the Free Thai guerrillas. Those Free Thai boys located Black Mac in a compound, right on the bank of the Chao Phya – that's the river that runs right through Bangkok. The Free Thai did some of their magic and got him out. Then they put him on a boat and went through the canals and down the river – all way to the Gulf of Siam. Right under the noses of the Japs! The OSS sent in not one, but two PBY Catalina flying boats. They landed those airplanes on the Gulf and picked up Black Mac. Took him to Ceylon and put him in another airplane that flew him to China. Chennault met him at the Kunming airport. Ed Rector was there too. Chennault never told Ed that Black Mac was on the airplane they were meeting. He let it be a big surprise! Can you imagine that? Ed had last seen Black Mac, looking very forlorn, standing in that clearing in the Thai jungle. Three years passed. Everybody thought Black Mac was gone. And then that airplane door opens, and there he stands, Black Mac."

Aloysious shook his head. "That's quite a story, Hawk," he said.

"Yes, it is. And it's all true. I was in Kunming then. It was Eddie Rector who told me all about it. Well, there's Miss Mouse. I see she has brought me my aeronautical charts. I guess we better get back to business, boys."

Hawk spread the map out on the table in front of them and flattened it with both hands. "Okay," he said, looking up at them over the spectacles he had just popped on his nose. "I have calculated and recalculated. I have enough fuel to get all the way down to here." He tapped at a red mark near the center of the map with his finger. "So getting there is not a problem at all. The problem is what do you do when you get there? Just where the hell do you land? Now, look at this map," he said, and they all looked down again. "There are lots of hills and few airfields. And all those are totally government-controlled. Unlike your Sparrowfart neighborhood, there are no uncontrolled airstrips in north Thailand that you can just sneak into. There are none at all. But look here." Hawk tapped another place on the map with his finger and their eyes went to the spot. "There was an old strip right here. It was closed down a long time ago. But then, recently, a movie company decided to shoot a film there. That strip is open now. Or let's say it can be made open – if you know the right people."

"And you know the right people, Hawk?" Aloysious said.

"I have contacts with those involved," Hawk said.

"Okay," Harry said. "You have a place to land the airplane in Thailand. But what then? Where do you put the P-40? That thing will draw a hell of a lot of attention. How do you keep it out of sight? And how do we ultimately get it out of Thailand when we want to?"

"Well, all of that is really quite simple." Hawk looked up, first at Harry, and then at Aloysious. The spectacles made his eyes big. Like a wise old owl. He went on. "It is quite simple if you have the right contacts – and just a little bit of luck. And maybe just a happy coincidence or two. It turns out the movie company is bringing in all kinds of props. That includes vehicles, container loads of things like that. An airplane is a vehicle, and as I have certain contacts, our P-40 will be registered as a prop.

It will be slightly disassembled and stored in a shipping container. Not much more than the wings will have to come off. Once the film shoot is completed, the P-40 will be returned to America with the other props. Except for my friends who will help with this, no one will be the wiser. When the shipping containers get to the West Coast, we take charge of the airplane again."

"What if someone starts looking for a lost airplane?" Aloysious asked.

"Well, I don't think that will happen, "Hawk said. "Somehow I don't think that Mr. Piggy will report his loss. At least not to Interpol."

"No, but he may have a lot of other people stirred up."

"You are certainly right about that, Sunny. And that is why I think it's important to get that P-40 to Thailand as soon as I can, and into that shipping container, hidden as a movie prop. The movie company will have so much stuff around that it will be well hidden."

Aloysious looked at Hawk for a long quiet moment. Then he nodded and smiled. Harry could hear admiration is his voice when he said, "It's a totally brilliant scheme, Hawk. It really is. I like the part where the P-40 becomes a movie prop." He looked at Harry. "There's no question in my mind that this will work," he said, then turned back to Hawk and added, "so long as nothing goes wrong. And assuming your contacts are responsible people who can keep their mouths shut." He turned back to Harry. "I like it. What do you think?"

"Sounds pretty good to me," Harry admitted. "At some point, though, I'd like to get to Thailand to see that movie set and how they pack the P-40."

Aloysious nodded. "I agree," he said, and turned back at Hawk. "In fact," he added, "I was asking why Harry can't follow you up there in the little airplane?"

"And I was saying, it is impractical." Hawk smoothed out the map again. "Putting aside the difference of speed – I mean the little silver airplane just couldn't keep up with the P-40 – but you are right, I could give Harry a compass course and he could follow on later. Meet me there. The real problem, though, is fuel. There will be three of us when we leave here to go up to Mr. Piggy's jungle airstrip. That little airplane will be heavy and can't take on a full fuel load. That's why I said it was impractical for Harry to follow me right away. What I suggest is that Harry bring P.C. back here and drop him off. Then he can take on a full load of fuel. He can carry extra if he needs it. We can calculate all that."

Aloysious looked at Harry. Harry nodded and said, "That sounds reasonable. I'll need help plotting a course."

"No problem," Hawk said. "I'll show you where to go. You don't want to land where I am. You go right to Chiang Mai, give the airplane back to my friend. He'll give you a car to drive to where I am at the movie set. I'll plot all that out on a map for you, Harry."

"Great!" Aloysious said. "That's a plan."

That night Hawk and Harry plotted out on a map of north Thailand the course that Harry would fly. As Hawk drew in a line that led toward the airfield at Chiang Mai, his pencil suddenly stopped in mid-course.

"Look here," he said to Harry. "This is where Black Mac went down. Your course will take you just a little south of there. It was right around this ridge where his airplane hit. That is really rough terrain, as you can see. All hills and jungle and nothing but animal trails that lead nowhere. Do you know they found Black Mac's airplane back in about 1990?"

"Yeah, I heard that, Hawk. I understand the airplane was all junk. The Royal Thai Air Force pulled it out."

"Yes, there was not much left. It was almost fifty years after it crashed that they found it. That is certainly rough ground." Hawk winced. He looked up at Harry with a small smile. "When you pass over that ground, son, you make sure you stay high. And you keep your propeller turning. You don't want to go down in that place."

"I sure don't, Hawk," Harry said, looking down at the corrugated section of earth shown on the map. "I don't have fifty years for somebody to find me."

Chapter 24

T he first gray light of dawn was just breaking over the hills, but all of Sparrowfart was there. The little silver airplane was loaded and gassed up. The three crew, having said their goodbyes, stood by the airplane door. Aloysious, Reggie, Mouse, and Bunster stood nearby, and looked solemnly on.

"Time to move," Hawk said, and motioned Harry to the seat on the left. "You fly, Harry. I'll do the navigating." P.C. squeezed into the back seat, next to the cargo.

When the engine was turning smoothly, and the nose was pointed at the distant hills, Harry pushed in the throttle. As they started to roll, Harry waved in the direction of his friends and took a last look at the crowd on the hill. It felt strange to be setting off this way, enroute to a major crime with a thousand witnesses to see them off.

The aircraft felt heavy. It was probably overloaded with the three of them, the heavy boxes of plastique, and as much fuel as Hawk judged they could carry. There was little else on board – a few water bottles and a small carry-on bag of personal things that Hawk would take with him in the P-40.

The little airplane just ran on and on across the old rice fields, gaining speed slowly, seeming not to want to leave the ground. "Just let her build up speed, Harry," Hawk said. They reached the end of the leveled strip of rice field that was the runway.

Harry eased back on the yoke; the nose pointed up, and the little airplane started to rise. Slowly. Tenuously.

Hawk held the map in his hand, but never looked at it. He must have memorized their route and knew exactly where they were. They stayed low, a hundred feet above the trees. There was no one down there to see them, but Hawk felt better if they were down where they would not be seen from any distance.

The jungle airstrip was not far by air, but it took a lot of time for a craft as slow as theirs. There was no conversation on this journey; each was alone with his own thoughts. After what seemed a long time, and when he judged they were maybe 15 minutes away, Hawk finally spoke. "I'll take it in ten minutes, Harry. I want to go straight in and cut the engine just before we reach the strip. Unless somebody is standing right in the middle of the field, looking in our direction, no one in the area will even notice us arrive. Flying that C-47 over here with Tommy was good practice."

When the ten minutes were up, Hawk took the controls and tucked the airplane in, just above the jungle canopy. After a couple of minutes, he shut down the engine. With no power, the airplane sank lower, heading down. Harry had just a fraction of a moment to feel concern when the airstrip popped up in front of the nose. Hawk set the airplane down on the grass and let it run toward the hangar. It stopped rolling about 50 meters short. They sat and listened.

"See anything?" Hawk asked.

"Nothing. I think we're okay."

"Let's get out. We need to roll the airplane just a little closer and get it pointed into the wind. Then we can unload."

In their pre-mission briefing, Hawk had explained how he expected things to go and the specifics of each man's role. Once they unloaded the plastique from the airplane, P.C. and Hawk would set the charge on the door. Harry's job was to stay with the airplane and keep a lookout for any unexpected visitors. If he saw something he didn't like and if it looked serious enough, he was to start the airplane's engine. That would be the signal for Hawk and P.C. to abandon immediately whatever they were doing and come right back to the aircraft.

Harry sat in the airplane's left seat and watched the far side of the field where he thought any patrol would appear. He could not keep from glancing over to the hangar where Hawk and P.C. worked, setting the explosives against the door. Everything seemed to be on track. As soon as the charge was set and ready to be detonated, Hawk and P.C. would walk down the side of the hangar, well away from the blast. After the explosion, P.C. would go directly back to the door, while Hawk would first stop by the shed where the generator was kept and turn it on. Harry's job would be to start counting down the 15 minutes that Hawk thought they had before the reaction force arrived.

Harry let his eyes sweep over the field. Everything was clear. He looked back again to Hawk and P.C, but there was little to see. Their backs were to him. They were bent over, and their bodies hid what they were doing. Just then a puff of smoke rose in the air above them and Hawk backed away. In P.C.'s hand was a section of smoking primer cord that he carefully lowered to the ground. That was it! The fuse was burning.

Hawk and P.C. walked down the side of the building, slowly and deliberately. Harry could not take his eyes from the smoke that crawled up the primer cord toward the explosive charge strapped to the door. He hoped he was far enough away. He turned to take one last look across the field when the smoke reached the charge.

BALOOOM !

The explosion was louder than he expected. Bells rang in his ears. The entire side of the hangar was hidden by smoke and dust. A small cloud of debris whirled above the door and slowly collapsed. He got a glimpse of P.C. running toward the door before he disappeared in the smoke. He could not see Hawk at all.

Belatedly Harry started the 15-minute countdown, pausing to turn the minute hand of his wristwatch to the top of the dial. Hawk was right about most things and Harry did not want to mess up the count. He looked back at the hangar. The smoke was clearing. He could see both Hawk and P.C. now, standing by the door. It looked like the door was still there and they were pushing at it.

Hawk suddenly turned and jogged over in Harry's direction. Halfway there he stopped, turned away from the hangar, and dropped down on one knee. He turned his face toward Harry. "One of the damn locking pins is still holding," he shouted. "P.C. is going to try again. How much time do we have?" He sounded far away.

"Thirteen minutes, fifteen seconds," Harry shouted back. Hawk got down flat on his stomach. They both watched P.C. walk away from a smoking charge at the corner of the door.

BLAAM!

It went off before Harry was ready. The fuse was short. Through the smoke and dust he could make out the gap where the door had been. "He did it!" Hawk shouted. He got to his feet and started for the hangar.

It was hard for Harry to just sit there and not to join them. He scanned the field again, but then a movement at the hangar caught his eye. The main hangar door was slowly lifting. He wondered about that, but only briefly. There was no sound from the generator that he could hear, but then there was little he could hear with all the bells ringing in his head. Harry turned back to scanning the airstrip.

His wristwatch told him they still had more than four minutes when Harry saw the first jeep drive into the clearing and stop. He looked back at the hangar. Nothing seemed to be happening. The jeep stayed at the edge of the clearing, probably waiting for the second jeep that was now emerging from the jungle. Together the two jeeps started across the grass, heading right for the hangar. He could see four men in each vehicle. What looked like a heavy machine gun was mounted on a rack above the windshield of one of the jeeps.

Without thinking, Harry shouted, "Hawk, P.C.! Let's go!" They probably could not hear him inside the hangar. Then reason returned. Harry reached for the starter and pulled. The airplane's engine started immediately, but its sound was drowned out by a much greater roar. Harry looked up at the hangar in surprise. The two jeeps heading for it were halfway there.

Then the P-40 emerged from the hangar, propeller whirling. It was all smoke and sound, like a huge beast on a rampage, bellowing in rage. The P-40 was not taxiing. The engine roared at full power; Hawk was taking off – right out of the hangar!

Harry watched in fascination as the distance between the P-40 and the jeeps grew shorter and shorter. The P-40 was moving faster now, but still not fast enough to break free of the ground. The jeeps coming toward it were moving fast too, getting closer and closer to the whirling propeller. For god's sake, Harry thought, Hawk and the jeeps were playing chicken!

Just when it seemed the two jeeps would plunge into the spinning propeller, they veered off, one to each side and Hawk went right up the middle. He kept the P-40 moving in a straight line, and within moments it lifted off the field, wheels retracting into the wings as it struggled for altitude.

"Got to go, suh!" P.C. was already in the right seat, door closed. Harry never saw him get in.

"We can't. They're in the way," Harry said, looking at the jeeps that straddled the piece of the airstrip that he needed to take off. "If we go now, we'll just be a target for them."

P.C. stared out the windshield. "Shit!" he said, quietly. The jeeps were stopped now, still facing the hangar. Their occupants had all turned, looking over their shoulders at the departing P-40. Suddenly, two or three of them started waving their arms and pointing in the direction the P-40 had gone. The jeeps started moving again, spun around and headed back in the direction they came, barely missing each other as they turned.

"What the hell are they doing?" Harry said. He knew, but he needed to reassure himself that what he was seeing was really happening.

"They're chasing him. They don't know what else to do, suh. It's our chance. Go, Harry!"

"Not yet. Not yet," Harry said. The temptation was great to open the throttle and get the hell out of there. But timing was critical; he had to be right on. He was sure they had not been noticed by the men in the jeeps. That was his margin, the small bit of time it gave him to do it right. They had one chance only. It had to be right. "Stand by, P.C.," he said. "We'll get out of here."

The jeeps stopped again and faced to where they had last seen the P-40. Harry looked in that direction too and scanned the sky. The P-40 reappeared, in a wide turn, heading back toward them. Near the edge of the field, not far from the jeeps, it started to turn again. Harry set the brake on the silver airplane, pushed the door open and stuck his head out to get a better view. Hawk was turning little circles in the P-40 now, and each one took the P-40 just a little farther down the edge of the field. Over the sound of his own idling engine, Harry could hear the P-40. Its engine was sputtering and backfiring. He quickly shut the door.

"He's in trouble," P.C. said as he watched Harry strap himself in.

"No, I don't think so. He's trying to decoy them. Lure them over there. If they move just a bit more, we may have a chance."

As they waited to see what would happen, P.C. said, conversationally, "There was a car in the hangar. It was beautiful. My second charge blew away its whole side."

"Oh, shit," Harry moaned. His spirits sank. At that moment, damaging something that was not even involved in their scheme seemed a greater sin than stealing Mr. Piggy's favorite airplane. If they were to be punished, it was for that.

The jeeps turned again, following in the trail of the P-40. It took them even farther from the hangar. They were chasing Hawk, and everyone in the jeeps was focused on the Flying Tiger P-40. They would never notice the small silver airplane on the far side of the field when it started to move.

"Make sure your seat belt is tight, P.C. A bit more and we're on our way." Harry kept his hand on the throttle and watched. The P-40's circle was wider this time and just a little farther down the edge of the field. The jeeps kept moving that way. "Hang on, P.C. Here we go!"

It was an almost perfect getaway, but not quite. The 'troops' in the jeep never heard their engine. Hawk kept his turns close to the jeeps and made as much noise as he could. The man with the machine gun was sweating heavily and cursed in frustration. He tracked the P-40 with his gun, but he was afraid to fire. He knew the importance of this airplane to Mr. Piggy. He did not want to be the one who damaged it.

No one in the jeeps would have noticed the little silver airplane if one of the younger 'troops' had not felt a sneeze coming. It was because of all the dust that had been raised by the P-40 and the jeeps. Before he sneezed, the young man politely turned his head to the side – and that was when he saw the little silver airplane scurry across the field.

The young 'trooper' finished his sneeze, wiped his nose with one hand, and with the other slapped the back of the man beside him and pointed. That man leaned forward and poked the machine gunner, who angrily turned around, ready to throw a punch. But then he too saw the little silver airplane stumbling into the air. His heart leaped. A target he could shoot and kill and not worry about. By now the driver saw the airplane and turned the jeep toward it. The machine gunner took aim, pulled the trigger and held it down, sending a stream of hot metal after the little airplane they were now chasing.

Harry was totally focused on getting the little silver airplane into the sky. As soon as he had the airspeed, he eased back the yoke. Just to make sure, he told the airplane what he wanted. "Up, up, up," he said. P.C. looked out the side window, watching something that Harry could not see. Harry sensed that not everything was going according to plan, and then felt the thuds of things striking the fuselage. The airplane shuddered violently and the plexiglas window behind him shattered and blew away. Over the howl of wind rushing through the hole, he heard P.C.'s voice.

"What the hell! What's happened, suh?"

"We took some hits." Harry realized he was shouting. "I think it's just the ass end." He looked at the instruments and moved the controls. "Everything is working. We'll be okay, P.C."

Harry did not really think they would be okay. It was a long way back, and they had just been hit by a lot of stuff. He had a vivid picture in his mind of the engine cowling jumping up when he felt the thuds. If something in the engine was hit, their chances of getting back to Sparrowfart were very small. One thing he had to do was to stretch out the flight, get as far away from the airstrip and the patrols as he could. The airplane was still flying, and that was a comfort. If he could get up higher, maybe he could stretch it all the way to Sparrowfart. What the hell! He looked over at P.C. and grinned.

They had another four or five minutes in the air, and then the engine quit. Just like that. Harry was pretty relaxed by then. Everything had been working fine; the engine was running smoothly. The sound of wind whistling through the hole where the window had been faded into the background.

"Shit!" Harry said. His voice boomed out in what seemed like total silence now that the engine noise had stopped.

"Shit!" P.C. said in agreement, his voice absolutely calm.

Harry went through the drill, trying to restart the engine, but with little hope that it would. All the while he looked outside, as he was supposed to, trying to find that open field his flight instructor always talked about. It was pointless, really; he knew that. There was nothing down there for as far as he could see in any direction, but trees and trees. Thousands of trees! Millions of them! And all bunched together. There was no clearing big enough to let a tree fall flat, let alone for an airplane to land. They were going down fast.

"Broken fuel line," Harry shouted. He was not sure; he said it for the record, an explanation for P.C. There was time for nothing else. The tops of the trees were getting close. One thing left to try. Pull the nose up in a landing flare just before they touched the trees. If it worked, they would land on the forest canopy and, with luck, get wedged high in the tops of the trees. If it did not work, it would not matter. It was their only chance. And the time to do it was right now!

Harry pulled back on the yoke and watched the nose start up. Then a big hand grabbed their tail and yanked it up instead.

The nose went straight down. The windshield showed nothing but leaves. It was so quick.

And so it ends, Harry thought. But none of his life flashed by his eyes, nothing at all, except the headline of the newspaper they would read back home – and wonder about:

'Local Antiques Dealer Lost on Jungle Trek.'

Tree limbs burst with the crackle of a hundred gunshots. Harry heard his own voice yelling, "Not trek, goddamn iiiit!"

Chapter 25

Later, when they finally got P.C. to talk about it, they got a reasonably clear picture of what happened that day, in the air and down in the jungle. Reggie handled the debriefing. Although Aloysious tried not to interrupt, he found it difficult at times.

"Harry did all right, suh, flying that airplane," P.C. said. "The takeoff was good. He timed it perfectly. They had their backs to us, the ones in the jeeps. They were far down the field. Hawk kept them distracted, flying little circles. That's what Harry thought. I wasn't sure; maybe Hawk had a problem. But Harry got us in the air and we were on our way home."

"And then what happened, P.C.?" Aloysious asked.

"Don't know, suh. We were spotted. I saw the bloke with the machine gun swivel around. He got his gun to bear and started firing. He never stopped. There were no tracers to help his aim. Didn't think he could do it. Thought he would burn out his barrel first. But he got us."

"How many rounds struck the aircraft?" Reggie asked.

"Don't know, suh. Three, four, maybe. Maybe more. Rear window blew out. Gave me a fright, that did. There were thumps. Strikes in the rear fuselage. And in the wing. On my side the wing had two holes. Small ones. Missed the fuel tank."

"Was there other damage? How did the engine sound?"

"No damage I could see, suh. Engine sounded fine. Harry worked the controls. He thought everything was okay."

251

"What happened then, P.C.?"

"We flew on. Then the engine quit. Harry tried to start it again. We were down low. Harry tried to land in the trees. He waited, tried to time it right. It could have worked, but something happened." P.C. fell silent and stared into the distance. He shuddered and turned away.

They were quiet for a while, then Aloysious gently asked, "What do you think happened, P.C.?"

"Don't know exactly, suh. Probably the landing gear snagged on a tree limb. The airplane twisted around. Flipped over. Went nose first for the ground. Broke a lot of trees on the way. The banging and crashing took forever. We were upside down when we finished. It was dark inside the airplane. Windows were smashed, blocked by branches, leaves, piles of rubbish. It was quiet then. Dark and quiet. I thought I was dead and buried."

"But you got yourself out." Aloysious said the obvious.

P.C. started talking again. "I lay there. I waited. I don't know for what. After a while I tried to move my toes one by one. And they worked. I knew I was alive then, and maybe not hurt too bad. Wanted to get out of the airplane, but I couldn't move. I was pinned down. My seat belt was still fastened. I lay there. It wasn't uncomfortable. Then I smelled the gasoline. I heard it dripping. That was frightening. There was nobody to light a match, but I didn't know how hot the engine was, or if there was an electrical short that could set it off. I remembered films in Hong Kong. An airplane crashed and there was always fire. People screaming and burning like torches. I scrambled then. Punched out a piece of side window with my fist." He held up his bandaged hand and they all looked at it.

"What about Harry?"

"Thought he was finished, dead. Didn't see him at first. He was twisted around, jammed under the panel. His seat broke loose, but the belt held."

"Did Harry say anything when the engine quit?" Aloysious asked.

"Yes, suh. 'Broken fuel line', he said."

"Did he say anything else?" Aloysious asked. His friend's last words were of great interest to him.

"When we hit the trees....One word, that's all I heard."

Aloysious, his voice solemn, asked, "What was that, P.C.? What did he say?"

"Hard to make it out, suh. We were crashing. It sounded like...like 'dreck'."

"Dreck," Aloysious said, "dreck?"

"Yes, suh. 'Dreck'. There was all this noise. Trees breaking, metal banging....When it was over, Harry just lay there, quiet. Everything was quiet. But the dripping, the gasoline dripping...."

"Did Harry speak German?" Aloysious interrupted, stopping both P.C. and a question Reggie was about to ask.

"German?" Reggie looked at him as he repeated the word. "Why do you ask, Aloysious?"

"Harry said 'dreck'. That sounds German. Isn't that the German word for shit? It's what Harry would say in a plane crash. It's appropriate."

"Yes," Reggie said, "quite," and looked thoughtful for a moment. He turned back to P.C. "Now then, P.C., you got yourself free of the wreckage, but then you went back to get Harry."

"Harry was wedged inside. Couldn't tell he was breathing. Had to crawl back through the window. The seat belt held him. When that was free, he was still stuck tight. Side of the airplane was pushed in. Pulled a panel back and then I could move him. Finally pulled him out. But only halfway first. He was conscious then. He said, 'Shit, P.C., that hurts'. I stopped pulling. Afraid I would pull him apart."

"But you finally got him out."

"After a long time. He wanted to get up. Said he wanted to pee. I said stay down, do it there. He said no, he wanted to see. See what? Blood, he said. He wanted to see if he was leaking blood from inside. Said he felt his guts were busted up. There was already blood everywhere. He had cuts on his head, on his leg. I had banged my head and it bled like a stuck pig. That's all normal. But Harry was not happy unless he could see if he was peeing blood. Finally, I helped him up. He peed and there was no blood. He was happier then. He relaxed. I didn't tell him, but I thought he could bleed to death inside and never see it in his pee."

"So you moved Harry and yourself away from the airplane."

"I was afraid of the Chinese patrols. Maybe that wasn't smart. They were Chinese, weren't they? Out of their element, they were. But I thought they might come for us. I wasn't expecting what came."

"When did you realize they were hunting you?"

"The next day. We couldn't move far from the airplane. Harry was in pain, a lot of it. We got maybe a hundred meters away; it could have been a hundred miles. I wanted to move south and west, aiming for Sparrowfart. Mostly we followed an animal trail. We found a creek. It was clean. I found a flat place we could spend the night, made a little shelter from leaves. That's probably what saved us at first. Couldn't see it from five meters away. Next morning I went for water. At the creek I smelled tobacco, cigarettes. Somebody was smoking. You can smell that a long way in the bush, so I wasn't sure how far away they were. I hunkered down and stayed quiet. They crossed the creek not far from me, and sat down. Three of them. They sat there and talked. I hoped Harry wouldn't move, or think it was me and call out."

"You knew they were bad guys?" Aloysious asked.

"Couldn't be sure, but it didn't look good. They weren't the Chinese 'troops' who shot at us. They were local people, but they wore military camouflage. Local hunters might wear an old camouflage shirt or trousers, but they never have everything. This bunch had the whole outfit. Even the boots. One had a rifle, a short one, a carbine really. The other two had long wooden spears. Ugly things. Pig stickers."

"You heard them talking. Did you understand them?"

"Not much, but enough. Languages get mixed up; I know a lot of words. They were looking for us, all right. They were hunters, local chaps, paid mercenaries of Mr. Piggy. Hired because they knew the jungle."

"How did they find you, P.C.?"

"Luck, I think. Luck and animal trails. The jungle is heavy there; it's hard to move. You chop your way or stay on the animal trails. That's what Harry and I did when we moved from the airplane."

"But how did they find where the airplane went down so quickly?"

"Maybe just luck. The hunters talked about the Chinese. The 'troops' knew their machine gun damaged our airplane. They saw the course we were headed. Maybe they calculated how far we would get. I thought we were out of sight when we went down, but maybe they saw us. From the hunters' talk, there were other teams. A half dozen teams could have been put down at intervals along our path. Somebody wanted us badly."

"Mr. Piggy," Aloysious said. "He must be really pissed off about now. Not only lost his airplane, he didn't get his hands on you."

"Did the hunters stay at the creek long?" Reggie continued.

"Not long. They hadn't found the airplane yet. When they started off again, I knew they would find it in half an hour. After that they would find us. I had to get back to Harry and move farther off the trail."

"And you got Harry moved?"

"Harry moved himself. He did his best. He walked; he had to. We moved farther up the creek. It was all we could do. Harry was too sick. Best I could do then was to backtrack and clean up our trail, hide our tracks. That was important; it bought us time. Night came and we stayed in the shelter among the banana trees. Had all the water we needed, but nothing to eat. Knew the hunters would find us sometime the next day."

"I expect that decided you to go on the offensive," Reggie said, a small smile on his lips.

"Had to strike first, suh. I needed to separate them, get the one with the carbine away from the other two. The man with the gun was the leader. He was the dangerous one. The pig stickers I could handle."

"Did you get them apart?"

"Not easy. Next morning, I saw them. I got where I could watch them work. The two pig stickers went in front. When they came to a thicket where a man could hide, they perforated it with their spears. The man with the gun stayed back, ready to shoot if they flushed anything. Every so often, they all stopped and the pig stickers sharpened the points on their spears. They had great long knives. The search was very methodical."

"Did they ever change places?"

"No. The leader, the man with the gun kept it. He was the dangerous one. An older man, an experienced hunter. Always alert and ready. He kept his weapon cocked and his finger on the trigger. Not a man to fool with. He made it difficult. To survive, I had to get him out of the way first. The pig stickers would be easy. They were young and knew nothing. Their spears were long and unwieldy. They would be easy to handle."

"How did you engage them?"

"It was a dance. The leader had a good idea of how far we could get from the airplane. He didn't know if we had injuries that could slow us down. And I left no trail for him. I even covered up the blood we lost by the airplane. He could not be sure how far we could go, or even in what direction. So he had to work his way out from the airplane. Do it methodically. He knew a man could only go so far off the trail in the time that had passed. He knew where a man could hide. He picked his places well, and the pig stickers worked it over while he watched. He was thorough. It was slow and tedious. But sooner or later he would get to us."

"You devised a plan?"

"My plan was to go high. Get on a tree above eye level, let the pig stickers go by, and then drop on the leader when he passed under the tree. If I could get him away from the gun, I could manage. I could take care of him and then the pig stickers. I had to separate him from his gun, that was my aim. I picked a place over the animal trail, near where I left Harry. It was the only place where a tree limb extended over the trail and was the right height. It was a leafy thing, gave me cover. When the pig stickers started spearing the next thicket, I used the noise to cover my climb into the tree."

"You did not have much choice. You did well under the circumstances." As he said that, Reggie looked toward Aloysious, who nodded his agreement.

"Not good enough, suh," P.C. replied. "It looked good when they started my way. The pig stickers walked right under me. Never looked up. The leader pointed out a thicket to probe. It was what I expected. One of the pig stickers started poking, and the leader moved forward, closer to me. I was ready. Another five steps and I had him. Then a sound, a voice! Harry! The pig sticker must have woken him. The leader stopped in his tracks, too far from me. He pointed the gun at the thicket where Harry was. The second pig sticker went there. He was ready to start sticking the spear. I didn't want that. I moved, dropped down - right in front of the leader. 'Now just hold on there, chaps!' I said. The pig sticker stopped in his tracks. He was in shock. But not the leader. He was calm, just looked at me, pointed his gun. I knew then I had made a mistake. I knew that in the next moment he would shoot."

"He had you, P.C., had you cold," Reggie said. "It was a near thing for you. But that was where Mouse came in, wasn't it?"

"Yes, suh. That was where Miss Mouse came in."

Chapter 26

T hat was where Miss Mouse came in all right, or at least as far as P.C. knew. Actually, Mouse's role in this jungle drama began days earlier, at the new airstrip at Sparrowfart. It was the morning of the day after Hawk landed the little silver airplane there. All but a few spectators had left their vantage point on the top of the hill for mid-morning coffee at the Small World restaurant, a recent Miss Mouse innovation. Mouse stood on the hill for a few minutes, studying the aircraft from a distance, and then walked down the hill for a closer inspection.

She slowly walked around the airplane. It was a simple little craft, all metal, with a high wing over a small cabin, perched on fixed landing gear. It looked in good condition; it was clean and obviously well cared for. She sat down in the shade of a wing to think.

Mouse knew little about airplanes. She did know that they did not fall from the sky without good reason. She also knew that on its planned mission to Mr. Piggy's jungle airstrip, there could be reasons aplenty for that to happen. There was nothing she could do about that. And besides, it was not the airplane itself that was her concern, but Harry and Hawk. Sato's position, as expressed to her, was that no harm was to befall either of them, at least no harm that could be avoided or prevented.

Sato was a man of great experience. He had lived many years and he was a realist. He once told Mouse that there were men who brought about their own destruction regardless of what others might do for them. Neither Harry nor Hawk fit that category, nor did Aloysious. Not that any of the three took a particularly cautious approach to life, but each one of them was calculating. Any plan they put together would have an excellent chance of success. There would be no major problems. Mouse's job, as she saw it, was to review their plans with an eye for minor flaws or omissions that might prove troublesome without her intervention.

She sat under the wing and thought about what she knew of Hawk's intentions. A stranger passing by would have instantly been struck by the beauty of the young lady sitting in the shade of the airplane wing. If he chanced to speak with her, he would have been impressed by her even disposition, intelligence, and common sense. On reflection, that would raise the obvious question: What was so lovely and competent a young thing doing, sitting under an airplane's wing in a town called Sparrowfart?

The casual observer might never guess, but Mouse's journey to Sparrowfart was not without its snares and pitfalls. The beginnings of her young life had not been promising. The third of five daughters of a rice farmer in north Thailand, she had had a happy enough childhood, but by her mid-teens, with her father passed away, she found herself in Bangkok, working as a massage girl. The crone who recruited her liked her looks and promised top wages at one of Bangkok's glitzier massage parlors. In no time she was the main support of her mother and four sisters. Each week, with religious dedication, she sent to her home in the north an envelope full of Thai banknotes.

She might have used up her youth kneading the flesh of rich old men had she not caught the eye of a talent scout for an escort service. The money was better, the hours shorter, and she was provided fashionable clothes at a modest markup. This was definitely a step up. She became the favorite of visiting executives who showed her off at elegant restaurants and expensive hotels during their stays in Bangkok. Her days passed pleasantly and her bank balance grew. Then one night she came to the attention of Sato.

Since he was the head of Black Lion Enterprises, an Asian trading powerhouse, Sato's presence was required regularly at social functions, a thing he was thoroughly bored with. He passed the time at these affairs by studying the character of his fellow guests, something he was quite good at. He rarely paid attention to the ladies at these affairs. Experience had taught him that most were of limited intelligence and the others dull and uninteresting.

But he did notice Mouse; he was aware of her from the start. She had been brought by the guest of honor, an important Tokyo banker. She was a beauty all right, but that in itself was not remarkable in a city full of beautiful women. What caught his eye was the way she carried herself. Despite her youth and tenuous social status – in a city where status really mattered - she moved through the room with dignity and grace. He eavesdropped on her conversations and, after a while, decided that her mind was probably as graceful and agile as her body.

Sato respected talent; he had uses for a smart, attractive young lady who could follow orders. By the end of the week Black Lion owned Mouse's contract. She continued to work as an escort at first, but was given special tasks, confidential ones. She carried them out in a way that exceeded Sato's highest expectations. He decided she was worth the investment of Black Lion time and money. He turned her over to experts to be tested. They determined that she had a very high IQ and an ear for languages; she was highly adaptable and could learn anything with remarkable speed. Her body was strong and agile, her reflexes extraordinarily quick. And the package all this came in was most attractive: a well-proportioned body, a face lovely and expressive, and a smile that could stop a man's heart.

She was introduced to tutors and taught as geishas were in Edo-era Japan. She learned to play musical instruments and proved adept at card games. She was encouraged to read widely and she understood what she read, even technical things. She was exposed to a half dozen languages and given courses in computers. She gained familiarity with certain devices that Black Lion found useful in areas such as surveillance and communications. In a relatively short time she acquired the accomplishments of what Sato had once called her: a state-of-the-art ninja in geisha's clothing. Although not one to admit such things, Sato was quite proud of her.

And now in Sparrowfart, as usual, she was trying to do her best. She would not be able to come up with her own plan until she knew the details of what Hawk intended to do, which was still several days off. For now, she would have to be content with the major component of the plan, the little airplane. She opened the door and looked at the instrument panel, focusing on the radios. They were excellent, but she also knew that Hawk would insist on 'radio silence' and the radios would not be used except in an emergency.

The thought of an emergency jostled something in her memory. She walked to the rear of the fuselage and near the tail saw a small whip antenna. It was what she was looking for. On the side of the fuselage below it was a small door that opened on the baggage compartment. Just inside, attached to the fuselage, was a small metal box with a three-position switch, the ELT - emergency locator transmitter. A small red indicator showed it was "armed." It looked good. She would remember to test the operation of the device and its batteries later.

That the airplane had an operating ELT was a good thing to know, and it would be factored into her review of Hawk's final plan. Later that would prove vital. The ELT would make it possible to locate the little silver airplane if it went down. An ELT was nothing more than a radio transmitter that stayed asleep until activated by the impact of a crash. Then it sent out its signal on several frequencies that were constantly monitored by satellites and rescue services. With direction finding, or DF equipment as it was called, the signal could be tracked to its source – and the crashed aircraft located. At the edge of the world where Sparrowfart was located, no one would be listening for an ELT signal. But Mouse knew that she could make that happen. She also knew that Black Lion's fleet of aircraft included at least one airplane with the DF equipment necessary to locate the source of an ELT signal.

Two days later she had the details of Hawk's plan. She went over it step by step and studied maps of the area until she had a clear picture of what would happen. She saw no flaw in the plan, but the one omission jumped out at her. There was no provision to rescue the little airplane's crew if things went wrong. In some circumstances that would not matter; there would be no possibility of rescue. But if it was only a question of the aircraft being disabled, a rescue might be possible. This was the one area where Hawk's plan would benefit from her intervention.

She sat down in the gazebo that afternoon, and calculated the timing of the operation. The little airplane and its crew was to take off from the airstrip at Sparrowfart at first light. If everything went as planned, Harry and P.C. could be expected back at Sparrowfart well before noon that same day. The only variable was the time required to get into the hangar.

Of course, things never go according to plan, so Mouse rounded out all the times and set noon as zero hour. This gave her a margin that precluded an unnecessary activation of the rescue plan if there was an unforeseen delay. If Hawk, Harry, and P.C. were grabbed at Mr. Piggy's jungle airstrip, no one would know of it for a long time, if ever. But if the little airplane crashed, they would find out very quickly, thanks to the ELT. She needed Sato's approval to place the Black Lion DF aircraft on standby. She would also need a helicopter and a crew that could accomplish a rescue.

She raised the rescue plan with Hawk and Harry and Aloysious, and got exactly the reaction she expected. Aloysious said this could all be organized "if and when" it was needed. Hawk said, "Young lady, such planning for misfortune brings nothing but bad luck." Harry looked at her thoughtfully.

She went ahead without their blessing and recruited Jock, who asked if he could bring his parasol; Bunster, who nodded as a look of grave concern slipped across his face; and Geoffrey, the little guy doctor, who simply said he would bring his full medical kit.

Getting Sato's approval was easy. He had already agreed to give Harry whatever help he needed, and he knew that Mouse would not request anything not absolutely necessary. And so, on the morning of the operation, the rescue plan was in place. If an emergency did arise, the plan could be activated at once. At Chiang Mai, in neighboring Thailand, the pilots of the DF aircraft were already onboard an hour before noon that day.

On the fateful morning, Mouse and Aloysious returned directly to the gazebo after watching the takeoff. The gazebo was the command center. Mouse had set up radio gear that would receive any transmission from the little airplane, although Hawk would allow that only in an emergency. There was also a separate receiver, a very sensitive one, tuned to the frequency on which the ELT would transmit - if it were activated. Because ELTs transmitted on very low power, Mouse doubted that the receiver at Sparrowfart would actually pick up a signal.

Under optimum conditions, Harry and P.C. could be expected back at Sparrowfart before 1030 hours. Mouse tried not to be concerned when 1100 came and went and there was no sign of them. Aloysious paced the walk outside the gazebo. The hand of the clock moved slowly after that. By 1130 Mouse had to do something. She radioed Chiang Mai and asked that the DF aircraft be prepared for takeoff. Unless she called it off, takeoff was at high noon.

The DF aircraft took off at Chiang Mai at precisely 1200 hours and was in range of the ELT in less than an hour. By then the little silver airplane's ELT had been transmitting for two hours with no receiver within hundreds of miles to pick it up. When it detected the ELT signal, the DF aircraft immediately alerted Mouse. Then it became a matter of locating the position of the crashed airplane, not an easy task given the heavy jungle and the need to stay well away from Mr. Piggy's jungle airstrip. But the DF operator was good and very quickly got a fix on the ELT's location, although the crew could not see the aircraft itself.

By then, the rescue helicopter was on its way to Sparrowfart. Mouse and her team were waiting at the airstrip when it arrived and quickly clambered aboard. Mouse had no idea what they were getting into, and whether Hawk, Harry, and P.C. were still together, or if Hawk had succeeded in absconding with the

P-40. She had to assume the worst and treat the area of the crash as hostile.

The immediate problem was finding a clearing big enough for the chopper to land. They never did find that, but not far from the area where Mouse wanted to begin her search, they found a ridge, a fertile place where plants grew well, but where the soil over the rocks was not deep. A day or two earlier, the weight of the vegetation broke a large patch loose and carried it down the side of the hill, leaving a small spot stripped bare of growth. It was not big enough for the chopper to land, but it could take a wire litter lowered by a winch. Given the compact size of rescue team members, the litter needed to be lowered only twice.

Mouse led the way down the hill. They could not be sure of exactly where the aircraft was, but they knew the general direction to get to it. Jock was no stranger to the jungle and eventually he took over the lead. At the bottom of the hill he had to cut a path for a dozen meters until they reached an animal trail where pushing through the brush became easier. That brought them to the stream that seemed to lead in the direction they wanted to go. At the end of the day, Mouse and her rescue team settled down for the night in a small clearing alongside the stream. They were not a hundred meters from where Harry and P.C. spent their first night.

It might have been a hundred miles. The jungle was very thick there, and the stream curved away from where they thought the airplane would be, and so they walked away from the stream. That was a mistake. Mouse's team spent the first part of the day heading north, and the jungle grew thicker and thicker. The animal trails ended and they had to cut their way. Finally, Jock said, "P.C. would never come though here. It's too thick. He would go where the animals go." Mouse knew Jock was right. They turned back the way they had come.

When they reached the stream again, it was Jock who heard sounds and smelled things that he knew were not part of the jungle. They camped again in the same place, but Jock and Mouse stayed awake most of the night and thought about what the next day would bring. They were not far from where Harry and P.C. were hidden among the banana trees. And although they had not seen anyone, they knew that they and their lost friends were not the only ones in this patch of the jungle.

When daylight started filtering through the trees, Mouse and Jock woke Bunster and Geoffrey and, with no thought of coffee, started to walk along the stream. And so it was that by mid-morning Mouse and her rescue team were moving into the area where P.C. was about to challenge the hunters.

Chapter 27

P C. dropped out of the tree and landed on all fours, just far enough away from the old hunter not to be able to reach him. "Now just hold on there, chaps!" P.C. shouted as he started to his feet. The hunter facing him was in his mid-thirties, not as old as P.C., but in local hunter terms quite old indeed.

He kept his face to P.C., but his eyes were everywhere, scanning the jungle in all directions, looking for signs of movement of others like P.C. – whatever he was! The hunter was a brave man; no one had ever questioned that. In his time he had faced down wild pigs and bears and, once, even a tiger, although it was a young one and had no experience of men. From the corner of his eye, he saw the two pig stickers, facing his way, frozen in place. There would be no help from them. Time stood still, and although he was brave he had never seen anything like what he faced now. It was as ugly as anything he had ever seen or even thought about. It was a Nat! It had to be.

Down on all fours, P.C. could have passed for a Nat among the Nats themselves. Dried blood streaked his face and matted his hair. His clothes were torn and in places hung loose in long strips. It took him moments to get to his feet, and his wobbling and lurching made him look all the more like a compact wild beast overcome with fury.

The hunter was not of the village by the casino, but he knew the village. He knew of the scourges it had suffered, and of its recent visitation by Nats. The Nats had been driven off, but the villagers still spoke in hushed tones of the Nat counterattack on a commandeered motorbike. A horrible thing! It was frightening just listening to the villagers talk of it. The hunter looked at this thing in front of him, this Nat, not sure what to do. A movement to the side caught his eye.

One of the pig stickers had started to move, the younger of the two, the one not so bright. The young were not strong believers in the mysteries of the forest as were the older people like the hunter. The pig sticker turned now, slowly. A little smile on his face made him look braver than he felt. If the old hunter would not shoot this thing, he would pierce it with his wooden spear. He had killed many animals with it, some big ones, and he knew he could kill this thing. He started toward it, but had taken only two steps, when a child carrying a parasol suddenly appeared in his path. He stopped, eyes wide with wonder.

The old hunter saw the child at precisely the same moment. "A little girl!" the pig sticker said, recovering from his shock. It had to be a girl. Her face was hidden by the parasol she twirled, but her eyes looked out coyly from behind it. The hunter looked at the pig sticker doubtfully. A sudden memory of something a villager said passed through his mind, and a chill washed over him.

"Maybe the other thing is a child too," the pig sticker said, and the hunter wondered how the man could entertain such an idea. "I will show you how to deal with brats like this," the pig sticker said and raised his spear. The little child lowered its parasol, and out of Jock's aged and ugly face came a horrible roar that overwhelmed the pig sticker as Jock ran right at him.

The pig sticker bowled over bushes and small trees charging through the brush in the opposite direction. Meanwhile, the second pig sticker, immobilized and standing like a statue since P.C. had dropped from the tree, suddenly found himself confronted by Bunster in his full Small World regalia – red jacket, epaulets, and peaked cap. Bunster shouted almost as loudly as Jock had, but his target refused to move. The young man certainly wanted to be elsewhere, but he simply could not move. Even his eyes had locked in their open position and he had to regard the apparition in front of him. His upper lip quivered and he felt a weakness in his bowels, but that was all that would move.

The old hunter watched in astonishment. He felt terribly alone. One companion had fled, the other stood frozen in fear. And now there was not just one Nat. There were three! He had to do something. In the past, when danger threatened, he killed. There was nothing he had met that he could not kill with his rifle.

The attack of the Nats had been Jock's idea. During their long night watch, he had discussed it with Mouse as a possibly useful tactic. By mid-morning, the rescue team was close to where the hunters converged with P.C. Under the cover of the noise made by the pig stickers probing thickets, they crept up to the edge of the trail where P.C. clung to the overhanging branch, and then watched as he dropped from the tree to confront the old hunter. When the first pig sticker moved against P.C., Jock went into action, with Bunster close behind.

Meanwhile, Mouse, crouched in the bushes, watched the action develop. She had evaluated the players and focused on the old hunter, the experienced one. She knew he would be the one from whom the real trouble would come. He had the gun and he was out of their reach. There was no way Jock, P.C., or Bunster could get close enough to disable him. The man had lived with that gun; it was an extension of his brain. Mouse knew he would use it.

Mouse was wearing jeans and a long-sleeved shirt. The clothes fit her well and she looked quite nice. Her concession to tramping around the bush was a pair of small but very utilitarian boots. She watched the action unfold and kept one eye on the old hunter. There was fear in the old man, but something else too, a grim determination to see this day through. The crisis was coming.

She stripped off her jeans and then her shirt, so quickly that half the buttons popped off. She pulled off her boots and then her underthings, which were simple but delicate-looking. She dropped everything in a little pile, boots on top. Then she reconsidered, slipped the boots back on and laced them. She stood up.

But for the boots, she was totally, beautifully naked. And when the old hunter started raising his rifle with the thought of eliminating three pesky Nats, she stepped out on the trail.

Those who have not spent time in the less developed regions of the world may believe that nakedness is not uncommon there, an impression perhaps encouraged by certain travel literature. The simple truth is that nakedness in such places is quite rare. Very small children may sometimes be seen running around bare-assed, but beyond a certain age, dignity and clothing go together. People may be poor and live far off the beaten path, but they do not go about naked.

Mouse was looking at him over her shoulder when the old hunter saw her. He shook his head as if to clear it. There was nothing there a moment ago. Now there was this...angel? A slim, curved, female form seen from the back, slim waist, shapely thighs – a beautifully rounded behind that seized his eyes and would not let them go. He tore his gaze away to look up at this being's face, framed by silken hair. The angel noticed him then, and turned. His eyes fell to her breasts, shapes more wonderful than he had ever seen. She stepped toward him, and he looked again at her face, her lips slightly parted in a smile. Beautiful, her face was beautiful, but he could not keep his eyes from ranging back down to her breasts, and then down over her stomach to the place where her thighs met. For a long moment he saw nothing else.

The arm that held the rifle dropped. The thinking part of his brain shut down. Now there was only instinct, the force that drove the animals he killed. Instinct shouted, 'Danger! Danger! Danger!' like a ringing bell. He did not hear. The voice of his experience spoke: 'This is not an angel come to offer herself! There is no free lunch! Succumb and you could find yourself mating with a wolf. Or worse!' He did not listen.

The angel was so close now. He reached to touch her breast. His fingers brushed the smoothest skin he had ever felt, and his groin exploded in blinding pain! The angel completed the whirl that had brought him into perfect range and let her deliver the kick of the flying stallion. Her aim was good. There was no mercy in the boot that caught the old hunter where it hurt the most. The carbine shot out of his grasp, sailed end over end, and crashed into the dirt next to Bunster, who picked it up and quickly handed it to Jock.

After a time, the angel and the three Nats faded back into the jungle, leaving behind a crumpled old hunter writhing on the trail, and a young man, fearful, bewildered, but fortunate, a witness to the mysteries of the forest, who lived to tell about them.

*   *   *

Harry looked up into the face of the angel and felt her touch on his head, up above his forehead where it hurt. His nose was pushed into Mouse's shirt, and she smelled good, a little sweet, like a fresh mango. There seemed to be buttons missing from her shirt, and a long piece of jungle vine held everything together. That was odd, Harry thought, but what did he know about women's fashion. "Hey, Mouse...," he started to say, but she shushed him, then got up and said something to one of the little guys.

Harry had been sleeping when Mouse suddenly appeared, and had no idea where everyone had come from – Jock, Bunster, the whole gang. Then Geoffrey, the little guy doctor, leaned over him and for a time poked and prodded him, and once in a while asked, "How does that feel, Mr. Harry?"

"It goddamn hurts. How do you think it feels?"

Geoffrey got him to move his arms and legs and tried to get him to sit up, and it all hurt. He was stiff and sore and felt like he had pulled every muscle in his body, strained every tendon, and broken a few bones just for good measure. The worst pain was in his back, and his chest hurt if he just tried to breathe. Other than that he felt great. He was alive after all, and that was reason enough to feel good.

"When are we getting out of here?" he asked.

"Soon, Harry, soon," Mouse said and tried not to sound worried. Harry looked beat up, but he had no serious injuries, at least no obvious ones. Geoffrey was concerned about his chest and his back. He was badly bruised, and there was a possibility of internal injuries. He did not want to move Harry, but they were going to have to. Yesterday Harry had already stumbled a good way down the animal trail with P.C. He had survived that, which was probably a good sign.

P.C. and Jock returned from their search for a possible pickup area, a place where the helicopter could land, or at least drop a litter to pick everybody up. They found a site not far away, where the stream widened and became two branches to flow around a small sandbar. There was less foliage there than in other places, and some overhanging branches could probably be cut to let the chopper in. If not, it was wide enough for a litter drop.

Harry decided on his own to stand up, and then was sorry he did. But he could walk. It was painful, but if he could walk to the pickup site it would be easier for everybody. It was not far to the place where the chopper met them, and the pickup was easy with Mouse talking the chopper in on a handheld radio. And before much time had passed, they were on their way to Chiang Mai.

Chapter 28

Black Lion maintained a suite of rooms for its senior executives in a small private hospital just outside the city of Chiang Mai. Harry was ensconced in the master bedroom, a suite within the suite, while P.C. got a slightly smaller room and Mouse moved into one of several guest rooms. It was more luxury hotel than hospital and had neither bad smells nor unpleasant sounds. There was even a kitchen, to which Sato assigned a chef, who specialized in Thai food, but could handle anything.

Once they were settled in, various medical specialists came in to poke and prod at Harry and P.C. and do X-rays and other procedures. P.C. was quickly pronounced fit, or at least deemed not worthy of greater concern, but Harry continued to be subjected to grave looks and huddled conversations. Late in the day, the highest paid and most serious looking of the specialists stood at the foot of Harry's bed and pronounced his judgment: "... injuries that may be quite painful for a time, but nothing at all serious."

As Harry understood it, body parts had been pulled and mashed, twisted and strained, but everything would heal up, eventually. In the meantime he would have to bear the pain that was a part of the process. Nothing could be done for him that would not be cured by rest. With that reassurance, he promptly fell asleep, despite pains that he thought would keep him from ever sleeping again.

He slept through the night, and woke up only when sunlight came streaming into his room. He lay in bed for a while and enjoyed the feeling of being sandwiched in clean, crisp sheets. There was coffee being made; he could smell it. He knew that when it was ready, Mouse would check and, finding him awake, bring in the coffee, together with bread rolls, marmalade – and a fresh morning newspaper. He realized how wonderful it was to be alive, to be able to look forward to these wondrous, ordinary things. That's what a near-death experience did to a man. He was completely changed! For now anyway. He doubted that it would last long.

The coffee really smelled good. He wondered why Mouse had not looked in on him yet. He felt a twinge of annoyance, then just stretched out in bed, and patiently tried to enjoy just being alive. That got old after a while. He could not wait anymore. "Hey, Mouse," he called, and when there was no response, tried again. "Hey, Mouse!"

"Where mouse, boss?" The man in the doorway was a big, muscular fellow with a broom in his hand. With his shaved head and hospital whites he looked like a genie. "Where mouse, boss?" he asked again. "I fix him quick." He shook his broom at Harry.

"Who are you?" Harry asked. "I thought Mouse was in the kitchen."

"No mouse in kitchen, boss. I keep clean."

Harry saw the problem. Language. It was always language. "Not mouse," he explained carefully, "Mouse! The young lady. She was staying in the room across the hall."

"Oh," the big man said, "lady. Pretty one. She go out, boss. You see mouse?"

"No, not mouse. Mouse!" Harry explained again. "Who did you say you are?"

"Jim-Jim, boss. I am cook for big boss, Japanese guy."

"I see," Harry said, not quite sure that he did. "When is Miss Mouse coming back? Is P.C. here?"

"Don't know, boss. Lady go out last night. Little man go too. Only Jim-Jim here. You want something, boss? Jim-Jim fix nice breakfast."

"Okay, Jim-Jim. Coffee and whatever. I need a newspaper."

It was a great disappointment. Breakfast with Mouse would have been the highlight of the morning, a great start to this new day, his new life. And where the hell was P.C.? When Jim-Jim brought him a newspaper, it was two days old, but he smelled ink as he opened it. It was unread and fresh as his new day.

Jim-Jim's breakfast was lavish. That raised Harry's spirits a bit, but from there on it was downhill, and the day soon started to drag. P.C. finally showed up just before noon. He had taken his discharge literally and struck out for the bright lights of Chiang Mai city. He looked terrible and probably had a hangover too. But he was so beat up looking, his face scratched and discolored, that Harry really could not tell. They sat and talked, mostly about P.C.'s night out. Harry was just starting to perk up when P.C. asked, "Heard from Mr. Hawk, suh?"

"No," Harry said, a little surprised. Then a feeling of terrible guilt washed over him. Hawk! He had not given Hawk ten seconds thought since the plane crash. He had thought only of himself. A glimpse of mortality and everything else slipped away into insignificance. "No, P.C.," he finally said, "I haven't heard anything from Hawk. Maybe Mouse has heard from him. Maybe that's why she went out."

"Don't know, suh," P.C. said, his eyes not meeting Harry's.

"Hmm," Harry mumbled. It made him think. During their last evening together at Sparrowfart, Mouse had exchanged telephone numbers and other information with Hawk that would let them get back in touch, once Hawk had the P-40 safely in Thailand. "They'll be in touch if they're not already," Harry said to P.C. "We'll have to wait till Mouse gets back."

"You don't think they got him, suh?" P.C. asked suddenly.

"Got Hawk? Who got him, P.C.?"

"Same chaps as winged us, suh. The Chinese gunners. Damned good shots."

"I don't know, P.C. I never thought of that as a possibility. They wouldn't have fired on the P-40, would they?" Harry thought for a moment. "You didn't see Hawk take any hits, did you?"

"No, suh," P.C. replied, "no, suh, not at all." This reassurance made Harry feel a little better until P.C. added, "Could have taken some damage from a stray round, though. Gone down in jungle like we did, suh."

P.C. decided to leave when two nurses came in to poke at Harry and make sure he took his pills. When they left, things really started looking grim. Harry ate just a small portion of a large lunch that Jim-Jim had made in the expectation that P.C. would stay. Harry was wondering what he would do with the rest of the day, when Jim-Jim brought word that 'Big Boss' was on the way and placed a bottle of five-star cognac on the table. Sato arrived just minutes later, with Mouse alongside, and Aloysious coming up behind, towering over the 'Big Boss'.

Jim-Jim poured large measures of cognac for everyone, and Sato raised his glass to Harry. He congratulated him on his escape from the bad things that had happened and those that could have happened. After an exchange of pleasant small talk, Harry raised the issue that was most on his mind. "I've been a little out touch. What's the word from Hawk? Have you been in touch with him, Mouse?"

Mouse just shook her head.

Harry looked from face to face, but no one said anything. "Do we know where he is?" he asked. "Do we know what's happened to him?"

"No." It was Aloysious who answered.

"He's all right, isn't he?" Harry asked, looking directly at Aloysious. "You don't think he crashed or anything?"

"No, we don't think he crashed, Harry. In fact, we're sure he didn't."

"I'll glad to hear that. You say he didn't crash...but you're not sure where he is?"

"He's in Thailand. We're pretty sure of that."

"Great!" Harry said, and relief washed over him. "Great. If he landed someplace in Thailand, he'll be in touch. He's got telephone numbers and all that, right, Mouse? He'll probably show up at that airstrip where the movie's being made. He needs to get old Number 36 hidden away pretty quick."

"I doubt we'll find him at that airstrip," Aloysious said, sounding so certain that Harry stared at him for a moment. "There's nobody there, Harry. The place was abandoned a long time ago - just like Hawk said it was." After a lengthy silence, Aloysious added, "And it's still abandoned. Nobody has been there in years. We checked."

Harry thought about that. "Well," he said, "the movie guys are probably late getting there. That's why Hawk went someplace else. He's waiting for them to show up. That's probably why he hasn't called in. He wants to get the P-40 under cover first. If you want to get hold of him, I would check with his friend right here in Chiang Mai. The guy who loaned him the little silver airplane. Shit, we're going to have to talk to that guy anyway. We busted up his airplane! I'm sure he'll know how to get hold of Hawk."

"That guy doesn't exist," Aloysious said and took a big swallow of cognac.

"What do you mean he doesn't exist?" Harry asked a little impatiently. "We had his airplane for god's sake. Mouse, you wrote down all the registration numbers before we scraped them off the airplane up at Sparrowfart. Check the records. I'm sure you can use the airplane ID numbers to find the owner's name and place of business."

"The airplane doesn't exist, Harry," Aloysious said again. "That's what I'm trying to tell you. The man who Hawk said owned the airplane doesn't exist. We don't know where Hawk got that airplane, but there's no record of it ever being in Thailand."

"Now wait a minute. A man's name doesn't match up with the airplane. So what? He probably did that for tax reasons."

"Harry, you're not listening to me," Aloysious said, talking louder now. "That airplane was not registered in Thailand. It never existed here. Hawk gave Mouse names and phone numbers - and other particulars of how he could be contacted once he was back here in Thailand. None of the information he gave us checks out."

Light started flooding the darker recesses of Harry's brain. "Oh, shit," he said, and after a pause, "Where do you think he is?"

Mouse spoke up. "We're sure he's in Thailand. But that's all we know for sure."

"Son of a bitch!" Harry exclaimed, the implications of Hawk's disappearance finally starting to sink in. "You say he's in Thailand. How do you know that? You haven't talked with him, you haven't seen him. Did he land hard and set off his ELT?" Harry tried to make a joke of it; the P-40 never had an ELT, but now it made him wonder. "He didn't have an ELT on that airplane, did he?" Some more lights flicked on. He looked at Mouse. "Or something like that?"

It was Aloysious who answered him, with a half-smile on his face. "Or something like that," he said. "Let Mouse tell you what happened."

Mouse looked at Sato. He nodded.

"When I reviewed Mr. Hawk's plan," Mouse said, "I realized there was nothing to cover the possibility of either airplane being lost in the jungle. I knew that the ELT on the silver airplane could help find you if something happened. But with the P-40 it was different. There was no ELT when it was built, and we did not think Mr. Piggy would install one."

"So you gave Hawk an ELT!" Harry jumped in.

Mouse did not answer. Sato looked at her and then turned to Harry. "Mouse is reluctant to speak," he said. "She gave P.C. a device that Black Lion finds useful." He turned back to Mouse and nodded. She looked at Harry, smiled, and went on.

"It was a small transmitter. It can be activated remotely, like the little radios that will tell you where to find a stolen car. I gave it to P.C. to stick on the P-40. We didn't tell you or Mr. Hawk. We didn't think you would be interested. We thought if there was a problem with the P-40, at least we would be able to find Mr. Hawk."

"You were protecting our investment," Harry said.

Mouse ignored that. "When you and P.C. did not come back to Sparrowfart, I sent the direction-finding airplane from Chiang

Mai to look for your ELT signal. When they found it, I asked the DF airplane to activate Mr. Hawk's transmitter. We got a signal. By that time he should have landed in Thailand, and the signal was coming from where we expected it, in the area of the airfield where he said the film crew was working. We did not do a full search to confirm it; we didn't want to draw the attention of Thai air control. Later we routed another airplane over the area of the abandoned airstrip. But there was nothing there, no airplane, no film crew. At that point the transmitter on the P-40 was no longer sending a signal."

"What happened? Why did the transmitter stop?"

This time Aloysious answered. "We gave that a lot of thought. The transmitter could have stopped by itself, just died, its batteries worn down. But that's not likely. Another possibility is that somebody found it and turned it off. P.C. stuck it on the fuselage near the wing root. It was small. It didn't look like anything, but somebody could have found it. Or...the P-40 was put into a shipping container just like Hawk said it would be. If that happened, the transmitter could still be sending a signal, but the signal would not get out of the metal box."

As Aloysious spoke, the pieces were falling into place. A long silence while Harry and Aloysious looked at one another. Finally, Harry spoke. "Airplane in a metal box is what it looks like to me."

Aloysious nodded. "Me too."

They both turned to Sato. He nodded.

They looked at Mouse, a pretty face tight with frustration. She nodded.

They were all agreed. Harry said it out loud: "He stole the goddamn thing!"

They shared a long silent moment then. Finally, Harry asked, "What kind of man would do something like that?"

Aloysious chuckled. "A man like you, Harry. A man like me. We all stole that airplane. Once, from Mr. Piggy. Hawk just took the opportunity to steal it a second time – from us."

"He saw an opportunity, and he took it," Harry said. He shook his head. "Son-of-a-bitch. I just can't believe that. But we'll get it back! We'll find the damn thing. That's our airplane!"

Aloysious sat back in his chair, staring at the ceiling. He looked amused. "Can you imagine," he said, "going from shipping container to shipping container in the Port of Bangkok, looking for that airplane? That's where it is by now."

"We can't just let him get away with it."

"I think he already has."

"Look," Harry said, trying to explain what he was thinking, "a guy like Hawk can't just walk into Southeast Asia, organize everything he needs to steal an airplane out from under our noses - and then get clean away with it. To do that, a guy needs...." Harry looked for the word. "Infrastructure!" he said finally.

"Infrastructure," Aloysious repeated. "Good word, Harry. I guess you mean friends and family. Sato-san, maybe you better tell him."

Sato turned to Harry. "Old contacts have told me about Mr. Hawk. He is not new to Asia, as you know. He flew in China and Burma during the war. But he was more involved here in Thailand than we thought. He flew here again during the French times in Indochina. Then during the Vietnam war he flew in Laos and in Vietnam. During those years he had his home in Thailand. He had a Thai wife, who was very well connected. He had friends among the Thai, among the Americans. Many of those people are still here, doing all kinds of business. If he needed help, there are many here to help him."

"Okay, so he had the infrastructure. Infrastructure and opportunity. That still doesn't mean we can't get the airplane back," Harry said stubbornly.

Aloysious leaned way back in his chair, still staring at the ceiling. He shook his head. "No, Harry, we'll never see that airplane again. Not in your lifetime. Not in mine."

"What the hell could he do with it? You can't just hide an airplane like that."

"You can," Aloysious said with an even voice.

"You can't!" Harry repeated, stubbornly. "The value of that airplane is in the condition it's in. The fact that it hasn't been rebuilt or restored. Right now it's totally original. Change anything and its value diminishes. You can't change the way it looks."

"You're right," Aloysious responded, "you can't change the way the airplane looks, but you don't have to. Look at your own field, Harry - antiques, ancient artifacts. A valuable antique disappears, drops completely out of sight. Where does it go? Priceless artifacts are stolen from museums and are never seen again. You know what happens to those pieces. They can't ever be shown in public again; they're too well known. And you can't change their appearance. So those pieces drop out of sight. And you know where they go, right, Harry?"

Harry knew. And because of that he looked exceedingly unhappy. He did not answer.

"They fall into the hands of the demon collector," Aloysious finally said. "A strange breed, the demon collector. He needs to possess a thing. But he feels no need to show it off. He needs to own it, to keep it - but where only he can see it and enjoy it. What I'm saying, Harry, is that Hawk - or whoever paid him - will put that P-40 where nobody will ever see it again - nobody but the demon collector who owns it now."

Harry sighed. "I know you're right, Aloysious. And that means there's big money involved. And big money means that airplane will get to where it's going and we can't stop it. And once it's there...that's the end of the story."

"The end of the story," Aloysious repeated as if reading that somewhere on the ceiling.

Sato started getting to his feet. "Perhaps the end of the story is a good time to leave, Ha-Lee," he said. "You are tired."

Harry started up. "Please, stay seated," Sato told him. "Mouse will see me out. We will speak more when you feel better. For now you must think only of getting well."

Harry did not argue with that. He felt weary, all used up. As soon as they left he could crawl back into bed.

Aloysious and Mouse walked with Sato to the door. In the doorway, Sato paused and turned back to Harry. "Things did not go as you wished," he said, "but you must not look on that as a failure. The important thing is that you tried."

"I'm sure you're right, Sato-san," Harry answered, "but I'm still a bad loser." As he raised his arm in a small wave of goodbye, he heard Aloysious say, "I need to talk with Harry. Mouse will see you downstairs, Sato-san."

After he closed the door, Aloysious sat down again. For a time he just poked at things on the coffee table, as if reluctant to get started. Finally he looked at Harry and said, "You're not drinking your cognac." Harry just shook his head. "How about a coffee?" Aloysious asked. "No, thanks," Harry said. He was not just weary now, he was feeling depressed too. He hoped Aloysious would not stay too long.

"I didn't want to say anything more in front of Sato and Mouse," Aloysious said. "I didn't want them to feel bad."

Harry looked up at him. "There's more" he said, "and you didn't want Mouse and Sato to feel bad?"

"Yeah, I think Sato probably thinks that losing the airplane was a just fluke - that Hawk saw an opportunity and grabbed it. Maybe Sato will figure it out after a while. I know Mouse will."

"Figure out what?" Harry asked.

"How bad we were taken by that old goat, Hawk."

"I think you already told me that."

Aloysious shook his head. He leaned far back in his chair as if to get more comfortable. "I guess what I mean is that there's more to the story than Hawk just seeing a chance to grab an airplane. A lot more than that. Hawk worked at it, and he did a magnificent job. They'll probably make this a case study at Harvard."

"Aloysious, what are you talking about?"

"I'm talking about Hawk. It wasn't just that he suddenly saw a chance to grab an airplane and took it. He had it all thought out. It was a well planned scheme, malice aforethought. He had the two of us figured out real well. He played us like a banjo. I don't know when the scheme started, but he was still working out the details up at Flying Tiger Land. Hawk was manipulating the shit out of us up there."

Harry tried to think back to how things went at Flying Tiger Land. "I don't know," he said. "What I remember is that we made an offer to Piggy for six P-40s. Then we decided Piggy was trying to scam us and we walked away from it."

"Tell me, Harry, why did we walk away from those six P-40s?"

"They weren't real. They weren't authentic."

"They weren't authentic? They weren't authentic because Hawk convinced us of that. When you first looked at those airplanes, you thought they were real. Even at the end you wouldn't say they weren't. It was only after Hawk expressed all his subtle reservations about them that you said you couldn't be sure. You deferred to Hawk's superior knowledge. We all did."

Harry looked at Aloysious, thinking back.

"Look, Harry, I'm not trying to lay blame," Aloysious said. "I'm trying to show you what I think happened."

"I understand. Go on."

"Okay, based on Hawk's comments, we couldn't be sure that the six P-40s we offered to buy from Mr. Piggy were authentic. Hawk didn't like the patina, as I recall. Remember that? We all wanted the Holy Grail, the real Flying Tiger P-40, and Hawk planted doubts about the airplanes at Flying Tiger Land. That's why Tommy flew you guys to the jungle airstrip to look at Number 36. So Hawk could make sure."

"Right," Harry said, "we went to look at Number 36. And we both agreed that Number 36 was authentic. So if Hawk wanted to grab an authentic airplane, it had to be Number 36."

"You're right, Harry, but only half-right. Number 36 was authentic, but that's not why Hawk wanted that particular airplane. He wanted Number 36 because it was the one airplane he could steal. All of Piggy's P-40s were probably real, but Number 36 was sitting out at that jungle airstrip, where security was kind of haphazard. The fact that Hawk has Number 36 now just proves that."

"You're telling me that all of Mr. Piggy's P-40s could be real? That we could have had the six of them, if we had just gone ahead and bought them?"

"You're catching on, Harry. Hawk couldn't let that happen. He couldn't let us buy the six airplanes from Piggy, because that would have cut him out. If we bought them, they would have been disassembled, packed in containers, and shipped to the States. The whole process would have involved a lot of people. Once the shipment was underway, it would have been too difficult for Hawk to get at any of the airplanes. Even before they were shipped, there was no way Hawk could steal a P-40 by flying it from Flying Tiger Land. The place is too remote to fly one away, and there was just too much security there. He had to do it in the jungle with Number 36. There, it was close enough to Thailand to fly it out. And it was all so easy. He had all of us to help him."

Harry thought about that. To hell with whatever medications he was on; he reached for his cognac glass. A healthy swallow and he started feeling better. "I like your analysis," he said, "and you're probably right. But it sure doesn't make me feel very good. One way or another, you and I have been thoroughly scammed."

"The man's a master, Harry. He did it all very professionally. You have to admire that in a man. I feel as bad as you do. But how would you feel if Hawk was just a bumbling amateur and did that to us? No sir, what Hawk did, he did well. It was masterful. That old man is a real tiger." He looked Harry directly in the eye. "It's no more than you or I would do. You know that. It's the golden rule, Harry: Do unto others as they would do unto you - if they had the chance."

Aloysious raised his glass. "It was like old times, Harry. I enjoyed it. You know, it's like Sato said: the important thing is that we tried to do it. That's the main thing. Hell, it was only an airplane, Harry. Piggy's got a bunch more at Flying Tiger Land. You know, now that we know those airplanes are probably real, maybe we can go back and re-negotiate our six-pack."

"Piggy may not be so pleased to see us right now," Harry said, just a trace of sarcasm in his voice.

"Yeah, well, he's probably not too happy with us right now." Aloysious took a big drink of cognac.

"Did I tell you...." Harry suddenly remembered, "We accidentally blew the side off his favorite sports car, the one in the hangar?"

Aloysious gave Harry a long thoughtful look. "Maybe we better let it rest a while," he said a little glumly. Then he brightened visibly when he added, "Did I tell you about my instant vintage wine scheme?"

Note

None of the original 100 AVG Flying Tiger P-40s survived the war. In 1990 wreckage of an aircraft was found in the jungles of north Thailand, not far from the Burmese border. It was identified as the AVG P-40 flown by William "Black Mac" McGarry when the AVG attacked the Japanese Air Force Headquarters at Chiang Mai, Thailand, on 24 March 1942. McGarry's P-40 was struck by ground fire and crashed before he could reach safety in Burma. "Black Mac" McGarry survived the war. The remains of his P-40 are on display at the Royal Thai Air Force Base at Chiang Mai. This wreckage is the only remaining relic of the AVG's P-40 Tomahawks.